PRAISE FOR THE MAGNIFICENT NOVELS OF
MICHAEL CURTIS FORD

THE SWORD OF ATTILA

"A massively long, brutal spectacle, supremely well-executed . . . again, Ford offers solidly researched and lustily violent military historical fiction."

—*Kirkus Reviews*

"An exhilarating journey into madness and destiny . . . this is first-class writing . . . impeccably researched, a surge of bloody excitement." —*Salem Statesman Journal*

"Michael Curtis Ford strips away the civilities of modern life. When you pull yourself out of the last page, you know you've been told one of our story's huge moments, by a master storyteller, whose stunning sweep and involvement is only matched by his expertise in breathing alive again our heroic and gory past." —rebeccasreads.com

THE LAST KING

"A swashbuckling account . . . solid fun: a good, old-fashioned adventure tale with plenty of action." —*Kirkus Reviews*

"Ford captures the Roman first century B.C. from a novel perspective . . . Battle scenes are described with great skill . . . a mastery of military history." —*Publishers Weekly*

MORE . . .

50¢

"Michael Curtis Ford's love for the ancient world emanates from every page: in his magical settings and spectacular re-creation of monuments and landscapes, in his bold portraits of the protagonists, and in his intriguing and swiftly moving plot." —Valerio Massimo Manfredi, author of the Alexander Trilogy and *Spartan*

"A swift and exciting story . . . Brutal, straightforward, exciting, and informative . . . a hair-trigger ride on ancient sands and hills. This is Ford's best so far, and only those who have read his first two know just how good that makes this book." —*The Statesman Journal* (Salem, Oregon)

"Powerful telling of historical drama. Michael Curtis Ford brings the Roman Empire to life. *The Last King* is complete with battle scenes and powerful storytelling about one of history's most feared warriors." —*Oregonian*

GODS AND LEGIONS

"Thanks to the author's excellent research of both his subject and era, the reader experiences this great man's transformation step by determined step. Highly recommended." —*Historical Novels Review*

"Powerful and passionate. A truly compelling story—one not just of gods and legions but of men." —*Library Journal* (starred review)

ST. MARTIN'S PAPERBACKS TITLES

BY MICHAEL CURTIS FORD

THE TEN THOUSAND
A NOVEL OF ANCIENT GREECE

GODS AND LEGIONS
A NOVEL OF THE ROMAN EMPIRE

THE LAST KING
ROME'S GREATEST ENEMY

THE SWORD OF ATTILA
A NOVEL OF THE LAST YEARS OF ROME

THE FALL OF ROME

A NOVEL OF A WORLD LOST

MICHAEL CURTIS FORD

St. Martin's Paperbacks

This is a work of fiction. All of the characters, organizations, and events portrayed in this novel are either products of the author's imagination or are used fictitiously.

THE FALL OF ROME

Copyright © 2007 by Michael Curtis Ford.

Cover illustration credit: *The Course of Empire: Destruction* (1836) by Thomas Cole (1801–48) / Collection of the New-York Historical Society / Bridgeman Art Library

Map by Jackie Aher

For information address St. Martin's Press, 175 Fifth Avenue, New York, NY 10010.

Library of Congress Catalog Card Number: 2007008900

ISBN: 0-312-94528-0
EAN: 978-0-312-94528-2

Printed in the United States of America

St. Martin's Press hardcover edition / May 2007
St. Martin's Paperbacks edition / October 2008

St. Martin's Paperbacks are published by St. Martin's Press, 175 Fifth Avenue, New York, NY 10010.

10 9 8 7 6 5 4 3 2 1

FOR EAMON, ISABEL, AND MARIE-AMANDINE

HISTORICAL NOTE

It has been said that if no period of Roman imperial history is so completely documented as the first century, no other is so poorly recorded as the fifth. Yet in the dim shadows that have survived through the ages, we can still discern the outlines of epic tragedy. The century opened with barbarians dominant at the imperial courts and among the legions' leadership; its midpoint saw Rome staggered by the invasion of Attila and his horde; the weakened empire then endured the relentless barbarian assaults and internal rebellions described in this book; and, finally, Rome finished out its terrible century, and long history, with a great stillness, as at a wake for a dead patriarch, with the heirs praying silently around the body, but keeping one eye open and fixed tensely on the others for control of the estate. By the close of the century, the western half of the empire had passed completely out of Roman hands, but this, perhaps, like a beneficial amputation, aided the survival of the eastern half, relieving it of serious threat from foreigners and invaders, and so strengthening it to endure an additional thousand years.

Definitive reference works on this period are hard to come by, and their descriptions of the events tend to contradict each other nearly as often as they agree. Perhaps the most useful overview of these times is Gibbon's indispensable *Decline and Fall of the Roman Empire*, from which, for me at least, all research must start, and from whose details and conclusions I vary only with great caution. The Anonymous Valesianus provides interesting first- or second-hand accounts of court gossip in the imperial household and biographical details of the main personages; and the ever-useful *Oxford Classical Dictionary* provides a number of source ideas for other, minor references that fill in some of the gaps. More modern historians who were useful include Otto J. Maenchen-Helfen, with his magisterial *The World of the Huns*; Peter Brown, with his *Augustine of Hippo*; and Paul Bigot, whose lovely early-twentieth-century sketches of the city of Rome as it would have appeared in antiquity were invaluable for determining the locations of ancient streets, bridges, and palaces.

Ultimately, however, where the historical record is lacking, or where my own research skills fell short, I had to rely on educated assumptions. This was particularly the case for Odoacer's early life among the Scyri, a mysterious tribe (even to the Romans) about whom virtually nothing has been written. Only the barest historical references exist for certain of the minor personages in this book, and even individuals who were the leading men of their day, such as Anthemius and some of the other later Western Roman emperors, fall surprisingly short on verifiable details. This affords great opportunities to a novelist looking to develop interesting plot points and characters without violating the *known* historical record; but it also exposes him to the risk of error from violating records that are known by someone, just not by *him*. I did my best to seek out available sources, but as they say, a book is never really finished, it is merely abandoned, when the author's research finally hits walls, either genuine or of his own making.

What remains, in the end, is to express my awe and appreciation for the tremendous research performed by historians and writers of the past, whose efforts I have shamelessly exploited; and my responsibility for any historical errors this book may contain, which of course is mine alone. The most I can hope for is that any shortcomings will lead the reader to seek out his own sources and research, and contribute to our growing body of knowledge of these fascinating times.

DRAMATIS PERSONAE

ANTHEMIUS	Western Roman Emperor
ARDERIC	Germanic commander of one of Rome's *confoederati* legions
BALDOVIC	Commander of Vismar's bodyguard
BASILISCUS	Eastern Roman admiral, loaned by Leo to command Western Rome's naval armada in attack against Gaiseric
CONFOEDERATI	Roman troops of barbarian origin, usually stationed in the empire's border regions
EDECO	Hunnish general and diplomat, a close associate of Attila; father of Odoacer and Onulf
ELLAC	Attila's son
GAISERIC	Vandal king, longtime enemy of Rome
GILIMER	Goth veteran of Rome's urban cohort, commander of Orestes' bodyguard
GUNDOBAR	Burgundian commander, close associate of Ricimer and later Odoacer
GUTHLAC	Gepid king leading a military alliance of Germanic tribes that included the Scyri

LEO	Eastern Roman Emperor
ODOACER	Hunnish/Scyri soldier, son of Edeco, brother of Onulf, who after exile travels west to Europe
ONULF	Hunnish/Scyri soldier, son of Edeco, brother of Odoacer, who after exile travels east to Asia
ORESTES	Germanic mercenary general, commander of Attila's bodyguard; father of Romulus Augustus
RICIMER	Germanic general, commander of all of Western Rome's military forces
ROMULUS AUGUSTUS	Western Roman Emperor
SEVERINUS	Hermit and holy man in the land of the Scyri
VISMAR	King of the Scyri, an eastern Germanic tribe

THE FALL
OF ROME

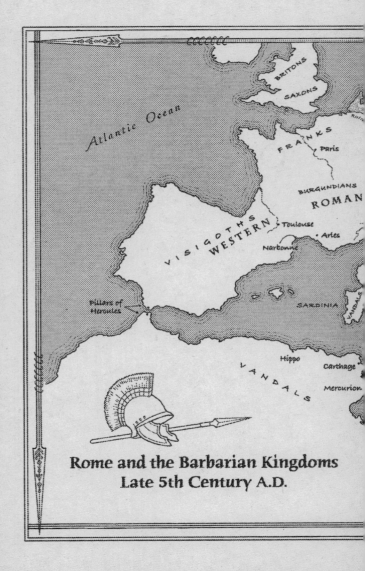

Rome and the Barbarian Kingdoms
Late 5th Century A.D.

Now I beseech those that shall read this book, that they be not shocked at these calamities, but that they consider the things that happened, not as being for the destruction but for the correction of our nation. For it is a token of great goodness when sinners are not suffered to go on in their ways for a long time, but are presently punished.

—2 MACCABEES

PART

I

*Non solum fortuna ipsa est caeca sed etiam
eos caecos facit quos semper adiuvat.*

(Not only is fortune itself blind,
but it even makes those blind whom it helps.)

—CICERO

CHAPTER ONE
453 A.D.

HUNNISH CAMP

I

The stars had long since turned their course in the late-autumn night's sky, and dawn itself would not be long in breaking; yet the massive camp on the Hunnish plain was lit as in broad daylight, with such quantities of torches and bonfires as would have done credit even to Constantinople. The brightness of the city-camp was matched by the noisomeness of its inhabitants, for every man, woman, and child, every dog, housebound fowl, and domesticated plains pony, every slave and master, every Hun and exiled Goth and German, were lifting their voices and spirits in celebration. Their songs resonated across the plain, and the dung fires reflected red off the low-hanging smoke, creating a hazy glow that could be seen for miles across the expanse of waving, summer-dry grass.

A party of mounted Hunnish officers, thirty in all, thundered in from the plain, past the grinning Goth sentries who raised half-depleted skins of *kamon,* their barley beverage, in mocking salute to the dusty riders. They pounded through the dirt-packed streets, scarcely deigning to look down from their foaming mounts, for their fierce expressions and hurried pace were sufficient warning for bystanders to clear the way. From all sides, drunken faces leered at them in the flickering light. Horns, whistles, and wordless shouts greeted the riders' arrival, and hands grasped at their soft doeskin boots, welcoming them to the festivities or pushing against them in the jostling. The horsemen's leader looked about in distaste, not at the poverty and filth the city exuded, but at the signs of wealth: the dandified young men meandering drunkenly, fingers burdened with rings and shoulders heavy with the fine silken fabrics by which they aped the fashions of those they conquered; the thin-shanked European and Arabian horses the Goth officers rode, rather than the homely yet reliable steppe ponies the Huns had bred for generations; the chalices of metal from which many of the celebrants guzzled imported wine, rather than the wooden bowls from which the elders sipped humble *airag,* the Huns' traditional beverage of fermented mares' milk. The leader, a middle-aged Hun of broad shoulders and uncommon height and physical strength for his race, frowned in disapproval. It was a culture gone soft, a people who valued shiny baubles over sturdy horses, drunkenness over conquest, Gothic frivolities over Hunnish austerity. Attila, he reflected, had made himself conqueror of Asia and sovereign of the scattered Hunnish clans, and of many unruly European tribes as well; but the price he had paid for this unity of purpose, this assimilation, was perhaps one the mighty king had not anticipated.

The group of riders forced their way through the throng to the wood-palisade gates of the palace. There, the sentries were Hunnish, of more reliable and sober countenance; they glanced at the riders' impassive faces, ordered them to halt, and dispatched a runner to the inner compound.

The horsemen slumped into the relaxed position they adopted when dozing on their mounts. Despite their seeming ease, however, their eyes remained wary, peering out from beneath the low-wrought rims of their battered iron helmets. Their leader slid off his panting horse, landing with catlike grace and unstrapping his helmet before even touching the ground. Without setting aside his quiver and war bow, he shifted impatiently on his heels, peering past the palace guards into the flickering shadows, where snoring bodies littered the courtyard and doorways like so many casualties of a battle.

Across the courtyard, a heavyset Germanic officer, armor glowing dully in the torchlight, emerged from the wooden palace doors and swaggered toward them. He shouldered through the drunken revelers, shaking his mane of reddish hair back over his shoulders, jutting his chin to expose a thick, dun-colored beard streaked with gray. He held a shining chalice in his right hand, but showed no intoxication or joyfulness. Indeed, his piercing blue-gray eyes were as alert and malicious as the last time the Hun had seen them six months before. He strode up to the horsemen and stopped in silence.

"What is happening here?" the Hunnish squad leader demanded abruptly.

The German stared contemptuously at the new arrivals, then nodded to the sentries at the gate, who relaxed their guard. As the Hunnish horsemen slid off their mounts, he turned pointedly back toward their leader.

"Good to see you, too, Edeco," he replied in flawless Hunnish. "This is how you greet me after six months away from camp?"

Edeco grunted in annoyance.

"I owe you no protocol, Orestes. Six months in Constantinople has made me sick of it. Unless your existence has more purpose than I remember, step aside. I must report to Attila."

"The king is celebrating his wedding. He will take no reports now. Did you not see the revelry? Or are you as drunk as the rest of the camp?"

"His wedding? He has contracted a new wife?"

"A princess of a Pannonian tribe," Orestes replied laconically. "Her father reigns over some river mud on the Danuvius. The wench will keep Attila warm for the next few nights."

Edeco glanced at him coldly as the two men began picking their way across the dirt courtyard toward the palace.

"A Pannonian," he scoffed. "No doubt loyal to Rome. And I see you yourself still wear a Roman citizenship ring, though you claim to serve Attila. You're Germanic, she's Germanic—I'm sure the arrangement held no conflict of interest."

"My father was made a Roman citizen years ago, and I am proud to wear his ring."

"Proud to wear Rome's ring?" The Hun's laugh was short and dry. "I once put a gold collar on a mongrel dog, which much improved its looks. But it was still just a mongrel."

Orestes stopped short.

"What are you saying, Hun? Germans are not dogs."

Edeco maintained his calm stride.

"So much the better for dogs."

"Hunnish scum . . ."

Edeco whirled on him.

"You are Attila's chief military commander. You spent the past year leading the troops on a second campaign against the Western Roman Empire. Yet Rome still flourishes. What have you to show for your efforts, besides a drunken army and another yellow-haired bitch for the king to marry?"

Orestes' face darkened in fury, and he tensed to lunge at the Hun, but warily dropped his guard as he saw Edeco's hand moved to his sword hilt.

"We reduced Concordia, Altinum, and Patavium to ashes," Orestes retorted angrily. "We captured Verona, as well as Vicetia, Brixia, and Bergomum. Even powerful Milan surrendered all its wealth to us—surely you received the news announcing our triumph. There in the palace we found a great mural of the Roman emperors of East and West seated on their thrones, dividing the spoils of Scythia. Attila ordered the city's artists to repaint the mural, to depict him towering over the two Romans as they poured golden coins at his feet."

"Such a staggering blow against Rome's artists," Edeco replied flatly. "And after Milan, how far did you advance into Italia?"

Orestes glanced away sullenly.

"We advanced no farther."

"I'm told you met the old white-beard Leo, whom the Christians call their Pope."

"Attila met with him, in private. He has discussed the matter with no one. I suspect Leo claimed Rome was plague-ridden, and that if we captured it, the Huns would not long survive. When Alaric the Visigoth sacked the city forty years ago, he died soon afterward. . . ."

"So you let the king be swayed by an old priest. But then you are Christian yourself, are you not?"

"As was your own Scyri wife," Orestes retorted, seething at the Hun's insults to his honor, "and as are your sons. Do you dare judge me? I did not see you in Italia advising Attila."

"No," Edeco replied. "Nor did you see any Eastern Roman legions attacking your back while you were most vulnerable. Who did you think dissuaded the Eastern Emperor Marcian from marching his troops from Constantinople and knocking you on your drunken arses while you were painting murals in Milan?"

"An easy claim to make. I didn't see any African war elephants swimming the Mediterranean, either. That doesn't mean you kept them away."

"We will settle this later, German. Just you and me."

Orestes smirked, and patted the hilt of his own knife.

"Indeed we will, Hun," he growled. "With great pleasure."

Two shadows emerged from the group of horsemen several paces back. A pair of young men stepped forward and flanked Edeco. Their tall stature and chestnut-brown hair were incongruous with their broad Hunnish faces and narrow eyes. Among the Huns of recent generations, bloodlines and parentage had become increasingly mixed. Yet despite their European features, their loyalties were clearly with the Hunnish squad leader.

"Is there a problem?" one of them muttered to Edeco, staring contemptuously at the German.

"No," Edeco replied. "We will report to Attila and then find our beds for the night."

"Your riders need not come," growled Orestes.

"These are my sons. Odoacer and Onulf are captains of the Hunnish cavalry, and they go where I command them."

"The king," Orestes insisted, "is not to be disturbed."

Edeco paused just short of the entrance to the palace. He turned to his sons, his voice betraying only a hint of his barely controlled anger.

"Release the squad. Let them tend their horses and muster

at dawn. Then you two come back, and remain here outside the door."

Without waiting for a response, Edeco then addressed Orestes.

"Enough of your chatter, German. Accompany me inside or tend the horses with my men, it is of no consequence to me. How stands the king?"

" 'Stands' is not an accurate word," Orestes muttered as he stepped angrily through the wooden doorframe. "He has been stone drunk for three days now."

Edeco paused.

"Drunk? The king does not get drunk."

Orestes shrugged.

"Since his defeat by Rome two years ago, the king has not been the same. And since our siege at Aquileia, he gets drunk. Often."

"Is he ill?"

"No, his body is well. He is past fifty, yet can still ride a day and a night without dismounting, and he remains the best bowman and roper of all the Huns. He suffers frequent nosebleeds, though the *qam* has examined him and claims it is a good thing, as it purges him of evil humors."

"Nosebleeds! If that's all he suffers at fifty, then he has no complaints."

"No, his body is healthy . . . ," the German repeated, as both men stepped into the dining hall of the plain wood-frame structure that was the palace of the Hunnish king. Edeco took in the sight with a glance and stopped short in amazement.

"It is his mind that suffers," Orestes continued in a low voice.

The Great Hall looked as if it had been hit by a storm, as three days of unmitigated revelry had left it a shambles. Broken dining tables and furniture lay everywhere, topped by semiconscious Hunnish and German officers sprawled drunk and snoring in the debris. The room was heavy with the stench of sweat and spoiled *airag* that had soaked into the carpets and soured. A thin, acrid smoke drifted through the air, the remnant of one of the large woolen wall tapestries that had caught fire earlier from a clumsily wielded torch. A young Hunnish warrior, whom Edeco recognized vaguely as a cavalry captain under the command of Attila's son Dengizich, struggled to his feet, glanced around blearily, then untied the drawstring at his waist and calmly pissed into a smoldering brazier, eliciting a hissing sound that caused him to grin in satisfaction. Zercon the dwarf crawled out from behind one of the toppled tables and scolded the soldier in pidgin Hunnish for his poor manners, and the warrior laughed and aimed the stream at him, causing the jester to scuttle back into his shelter.

On the dais at the head of the room Attila sat in his wooden throne, head slumped forward onto the table, hands spread before him. Edeco glanced around carefully, astonished at the lack of security—any peasant with a grudge could easily walk into the palace, dispatch the king, and walk out again, waving the bloody knife before him, and nobody would even think to stop him. Before assuming his diplomatic duties, he himself had been commander of the king's bodyguard—and a lapse such as this would have meant execution for him and all his men on duty that night. Now, his old responsibilities had been assumed by Orestes. Different commander, different discipline, obviously different results. But then, Attila himself was a different man as well.

The only alert faces in the entire room were at Attila's right side. There sat a young girl, perhaps fifteen years of age, her long golden hair dressed in complicated braids and wound tightly around her head. She wore a shimmering gown of pink and light blue, decorated with intricate patterns of glass studs and ornately embroidered hems. She sat immobile, the plate and goblet in front of her untouched, trails of dried tears marring her plump face as her gaze shifted between the sodden king sprawled on the table beside her, and the new arrivals.

To her right was an older man, clearly the maid's father, the Pannonian king, by the familiar way he touched her elbow and leaned over to whisper in her ear. He, too, wore imported finery, perhaps a wedding gift from Attila himself, and his face reflected not the sorrow and despair Edeco could see on the daughter's, but rather stoic detachment, resignation at losing the girl, tempered by satisfaction at making a valuable political alliance by betrothing her to a powerful monarch.

"Ildico," Orestes said. "The bride. She has sat there for three days now, scarcely moving, her food and drink untouched. She fears the wedding night, no doubt."

"Which is when?" Edeco asked.

Orestes smirked again as he glanced at the unconscious king.

"Tonight."

Edeco shook his head, in amazement and shame.

"A princess," he muttered as he looked around the room. "A princess of swine. Orestes, you are commander of the guard, yet all your men are drunk. I myself will pick the valuables out of this trash."

Turning his head, he gave a sharp whistle, eliciting angry curses from the dozing men around the room. Immediately Odoacer and Onulf stepped into the door, eyes wide at the scene of debauchery.

"Escort your king to the wedding tent," Edeco ordered them.

The two young men nodded silently. Stepping over to Attila, they lifted him between them, draped his arms over their shoulders, and began half-walking, half-dragging him across the room. Ildico and her father rose and began to follow, and Orestes and Edeco fell into step behind.

The wedding tent was a circular structure of felted wool constructed in the center of the outside courtyard, in full view of all the palace inhabitants and Attila's other local wives, who numbered some fifty. It was a ceremonial structure, reminiscent of the Huns' traditional lodgings on the plains during the summer horse-roping campaigns, yet it was far from the modest shelter used in those workaday environments. Every fiber of it was draped with brightly hued carpets, pennants, and blankets, like a colorful jewel set among the otherwise drab wood-plank structures of the palace compound. It had been erected in the courtyard at the very beginning of the wedding ceremony and would stand like a threat or an invitation until the morning after the marriage's consummation. On that day, after publicly displaying the bloodied marriage sheets as evidence of the new bride's virginity and the king's virility, the festivities would be declared at an end, the tent would be disassembled, the camp-city would return to its normal business, and the new bride would be shown to her future accommodations, the women's quarters with the king's other wives.

As the small party stooped through the tent's low door and entered, Ildico began sobbing loudly and her father commenced wringing his hands, his carefully cultivated reserve vanishing as he saw the feather-filled floor mattress on which his daughter would lie with her drunken new husband.

"How will he consummate?" the Pannonian king asked in anguish, looking at Orestes in hopes the fellow German might sympathize with his plight. "With all due respect, the King of the Huns cannot even walk! If he cannot do the deed, there will be no blood on the sheet in the morning to prove my daughter was a virgin, and people will suspect her virtue!"

The brothers dropped Attila onto the mattress, then stood. Orestes bent to pull off the king's boots.

"There will be blood on the sheet, old man," Orestes growled, straightening Attila's legs. "We'll take it from elsewhere if we have to. Watch that it's not from you."

"But my daughter cannot lie with him in that state! It will be impossible!"

"She will not lie with him anyway. Attila takes his wives standing."

"Standing? Like an animal? This is how the Huns treat their women?"

Orestes glared at him, in no mood to explain to this petty king, this tribal chiefling, how Attila's recent nosebleeds were exacerbated when he exerted himself horizontally. Custom had nothing to do with Attila's new predilection for a vertical position in things sexual. It was, rather, a question of hygiene.

"You insult the king," Orestes replied. "You may now be his father-in-law, but you insult him, before your daughter has even proven her worth." He grinned maliciously. "Your people are farmers, you should know animals: an ox plows a deeper furrow standing up than lying down."

At these words Ildico, who had slumped in exhausted silence on a rug against the wall, blanched and burst into a new round of sobs.

"I've had enough," Edeco said in disgust. He gestured for his two sons, the girl's father, and Orestes to exit, and then, taking a last look at his snoring commander and the terrified bride, he, too, stepped out into the warm night air and closed the door behind him.

Outside, as the party dispersed to their separate quarters, he took his sons aside.

"Six hours still until dawn," he muttered, "and there's not a guard in the entire city I can trust tonight to stand watch at the king's door. You two stay. I know you have been riding all day, but you are young—it is an old man's prerogative to go to bed, and that I will do. I will be at the king's apartments, in the palace. And I will send a relief at dawn, if I can find one sober."

The brothers nodded, and Edeco strode off, suddenly feeling the full weight of his own fifty years, and of the efforts he had made of late, both physically and mentally. He was a Hun, he reflected, born for riding, for the steppe, for hunting the fleet-footed antelope, and the even fleeter-footed Persians and Alani. No man is meant to survive under roofs day after day, eating delicacies and being primped by eunuchs until his muscles grow soft and his will dissipates like smoke—yet that was precisely how he had been living the past six months in the Eastern Roman court, spinning tales and pulling tricks and performing feints and lies, like Zercon the palace dwarf, all to convince the Emperor Marcian of Attila's peaceful intentions toward Constantinople, even as the massive Hunnish army marched upon Marcian's co-emperor in Rome. It was not as difficult as it might sound, for Edeco had learned long ago that most men will believe that which is easiest to believe—and it was much easier for Marcian to simply do nothing and enjoy the pleasures of his court, than to see the clear truth: that half the Roman world was being viciously mauled, and that once it had been dispatched, the victorious Hunnish army would turn its sights on the other half.

Admitting this was simply too difficult for Marcian. It would require effort, mustering the army, calling in the border garrisons, engaging new recruits—all of which are expensive, and time-consuming tasks. Much easier to ignore the problem and trust that the Huns truly meant no harm to the Eastern Empire—which it was precisely Edeco's job to convince him of.

But in those six months Edeco had grown soft and weary, and he felt the strain. So, too, had his sons—fine, strong lads, the only vestige of the one wife he had married of his own choosing, a Scyri slave girl he had captured on a raid into eastern Germania a quarter of a century before and whose name he had not mentioned since her death years ago. The two younger men had been frustrated at their prolonged exposure to the decadence and filth of city life in Constantinople, but had never uttered a word of complaint in his hearing. Yet the look on their faces when he received word that Attila had retreated back to his camp, and that there was no longer a need for the Hunnish embassy in Constantinople, was one of utter delight. As joint captains of the small cavalry squadron that traveled to the Eastern Roman capital, they had raced off to inform their troops, and within an hour the squadron had packed its gear and was ready to depart. That was a month ago—a month of hard riding, difficult river-crossings, and wormy hardtack purchased at inflated prices from stony-faced market crones displeased at having to deal with Huns, even those merely passing through their miserable trading villages. A month spent on the bony, ridged backs of the tireless Hunnish steppe ponies.

It had been the best month of Edeco's life.

Before he was even aware he had fallen asleep, he felt a hand shaking his shoulder. He struggled to clear his mind and open his eyes.

"Father."

It was Odoacer's voice. Edeco rubbed his eyes and looked around. It was still dark, and the room was lit only by a faltering torch. He was lying on his old cot in the guard-room just outside Attila's empty bedchamber.

"Father!" his son repeated. "I think the king is unwell."

"Unwell?" Edeco repeated. "What do you mean? Where is Onulf?"

"Onulf remains at the wedding tent on guard. The girl is weeping."

The older man scoffed.

"Weeping? It is her wedding night, she is a virgin, and she is locked in her room with a drunken king. Wake me if she's *not* weeping—then I will be worried."

"No, Father—she is frantic. And there is no sound from the king. He does not laugh, nor even beat her to silence her."

Edeco considered this a moment.

"And did you enter to see if there is a problem?"

"I dared not. What if there was no problem, and I entered at the wrong moment? The king . . ."

"Meet me at the tent in a moment. Find that Germanic idiot Orestes and tell him what you have just told me. I do not wish to be the only man to interrupt the king while he is 'plowing his furrow.' "

A moment later the four men stood outside the tent door, listening as the girl inside sobbed loudly. Their whispered entreaties to her through the heavy felted walls had been to no avail. Either she did not hear, or she was ignoring them. Carefully testing the door, they found it barred from inside, and so impossible to stealthily insert a head to inquire. Orestes glanced at the sky.

"Dawn in one hour," he said tersely. "The wives in the women's quarters are already awake and restless . . ."

"They are always awake when Attila takes a new wife,"

replied Edeco. "They are praying she will beget dwarves who will not compete with their own children."

"Nevertheless," Orestes continued, "the girl's infernal crying will soon have the entire palace staff talking, and then the city itself. It must be stopped."

"It must *be* stopped?" Edeco glared at him. "Are all Germans as helpless as you?"

Without further discussion, he drew his dagger and thrust it into the fabric of the tent at the level of his eyes. Inside, the girl's crying immediately ceased. With a quick sawing motion, he drew the blade horizontally across the fabric wall, and then straight down at a right angle, cutting to the plank flooring on the bottom. Without further hesitation he stepped inside.

All was as they had left it, down to the guttering Roman-style ceramic lamps on the table. The girl herself had scarcely moved from the corner rug where she had first thrown herself upon entering the tent hours earlier, and now sat motionless, watching the intruders with wide, tear-filled eyes. Warily, Edeco looked on every side for threat or attack before finally settling his gaze on the middle of the room. The king lay on the bed just as they had placed him earlier. Nothing seemed to have changed.

Annoyed, Edeco seized one of the small lamps and stepped forward, followed close behind by Orestes. The king had slept through his wedding night. Unfortunate, but not unexpected, and certainly nothing to have merited Ildico's frantic sobbing.

"What in Hades are we in here for, girl?" Orestes snapped. "What is the reason for such disrespect for your new husband . . ."

His voice trailed off as the two men approached the bed and looked down. In the shadows they had seen nothing, but now the glow of the lamp reflected a dark, spreading stain on the sheet beneath the king's head. Edeco set down the lamp and seized the king's shoulders, pulling him to a sitting position.

As he did, his head slumped forward and blood poured

from his mouth into his lap in a thick, gurgling stream. The girl shrieked and hid her head beneath a pillow. Edeco stared wordlessly and Orestes froze, before he, too, grabbed one of Attila's shoulders and helped to gently lay him back down on the bed. Blood continued to flow, and the king stared upward, eyes glassy in the dim light.

Orestes stood up and strode to Ildico, drawing his dagger. The girl's eyes opened wide, and she fell silent, her face glowing white in the dim lamplight. The German's eyes narrowed and flashed fury as he seized her hair and jerked her roughly to her feet.

"Decades of battle failed to destroy the mighty Attila," he growled, "yet this treacherous hellcat has done in her own husband on her wedding night." He threw the girl's head back and raised his blade to her pale throat.

"Wait," Edeco ordered, still examining the cadaver on the blood-drenched bed. "The girl is not at fault. The king has drowned—a nosebleed, while he was drunk. In his own blood, he has drowned!"

Orestes paused for a moment, then grudgingly released the girl, who collapsed onto the strewn carpets where she had spent the night. Edeco stood and stepped back from the king's bed, staring stony-faced at the cadaver. Then, without a word, he crossed the tent, shouldered past the dumbfounded Orestes, and stepped back out the slit he had made in the wall. Standing between his two sons, he gazed around in silence, glancing up at the reddening streaks of the sky in the east, listening to the soft morning sounds of the enormous camp, the murmur of women stoking cooking fires, the cackling of the domesticated Persian fowls awaiting their ration of seed. He sighed, a slow expulsion of breath from the depths of his chest. After a moment, seizing a handful of hair at his temple, he grimaced, and pulled it in a bloody clump from his scalp.

Lifting high the sacrifice of pain, he raised a shrill, keening wail, calling out his own name in his lamentation of the dead. For a moment, the camp fell silent, and then other voices, too, lifted in song, the ancient Hunnish hymn of mourning. As yet, the people did not know for whom they cried, knowing only that it was for a man of merit, for the swelling song had originated in the throat of Edeco, one of the great men of the Hunnish nation, and a man of Edeco's rank did not cry in mourning except for a man of merit to him.

II

The ceremony was of a majesty not seen since the death of Attila's brother, Bleda, years before. Three miles from the city, on a bier set in the midst of the expansive plain, Attila's body lay sheltered under a brightly colored, silken pavilion, the sides left unfastened at the bottom to flutter and flap in the gusting wind, alternately exposing and obscuring the body where it rested. For hundreds of paces around the bier, the city's population shambled in a circle, moaning and weeping, the tears profuse, the grief genuine. Women and old men bared their backs, flagellating themselves with thorn branches and leather horsewhips until their skin was rasped and raw, while younger men used daggers and swords on themselves to inflict deeper cuts, a more profound sign of mourning for their fallen king. Even foreign emissaries participated in the rite. The small collection of Persian, Vandal, Suevi, and Ostrogoth noblemen, in the court finery of their respective nations, were given places of honor in the front ranks of the circle of mourners, yet they, too, were compelled by stern-faced Hunnish cavalrymen to rend their garments, bare their chests, and perform at least cursory rivening of the skin.

In the space before the front ranks of observers, Attila's greatest mourners formed up, a picked company of Hunnish cavalrymen, who wheeled round the fluttering bier in a direction contrary to that of the circling townspeople, chanting the ancient Hunnish funeral song in honor of their nation's hero. The horsemen weaved and dodged among one another in intricate patterns, some standing on the broad, flat backs of their mounts, others dipping low to the ground, clinging to their horses' sides with merely one heel and a hand on the mane, the skillful maneuvers of a people born to the horse. As they rode, they hewed to the ancient Hunnish custom and ritual, gashing their faces with daggers, bewailing their leader not with womanly tears of sorrow, but with the thick, red blood of warriors.

For three days the riders performed their incessant wailing and wheeling, while each night, after the mourners returned to the city to attend to their needs and break their fasts, skilled Maeotian embalmers worked to preserve the king's body for its coming trip to the afterlife. Unlike Bleda, and Attila's father, Mundzuk, and his uncle Rugila before him, the body of this king was not to be consumed by fire. In life he had been a hero, a man measured above other men, a living god unsurpassed even by those in the heavens. It would be unseemly for his body to be burned and destroyed like that of any other living creature. A god he had become, and a god he would remain, preserved and entombed forever, by the orders of his now godlike offspring, Attila's eldest son, Dengizich.

On the fourth day, the king's body was lifted from its bier in solemn ceremony and placed inside a silk-lined coffin built of thin-planed Danuvian river oak and plated with polished gold, scrupulously crafted by Gothic artisans in the city who had been diverted from their regular tasks as makers of weaponry, armor, and jewelry. This box, in turn, was inserted into a tightly fitted container, plated with burnished silver, representing his status as a mighty king and father of his people. Finally, the whole was sealed within a third coffin of solid iron, for it was by this metal that he had subdued nations. This box was heavier than the first two combined, its lid and joints sealed against the corruption of outside air and other humors by carefully applied molten lead. The entire construction, weighing well over a thousand pounds, was lifted on poles by strong men, and placed atop a wooden wagon borne on iron-shod wheels and drawn by massive Germanic workhorses imported from distant agrarian tribes as beasts of burden. Two more wagons were laden with additional gold and silver—coins and more coins, jewelry and even raw nuggets preserved as they had been found, without smelting—as well as other precious objects, fine war bows and ceremonial blades, unusual swords and battle-axes of distant provenance, and gold-plated skulls of past enemy rulers who had been taken and killed in battle, all to ease the king's transition into the afterlife. Attila's dozen or so senior *logades,* his Chosen Men, warlords and generals, dipped deep into their personal coffers to contribute to the king's passage, and two additional wagons were filled with their donations: silver goblets and trays, bridles studded with precious stones, Indian pearls, even perishable luxuries imported from distant lands by camel train: black peppers and dates, fine linens, and embroidered hangings.

Two cavalry units were mustered, of a hundred men each—one squadron Germanic, led by Orestes, the other Hunnish, led by Edeco, in accordance with the funeral instructions expressed by Dengizich for his father's *strava.* To assist in their task, each horseman was assigned four spare mounts from the royal herd. Fifty of the strongest Alani palace slaves were collected to attend to the casket wagons; and the city's chief shaman, the elderly *qam* who had presided over the funeral rites, was called to bless the assembly, and to accompany the men on their journey. Without further ceremony, the funeral cortege set out for the burial.

Odoacer trotted his horse to the side of his father's animal, to which he had been summoned.

"We are nearly there," the older Hun said tersely.

Orestes, who rode silently at Edeco's other side, glanced at him sharply.

"Nearly at the place of burial?" he asked.

Edeco stared straight ahead.

"Nearly at the campsite," he replied. "Two days from the place of burial, at the wagons' speed. The two cavalry squadrons will wait at the camp under Orestes' command, while I accompany the slaves and treasure wagons to the burial. If all goes well, we will return to the campsite in four or five days."

"I will go with you to bury the king," Orestes said. "Your son can command the horsemen in the camp until I return."

"I have fifty slaves to accompany me. Attila was a Hunnish king, and I will give him a Hunnish burial. I do not need your assistance, unless you plan to wield a shovel."

The German half turned on his horse and glanced back at the five wagons lumbering slowly behind in the rutted road. Dusty canvas tarpaulins sheltered their contents. He turned back to Edeco.

"Attila was king of my people as well as of yours," Orestes replied. "And now he is king of neither. I will go with you." Setting heels to his horse, he cantered away, up to the head of the caravan, as Edeco glared at his back.

Odoacer watched his father's reaction thoughtfully.

"Leave me at the camp with the troops," he said after a moment's pause. "I have captained such a number of men before, both Huns and foreigners, and Onulf is commanding even more men in the capital now, until we return. Orestes can travel with you. I do not need his presence."

Edeco glanced at his son and smiled thinly.

"I have complete confidence in your ability to command two hundred men for a few days," he replied. "That is not why I objected to Orestes' coming. The truth is, I do not wish him to know the burial site." He shook his head. "Nevertheless, he was commander of the king's guard and cavalry, and is my equal in rank. I cannot prevent it."

Odoacer looked at him in puzzlement.

"Why would you wish to?"

Edeco gazed into the distance with a half smile.

"The burial site—it is sacred ground. A cave set in the side of a cliff, invisible from the plateau above and the canyon floor below. It is accessible only by a narrow ledge cut into the rock."

"And it is sacred?"

"Very. Ancient paintings cover the walls, magical paintings—naked men hunting animals never seen in these parts, hairy elephants, lions with tusks. The farthest recesses of the cave contain strange bones, crumbling with age. Such a place can only have been inhabited by gods."

"What kind of bones?" Odoacer asked, wide-eyed.

"Many kinds. Men's bones—enormous skulls with ridged brows, thick thighbones such as no man has today but for giants in traveling circuses—mixed with bones of creatures, tusks, skulls of oxlike animals. The cave is so dry, some still retain vestiges of skin, as hard as the bones themselves. Yet there is a small spring nearby. It is a silent place, and secret. A fitting place for a king to be buried."

"And you wish no other man to know of it."

Edeco sighed.

"It is done. Orestes will know of it, whether I wish him to or not. Despite everything, he was loyal to Attila, and he would follow me to find it. So he will know of it."

They camped that night at the edge of the canyon that interrupted the grassy plain they had been traversing to that point. The next morning, the wagons were unloaded, and their contents distributed among the Alani slaves, who were roped together in a long line, bearing the valuable treasure in packs slung over their shoulders, or in large, stiff baskets perched upon their heads. The most precious cargo of all—the cadaver of the king, sealed in the threefold coffin—was mounted on two stout poles, its weight distributed across the broad shoulders of the expedition's largest slaves, who despite their great strength, still staggered and rocked their cargo precariously as they trod the uneven ground. Only Edeco and Orestes remained mounted and armed, saddlebags empty but for the spare weapons they carried, backs unencumbered but for their Hunnish war bows and shields. As the sun rose blood-red over the horizon, the party set off, descending rapidly from the high plain to the labyrinthine passages of the lower canyons. They quickly dropped out of sight of the Germanic and Hunnish soldiers peering at them over the lip of the cliff on which they stood.

Four days later, the burial party returned to the campsite and the waiting soldiers. Upon their arrival, before saying a word, Orestes assembled the men of the camp in a half circle at the lip of the canyon, as if to give a speech. The Alani slaves, sweating and filthy from their descent and return from the canyon, stood on one side of the assembly, at the edge of the cliff, with the Hunnish and Germanic soldiers a short space away. All eyes were on Orestes, who stood with the soldiers. Normally, the slaves were not included in such events, but were hobbled like horses or chained in groups of three or four at the rear of the camp until needed. This time, as they congregated, the Alani glanced around in some consternation. Edeco observed them for a moment, then turned away.

"Align the men in formation," Orestes ordered quietly.

"Infantry formation," Odoacer called, and the two hundred troops separated into two companies, Germans to the left, Huns to the right. The Alani milled before them, some squatting in fatigue.

"Draw bows," the older man commanded the troops.

Odoacer watched silently, in growing concern, as the men unslung the weapons, strung them in a single, fluid motion, and nocked arrows to the strings. The slaves, suddenly fearful, began shouting, clustering together at the cliff edge, as far from the wall of troops as they could get without falling off.

"Fire at will!" Orestes ordered.

The soldiers hesitated, glancing from Orestes to Odoacer, who had been their commander for the past several days when the older men and slaves had been in the canyon. Odoacer opened his mouth to question the order, but Orestes broke in, glaring at the troops.

"You will follow *my* command," Orestes said menacingly. "The slaves are no longer needed. *Fire at will!*"

Odoacer stood watching in silent horror, and Edeco turned away in disgust.

The air filled with a sibilant hiss as two hundred arrows found their marks. There was scarcely time for the cowering slaves to cry out before their voices were silenced. Several, in the rear of the group, fell or jumped over the cliff edge, dragging with them a dozen more who were chained to them, but no sound was heard as they fell to the canyon floor. The remainder crumpled and collapsed where they stood in an awkward heap, elbows protruding into the ribs of their comrades, shocked eyes staring glassily into the soldiers' impassive faces. The bowmen remained tense, in firing position, some having already drawn and nocked a second arrow by sheer force of habit. All was utter silence, but for the distant rushing of the wind and the snuffling of the curious horses behind them.

Orestes nodded in satisfaction and turned away.

"Push them over the edge," he ordered. "And roll the wagons over as well. Then we depart."

The elderly shaman who had accompanied the horsemen thus far slipped off his mount, and warily peered over the edge of the precipice, seeking signs of the dead below, or perhaps of their souls. Odoacer wondered briefly the form these might take, whether vapors, like clouds, or wisps of shadows, bewildered shades flitting silently and hesitantly from rock to shrub along the cliff wall, fearfully gaining their bearings before ascending or descending to the afterlife. The elderly man began his slow, droning chant for the dead, as a soldier approached with a spare horse for the final sacrifice, and Odoacer put such thoughts out of his mind.

He turned and found his father watching some distance away, and the two made their way to where the Hunnish horsemen stood patiently waiting for them, packed and mounted. Edeco's silence was absolute, but he sensed the questions forming in his son's mind as they walked along.

"Fifty-two men knew the location of Attila's tomb," Edeco said simply. "Fifty-two men knew of the treasure heaped around the caskets, knew the caskets to be constructed of precious metals, knew what they contained. Fifty-two men knew of that holy site."

Odoacer nodded silently.

"And now only two know."

Edeco glanced at Orestes, who was still breaking camp with his troops. The German's mood seemed unaccountably cheerful, and he could even be heard laughing at some joke, despite the somberness of the moment. Edeco turned back to his son.

"Only two," he replied flatly.

Within an hour, nothing was left to indicate the presence of the troops but the flattened grass and the puddles of blood at the cliff edge. The horsemen thundered back across the plain toward the Hunnish capital, to begin a new era, under a new king, and the cliff top reverted once again to the possession of the screeching eagles and the rushing wind.

III

Odoacer sensed the change even before the sun rose.

For three days the troops had kept up a steady canter toward the capital, each man changing horses at regular intervals, stopping neither to eat nor eliminate during the daylight hours—for the Huns had long before taught their allies that all things of men could be performed on horseback, or delayed until nightfall and then completed on solid ground. The Germans kept largely to themselves, leading the spare horses, and setting the pace in accordance with the men's and the animals' fatigue. The Huns preferred to sprint off and spread out at the start of each day's stage, ranging far as scouts and hunters, identifying the optimal route, spying out potential enemy encampments, shooting game to be shared later. At night, the two groups camped apart—sometimes by only a hundred paces, other times by a greater distance, depending upon the lay of the land and the location of the water. This had several advantages: the blaze of cooking fires spread over a wide swath of terrain would give enemy spies the impression of a larger group of men; the party would be less vulnerable to surprise attack, because an enemy would have to split its forces to cover a broader front; most important, the Huns simply preferred to sleep apart from the Germans, whom they mistrusted and disliked as being noisy and quarrelsome. The antagonism between Edeco and Orestes had filtered down to the men, and with Attila dead, there was

no longer a common bond, no shared leadership or mutual
enemy to join their interests. Tonight, the two parties slept
a half mile apart, out of hearing range of one another,
connected only by their horses, which mingled and grazed
together, gravitating naturally into a large group for safety
from predators, and watched over by two pairs of sentries
from each set of troops.

When Odoacer woke, wrapped in his cloak in the grass, he
could feel a difference. A herd of a thousand horses makes a
certain level of noise, even at night. Never was the darkness
free of the whinny and snuffling of mares as they called to
their mates, or of the snorting of stallions as they encroached
upon each other's territory or approached the females. Yet
this night was different. It was not silent—darkness on the
steppe is never silent, always there is the cooing of ground
birds, the yipping of foxes, the rustling of small life in the
grass—yet it was different. There was no sound of horses.

Odoacer stood. Peering into the darkness, he saw other
Huns nearby doing the same, and a few had already begun
trotting away from the creek by which they had been sleeping, in the direction where the horses had last been seen.

"Father!" he said, in a loud whisper.

"Here," Edeco grunted, from an unexpected direction.
Odoacer turned and stared into the dim light cast by the
banked coals of the campfires. His father emerged from the
darkness with a large bulk over his shoulders. Lumbering up
to his son, he dropped the body of a man at his feet. Odoacer
looked down uncomprehendingly, and bent to examine it,
but Edeco stopped him.

"He's dead," he said gruffly.

"Dead? What . . . ? Who . . . ?"

Other Hunnish troops began gathering, staring silently at
their dead comrade. As Odoacer looked more carefully, he
noted a gaping gash at the man's throat.

"Isn't that one of the men assigned to watch the horses tonight?" Odoacer asked.

"It is," said his father.

"And the horses . . . ?"

"Gone. Taken or scattered. Probably both. I would need a torch to examine the tracks."

"But who? Where are the other guards?"

It was a question that need not have been asked, for he already knew the answer, even before the single surviving Hunnish sentry staggered into the camp, bleeding heavily at the throat.

"The Germans," he whispered, blood gurgling from the wound. "The Germans—they are gone!"

Over the next day, several dozen horses wandered back into the camp. By examining the tracks, Edeco reconstructed the events of the night before: Orestes had resolved to leave with his men, and to avoid being followed, had taken as many of the horses as possible in the darkness. Stealing them all would have been impossible—each man would have had to lead away ten animals, while simultaneously avoiding or killing the Hunnish sentries and herdsmen. No, the treacherous Germanic leader must have ordered his sentries to approach their Hunnish counterparts under the guise of a question or conference, kill them silently, and then, when all chance of warning had been eliminated, sent in the remainder of his troops to capture as many horses as possible and walk them away to a safe distance. Those that resisted, or that were simply grazing too far distant to round up easily, were scattered with whips and sling-stones into the grasslands to prevent the Huns from following, or even from returning to the capital city.

Understanding the night's events was not difficult. It was the outcome that worried Edeco.

"Odoacer, take the troops back to the city. Have the men double up on the horses, or run alongside on foot."

"With so few horses, the return will now take much longer."

"It doesn't matter," said Edeco.

"And you?" Odoacer replied. "What will you do?"

"I will take ten men. One horse each."

"Where—to follow Orestes? With ten men? That's suicide."

"No, not to follow Orestes," Edeco replied. "With his spare horses, and two days' head start, we would never catch him."

"Where then?"

"To the tomb. Because . . ." He paused.

"Because," Odoacer completed the sentence for him, "only two know the location. I will go with you. There will soon be three who know."

Edeco hesitated for a moment, then shrugged. "As you wish."

The small band of Huns retraced the route they had just traveled from the cliffside campsite, trotting easily and carefully, warily examining the signs left by Orestes' troops as they rode. The trail was not difficult to follow: the Germans had not even bothered to disguise their route. Odoacer rode beside his father, his expression tense and bitter. He glanced at Edeco, but if the older man was angry or worried, he did not show it: his weathered face remained as calm and impassive as ever, though for hours on end he rode in complete silence, eyes fixed on the distant horizon.

The turnabout in route and fortune brought with it other hardships. The quantities of dried meat, carefully calculated to last just long enough for the trip to the tomb and back, were soon exhausted, and the Huns' progress was slowed as they were forced to hunt antelope and dress their kills. Odoacer briefly consoled himself with the thought the Germans would face the same delay, until his father pointed out why they had taken with them so many spare horses—the slower and younger ones could be culled and butchered for food. After an entire day and night without spotting any game, Edeco ordered the men to revert to the ancient practice of their forefathers when traveling swiftly through barren lands—each rider gently incised the large vein in his mount's foreleg, draining a bowlful of the steaming crimson liquid, and mixing it with milk from the udders of the mares. Odoacer and the younger riders had never performed such a task, but the older men, those who had ridden the steppe years before the Huns had become a great tribe under Attila, tapped their horses' veins with practiced smoothness and gulped down the frothy mixture with relish. Odoacer soon acquired facility in the technique and, with enough hunger, gained enjoyment in the drink.

After five days' ride they arrived again at the base camp from which Edeco, Orestes, and the slaves had descended into the canyon earlier. Orestes' party, too, had returned here, several days before; and from the volume of waste in the latrine, they could not have stayed more than half a day, at best. Edeco did not even dismount, but continued immediately toward the steep path that wended its way down the slope to the canyon floor. His comrades followed without a word.

Arriving at the bottom an hour later, Odoacer looked about, disoriented by the dark shadows and the jumbles of boulders, tipped logs, and dry streambeds that seemed to veer off in every direction. A foul smell assailed his nostrils, and without thinking, he dismounted and stepped a few paces into the shadows at the edge of the cliff to investigate. There, he encountered an enormous mass of rotting cadavers, limbs entwined about limbs, bones and skulls crushed, broken arrows emerging from the bodies. The mountain of decaying flesh was topped by a single grinning horse's head, leathery lips pulled back from yellow teeth, emerging from the stack of human forms like the head of a centaur. Oddly, the entire heap seemed to shimmer and heave, and Odoacer approached more closely to what he realized was the place where the massacred Alani and sacrificial horse had been pushed from the cliff top above.

Toeing the nearest corpse, he found it roiling with an army of maggots, and he stared in fascination at the voracious corruption. A million shiny, white creatures writhed and turned, each struggling to free itself from the mass of its fellows and gain its own meager scrap of flesh on which to feed, reaching blindly, coiling above the others, grasping for a hold the air itself could not provide. Taken as a whole, viewing the entire mound of corpses, the movement was indistinct, of a subtlety that deceived, that fooled the eye into seeing, one moment, a scene of quiet death, and the next moment, a teeming, ferocious life. Yet focusing on a single gleaming worm was impossibly mesmerizing, like observing a single mote of dust in an entire cloud of it, and the creatures' sound—for now he realized there was a sound emanating from the churning mass—was hypnotic, a low hissing, like meat roasting in a fire. With great effort he tore his eyes away, walked several paces, then knelt and retched. After a moment he looked up to see his father observing him and gesturing to him. Shaking his head to clear it of the sight, he mounted his horse and followed.

It was some time before he found words to speak.

"Father, could the Germans have found their way without a guide?" he asked hoarsely. "It is a labyrinth, and Orestes had only been here once."

Edeco shook his head.

"Orestes had no need for a guide when he returned just now. Our trail with the fifty slaves and the burial party was quite visible, as it still will be for a month or two. Look." He pointed to a mound of dried dung at the side of the trail, left by one of the horses on the earlier trip through the canyon. "No, Orestes had no need for a guide."

"How far is the cave?" Odoacer asked.

"It took me three days to arrive there with the slaves before, while bearing the coffins on their shoulders. It should take us about half a day on horseback."

For several hours they rode in silence, carefully picking their way through the jumble of boulders and thorny scrub on the canyon floor. Just as the sun dipped into its last quadrant, Edeco looked up.

"We are here," he said simply.

Odoacer looked up, carefully scanning the cliff walls above him.

"I see nothing."

"The entrance is invisible from the canyon floor. Come."

Dipping into a narrow gully to the side, like an alleyway off a city street, they found a rocky ledge traversing up the cliff face, barely wide enough for a man to walk without turning his shoulders.

"The best way to enter the cave is by climbing that trail," Edeco said. "Leave the horses and men here—we'll go up alone and return the same way."

Scrambling up the narrow rock face, grasping tenuous roots and shrubs, they finally arrived at the top, dirty and scraped.

"You couldn't have carried the triple coffin up that way— it would have been impossible," grunted Odoacer.

"No. A few of the slaves stayed at the bottom with the coffin and treasure, while the rest of us climbed up to arrange the ropes. We had long poles with us, the ones used to carry the loads. We lashed them together into two cranes, which we mounted at the mouth of the cavern here. We let ropes down from the cranes to the slaves below, who attached them to the coffin. Then it was merely a matter of hauling it up the side of the cliff to the cave entrance, and swinging it in."

Odoacer bent and struck a flint, quickly starting a small fire with a tuft of dry grass. As he fanned the flame, he looked out over the canyon. The sun was just setting over the distant western rim, and the dim, elongated orb was perfectly aligned behind an oddly symmetrical clump of shrubs, reminiscent of a cottage or small tower, the only plant life visible for miles in either direction along the far canyon lip. He marked the sight—almost as if the bushes had been planted purposely in alignment between the setting sun and the mouth of the cave, just as shamans sometimes mark the points of the winter and summer solstices with stacked rocks or mounds of rubble. He knew that was not the case here, for this day was of no astronomical significance, and within a few weeks the sun would be setting farther to the northwest and would no longer be aligned with the wilted greenery. Nevertheless, the reminder of the solstice brought to mind the melancholy he always felt on such occasions, the passing of the seasons, the end of a year or of an era, the beginning of another.

"Fire ready?" Edeco grunted.

Odoacer toed the flame. After a moment he had lit two

withered roots, handing one to his father. Edeco bent and ducked into the low, dark hole in the rock. Following his father's lead, Odoacer angled his own stick to create maximum flame, and passed through the opening. Scraping his shoulder painfully on the rock wall, he planted his feet, stood slowly, and allowed his eyes to adjust to the dim light.

Already his father was carefully moving forward over the sandy cave floor. Raising his fire-stick, Odoacer, too, stepped into the cave's depth, then suddenly stopped short. The great iron coffin lay on a crude pedestal of four rocks that had been rolled against the back wall. It looked just as he remembered it, but for the grimacing human head mounted on the top, staring at him with empty eye sockets.

"What . . . ?" Odoacer began, surprised.

"One of the slaves." Edeco shrugged. "Died when his rope broke. We thought mounting the head on the coffin might frighten away unwanted visitors. I see we were wrong."

Odoacer examined the iron.

"The coffin is undisturbed. The seal has not been cracked."

"No, the Great King has not been touched. Probably the coffin was too unwieldy for Orestes."

"Then why did he come?"

"What do you see around you?" Edeco asked.

Odoacer looked.

"Nothing . . ."

"Precisely. The gold, the jewels, the garments, everything the king needed to ease his passage—gone." Edeco looked around the cave once more, briefly, as his torch began to sputter out. The floor was bare, without even a dropped coin to indicate the existence of the treasure that had been there. "It is as if we had never brought it," he muttered.

Odoacer squatted and stepped back out the cave entrance. He gazed into the vast canyon, shrouded in the shadows cast by the dying light, and at the sheer drop to the floor below.

The treasure of an entire nation, the passage toll of a dead king, the ransom and plunder of decades of warfare—gone, in a single night of unguarded horses. Like the heat of a fire left carelessly untended. His heart swelled with anger, thirsted for vengeance.

"Orestes will die for this," he said, preparing the ropes for the climb out. "I vow he will die, and will burn for eternity in his god's hell."

Edeco stepped over to his son at the cave entrance and calmly took the coil of ropes from him.

"It is too late to return to the canyon floor tonight," he said. "It would be dangerous to climb out in the dark."

Odoacer eyed the cave, peering into the darkness as if in a daze.

"And what would you have us do?"

Edeco shrugged and lay down on the stone floor at the cave entrance.

"Vengeance is not ours to have," he said. "At least not tonight. Orestes' hell will wait. For now, we sleep in the shelter of our king."

They spoke no words until far into the next morning, after they had clambered down at sunrise and rejoined their men on the canyon floor for the somber return to the steppe. The story they told shrouded all in anger and disbelief.

IV

Odoacer smelled the trouble, or rather noted the absence of smell, long before they returned to the capital. Normally, on a fair autumn morning, the fetid, low-lying smoke of the dung and turf fires would hover far over the steppe, casting a wispy, grayish pall, collecting in low areas and swirling in breezes, dissipating only when the heat of the sun warmed the ground, drying the night's dew and causing the wind to spring up and issue from God's storehouses beyond the horizon. The Huns were swift-riding in warfare, stealthy on the attack, stolid and silent when moving camp to the winter ranges along the Danuvius when the cold crept down from the north—and wary when traveling in their family clans, like packs of ranging wolves or herds of wild horses roaming the steppe. Nevertheless, when gathered in the great assemblies around the royal household—as they did twice a year for ropings and festivals, or during momentous occasions like the death of a king—at those times, stealth was cast to the wind. Ten thousand fires would be lit, the air would ring with shouts of celebration or the keen of mourning, bawling animals would be slaughtered by the hundreds for food or for sacrifice, and smoke from the cooking fires and holocausts would suffuse the low, still air of the steppe for many miles.

Yet today, scarcely three weeks after they had left the great camp to bury the king, none of this was evident. Even as the riders came in sight of the shallow valley, the air remained clear, though the breeze had scarcely begun to lift. No sentries emerged to challenge or greet them; no bands of boys shot blunted arrows tipped with dirt clods into their horses' flanks to startle them. Most ominously, no camps of garrison troops—whether Ostrogoth, German, or Hunnish— were stationed in the outposts of the sprawling city. The camps were there, but uninhabited—tents removed, latrines filled with dirt, corrals emptied of stock. Edeco rode straight through without glancing to either side, his face cold and expressionless, but Odoacer and the accompanying troops surveyed the scene in deep puzzlement.

It was not until they approached the makeshift city gate—a wooden wagon bed turned on its side and hinged crudely to the palisaded walls—that they saw their first sign of human life. Odoacer's brother, Onulf, sat his horse at the half-open entrance, his lean body framed by the sharpened stakes of the walls on either side, watching silently as his father and brother approached. Though only a year younger than Odoacer, his face in the past month had aged considerably, and his eyes had the weary, suspicious look of a man who has seen too many battles and received too little plunder, and who now despairs.

Edeco signaled the troops to halt, and he and Odoacer walked their horses slowly to the gate. Edeco approached in silence, and then questioned with his eyes, his glance flitting around the space where the Germanic troops had once been lodged, and then back to Onulf's face.

"Gone," his son said simply. "We awoke in the night two weeks ago and found them breaking camp, preparing to leave, as if commanded to do so—yet we could not imagine who would have given such a command, as Orestes was with you. Dengizich ordered the Hunnish troops to stop them, but before we could deploy, the Ostrogoth camp, too, began to disassemble."

"There is no solidarity between the Ostrogoths and the Germans," Edeco replied. "Certainly not without the Hunnish command to force it."

"We could not force it," Onulf replied. "You were absent, and the king's two sons already at the palace, Dengizich and Ernac, fell to squabbling with Ellac, who arrived just after you left, with his clan of Acatziri Huns from the east. Others arrived as well—Emnetzur, Ultzindur, Hormidac, and some more distant kin. The city is filled with warlords and their troops, openly dividing the king's mandate among themselves, trading nations and peoples like baubles, threatening even to kill one another's followers."

"They are dividing the land? Dividing the steppe?" Edeco asked, incredulous that such a thing could happen so soon after Attila's death.

Onulf measured his words carefully.

"No, not the land—the peoples who occupy it. Land without people is of no interest—it is men that are needed. Many Hunnish warriors and clans unaffiliated with Attila's sons have already fled the city in fear. The Angisciri and Bittugure Huns have departed, and the Bardore are preparing to go. We thought that was why the Germanic allies had marched out as well—they did not wish to be divided among Attila's sons. Until your other troops returned from Attila's burial several days ago, riding double on their horses for lack of animals. Then we understood."

"And what did you understand?" Edeco asked.

"What the Germans had known all along. Their main

force left here the same day Orestes broke with you. He had planned it all in advance. The timing had been prearranged."

"And did you learn where Orestes went?"

"We guessed, and your eyes now confirm it. Father, the Hunnish Council is expecting you."

"They are in session now?"

"They have been in the palace for three days."

"They sent you here to tell me this?"

"Yes, and I have been waiting." He looked grimly at his brother. "And they call for Odoacer to appear as well."

"Then we must not disappoint the Council," Edeco said as he heeled his horse forward, and Odoacer fell into step beside him.

Odoacer could not understand it: the Great Hall had scarcely changed since he had seen it nearly a month earlier, the night of Attila's death. Tables and chairs were still upended, though pushed haphazardly against the walls to clear space in the middle of the room. The vomit and spilled wine from the celebration had been cleaned, though a vestigial sourness lingered in the air, mixed with smoke from a smoldering brazier in the corner and the rank odor of unwashed men. *Had no one thought to restore the hall to a condition befitting the king of the Huns?* he asked himself. *But who is the king of the Huns?*

He forced his attention back to Attila's eldest son, Dengizich. He was the king's apparent heir—yet his younger brother, Ernac, Attila's favorite, was seated beside him on an identical throne, looking scarcely older than a boy, but with a hard, intelligent cast to his eyes. Ellac, an estranged middle son, a hulking, heavy-browed warrior who led a powerful tribe of horse thieves and raiders in the east, stood imposingly between them, apparently unwilling to cede any notion of authority to his older and younger brothers. And what had Onulf said—that other kin, too, claimed a share in command of the empire? The elderly counselor Hormidac sat cross-legged on a side bench, leaning sleepily against the wall a few steps from Emnetzur and Ultzindur, the young and powerfully built sons of Attila's stepbrother, who jointly controlled the critical fortresses of Utus, Oescus, and Almus in lower Dacia. They and a dozen or so other chieftains sat attentively, eyeing the newcomers as they approached the dais.

There were no greetings or preliminary words of welcome as was customary at tribal councils under Attila. Rather, a stony silence prevailed, as all eyes fixed unblinkingly on Edeco and Odoacer. After a long moment, the stillness was broken.

"We did not burn the body on a pyre during the *strava,* as is customary," Ernac intoned, his harsh voice and sharp gaze belying his youthfulness. "Since the king had become a god on earth, the *qam* revealed he should be left intact to assume his rightful place among the pantheon."

"True," agreed Edeco.

"You were instructed by the Council to bury my father's body in the Cave of the Holies—a place only you and my father knew. The burial slaves were to be sacrificed to the last man, to eliminate any memory of its location."

"Also true."

"And yet," Ellac broke in menacingly, "you allowed a barbarian to witness the burial, and then to escape. A vast treasure, enough to purchase an empire, was stolen from under our very noses. And now half of Germany will know where the king's body rests."

Edeco took a deep breath.

"It is one thing for the traitor Orestes to flee to Germania with a small band of plunderers," he said. "It would be quite another for him to return to Hunnia with a force large enough to challenge us, then find the site to desecrate the tomb. The king's coffins are intact, Attila's body untouched by all but the gods."

"For now," Ellac snorted. "What about the future?"

Edeco held the younger man's contemptuous gaze.

"The way to the cave is difficult," he replied, "a labyrinth of ravines. After the traces of our own passage fade, the route will be impossible to find again. Orestes certainly will

not be able to explain it to anyone else. The secret is safe—
it is known only by him, and it will die with him—"

"No," Dengizich interrupted, in a tone so soft the entire
room fell silent and all leaned forward to better hear. "No,
there is still one man living, in Hunnia, who knows the secret. Perhaps two." He glared pointedly at Odoacer and then
shifted his gaze back to Edeco.

"The penalty for betrayal is death," Ellac spat, eyes full of
venom.

"I will seek out the German!" Odoacer blurted. "He is the
one who must die, and I will—"

"Silence!" Ellac cut him off. "You were not asked to defend yourself, pup!"

"And yet," Ernac interjected, "the Council is divided as to
your fate. It is not that we believe death too harsh. On the
contrary, some of us think it perhaps too lenient . . ."

"Exile, to roam with the wolves for the rest of their lives,
would be more fitting," old Hormidac wheezed from the side
bench, and several of the elders nodded their heads in agreement.

"We will continue to discuss your case," Ernac continued,
his boyish face hardening, "and render a decision by sunset
tomorrow. In the meantime, you and your sons will remain
confined in your family compound, forbidden to emerge,
even into the rest of the city, until authorized by us."

Ellac glared at his younger brother with evident disgust at
such leniency, but Ernac ignored him and, looking up, nodded slightly to the Hunnish guards at the door.

"My men will accompany you to your compound," Ernac
said. "You will not be bound, for now, but you will follow
their instructions completely." Four guards stepped up to
Edeco's and Odoacer's sides, and the two men turned and
strode with this new escort out the main door. Outside, Onulf
waited with his own escort of guards. Looking at his father
and brother, he shrugged in resignation, and they began the
long walk out the palace courtyard, through the inner gates,
and across the city to Edeco's family compound.

The streets were silent and half deserted. Oddly, there were no Hunnish men to be seen. The absence of foreigners was understandable—the Ostrogoths and Germans had abandoned their camp earlier, and thus the city as well—its markets stood empty, the makeshift taverns where the German officers gathered when off-duty were silent and dark. Even the brothel tents, set up in vacant lots in random clusters, wherever the roving bands of Greek prostitutes found space when the city gathered after the spring arrival of the herds, flapped empty and forlorn, the jaded women sitting outside the tiny shelters unable to disguise the worry in their faces. Wary eyes peered from the dark doorways of the log huts and felt tents—eyes of women, shooing their youngsters inside, eyes of children, frightened at the guards and prisoners marching past them. Onulf seemed to read his father's and brother's thoughts.

"The three brothers ordered their supporters out of the city—to separate camps, on different sides."

"What, for war?" Odoacer asked. "Has it come to that, then? Attila scarcely dead, and his sons already picking over the scraps?"

"No, not yet," Onulf responded. "There is still a pretense of civility between them. They said it was to bring in the horses for the winter—the Roping. Yet I'm sure it was to identify their own followers, gauge their own strengths. And to prevent their men from being corrupted and turned by the others."

"But the Roping is a festival," Odoacer argued, "with contests and feasting. The women and children watch and participate, yet I see them here, hiding in their huts. This is no Roping."

Onulf concurred with a nod of his head. "Not this year."

Rounding a corner in the muddy streets, they came upon the wooden palisade of Edeco's compound, a four-sided log wall nearly as high and sturdy as the one surrounding the royal palace, though not as extensive. The front wall and two side walls faced the muddy streets of the Hunnish camp, while the rear palisade looked out on the small river, a tributary of the Danuvius, which wound across the steppe and provided the camp its main source of water, as well as some fish. The broad portal stood wide open, and the pair of Hunnish bodyguards who customarily stood beside it were nowhere to be seen.

"What is this?" Edeco asked, as he and the others strode up to the gate and passed directly through, without hesitation or challenge. Just inside the doorway he stopped short, as did his guards, who were clearly as shocked by the sight before them as he was himself.

Inside the compound, the spacious wood-plank structure that for years had served as Edeco's home, carefully assembled and disassembled upon each move of the camp to new grazing grounds, was gone. Nothing was left but a low, black pile of charred beams and curled felt roof-flaps, swaying forlornly in the soft breeze, refusing even to smolder or to smoke, merely lying in cold accusation.

Edeco and his sons stared about, taking in the sight. There was no time to reflect, however, for suddenly an arrow hissed from the ruins of the house and slipped silently into the throat of the guard next to Edeco, dropping him to his knees as blood spurted over Edeco's feet. The others, guards and prisoners, leaped back outside the gate, behind the shelter of the palisade.

"Ellac's men," one of the guards exclaimed, all distinction now of rank and royalty effaced. "They were waiting for us. Run, back to the palace!"

"No!" Edeco ordered, seizing his sons' arms. "They'll expect that, waiting in the street . . ." But it was too late. As their six guards raced around the corner, they were cut down by a hail of arrows from an unknown source, out of Edeco's sight. The guards fell in a heap in the muddy street, dead before they hit, as neat and still as if they had been stacked by executioners to be readied for burial.

Edeco, Odoacer, and Onulf did not linger to investigate. They immediately stepped back inside the portal, slamming it shut behind them and barring the door against the bowmen in the street. Whoever was still inside the compound with them would simply have to be dealt with, and perhaps it would be within the three men's strength and ability to do so. Judging from the number of arrows shot at their guards a moment before, the force attacking from outside the compound would be more than any three men alone would be able to handle.

"There—to the stable!" Odoacer exclaimed, pointing to a detached wooden outbuilding on the far side of the courtyard that had not been damaged by the fire.

The three sprinted across the compound, arrows whizzing past. Just as they reached the door of the small structure, Edeco grunted and stumbled. Odoacer caught him under the arm and dragged him through the door into the unlit room, while Onulf slammed shut the door and braced a heavy board against it on the ground. Immediately, a half-dozen arrows thudded into the wood on the outside, the iron tips of the warheads penetrating the barrier with small spurts of splintered wood, like nails being driven through by a hammer.

Odoacer glanced around at the structure, which had not been occupied by livestock since the men had departed for Constantinople months before. Seeing no danger inside, he laid his father on the dirt floor of the structure and peered at him through the striped sunlight filtering through gaps in the planked ceiling. The arrow had pierced the back of his neck and emerged in the front just above the collarbone, and though it had not killed him, he was gasping for breath, the windpipe penetrated. Blood frothed and bubbled at the opening in the throat, which emitted a hiss as the air escaped from it.

"Father!" Onulf exclaimed, horrified at the wound. "Father!"

The thudding of arrows on the door was replaced by shouts and a loud pounding, as men outside began beating on the wooden barrier. The door was stout, but it would not be long before an axe was found and a true attack could be mounted. Odoacer looked down at his father. The older man's gasping was weaker, his face turning a dark, ashen gray.

"We have no time," he said to his brother quietly. "I'll do

what I can. Barricade the door. Then look to the feed drop on the other side."

He bent down to Edeco, stifling the emotions, the anger and fear that welled up inside him, constricting his stomach. *Don't think!* he commanded himself. *He's a man like any other.* Turning his father on his side, he seized the back of the arrow where the fletching emerged from Edeco's neck, and gently snapped it, striving to hold the shaft steady where it was lodged in the neck. With the shaft now broken clean, he grasped the arrowhead where it had emerged in the front, and smoothly pulled the shaft through, careful not to further enlarge the opening.

The air hissing from the lungs became a full gurgling sound, as blood flowed copiously from the hole now that the main obstruction had been removed. Odoacer glanced at his brother, who was furiously lodging wooden planks against the weakening door and bracing them into the ground.

"How long can you hold them?" he asked, surprised that his voice sounded so calm.

"The door can't open, but they'll smash through it," Onulf replied with a grunt. He was interrupted by a crash as an axe head penetrated the wood next to his shoulder in a shower of splinters. "Or through the wall itself . . ."

Odoacer nodded. "We have to go, then," he replied calmly. Ripping a strip of cloth from the hem of his tunic, he bit off a small section, rolled it into a ball between his teeth, wetting it with his saliva so it would remain hard and compact, then inserted it into the hole below Edeco's throat, pushing it with his thumb until it almost disappeared inside. Biting off another piece, he did the same thing to the hole in the back, then wrapped the remainder of the linen strip gently but securely around his father's neck to hold the two tamps in place. Immediately blood began seeping through, staining the strip a bright crimson; yet it was flowing more slowly than before. Edeco's face remained gray, but lightened slightly, and as much as he gasped and wheezed, some air appeared to be penetrating to his lungs. Odoacer peered into his father's eyes, glassy and dilated.

"Please live," he muttered.

Another axe smashed through the wall near his head. Odoacer looked up.

"Onulf—the feed drop: climb up and open it."

His brother looked up to the small door on the upper half of the far wall. It was perhaps an arm's-length square, with the bottom edge at just over the height of a man's head. Cut into the outer wall of the compound, it was so placed that cut grass and grain could be shoveled into the stable by a slave standing on the bed of a wagon outside, without having to disrupt the compound by entering through the main portal with braying mules and rumbling cart. The door was thick, barred with an iron rod to prevent thieves from passing through the opening, and as strong as the palisaded wall itself.

Onulf seized a rickety stool from a corner and leaped upon it, using the hilt of his dagger to pound back the rusty bar from the fittings in which it had become stuck during the past several months of immobility. Outside the stable's main door, the pounding and smashing of the axes increased in tempo as the attackers heard the activity inside.

Finally edging the bar aside, Onulf gave a mighty push on the stout door, which also had become stuck in its tight fitting. With a whine of the unused hinges at the bottom of the opening, it pushed open from the top and dropped down against the outside of the wall, just as the stool fell away from his feet. Falling heavily onto his chest on the lower sill, Onulf swore under his breath, his head out the opening.

"No one in the road," he whispered hoarsely.

Odoacer nodded from below. "They must all be in the compound. Let's go."

Onulf pulled himself through the opening headfirst, somersaulting and landing on his feet on the road outside. Inside, Odoacer lifted his unconscious father, and without time for gentleness, raised the limp body above his head like an athlete hefting a large stone. Staggering to the feed door, he passed Edeco's head and shoulders through, rested his weight on the rough wood of the lower frame, and then shoved forcefully on the legs to push his father's lower half through. He heard a grunt and shuffle on the other side of the wall as Onulf caught him. Then swiftly hoisting himself up to the opening, he tumbled through headfirst, tucking at the last moment to land on his shoulders, then rolling swiftly onto his feet.

Scarcely a hundred paces away rolled the flat, muddy river, its level low after the long summer dry spell, and in the distance, along the bank, a herd of horses stood knee-deep in the water, drinking, after their two-day walk from the eastern grasslands with two herdsmen in preparation for the winter season.

"That's our escape," Onulf said, glancing at the rugged, hook-nosed steppe ponies, his voice muffled by more frantic pounding on the walls of the stable behind them. He lifted back the door through which they had just emerged, and with a mighty shove, lodged it back into place, as tightly as they had found it a few moments before. "That'll keep them guessing, when they finally break through."

"Which will not be long now," Odoacer replied. "Come on. I'll take him first—hoist him up."

Onulf lifted Edeco under the arms and placed him on Odoacer's back, arms dangling down. Odoacer grasped the wrists firmly, and felt a warm trickle of blood on the back of his neck from his father's wound.

"Go," Odoacer said hoarsely, "get the animals. I'll catch up."

Onulf raced toward the herd, with Odoacer staggering behind, his burden weighing him down in the sticky mud of the riverbank. Ahead, he saw Onulf charge up to the startled horses, where he was challenged by the two young herdsmen, Ostrogoth slaves. It was no hard task for him to seize one of the men, pull him off his horse, and slip the man's own dagger into his throat. Seeing this, the other herdsman raced away, leaving the animals milling and confused. Onulf leaped upon the dead rider's horse, the only one with any equipment—a saddle blanket, a length of rope, a small cloth bag of dried meat—and hurriedly separated out a dozen other animals from the herd. These he drove back to Odoacer, now breathless and staggering from his load.

"So many?" Odoacer looked up, surprised.

"As many as we can handle. Quick, put Father on one and stay here with these."

Odoacer draped his father across the bare back of one of the animals, tying his wrists around the horse's neck with another strip of linen he had ripped from his garment. At this rate, he thought grimly, he would soon be wearing little more than a loincloth. Onulf, meanwhile, had charged back to the main herd on his chosen mount, shouting and waving his hands vigorously, frightening the animals in the water, who broke from him as if he were a madman, splashing farther into the shallow current and then charging up the opposite bank and out of sight. He quickly raced back to where Odoacer was binding their father to the horse. Far behind, at the palisaded wall they had just left, the feed door had been pounded open by the attackers who had broken through into the stable, and an angry head now peered out at them. Curses drifted to them on the breeze.

"We'll follow the herd across the river," Onulf said. "If we catch them, we'll drive them along with us, west. If they've veered off in the wrong direction, at least we'll have prevented Ellac's men behind us from using them. The idiots will have to run back to the palace, explain their story, find their own horses, and organize a chase party. That will give us a head start."

"We have an injured man," Odoacer reminded him.

"But plenty of spare mounts," Onulf shot back.

There was nothing further to say. Grasping his horse's mane in one hand, Odoacer squeezed his thighs tightly around the animal's girth as he had when learning to ride as a boy, without saddle or stirrups for balance. He leaned over to slap the rump of the horse bearing his father, which leaped forward in fright, and then drove the small herd of half-wild ponies splashing furiously into the river, drenching all three men to the skin with brown, frothy water, washing from his hands the spilled blood of his father, the manure-encrusted dirt of the stable floor—and the dust of the once-mighty Hunnish camp, the land of his ancestors. He looked back as the horses pounded through the grassland, following the much larger herd of their brethren they could hear and smell ahead of them. Hunnia, he knew, was dead, as dead as its king, Attila. His father had served Attila well. For the sons, however, it was time to seek new masters.

CHAPTER TWO

Four Years Later, 457 A.D.

ROMAN GARRISON, ARGENTORATUM,
EASTERN GAUL

I

"I don't like it, my lord," the captain muttered.

The flat-bottomed scow, rowed by a crew of hired sailors across the lazy expanse of the Rhine, glided smoothly up to the dock below the city of Argentoratum. A dozen legionaries in full mail lined the quay, staring coldly as the sailors nervously cinched the boat tight to the pilings. The captain had lived on the river his entire life, doing good business in trade goods among the various Germanic tribes of the eastern bank, transporting pelts, cloth, ice, and other merchandise. Yet he could count on one hand the number of times he had been permitted to tie up on the west bank, the Roman side. Even today, as his vessel crossed the centerline of the river a few moments before, he had been rapidly accosted by two Roman patrol cruisers of the Rhine fleet. He was unsure whether it was an escort of honor, given the rank of the man he carried, or an assault squadron. The armed legionaries on those vessels had stared at him with eyes as disdainful and suspicious as this squadron on the dock.

"I'm not paying you to like it," Orestes replied coldly, gazing up to the quay with a calm, neutral expression as the sailors stored their oars and prepared to disembark. "I pay you to ferry my men over, and to wait for me here. If all goes well, I'll return before nightfall."

"I pray you do, my lord. I don't relish spending the night on the Roman side."

Orestes did not answer as he clambered up the ladder to the rough planking of the quay, followed by the three Germanic officers accompanying him. As he eyed the clean-shaven legionaries awaiting them, with their spotless tunics, newly polished mail, and stiff, new leather, he disguised the envy he felt—not for these troopers, but for the officers commanding them. It was the genius of the Roman legions: their ability to take rough country boys, from Tuscany or Syria or even Germania, scarcely able to speak Latin or count to ten without using their fingers; and by training and discipline and not a few well-timed beatings, to turn them into these men, dispassionate and reliable, capable of marching a day and a night without complaint, content to live on biscuit rather than demand meat, cool and professional in every way. If he had an army of men like these, like these Romans, instead of the unwashed rabble he was cursed with, he could rule the world. Today, he vowed, he would take his first steps to that end.

Orestes' comrades assembled on the dock, their appearance in starkest contrast to that of the Romans. All had dressed in their finest gear and weapons, with Orestes resplendent in a flowing cape of soft sable fur, befitting his rank as clan chieftain. His trousers were of the finest woven wool, tucked neatly into the high leather boots he had taken care to clean the night before. The weather was mild, so beneath the cape he wore only a light linen vest embroidered with colorful scenes of Germanic legend. His hair was long, much longer than during his years with the Huns, when caring for it during the long journeys by horseback was an unnecessary vanity. Now he allowed it to flow to the middle of his back, the gray streaks carefully plucked out or dyed, and he dressed it casually in two loose braids tied at the bottom with bits of bright cloth. His greatest extravagance, however, was his mustaches, which he wore untrimmed: magnificent swallow-tailed brushes that flowed over his lips in two long, auburn trails, swaying like tusks below either side of his jaw.

"Lord Orestes?" The decurion commanding the Roman squadron stepped up. "The commander bids you come to him. He informs you he has been away from the garrison reviewing the outposts, and so did not receive the dispatch announcing your arrival until this morning. He has therefore not had time to prepare a welcome befitting your rank." The officer stared deprecatingly at the barbarian attire and unruly hair. "But he conveys that if you will excuse him that protocol, he will attend your petition."

"You will take us to General Ricimer now?" Orestes replied in lightly accented Latin. The decurion eyed him with slight surprise.

"*Count* Ricimer, if you will. He has recently been given command of all the Western Empire's military forces. Hence his passage through Argentoratum. He is touring all the military garrisons along the Rhine. He will be staying only tonight, so I would advise you to present your petition quickly, as he is a man of little time and no patience. My troops will search you for weapons."

Orestes held out his arms as a pair of legionaries patted him and his men down. Swords and daggers were removed, and tossed casually back into the waiting vessel. He then looked down off the pier, and gestured for one of the sailors to hand up a tightly wrapped canvas bag that had been stored under one of the benches. As the sailor dropped it on the dock, Orestes turned contemptuously to the decurion.

"Your men will carry this bag."

The officer's eyes glinted with anger, but seeing the determined expression on the face of the Germanic chieftain, he grudgingly grumbled an order to his men. One of them bent with a grunt and slung the satchel over his shoulder. The legionaries then fell into formation, surrounding the visitors in a square, three on each side, and without visible command from the decurion, they fell into a precise parade-ground march step that again raised Orestes' admiration at the discipline of even these, the most common soldiers of the legions. With tramping rhythm, silent but for the crunch of the gravel and flagstones beneath their feet, the decurion led them away from the wharves, past the thick stone walls protecting the city, and into the winding streets comprising the main garrison of the Eighth Augusta Legion of the Western Roman Empire's Army of the Rhine.

II

Count Ricimer was a man whose hour had arrived and, to his mind, in the fiftieth year of his life, none too soon. Raised since boyhood in the court of Ravenna under the Emperors Honorius and Valentinian, he had a knowledge of the inner workings of the empire's politics that was second to none, including that of the late Count Aetius, in whose shadow he had lived for most of his life and under whose command he had fought skillfully against Attila's forces at Campi Catalaunici four years earlier. Yet Ricimer was no born follower. His maternal grandfather had been the Swebian king Vallia, a terror and later an ally of the Romans many years earlier, and his mother, a princess of the tribe, had married into the Roman nobility. From that side of his family he had inherited his tall stature, widely spaced eyes, and square jaw typical of the men of his tribe. As a young man he had been known as a risk taker and a brawler, and it was his reputation for impetuosity, perhaps, that had kept him from rising through the ranks as quickly as he might have. Instead, for years he had chafed under the rule of those who, by fortune or skill, had been promoted ahead of him.

Yet with the recent deaths of both Aetius and Valentinian, Roman military leadership had fallen into turmoil. Outsiders had exploited the vacuum. The previous year, Gaiseric and his Vandal hordes had invaded Rome from Africa, rampaging through the city and causing the death of the Emperor Maximus before leaving the city waste. The Patrician Avitus had been acclaimed emperor, and since that time generals across the empire had been eyeing him, and one another, and themselves in the mirror, maneuvering to maintain the positions they had attained, or to rise to the highest level of all— general command of all the legions.

For now, at least, this contest had ended. Avitus had been murdered, and by a stroke of good timing, Ricimer had been in the capital that very day and had taken control of the legions before chaos could ensue. The competition was over; Ricimer had won. There only remained for him to consolidate his control by placing on the throne a man pliable to him and acceptable to the Senate, a role handily filled by one of his old military comrades, Majorian. Ricimer's ambitions were fulfilled—absolute military control, and de facto political rule through his friend. Now, however, the hard work began: that of molding the empire, whose glory had declined in recent centuries, into a power worthy of his own ambitions. He had resolved to begin this task with a tour of the legions. He would calculate the military's strengths and weaknesses, particularly on the empire's borders, and identify those commanders on whom he could count for support—and those who would have to be removed.

As the company of Germans was ushered into the small conference room of the aging mansion that served as general staff headquarters, Ricimer greeted them politely though distractedly, resentful of this diversion from his more urgent tasks. He was expected at the garrison of Moguntiacum, forty miles down the Rhine, the day after tomorrow, and knew that unless he completed his inspections here soon, he would be late, and he despised being late. Delay simply allowed rivals and subordinates more time to prepare for him, to plot against him, to devise excuses and shams to hide their shortcomings, which would take him weeks to unravel. If possible, he always preferred to arrive at his destination a day or two early, if only to see the expression on the face of the local commander, often as panic-stricken as if he had just been informed that barbarians had infiltrated in the night and set fire to the command hut. Yet already it was clear that arriving early at Moguntiacum would be out of the question. Ricimer was quickly learning that his new title of count involved not only military command, but diplomatic duties as well. He resigned himself to these additional burdens, set his jaw, and greeted the visiting delegation.

Orestes stepped forward from his escort and strode to greet Ricimer with a handclasp.

"May I be the first from my tribe to congratulate you on your promotion," he said. "God willing, our peoples will enjoy many years of peace and cooperation with one another." As he released Ricimer's hand, he crossed his arms before his chest, ostentatiously displaying the gold Roman citizenship ring he wore on his right forefinger.

Ricimer eyed the German, lingering for a moment on the ring. He considered himself a good judge of character by first impression, yet this man, Orestes, posed difficulties. His manner and looks were barbarian to the extreme, yet his cultivated Latin indicated an educated background, and his Roman citizenship meant he would have to be treated carefully—if not as an equal, then at least as a military colleague. Inwardly, he sighed. This would not be a matter of a quick presentation of credentials, exchange of gifts, and a farewell. He mentally struck the entire afternoon off the calendar.

"It is my pleasure to receive you, General Orestes. I have heard a great deal of you and your people, though I was not aware of your Roman ties until now. You are a citizen, I see?"

Orestes nodded.

"I was born in Gaul, the son of an exiled Alamanni prince. My mother was the daughter of a Roman provincial magistrate, who arranged for my citizenship when I was a young boy, before my father took me back across the Rhine."

Ricimer gestured halfheartedly around at the sparse room. "Forgive my rustic welcome, as my schedule is in a bit of disarray. Would you accompany me on a short tour of the garrison?"

Orestes assented, surprised at the invitation, but only slightly. The facilities at Argentoratum were hardly a secret— the city had been a Germanic trading center for many centuries before the Romans had assumed control. Many of Orestes' older tribesmen still remembered the streets, taverns, and docks, though they had not visited in decades. Although this invitation constituted no great disclosure, Orestes was nevertheless intrigued, for it meant that Ricimer acknowledged him as a commander in his own right. The plan was being accomplished more easily than he had anticipated.

As they stepped outside, Ricimer led his staff and the visiting Germans directly to the parade ground, where a detachment of recruits from the nearby provinces was engaged in exercises involving the rapid assembly and disassembly of artillery pieces. Orestes observed the maneuvers, genuinely impressed.

"I fear the drill is unnecessary," he remarked. "Your men have already mastered the routine."

"No drill is unnecessary," Ricimer responded. "Even if it is not required directly for military preparedness, it keeps the men occupied, maintains discipline. That is especially important for local auxiliary troops, our largest contingent here on the border. It 'Romanizes' them, converts them from barbarians—foreigners—to full-fledged Roman legionaries. But in this case, the soldiers are already trained, as this unit was formed some months ago. The drill is not so much for them . . ."

Orestes looked at him quizzically.

"As for the officers."

"The officers?" Orestes asked.

Ricimer hesitated a moment before continuing.

"I see no reason to hide from you the fact that with the change in administration in Ravenna, a number of officers have been recalled or transferred, and have now been replaced by new staff."

Indeed, Orestes observed that the artillery troops were actually drilling themselves. The young tribune overseeing them stood with jaw jutting in a commanding expression, but silent except for the occasional quiet comment to the centurion standing at his side.

"Paquius Proculus," Ricimer said, as if reading Orestes' mind. "Newly appointed from a staff position in Ravenna. His first field appointment. One of my more capable young officers, yet never commanded artillery. He's a fast learner, though."

"How ironic," Orestes murmured quietly.

"What do you find ironic?" Ricimer asked evenly.

Orestes pondered for a moment before speaking.

"Simply that your situation almost precisely mirrors my own," he replied. "Your military situation, I mean, the state of readiness of your troops."

Ricimer smiled. A comparison between his crack troops and the Germanic hordes, by a Germanic chieftain, no less, would be entertaining.

"In what way?"

"Your officers are inexperienced. Yet your men are superbly trained, even the Germanic auxiliary recruits among them. An admirable force, Count, worthy of the very finest leadership Rome can assign to them, and I have no doubt your new officers will soon be up to the task."

"And your situation?" Ricimer pressed, enjoying the German's analysis despite the thinly veiled arrogance he sensed in the man's bearing and tone.

"My situation, of course, is the complete opposite. My officers are supremely competent."

At this, Ricimer could not help but glance to the side where the other Germans stood a few paces away, chatting quietly with his officers. *Competent?* he wondered in amusement. He examined the long, flowing mustaches, the auburn braids hanging loose down their backs, the greasy leather traveling boots, the battered mail tunics, and the taut muscles, hard despite their age—not one of them was younger than fifty, yet each, he wagered, could easily take down an average twenty-year-old Roman legionary in a wrestling match. *Strong, perhaps. But competent as commanders?*

"Supremely competent," Orestes repeated, "with many years of experience at warfare, among the Huns, against opposing tribes—some of them even against Rome." He smiled. "Yet my men, my common soldiers . . . ," he shook his head sadly.

"The Germans are renowned for their strength and bravery," Ricimer prodded.

"True. Individually, we are unexcelled as fighters. Yet the men are undisciplined and untrained, unaccustomed to cooperation, to working with one another, even to rising in the morning at a decent hour. They are fierce alone, but clumsy as a unit. Brave, but stupid. They would have been completely incapable of rapidly assembling complex machinery like your artillery recruits here."

"Interesting," Ricimer responded, turning and gesturing to Orestes to follow him. "It is time to dine—would you and your staff care to join me?"

Orestes fell into step beside the count as they walked slowly back toward the palace.

"I think not. I assured the boatman we would return before nightfall. His sailors fear spending the night on this side of the river."

"I see."

They proceeded in silence to the massive wooden doors of the building, which a pair of sentries opened to them, saluting smartly as they passed inside. Followed by the other Germanic chieftains and Ricimer's aides, they strode down a nearly empty corridor, the Romans' hobnailed sandals clacking loudly on the stone floor, while the Germans' soft leather boots padded almost noiselessly. They turned into a large reception room with braziers at either end emitting a cheery warmth. Orestes noted that the canvas bag the legionaries had carried from the boat had been brought in and tucked discreetly into the corner, the lacing of its leather buckles and tie-downs still intact. Ricimer strode to a small table in a corner and rang a bell. A steward appeared, bearing a large, wrought-silver flagon.

"Drinks all around, gentlemen," Ricimer announced, as the servant produced goblets from a sideboard and began filling them with a honey-colored liquid. "I greatly enjoy the local wines, and I trust you will accompany me in drinking as much of them as I can during my short stay in this country."

The men smiled and stepped forward, each taking a cup

and toasting his neighbor, before falling into amiable chatting. Ricimer, however, looked straight at Orestes.

"Come with me, General, for a moment."

Orestes set down his drink and followed the count through a nearby door, which led to a smaller room, as elegantly furnished and as warm as the reception salon they had just left, but much smaller, with scarcely enough room for a small rectangular table and a chair on either side. Ricimer closed the door behind them and gestured for Orestes to sit.

"So," Ricimer said, when they were both seated. "I appreciate your greetings, General, but I sense there is something more to your visit. Let us talk now, just the two of us, in honesty and confidence. Precisely why have you come?"

Orestes looked across the table. Faintly, in the background, he could hear the voices of his men, becoming louder and more relaxed as the wine and the warmth of the room had their effect. He regretted neglecting to bring in his own goblet, but there would be ample opportunity to drink later, if all went well. If all did not go well, he would most likely be dead.

He smiled. "I come to report a crime against the state."

"The state?" Ricimer asked, puzzled. "Which state?"

"Rome, of course. A betrayal of the empire by a Roman citizen. First, however, I would like to know the punishment for betrayal."

Ricimer paused and frowned.

"The punishment? That depends. Betrayal comes in many forms. Barbarian towns are full of Roman merchants trading with the enemy, foreign armies are full of ex-Roman soldiers, hired as mercenaries. It is especially common these days, with the borders in flux, yet it is nothing new, nor any cause for great deliberation. If we catch conspirators or traitors, we generally put them to death as expeditiously as possible, to prevent their imprisonment from being a further burden on the state. As I'm sure you are aware"—he nodded at Orestes' gold ring—"being a Roman citizen yourself."

Orestes remained expressionless, but for a vague smile.

"And can convicted traitors ransom their lives instead?"

"Few have money, or they would not have committed betrayal in the first place, no?"

"But if they did?" Orestes pressed. "How would the ransom be calculated? Would it even be accepted? Can one man wipe away his guilt through monetary compensation, while another man, in penury, redeems himself only by paying with his life?"

Ricimer's eyes bored into him.

"An interesting question," he mused, "and I am not sure I am sufficient philosopher to answer it."

"Please make the attempt."

Ricimer leaned back in his chair, gazing at the ceiling.

"Christianity tells us that every man's life is priceless," he replied laconically. "Yet the state acknowledges—indeed *insists*—that every man's life has a monetary value. I would even venture to say that the government could not function were that not the case. If a pedestrian is struck and killed by a cart, then his widow can be placated by a payment from the driver: more if the victim is a wealthy merchant, less if a common laborer, a great deal if a senator. The state, through the courts, sets a precise value in the form of a judicial award."

"Is that not presumptuous, for a judge to thus play God?"

"Perhaps," Ricimer replied, "but do we not all play God, in our own way? We assign monetary values not only to the lives of others, but to our own as well. Whenever we take a risk, whenever we cross a street, whenever we swim in the ocean, or throw ourselves into battle, we are assigning an intrinsic value to our lives, and multiplying it by some intrinsic probability of death occurring from that activity, to determine the precise cost of the risk and measure it against the potential value of the gain or pleasure. If the risk of dying in the current is greater than the pleasure afforded us from the swim, then we will not enter the water. An economic reason, if you will, to explain why generals of the patrician class remain in the rear of battle, while common soldiers of more humble birth fight in the front lines. Not the only reason, of course. But one reason."

Orestes observed him impatiently, drumming his fingers on the tabletop. "So in a word . . . ?"

"In a word: I would be dishonest were I to tell you that a traitor's life could not be ransomed, for a sufficiently large sum. Who is this scoundrel you speak of?"

"Myself."

Ricimer let out his breath in a slow sigh and then smiled. "Ah. Then this is not an accusation so much as a confession. I am not a priest, General. And you are under a safe-conduct while visiting me here at Argentoratum. So you have nothing to fear, or to confess, for that matter."

"I assisted Attila for many years. I fought against Aetius at Campi Catalaunici."

"Then you fought against me, as well. Fortunately, you lost. Had you won, I would have considered your crime greater. Nevertheless, as you rightly point out, it was a crime for a Roman citizen to fight against his own nation. However, you are seeking to make amends, so I am willing to consider it. I will have one of my subordinates discuss terms with you this evening. In any event, I must make my own preparations, for I leave tomorrow at sunrise."

Orestes leaned forward.

"Count Ricimer, I will be frank with you. I mentioned our mutual problems earlier today. We both know you have highly trained troops, led by incompetent officers."

He ignored Ricimer's visible wince at these words and pressed on.

"My clansmen are pressing at the river, at your border, as are the other tribes along the entire length of the Rhine, and along the northern bank of the Danuvius. They have broken through in the past, and they will do so again. I guarantee it."

"Are you threatening me?"

Orestes smiled.

"Merely stating the obvious, Count. My own problem, as I have said, is the mirror image of yours. My chieftains are skilled, but my men are useless. Unworthy of my officers."

"So."

"I can resolve both our problems at once."

Ricimer stared at him coldly.

"You are suggesting combining your skill at command with my troops' skill at warfare? That you wish to join the legions? *Command* in the legions?"

"I am a citizen. You are the commander of the military forces of all Rome. The talent and the connections are there. This would not be a difficult thing for you to arrange."

"On the contrary, we already agreed you are a criminal, and your threat just now did little to dissuade me of that opinion. I believe it would be a *very* difficult thing to arrange, even if I were disposed to do so."

Orestes calmly continued on, as if he had not heard.

"I also would require that my chieftains be given senior positions of command, perhaps twenty at the level of tribune or higher. And that their families be allowed to immigrate and be given immediate Roman citizenship as well."

Ricimer's eyes narrowed.

"You are suggesting . . . ," he said, his voice a mixture of amusement and incredulity, "you are asking . . . you are *demanding* that I open the floodgates to your entire tribe, allow your rabble to invade Roman territory, as they did in my father's generation, but without having the inconvenience of having to wait for the river to freeze over first?"

"Of course not," Orestes replied coolly. "Not the entire tribe. I recognize there are limits even to your power. My immediate clan only. A thousand men and their families."

Ricimer stared at him for a moment, dumbfounded, then shook his head with a wan smile, as if resignedly acknowledging the punch line of a poor joke.

"I admire your brazenness," he said finally. "If you were not under a safe-conduct, I might have you arrested, not for betrayal, but for lunacy."

"Oh, I am deadly serious."

"That only confirms my conclusion. You see, General— you are proposing not only that I pardon your crime, but that I commit one of my own."

"I fail to see how engaging an experienced commander,

and a Roman citizen yet, can be considered a crime. Clearly Rome needs such commanders."

"And yet *I* fail to see the advantage to me—to Rome—of accepting your entire long-haired horde, apart from gaining a couple of dozen officers of dubious competence."

Orestes held Ricimer's stare unblinkingly.

"We have other resources."

Ricimer raised an eyebrow, but remained silent.

Orestes abruptly stood and stepped out the door. The conversation and laughter in the adjacent room fell suddenly silent.

"Bring me the purse," he ordered one of his men.

Behind him he heard the scraping of a chair as Ricimer stood, shaking his head in annoyance that this petty chieftain could think to so easily bribe the commander of the Roman legions. Orestes stepped back into the room, accompanied by a Germanic officer who slung the large canvas bag onto the table. It landed heavily, with a hard thump that made the furniture's spindly legs shudder. Ricimer blinked in surprise— the bag clearly weighed a hundred pounds or more. Behind him, Orestes could hear the shuffle and coughing of the other officers, as they crowded in curiosity at the open door.

"What is this?" Ricimer demanded. "Open it."

"You may have the honor. I was disarmed by your men when I landed at the riverbank."

Ricimer seized the dagger at his belt, and ignoring the leather lacing stretched tightly around the shapeless contents, he jammed the blade directly into the canvas itself, slicing it open like the belly of a goat. Hundreds of gold coins spilled out with a clatter, pouring onto the small table and then the floor, rolling with a metallic hum in diminishing concentric circles. Not a sound was heard from the thunderstruck Romans in the doorway. Ricimer remained motionless until the last coin rolling lazily on the floor had tipped onto its side. Then he picked one up from the table and examined it carefully.

"These are not coins I have ever seen."

"You would not have. They come from distant lands: India,

China. Some are centuries old. But they can be melted into new coins, Roman coins. Perhaps with your own likeness on them."

Ricimer pondered this in silence, his eyes ranging avidly over the shimmering pile on the table.

"We can perhaps make arrangements for your clan," he said softly.

"Perhaps?" Orestes inquired, eyebrows raised.

"Perhaps."

"I have many more such purses, in safekeeping. Identical to this one."

Ricimer looked up for the first time since the bag had been placed on the table, and smiled humorlessly.

"We can make arrangements. Tell me, General: This money—I have heard rumors that Attila's burial—"

"No one is pursuing this money!" Orestes interrupted, the sharpness of his tone betraying his impatience. He fell silent for a moment, regaining his composure, then continued calmly. "Its source is no man's concern but my own."

Ricimer stared at him hard, lips pursed in thought, then looked back down at the table.

"The Huns' gold," he mused. "Attila's gold. Rome defeated him once in battle, and then repelled him from Europe again a year later. This, then, is Attila's third loss to Rome. A posthumous loss."

Orestes nodded, and then with a glance at his men beyond the doorway, he and the Germanic officers strode out, through the palace, and down to the vessel waiting for them at the quay, this time unaccompanied by the Roman guards.

CHAPTER THREE

Later the Same Year, 457 A.D.

SCYRI CAMP

I

From the hilltop overlooking the River Nedao in this remote corner of Pannonia, Odoacer gazed about in satisfaction. The allied troops—thirty thousand strong, a powerful confederation of the Gepidi, Rugi, Suevi, and Heruli tribes under the leadership of the Gepid king Guthlac—were arrayed in a flexible battle formation. Fronted by a deep trench and palisades of sharpened stakes laced with thick coils of thorn branches, the Scyri heavy infantry was poised and tense in the center of the allied lines, consolidated but not bunched, prepared to break out into separate units of ten or a hundred soldiers, as the fluid battle circumstances dictated. The formation had been devised by Odoacer himself, who though young, knew more of battles and victories than the Scyri king had absorbed in an entire lifetime of defeat and flight, of leading his demoralized and impoverished people from refuge to refuge in search of a haven from invaders. King Vismar's battle strategies had always been defensive, premised on reaction and fear, exercises in futility and frustration. Yet somehow, Odoacer's arrival three years ago had changed all that, quickened the old king's blood, given impetus to his determination to serve his people well, by leading them well in battle.

This same determination had been taken up by others as well, by the Scyri officers, and even by the newly recruited infantry, who were now acting as young troops should—aggressive, boastful, eagerly sharpening their spear tips, as enthusiastic as if they were facing a prize boar in the field. Indeed, their confidence greatly astonished the other nations' troops, and even the Scyri king himself. Vismar had warned Odoacer about his inexperienced soldiers—many of them had never fought a single combat, as the tribe had spent the past ten years in silence and anonymity in their marshes north of the Danuvius. But Odoacer had dismissed the old man's concerns, and doggedly carried on his training of the men.

He looked around again. The battle deployment he had devised was as neat and effective as any Attila would have made of his own confederations and clans, though Odoacer himself had been too young to serve under the great king in battle—his only information had come from his father, from the stories told by the old ones around the wintertime council fires, from the chanted histories of great battles fought and won in the misty past of his former tribe's history.

The flexible movements and separable units of small, independent squadrons of fighters—this was the classic Hunnish battle tactic, the method that in two generations had allowed the Huns to rise from a mere roving steppe clan to lords of the most powerful nations of Asia and eastern Europe. Yet the other techniques he was now employing—the entrenchments, the hilltop fortress where he had prevailed upon the king and their allies to make their stand—these could not have been more different from the Hunnish methods in which he had drilled and practiced as a youth. Such static, defensive measures he had learned from men who had fought at the Campi Catalaunici under Attila. It was these tactics—the stakes and the deep trenches; the stolid stands of crack infantry in the front, with ample support and reinforcements; the large stores of supplies in the camp behind them, of food, water, and spare weaponry, allowing them to dispense with vulnerable supply lines or the need to take plunder where they traveled merely in order to survive—these were the tactics that had allowed the Romans to defeat his former countrymen in that epic battle, even though, by all accounts, the Romans as fighters were far inferior to the

Huns, laughable as horsemen or archers, competent only in hand-to-hand combat and in engines of artillery. These were tactics for which the Scyri and other Germanic fighters were well suited, being physically large and fearless in swordplay and direct combat, and living in fixed villages requiring defense and fortification. These were the tactics Odoacer sought to reinforce, rather than the speed and ability to cover long distances that the Huns' nomadic civilization required.

But what differentiated this army from previous Scyri forces was the innovation Odoacer had pressed upon Vismar, which the old man had accepted reluctantly at first, but with increasing enthusiasm over the months of training: Hunnish-style cavalry. Odoacer glanced down the hill toward a thicket of trees on his right flank, behind which he could glimpse his horse units waiting restlessly. The Scyri had long used horses for other military purposes, of course—transporting loads, travel by officers, reconnaissance—but never as a true fighting force, one that could actually take a leading role in combat, as the Huns had always used them. And it was here that Odoacer had been able to draw on his own past knowledge, his experience as a Hunnish cavalry officer, and most important, his skills as a rider. This was the reason for the months he had spent carefully selecting and training his horsemen, all of them from among the smallest and youngest and wiriest of his Scyri troops, those least fit for infantry duty, who would have been the first to die in a pitched battle of heavy axes and swords, but who would serve well in the role he had in mind.

For the past two years he had drilled them in the techniques: stay on your horse at all cost; space yourself widely from your fellow riders so as to flank slower-moving infantry; weave and dip to prevent enemy archers from locking aim on you; throw your animal directly into groups of enemy foot soldiers, remembering that men, when terrified, always cluster close to their fellows, leaving them even more vulnerable than when suffering from the weakness and stupidity of terror alone. Slash downward on the enemy's heads, for their stiff armor prevents them from raising their shields and swords high, and their helmets block their vision. And again, *never* leave your horse.

Odoacer's newly trained Scyri cavalry were scarcely five thousand strong, a number Attila would have viewed as risible, scarcely more than a personal guard—but it was five thousand more horse troops than the Scyri had ever had in the past, and more important, five thousand more than the enemy expected them to have now. Most critical of all, they were five thousand men who had been taught that the Scyri destiny was no longer to flee and dodge, no longer to fear more populous tribes, no longer to tremble at the sight of more experienced warriors, with larger battle-axes and stouter shields. Odoacer had taught these men to ride, had formed them into a cavalry unit second to none among the Germanic tribes—and in their pride and gratefulness at their newfound power, these young men looked upon Odoacer almost as a god, or at the least as a gift *from* God, who had dropped upon them from heaven itself. They would follow him to the ends of the earth.

Odoacer knew that clever tactics alone might not win a war—Catalaunici had proven that. But he had long reflected, fascinated, on that terrible battle between the Huns and the Romans in Gaul. Indeed, it had become a kind of obsession for him. Grilling survivors, recreating battle diagrams, reading written accounts—he had convinced himself that the Hunnish way of fighting, as dramatic and as terrifying and as effective as it might be to lesser tribes, was no match against either other Huns or the Romans themselves. Yet by the same token, the Romans' method of static entrenchments was not invulnerable. There had to be a better method, a melding of the two, just as Guthlac was now melding Vismar's people and the other river tribes into a great confederacy. There *had* to be a new alloy of battle techniques that would take two inferior methods and make them one, a superior one, the best. And in developing the strategy for this new army, Odoacer had demanded nothing less, in the way of tactics, training, and drill, than the very best.

Hence the trenches. *And* the horses.

The enemy knew he was here. They knew who he was, whence he had come, how long he had been here. They knew of his trenches, and were determined to destroy him anyway. But they didn't know about his horses.

According to the scouts, the enemy would arrive before the sun reached its zenith, and indeed he could already imagine he felt the ground shuddering slightly under the weight of their approach. Again he looked down the long line of troops, massed behind their earthen fortifications, and he saw that all was ready. Keeping the men on edge before the enemy was even in sight would simply tire them. He spoke quietly to a waiting aide, ordering him to inform the officers to put the men at ease, to distribute rations of watered wine and biscuit to calm the nerves, a technique used by Romans before impending battle. There would be time enough for the men to be on the alert when the enemy approached more closely.

Dismounting, he strode to a nearby tree and leaned against it, pulling out his own water skin and a chunk of stale bread. Simple fare—but fare for which he would have given his entire inheritance nearly three years ago when crossing this very range of hills. Not that he had had any inheritance then, or so he thought. To his knowledge at the time, his only possessions were the tattered and threadbare clothes on his back, and six exhausted horses, his share of the herd they had taken after the attack by Ellac's men. As he had done every day for the past three years, he thought back to that terrible time.

II

The two brothers had driven the stolen horses fifty miles without stopping, straight through the night, splashing miles through streambeds to hide their tracks, splitting up at blind valleys and doubling back separately, circling around to traverse again the same trail—every trick they had ever learned to disguise their path and confound their pursuers. Edeco was conscious the entire while, eyes wide as he slumped over the neck of his horse, wrists tied beneath the animal's neck and ankles beneath its girth to keep from slipping off. He stared steadily at Odoacer, who galloped at his father's side, while Onulf ranged to the rear and along the flanks of the small herd, guiding the half-wild horses, using his length of rope to link together several of the stallions he sensed were the leaders, compelling the mares to follow. Occasionally Edeco would attempt to speak—a breathy rasping, or perhaps merely a cough. Odoacer could not be certain, because his father, with hands bound, could not supplement his croaking with gestures. The most Odoacer could do was to rein in their horses for a moment at the streams they crossed, offer his father a bit of water from cupped hands, and drizzle some over his dusty head to cool him off.

Thus passed a night and a day, and as dark descended on the second night, the two brothers looked back and saw that the distant dust cloud raised by their pursuers, by Ellac's men, was gone. Dissipated, perhaps, when the chasers had stopped and made camp for the night. Onulf calculated the distance between the two parties to be at least twenty miles. The pursuit was not over; the tracks of their dozen horses could not be hidden for long, and the chase would surely resume at first light. But it was suspended, and for now, they could sleep.

Edeco had suffered in silence during the harsh ride, his only sound being gasps of pain, as the brothers rotated his mounts to keep from straining any one animal. But when they untied him and lifted him off at their campsite for the night, he was dead, his face the dark purple of a man who has suffocated, and Odoacer wondered with sudden grief how he could have failed to notice the color of his father's skin, despite the dimming light. When he laid Edeco on the ground to unwrap the dirty linen strip from his neck for examination, he found that the ball of fabric he had hurriedly pushed into the hole in his father's throat to stop the bleeding had disappeared—fallen into the cavity during the horse's jostling, blocking the windpipe. The sons' desperate measure to save him had eventually killed him.

Odoacer knew he had done the best he could under the

circumstances; yet the deep emptiness in his heart felt constrained, more a sense of bewilderment, a lost opportunity, than the overwhelming sorrow he expected he should feel at the death of his father. He looked up at Onulf, saw his brother's face twisted in grief, his dusty cheeks damp with tears, as he stepped forward to help lift their father's body to the ground. Odoacer wondered that his own tears did not come to him, that his own grief felt so vacant and dry. Perhaps, he thought, the tears would come later. Perhaps the thoughts of vengeance, the hate for his pursuers, had pushed them aside. The fatal chain of events—the desecration of the burial cave, the burning of his family's compound, ultimately the very death of his father—were all ultimately due to Orestes, and Odoacer knew that his grief could never be completely felt, nor entirely assuaged, so long as revenge remained to be exacted. Orestes, he knew, must pay.

The Sacred Cave was in the direction they were fleeing, and their decision was easy. Before sunrise they had remounted, with Edeco again bound to a horse by wrists and ankles, though now his head and body were covered by his own stained woolen tunic, torn along the seams lengthwise to form a rough funeral shroud. Upon arriving at the campsite on the cliff-edge where the burial party had stayed several weeks before, they paused, and Onulf peered down the rocky trail descending into the gully.

"You're mad," he said simply.

Odoacer knew he was right. It would be impossible to lead twelve untrained ponies with a corpse down that track. They rode away from the campsite, clinging close to the cliff-edge as Odoacer anxiously scanned the shapes and formations of the rocks below, the contours of the canyon edge beneath them, and the jagged, purple lip on the opposite side. After two hours' ride, he found it—the lone shrub, stark against the evening sky on the distant western edge of the canyon. Pursing his lips, Odoacer examined the sun, calculating where it would set over the western horizon, and adjusting that point slightly to the south, where it would have been several weeks earlier. He dismounted.

"Right . . . here," he said, and stopped, staring at the cliff before him. He walked warily to the edge, careful to avoid the crumbling lip, then dropped flat on his belly and crept forward until he could peer over. "That's it," he said confidently, "about twenty arms'-lengths down. I see the poles they used to lift the coffin below us. You still have the ropes from the horse herders?"

Onulf looked at him, surprised.

"You found the Sacred Cave? From the *top*?"

"I used a mark—that strange bush across the canyon."

"Then why did Father and the slaves hike three days on the canyon floor to carry the casket?"

Odoacer shrugged. "At the time, Father himself didn't know the way to the cave from the cliff top—he and Attila had discovered it forty years earlier only from the canyon floor. And after depositing the coffin, it would have been impossible to climb to the top with fifty slaves—there is an overhang. In any case, the return back to the base camp along the canyon floor only took them half a day, without the load."

"So why didn't you and Father return along the upper route when you were following Orestes after the Germans broke away? That would have been faster yet."

Odoacer considered this. In fact, he had wondered about it himself at the time, but acknowledging his father's black mood while following Orestes, he had not wanted to interrupt his thoughts. Now, however, he understood.

"Because even if Father did know how to get here from the cliff top, he knew Orestes' party would be taking the bottom route. It would have been faster for the Germans to carry the treasure down the cliff trail on their backs and out the lower path, than to hoist it up to the top with ropes, piece by piece, and all their men besides. Perhaps Father sought to intercept them, to ambush them somehow. But we missed them anyway. Hand me that rope."

That night, Onulf stayed with the horses at the cliff top, keeping a wary eye out for signs of torches, or the thunder of approaching hooves. In the cave below, Odoacer carefully placed Edeco's body on the surface of Attila's still-intact coffin, the one a sleeping and slack-jawed guardian of the other. For the second time, he spent the night in the dark cavern with his father and his dead king by his side. In the morning, as the dawn's first rays shot over the cliff-edge of the canyon behind him, lighting up the layers of color on the cliff walls opposite, he dropped himself down to the canyon floor, trotted along the ravine bottom until he found a narrow goat path ascending the other side, and clambered up to the far lip of the canyon. There, with a large rock chipped to an edge, he spent a quarter of an hour hacking at the trunk of the bush he had used as a landmark, until the rubbery green wood gave way, and he was able to break the shrub off at ground level and push it over the cliff. Never again would the cave be found by such markings. He scrambled down after it, returned to the Sacred Cave, and hoisted himself the rest of the way up by the rope.

To Onulf's questioning glance, he said nothing. Then, seeing movement out of the corner of his eye, he swiftly strung his bow, notched an arrow, and shot.

The steppe hare was the first food they had eaten in three days. Out of fear of attracting attention from the smoke of a cooking fire, they skinned and ate it raw, then threw the bones and offal into the canyon below. Before the sun had risen two fingers above the eastern horizon, they had mounted their horses and driven the herd back out onto the plain.

That night, as they camped beside a stagnant pond, the brothers considered their prospects. They agreed they would have to start new lives—there was no going back for them— but beyond that, they differed. Onulf felt their best chance was in a vast city—Constantinople perhaps, where they both had most recently sojourned with their father while representing Attila to the court of the Eastern Roman emperor. There, they could blend with other men of distant provenance and strange features, with Nubians, Indians, Berbers, and Greeks; locate employment or patronage, perhaps even find or purchase wives for themselves; and live out their lives in peace. Odoacer was swayed by the prospect of starting with anonymity, of creating a new identity, though the thought of doing so among the teeming, sweltering masses of Constantinople repelled him.

"First, we will find Orestes and kill him," Odoacer said.

"No. Our first duty is to survive," replied Onulf. "We are still being pursued, and Orestes has too far a head start on us."

"Nevertheless, revenge must be ours. For Father, and for the Huns."

Onulf shrugged.

"It is impossible. We will lose our lives. What vengeance is that?"

The next morning, at first light, Onulf rose, washed his face in the fetid pond water, then silently separated their small herd into two groups, while Odoacer lay quietly on the ground, wrapped in his thin tunic, watching him. Onulf was scrupulously fair, several times swapping horses between the two halves, balancing for mares and stallions, strong runners and weak, separating rivals, keeping mothers and foals together. Finally, when he was satisfied with the result, he turned to his brother, face expressionless but eyes questioning. Odoacer stood up, smiled slightly, and gripped Onulf's forearm tightly for a moment; and then both men mounted, rounded up their spares, and parted ways, as quietly and naturally as a nut falls from a tree, or a young fox wanders from its brethren to find a new home. Onulf set off to the southeast, circling wide around the location of the distant Hunnish camp, toward Constantinople; Odoacer to the southwest, to a location that was, as of yet, only a vague, shimmering idea in his mind.

This idea was Noricum, a region of which his mother had spoken to him as a child, a forested and marshy land along the middle Danuvius where dwelt her ancestral people, a Germanic tribe known as the Scyri. Beyond his mother's own name, Gethilde, and a few child-words of her tongue, he knew nothing of this people, for as a boy, he had never had the slightest interest in her nostalgic, dreamlike stories. Gethilde had died of a fever when he was but four, and his memory of her was strange, in both its excruciating detail and maddening vagueness: skin so pale as to be almost translucent, with tiny blue veins showing spidery and vivid at the breast; dull yellow hair, wound in long tresses around her head; and large eyes, sad and hollow when she looked at him, limpid pools that conveyed a deep melancholy for her own lost world and her sons' absence from it. No further recollection of her did he have. He heard later she had been a princess of sorts, though what that might mean to a distant tribe like the Scyri he had no idea; nor did he know even whether that was true, or whether it was mere family legend told by his father to boost the standing of his sons' bloodlines in the eyes of his fellow Huns.

After two days his path crossed a faint pair of wagon ruts, which he followed to an abandoned hamlet, apparently pillaged years before by marauding Goths. Now it was inhabited only by a pack of half-starved dogs, and an itinerant Germanic trader who had stopped for the night with a wagonload of cheaply fabricated iron goods, cookware, and other products he was transporting from Constantinople to the isolated villages of the interior, in hopes of thus eking out a living. Odoacer had no currency with which to purchase anything, but he offered the man one of his horses in exchange for a dried hock of pig and his supply of a few dozen iron-tipped arrows. It was an extravagant trade, for the horse was worth ten times what he was asking in return; yet the merchant, thinking himself clever and oblivious to the anger glinting in Odoacer's eyes, disparaged the horse's breed and demanded instead two animals in exchange for his paltry goods.

Odoacer was tempted to kill the man outright and simply take what he needed. Instead, he tied him loosely to a tree, stuffed a fistful of grass in his mouth to silence his cursing, and took the ham and arrows, as well as a small cooking pot, a pair of daggers, a piece of flint to replace the worn-out chip he carried, a rough woolen blanket, the man's own water skin, and a handful of small copper coins, by which he might purchase smaller articles in the future without having to offer an entire horse in exchange. Before he rode away, he tied one of his horses to the man's tree, one that had recently pulled up lame. The animal would never again be a runner, but was sufficiently strong as to pull the trader's wagon. He then thundered off down the road with his remaining animals. The merchant, he reflected, had still gotten the better part of the deal.

Odoacer passed the winter in a stone-walled animal stall he found in another abandoned hamlet. Daylight was scarce, and the nights long and bleak. When the cold wind became too harsh even for the smoky turf fire smoldering in a corner of the rude dwelling, he brought two horses inside and positioned them beside him, as a Hunnish peasant family would have done, to warm himself by their body heat. The ponies, grateful to be sheltered from the icy blasts outside, would stand thus a day and a night without moving, save for the forceful streams of piss they occasionally loosed onto the hard-packed dirt floor, which Odoacer channeled outside the building by means of a shallow, hastily dug gutter along the walls. He spent many hours lying awake on the cold ground, wrapped in his blanket and staring up at the horse's underbelly over his head, wondering about Onulf and thinking of his father. With the arrival of the spring rains, he threw his belongings into a rabbit-leather bag he had painstakingly sewn over the winter, and rode off, not bothering to look back at the ramshackle hut, for despite the months he had spent there, he had developed no fondness for it.

Upon arriving at the River Morava, a northern tributary of the Danuvius, he followed its broad, muddy flow downstream for several days, for want of a suitable crossing point. Unable to find a ford, he became impatient at the growing bogginess of the terrain, in which the river sometimes seemed to disappear for miles into trackless marshes before emerging even more lethargic and mephitic farther down. Finally, he came across a small settlement, built precariously on rafts of light pine designed to draft only a few hands' depth in the soupy water, but able to carry heavy weight—each fisherman's family, thatched hut, and possessions, as well as several barrels containing the eels they had trapped live and were bringing to market.

Approaching the tiny, mobile village, Odoacer hailed the nearest eelman, who was squatting on his craft mending one of the nets used to catch his quarry. Gesturing to him with signs, and speaking a pidgin Germanic, he made the man understand that he wished to cross to the other side of the marsh. The man pointed to the cooking pot, which Odoacer regretfully understood was to be the payment for the journey, and when he nodded his assent, the man emitted a low whistle, and from out of the neighboring huts and rafts emerged a crowd of children, naked and filthy, gap-toothed and grinning, who raced up to Odoacer and began chattering at him incomprehensibly, extending their hands for gifts, and stealthily patting his clothing and pockets in search of food and coins.

Odoacer stood stiffly, repelled by the urchins' aggression, yet unwilling to offend the man who had agreed to ferry him, until a moment later the man growled at the children in his guttural tongue, and they immediately backed away, eyes still fixed avidly on the tall stranger. The eelman then beckoned for him to step aboard his raft, and after a moment's hesitation, Odoacer tied the ropes of his horses into a single tether, looped it over a stanchion at the stern and, with the children's assistance, pushed off the muddy bank, as the horses stepped nervously into the water behind. An hour's worth of poling through the murky current, followed by the animals, who alternately swam and walked in the shallow places and sandbars, brought them safely to the other side, where the cooking pot changed hands, and the eelman gruffly pointed to a muddy track along the bog edge, which he gestured for Odoacer to follow.

Within a half-day's journey, Odoacer encountered the first signs of true civilization he had seen in nearly six months, and though reluctant to enter the city he knew he was approaching, he was unable to avoid it, for the surrounding terrain was so fetid and marshy he was forced to remain on the road. As he passed through the squalid hamlets and farmhouses outside the town, the inhabitants stared openly, without uttering a word, which he attributed not so much to rudeness as to astonishment at seeing a stranger entering their midst. As the number of dwellings grew denser, the inhabitants became more open in their pointing and whispering, and he realized their behavior went beyond mere surprise. Looking down at his filthy tunic and leggings, he realized they had grown threadbare and nearly transparent from constant use, and that his doeskin riding boots were in tatters, their soles flopping forlornly from the uppers as he rode, like a pair of wagging tongues. There was nothing to be done about it, and as long as he was not freezing or spreading the plague, he could not understand why these ragged tribesmen should care what he wore. He clucked his tongue to encourage his horses on their slow trot, glancing distastefully at the boglands on either side, unfit for riding or cultivation, suitable only for wretched, defeated people such as these.

Just outside the city's crooked, wood-palisaded walls, he found what he was looking for: a rough stable that rented horses to passersby. In this case, he prevailed upon the reluctant owner to take charge of Odoacer's own horses, and to give him sleeping space on a bench in the house, in exchange for a handful of his scarce copper coins, which he slapped onto the tabletop as a down payment for the horse's forage. He pointed out that the horses themselves would be adequate surety for any further expense they might require.

As the stable-owner was considering the proposal, a pair of young children, a girl and a boy, tumbled laughing into the room from outside and stopped short when they encountered the tall, shaggy-haired stranger speaking haltingly to their father. As Odoacer turned to step back outside the small shed, the little girl spoke up.

"Sir—your arse is showing."

The boy stifled a giggle and they both continued to stare, half fearful, half amused. Odoacer turned back to the father, who was also looking at him.

"This is true," the man said gravely. "A man cannot be seen

in the streets in such a state, nor can a Christian let a man be seen in such a state."

He ducked through the back door of the dwelling into the adjoining house, leaving Odoacer standing uncomfortably in the wide-eyed stare of the children, and returned a moment later with an old tunic, worn but patched. He tossed it to the newcomer.

"Wear this, until my wife can repair your breeches."

Mentally, Odoacer knew, the stableman was adding another copper to the account, but he shrugged resignedly and pulled the tunic over his head, while stepping out of his old clothes and kicking them into a corner. It would not be an auspicious start to walk through the city frightening children.

"What is the name of this place?" Odoacer asked, after changing his clothes.

The stableman stared at him dumbly, until the little boy piped up.

"Soutok," the youngster said with a serious expression on his face. "We're Scyri."

Odoacer gravely nodded his thanks.

Stepping outside, he paused for a moment before passing through the open wooden gate into the town itself. Apart from the need to purchase some supplies—a new set of clothes, obviously—and to sell a horse or two to pay for them, he was not sure why he had come, what he wanted. Though he had been away from civilization for many weeks, this place hardly brought to mind what civilization was like. What he saw of it repelled him even more than most cities. At least in Constantinople, his very strangeness had allowed him to blend in anonymously. There, *everyone* was strange, which allowed one to retain one's own sense of dignity and privacy, though surrounded by a million bustling people, with their smells, habits, quirks, and ailments. Here, in this remote marsh town beyond the reach of Huns or Romans, the combined wealth of the entire population would scarcely have turned the head of a single middle-class merchant in Constantinople; the numbers of malnourished children, clubfooted adults, and drunken soldiers were seemingly greater than the number of hale citizens; and the ramshackle buildings, filthy streets, and withered market vegetables evinced a lack of energy and ambition that seemed incomprehensible, given the number of beggars and idle shop-mongers who stood staring at him from the alleys. Yet here, of all places, he felt particularly suspected, almost incriminated, as if by merely setting foot on their streets he had somehow violated an understanding, upset these people's lives, invaded some precious space they were protecting for themselves.

No, he could scarcely understand what it was that had drawn him to this city in the first place, and what was keeping him here now any longer than it would take him to purchase his supplies. But at the same time he had a confused idea, an understanding, that there was something here, something of *him* here among these people, among his mother's people. Half the blood in his veins originated from this stock, the chestnut color of his hair rather than the black of his father's, the gray of his irises that contrasted with the narrow Hunnish cant of the lids. Half of him. Perhaps it was a half he would not want, a half that would serve no purpose in his life. He didn't know.

The people stared at him curiously, some with outright hostility, a sentiment that, upon reflection, he could begin to understand. Once a proud people inhabiting a wealthy and fertile land of river deltas farther east, the Scyri had been repeatedly bested by the Huns in battle and eventually lost possession of their homeland. This was a story he had often heard told and chanted as a boy, sung by the old men in their round huts on winter nights as they slurped hot milk from bowls. His father had proudly joined in these stories, though when the subject of the vanquished Scyri came up, his mother had always found tasks to perform outside the room, for it was her story being told, her people being conquered, her brothers fighting fruitlessly against the ever-victorious Huns—and she part of the plunder triumphantly carried back, tied sobbing across the haunches of Edeco's horse, and later giving birth to Edeco's sons.

This story Odoacer knew, for it had been engraved in his memory since he had been old enough to understand speech. What he had never known, never even considered, was her side of the story, the story of those survivors who, refusing to live under the Huns' domination, like the Alani, or to ally with them and fight their conquerors' wars, like the Ostrogoths, had simply disappeared—picked up their meager possessions and walked west, up the flow of the Danuvius, out of their ancient homeland, beyond the reach or desire of the ravaging Huns. They had moved without a sense of bitterness or resentment at having been treated unjustly— harshly perhaps, unluckily, but not unjustly—for such was the way of the world, and indeed as the Scyri moved west they displaced other tribes and peoples before them, peoples even weaker than they; and indeed, these peoples the Scyri had no compunction against enslaving, absorbing, or killing, as the Huns had done to them. It was not a question of just or unjust—it simply *was*. The Scyri rolled west over their victims, as the Huns had rolled over them, as no doubt some even more powerful enemy in the east threatened to do to the Huns; and they stopped moving west when they found that fragile balance point, when they met with resistance, rather than fear, among the tribes they encountered, and when the distance they had traversed caused the Huns to lose interest in further pursuit.

Thus, Odoacer reflected, the Scyri had something in common with himself.

For three days he wandered the streets of Soutok, retracing his steps, encountering the same curious and hostile eyes, and feeling the same sense of restlessness and repugnance, yet unable to tear himself away. His conditions were far from comfortable—the bench in the stableman's hut was knotty and hard, the man's children cried at night, and the wife had made no move to repair his breeches—yet he nevertheless felt drawn to this city. Perhaps, he told himself, it was that every man needs a tribe, and that having been forced to abandon his own, something inside him longed for this one instead. He hastily rejected this idea. If he were indeed longing for human warmth—which he doubted—he could easily have chosen more amenable company than this wretched lot, where the people would just as soon rob him of his few coppers, while laughing at his buttocks, as provide him with companionship. No, it was not that. Blood was drawing him, the blood of this people, this people that was his mother's, and therefore his. . . .

His thoughts were interrupted as two strong hands gripped his arms. He tensed, his initial instinct being to draw a weapon or to flee. Yet glancing from side to side, he realized flight would be useless. He was accompanied by two large guardsmen, unaccountably sober, bearing the same rusty and ill-assembled mail armor and weaponry as those he had seen loitering casually around the ramshackle building he assumed was the local king's palace. The three of them continued striding at the same easy pace at which he had been moving before their leather-gloved hands had seized him, as if he had simply encountered a pair of friends in the streets. After a moment, he ventured some words to them in the rusty camp Latin with which he had struggled over the past few days, during his haggling with shopkeepers.

"Where are we going?"

The guards seemed not to understand him, and in truth, he saw no reason why simple soldiers should understand a foreign merchants' language. The one to his right, however, glanced at him briefly, tightened his grip, and with a guttural order, nodded in the direction where, he knew, lay the ramshackle palace. Interrogation by the guards' captain, he assumed, would be the order of the day, most likely followed by a beating or brief imprisonment, then a stern ejection from the city for the crime of being a foreigner. He hoped resignedly that the stableman would care for the horses until he returned.

After passing through the palace gates he was taken to an interior courtyard, surrounded on three sides by squat, unobtrusive stone-and-mortar buildings. There, he was led to a domelike structure in the corner, built of flat stones stacked atop one another in an overlapping pattern to create an inward slope to the walls, capped by an angled keystone in the center of the rounded roof. The stones of this one-room hut were much more weathered, their lichen- and age-stains deeper, than those of the surrounding buildings. He looked at it with idle curiosity as they approached. Clearly this stone beehive had been here much longer than the rest of the city—perhaps built by the original inhabitants of these parts, troglodytes or others who had long since disappeared but had left traces of their passing—bones, strange statues, the foundations of ancient buildings, or even, as in this case, an entire structure: a house, a holy place, or . . .

He was thrown roughly to the ground and the stout oaken door slammed shut behind him.

A prison.

The darkness was not absolute, for the poorly dressed stones allowed sunlight to penetrate in thin, narrow shafts like streams of whey through his mother's course filtering fabric. The room was wide enough that he could lie down if he chose, or even stand if he did so in the very center, where the ceiling was highest. The earthen floor was hard-packed and reasonably clean, without waste or stench from previous prisoners. There was a large stone block on the floor near one wall, presumably to sit on. He was not chained, nor had he been beaten or tortured. He supposed things could be worse, and undoubtedly would have been had he been caught by Ellac. Yet he did not know what the future might bring, how long he might be kept here. He sat on the stone block and waited.

By the angle of the beams of light slanting through the stones, he figured there were perhaps two hours of daylight left, when he heard footsteps outside. These were accompanied by a grunted order to the guards, and then rustling at the door as a small peephole was slid open and eyes peered in to stare at him. He resisted the temptation to shoot out his hand and poke them, or to throw dirt from the floor. Instead, he sat quietly on the stone block, ignoring the watcher, until finally, with another grunted command, the bolt was shot from the outside and the door thrown open. The room's interior was flooded with bright, low-angled sunlight shining directly through the open door, only slightly blocked by the imposing figure who stepped into the doorframe, his expression and the details of his mail shirt darkened into a glowing silhouette, with the sun behind him. Odoacer squinted, and stood up.

"You speak Latin?" the man growled. Odoacer nodded. "I am Baldovic, captain of the palace guard."

"On what grounds do you arrest me, and hold me in this prison without water?" Odoacer asked, his tongue stumbling over the Latin phrase he had carefully prepared in his mind while waiting for this moment.

Baldovic laughed.

"A prison?" he repeated. "There are a hundred domes like this behind the compound, which are used by the palace guard as barracks—except they shelter four men each. You should be thanking me for giving you a room of your own, rather than complaining."

"I am not complaining. I ask why I am being held here."

"Because you walked into our city with your arse showing."

At this, the guards outside roared with laughter, and Odoacer could see the shoulders of his interlocutor shaking with a silent chuckle. Finally, Baldovic gestured for the noisy guards outside to be silent.

"Because," he continued, stepping further into the hut, "you are a Hun."

Odoacer was nonplussed.

"And it is a crime in your pissant city to be a Hun?"

The officer's expression hardened, though he ignored the insult.

"Moreover," he said stiffly, "I have noted that you are a wealthy man, yet you dress as a field slave. This means you are either mad, or a thief. Either case is grounds for interrogation."

"A wealthy man?" Odoacer looked at him questioningly.

"You arrived from the east with a number of your ugly ponies and are keeping them outside the walls. Oh yes, we have had a little chat with the stableman. You rode alone, yet have more horses than any Scyri but the king himself. And you carry coins stolen from a Scyri trader several months ago. We have spoken with him, and with the shopkeepers with whom you have done business in this city."

Odoacer pondered the man's perception of wealth. In Hunnia he would have been considered laughably poor indeed for possessing only a handful of horses. But among this wasted and poverty-stricken people . . . Mentally he berated himself for entering the city so conspicuously and not selling or hiding the horses first.

"The king has decided to hold you in custody for the time being," Baldovic continued, taking off his helmet in the close quarters and dropping his shaggy head down close to Odoacer.

Odoacer stared at him unblinkingly.

"Horses and coins—there is no offense in that."

"So you are not wealthy?"

"If I prove I am not, will I be released?"

Baldovic paused for a moment.

"No."

"Why not?"

"Even if you are not wealthy, you are worth money to the king—or at least your face is. Gray eyes, brown hair, yet Hunnish features. It is precisely what Ellac's message told us to watch for. You are potentially quite a valuable commodity, Hun, with a sizable reward on your head. Your wealth is merely what attracted our attention to you." He straightened and gestured around him with an expansive sweep of his arm. "And in comfort, no less! No doubt the king himself will be paying you a visit soon."

Laughing again, Baldovic strode out the door, closing it roughly and slamming the bar home. As the guards walked away, Odoacer could hear their faint, mocking voices filtering through the stones of his cell.

". . . because his *arse* was showing!"

It was past midnight—he could tell by the slant of the moonlight, this time, beaming through the cracks—when he again heard the crunch of steps in the sand outside. He did not bother rising from where he lay on the dirt floor, though he had not been asleep. He remained still while the peephole opened, and felt the guard's gaze upon him for a long moment before the iron bar outside was noisily slid through its rings and the door opened.

Baldovic stepped in, followed by two more guards, whom Odoacer assumed, from their well-maintained and matching mail armor, were the bodyguards of a high official. They were followed by an elderly man, tall but stooped, and also wearing a mail tunic that may once have fit him well, but now hung loosely upon his frame like the tattered rags of a scarecrow. The four crowded around Odoacer's prone form, and Baldovic toed him roughly in the ribs.

"Up, Hun," he growled. "Stand before Vismar."

Odoacer opened one eye balefully, then slowly and with great deliberation rose to a standing position in the center of the dome. He was the same height as Baldovic and the old man, and half a head taller than the two guards, who moved in closely, hands on sword hilts.

The king peered at him through the shafts of moonlight, and Odoacer could see his eyes widen in interest.

"So this is the man Ellac seeks?" the old man asked finally.

Baldovic nodded.

"I am sure of it, my lord. I have made all possible inquiries. The stableman is being held in the cellars, if you would care to question him."

The king nodded, but continued to stare at Odoacer.

"I wish to see him in the light," he muttered. "Bring him out to the torches." He turned toward the doorway, followed by one of the guards, while Baldovic seized Odoacer's arm and jerked him toward the door.

Odoacer pulled back.

"I will go nowhere until I am given water and a chance to speak in my defense," he said, in a voice hoarse with thirst but steady with determination.

Baldovic glared at him and ordered one of the guards to take his other arm.

"You are in no position to make demands, Hun," he growled, and pushed him toward the door. The king, however, who was just ducking through, turned and peered back into the hut.

"He is right," the old man said. "Prisoner or guest, he must have water. Your defense, however," he said, glancing dismissively toward Odoacer, "is out of my hands."

The five men emerged from the hut and paused while a guard strode to the well in the center of the courtyard, picked up a ladle from a bucket resting on the stone ledge, and brought it over, slopping half its contents on the ground before arriving. Odoacer seized it in his hands and brought it to his lips, drinking the cool liquid greedily, and lifting his face to drain every drop before handing the ladle back. He nodded with satisfaction, and then with Baldovic and the other guard pinning his arms to his sides, they walked over to a torch fastened to a sconce in the wall of one of the buildings fronting the courtyard, sputtering dim flames into the night sky. Pushing Odoacer toward the light, the guards roughly turned him and backed him up to the stone wall. The king approached gingerly.

"Careful, my lord," Baldovic growled. "He is not fettered. Do not step within range of his kicks."

Odoacer glanced sideways with undisguised contempt.

"I do not attack unarmed old men . . ."

"Wait!" the king exclaimed. Odoacer turned to face him, but the old man reached up and gestured to him to hold still. "Don't move," he said. He reached out to Odoacer's face and gently gripped his jaw, turned it back toward Baldovic, who looked at him in turn with an expression of contempt.

"That forehead," the king whispered, "with the peak of hair in the middle. And look—the shape of his ear, large and fleshy. Unusual for a Hun."

"He's a mongrel," Baldovic spat. "Half Goth, or some other rabble. The Hunnish camp is full of such bastards. There's not a purebred in the lot of them. He'll fetch the reward Ellac is offering."

At mention of Ellac, the king's face suddenly went hard,

and he let drop his hand. Yet he seemed unable to tear his eyes away, and slowly Odoacer turned his head and faced the king in full.

"Who is your father, Hun?" the old man asked softly, a hint of a tremor in his voice.

"Edeco," Odoacer answered, "of the clan of Attila, a general of the king's armies and lately his chief ambassador to the Eastern Roman Empire."

"Your father lives?"

"No, he died last year, at Ellac's hands."

"So, you do flee Ellac."

"I remain alive in order to kill him."

The king nodded sagely.

"And your mother?"

"She, too, is dead, many years ago."

"She was not a Hun."

Odoacer paused long before answering. "No, she was said to be of your tribe, taken in battle . . ."

"How long ago?"

"The year before I was born. Twenty years ago."

"Her name, boy . . . what was her name?"

Odoacer stared at the king. Vismar's eyes were fixed and unwavering, looking at him as if he were an object to be coveted, or destroyed. He held the old man's gaze unflinchingly in his own.

"Gethilde," both men whispered at the same time.

The eyes of the guards opened wide and their grips relaxed. The old man stepped up to Odoacer, but this time the guards made no move to stop him, and then he reached up, placing his leathery hands on either side of Odoacer's head, pulling his face toward him to give him a warm, smacking kiss on the forehead. From the corner of his eyes, Odoacer could see the guards bowing their heads and kneeling toward him where they stood.

"A grandson," the old king murmured. "My grandson lives."

Odoacer's head swam, with hunger and amazement, and the king then grasped the sleeve of the younger man's ragged tunic in his gnarled old hand, turned, and led him slowly into the palace.

III

Odoacer's reverie of this day more than three years earlier was broken by a messenger thundering up on one of the Hunnish ponies he himself had brought upon his arrival in Noricum. His small herd had not been put to use among the nascent Scyri cavalry, for even with as ragged and hodge-podge a collection of animals as they had, the stout, squarish Hunnish breed stood out so acutely as to almost resemble another species. Instead, Odoacer had put his horses to administrative use, for which he found them to be well-suited: tirelessly running couriers and scouts from one end of a battle line to the other, galloping effortlessly in the hot sun for hours without pause to graze or drink. It was constant, unremitting work that would have blown one of the larger, more fragile Germanic horses with which the cavalry was otherwise equipped, though those animals thrived under the conditions of combat—short, intense sprints with acrobatic wheeling and leaping, followed by long periods of delay, when they could recover from their bursts of activity.

The messenger reined in his horse where Odoacer sat leaning against the tree.

"King Guthlac seeks your presence, my lord," he said brusquely, then with a brief salute, he wheeled and galloped off to his next commission.

My lord. Odoacer strode toward his own Hunnish mount, named Fly-by-Night, the mare born during the winter he had spent in the abandoned hut on the steppe, whose twin brother he had eaten to survive a blizzard. He allowed himself a rare smile. How the Fates had favored him since his arrival in Soutok, penniless and in rags. Yet he did not believe in the Fates. He was not even sure whether he believed in God. For now, his trust was in himself alone, and in his grandfather.

He galloped to the king's station just behind the center of

the infantry lines, a sprint of nearly five miles that would have left a Germanic horse gasping and trembling at the knees, though his was barely winded. He passed Baldovic among the tight circle of aides surrounding his grandfather, King Vismar, and the man gave him a curt nod. Since Odoacer's elevation from beggar to crown prince of the Scyri tribe, Baldovic's demeanor toward him had improved considerably. Yet even now, years after the rude treatment and insults Baldovic had offered him when he had first been taken prisoner, the captain's embarrassment had not receded. At first, when Odoacer was assured by the king of his officer's loyalty and competence, he had tried to put Baldovic at ease, shrugging off his clumsy apology with the comment that he had simply been following the king's orders, doing his job. Later, however, Odoacer ceased trying to efface the awkwardness between them. In the end, he concluded, Baldovic's coldness toward him was probably to his benefit. In his past life, with the Huns, Odoacer had always been amazed and appalled at how easily Attila could share in wild bouts of hunting, drinking, and gift-giving with his guards one night, and then coldly send them to their deaths in battle the next morning. Perhaps, Odoacer thought, it was actually the camaraderie that was premeditated, a kind of calculated farewell, because Attila knew they would be killed shortly afterward. All in all, he decided, if one had to order a man to die, it was better—both for one's conscience and for the professionalism and dignity of one's rank—to maintain some distance in the relationship beforehand.

Odoacer's grandfather, lanky and stoop-shouldered on his horse, mail tunic hanging as loosely as ever, but face composed and hands steady, reached out to seize Odoacer's shoulder, to guide him in closer to where he was speaking in confidence to Guthlac, the leader of the allied Germanic forces. Odoacer had not yet been formally presented to the Gepid king, and now he looked at this famous warrior closely, taking in his powerful frame, the finely wrought mail with the brilliant gold links interspersed among the iron in an intricate pattern, the gold-plated shield embellished with designs of mythical creatures.

"Baldovic reports the enemy is arriving," Vismar said. "The last two scouts have just ridden in from reconnaissance. There." He pointed toward the low ridge of hills across the valley atop which his troops were entrenched. "I can see the dust they raise."

Odoacer squinted. More impressively than the dust, he could see the flocks of birds issuing up from the trees beneath which the enemy was approaching. He stared for a moment, gauging distance.

"They ride fast," he said. "They know where we are located, and no longer pace themselves."

Guthlac scoffed, and reached down to pat his horse, which was quivering with excitement.

"I have not kept our location a secret," the allied king replied. "My own troops have traveled far to reach this site, as have the Rugili and Heruli. The cooking fires, the cut timber on the flank of the hill facing their arrival—all is known to the enemy."

"Not quite all, Your Majesty."

Guthlac dropped his eyes from the distant hill and peered at Odoacer, his pupils so tiny in the bright sunlight as to appear like needle pricks, almost disappearing in the watery, blue-gray irises, giving the effect of a statue whose bulbous, rounded eyes have been formed but not yet painted to give them realism and life. It was the first time he had truly looked at Odoacer, and he seemed surprised, a reaction Odoacer often encountered from strangers. Though since his arrival among the Scyri he had adopted the appearance of his kinsmen—the long, drooping mustaches, the hair dressed in two braids, the mail armor and heavy boots rather than the leather gear and moccasins he had favored in his youth— there was little he could change about his Hunnish face and eyes. After the first look, men became accustomed to his features. Yet it was the initial encounter that caused consternation. Guthlac stared at Odoacer, then glanced at Vismar, as if

for reassurance that the Scyri king's confidence in his grandson was well founded.

"Your cavalry is well hidden from the enemy's eyes?"
Vismar asked. "You have but five thousand horse . . ."

"Five thousand *men*—on horses. The finest men in the
entire allied army."

Guthlac snorted.

"I saw them when you arrived two days ago. They are
certainly the *smallest* men in the army. Scarcely boys."

Vismar held up his hand to his colleague in a gesture of
reassurance, then turned back to Odoacer.

"But if they are, as you say, the finest men, then all the
more dangerous this venture of yours. We could lose the very
cream of our forces—and the best of our animals. Our *only*
animals. The Scyri could never replace five thousand horses
if we lost them. We would be . . ."

"Grandfather . . ." Rarely did Odoacer call the king by
this name. Perhaps it was hard for him to do so, having come
to know the man only long after he himself was grown, long
after his childhood. But he used the name now, and behind
the liquid blue eyes Odoacer saw a flash of surprise, and
pleasure.

"Grandfather—yes, the Scyri might be destroyed if these
cavalry are deployed and lost. But the entire allied army will
most *certainly* be destroyed if we do not deploy them. My
lords: we did not ask for this battle. Our nations were driven
here by our enemies, and these same enemies seek to drive us
out again, from land that is not ours but is at least empty, into
land that is still not ours, but is inhabited by other peoples
who will fight to keep what is theirs. We have no choice."

"I do not want my people to suffer because of this," Vismar responded cautiously.

Guthlac glared at him.

"It is too late to have such thoughts."

"They will not suffer," replied Odoacer. "They cannot."

"How can you say this?"

Odoacer pursed his lips as he stared across the valley to
the ridge on the other side. The flocks of crows frightened

from their roosts in the trees were all the closer, and now he thought he could even hear their angry screeching.

"Because if we gain victory this day, our people will be celebrating. And if we lose—"

"Our people will be dead," Vismar finished for him.

Guthlac wheeled his horse. "Enough talking," he growled. "We have preparations to make. The plans have been laid. I leave you Scyri to hold the center. And"—he looked directly at Odoacer—"I expect greatness from your cavalry."

As he galloped away, Odoacer turned back to Vismar.

"All is prepared, Grandfather. Give me your blessing on this."

The king looked long at him, and placed his hand on Odoacer's head.

"For twenty years I did not even know I had a grandson. My own sons killed in battle on the same day my daughter was stolen from me, my tree cut off at the root, my honor and lineage as a king eliminated. Now a grandson has appeared—as if dropped from the sky, born already a man. And just as suddenly, he, too, might be taken away. I should have no right to grieve at losing something I thought I never had in the first place. Yet still I grieve."

"The battle has not even been fought."

"You have my blessing. Go."

Odoacer kicked heels and wheeled his horse, urging Fly-by-Night back into the long sprint to the distant copse of trees, behind which five thousand horsemen silently waited.

They swept from the woods at the bottom of the valley like a surging tide, galloping across the broad gravel bars on the far bank of the meandering Nedao, on a front half a mile wide. Their force was thirty thousand strong, the same as the Germanic allied army, yet all were mounted on strong-legged steppe ponies. From the Germanic fortifications a mile from the crossing, the ground around the river seemed to suddenly come alive—seething with men and horses, the bare gravel darkening like a shadow or a stain; and yet still more men poured from the woods on the far bank, driving enormous herds of spare horses, the secret of the horde's ability to travel day and night without pause, at a speed that would kill other armies. They were presaged by an enormous flock of cawing birds, crows and starlings shrieking shrilly in protest and fright, as effective a war cry as ever an invading army itself had launched.

At the river, the attackers barely slowed; the lead ranks of horses surged into the water in a cloud of spray and foam, while others leaped in behind them. In a moment, the entire force was in the water, churning across the shallow brown stream, hooves treading the rough gravel bottom but for the narrow stretch in the middle where the animals lifted their feet and adeptly swam, the riders leaning low to maintain a good center, and then sitting upright as the horses found their footing and heaved themselves out on the other side, flanks glistening, quivering with chill. Without hesitation, scarcely panting from their effort and in the same close formation as when they had first emerged from the trees, the lead horses sprinted across the nearer gravel bank. The hillside facing them was longer and flatter than the one they had just descended through the forest, with only the occasional shrub or isolated tree to break their view of the Germanic troops who awaited them, transfixed, at the top.

The screeching birds swooped up from the path of invasion and scattered into the vast, cloudless sky, and their screams faded into the distance. Not so the army below, which sprinted ever closer, the riders loosening their formation as they wove in and around one another, tracing complex threads and paths, veering but never touching. Their signals were unseen and unheard, but rather sensed and felt, imbued in each rider from years of training and practice, imbibed in the very milk they had drunk as infants, from their mothers and from the mares, rendering them one with their horses, and one with each other, as close to a single living organism as it was possible for thirty thousand men to be.

The Huns had arrived.

Vismar had always known it would be so. A generation ago, the Huns had driven his nation out of his ancestors' territory, and since then had crossed the new Scyri homeland several times in pursuit of larger targets in the west and south: Constantinople, Gaul, Italia. Never had they bothered to plunder more than a few villages in Vismar's new land. Yet what Vismar feared was not the day the Huns became stronger, but the day they became weaker—the day the larger quarry seemed too ambitious for them, too distant, too powerful, too populated for the weakened Hunnish tribe to conquer. That would be the day the Huns would seek easier targets. And now with Attila dead, his clans dispersed, his Goth allies undecided, that day had arrived: the day of the weaker, but perversely more dangerous Huns, led by a new chieftain who, over several years of internecine warfare, had risen to command these steppe horsemen: Ellac.

As the enormous body of riders thundered up the shallow slope of the hill, Guthlac, Vismar, and the other Germanic kings galloped behind their respective lines, calling to the allied archers to stand from where they lay prone in the grass awaiting the enemies' approach. The hilltop suddenly bristled with warriors, deployed along the entire length of the battle line, bows strung, arrows aimed high.

"Loose!" Guthlac bellowed, and his cry was taken up by the heralds and officers and relayed in both directions up and down the line. The air suddenly filled with the hiss of arrows, arcing high into the sky in that careful calculus of trained archers, then down into the freefall that lent the missiles their deadly impetus as they fell on the enemy from the great height to which they had been shot.

The attackers were still too distant for the archers to pick out individual targets—the purpose of the volley was to decimate, like artillery, to land in the thick of the invaders and, by dint of sheer numbers, of both arrows and targets, to wound a percentage of men, to exact a toll that would increase as the attackers drew steadily nearer and the archers' aim became more deadly.

Yet the horsemen, too, had their defense—their constant weaving and threading as they advanced at the gallop, at a speed that left an archer dizzy if he focused on any one individual rider. Spacing themselves, keeping maximum distance, they varied that distance as they rode so that the arrows fell into the broad gaps between riders, only a few actually reaching a living target. The victims' cries of pain were drowned by the bellows of rage from their comrades, and the volley of arrows seemed only to spur the horsemen on, to increase the ferocity of their attack, to encourage the complexity and the sheer, violent beauty of the intricate paths they rode.

Again a volley was ordered, and again the sky bristled and hummed with whizzing arrows, this time speeding on a flatter arc, closer to the ground, as the attacking Huns had covered that much more of the distance separating them from the defenders. This time, too, more arrows found their marks among horses and riders, and a score of animals in the front ranks tripped and fell, whinnying shrilly in agony as they slammed jaw-first onto the rocky soil, their riders skidding and tumbling behind them, some dead of wounds before they hit the ground. A faint cheer rose from the Germanic lines, but Guthlac cut it off with a sharp glare and a new, terse order.

"Loose at will!" he bellowed, and this was the command for which every archer, indeed every man in the army, had been waiting. Now it was the marksmen's task, and they squinted and pursed their lips as they loosed arrow after arrow into the approaching enemy lines, observing their targets carefully, discerning the rhythm and rate of their choreographed runs, anticipating the left feint, the right cut, before they happened, calculating that as the rider swerved and leaned his tight turn into the gap left an instant before by a fellow rider, he would be met with a Germanic arrow to the face, toppling him from his animal and confounding the riders behind as they leaped over the writhing body of their fallen comrade. Again and again the archers shot, two arrows to the breath, three, four, scarcely breathing at all in their close concentration, minds working furiously to break the code of the attackers' rhythm, to discern the hidden patterns governing the careening path of the fast approaching horse troops.

More Hunnish riders fell, and the allied foot soldiers waiting impatiently behind the entrenchments broke into an enthusiastic cheer; yet the cry died in their throats as the horsemen continued to surge forward, for though the front ranks were nearly destroyed, those in the rear rode fearlessly into their places, resuming the damnable weaving and dodging of their fallen brethren. The advance was closer now—specific faces could be picked out, the rolling white eyes of individual horses, even the ritual scars on the cheeks of approaching riders. The archers were having their effect—the attackers were falling by droves—but it was not enough. The Huns urged their mounts forward at breakneck pace, leaping over those fallen before them, reducing the effectiveness of the deadly barrage of arrows by the sheer speed of their approach: the faster they arrived at the forward lines, the fewer arrows the Germanic archers would be capable of firing. The strategy was simple—to charge directly into the teeth of the defense.

The barrage of arrows slowed, at first imperceptibly and then noticeably, as the archers ran low on missiles, and then exhausted their supplies altogether. Vismar stood watching, shoulders thrown back from their customary stoop, mouth set in a grim line. Never had he seen an enemy withstand such a bombardment, yet still they came, scarcely bothering to raise the small leather-and-wood cavalry shields they bore strapped to their arms.

"Javelins, stand!" Guthlac roared, and again the hilltop came alive as twenty thousand infantry stood, these men taller and heavier than the bowmen, oaken shields wielded before them, each shield-hand gripping three iron-tipped ashwood shafts, with a fourth poised for launching in their right fists.

"Javelins, throw!" With an audible grunt rippling along the length of the defense, a line of shafts flew directly toward the broad chests of the onrushing Hunnish horse.

With high-pitched screams of agony, the animals reared and wheeled at the impact of the hurtling wall of missiles. The javelins came in steady volleys, one after the other, as the Germanic troops settled into their rhythm: hurl the weapon, drop to one knee, second rank throw and drop to its knee, third rank throw, and remain standing as the first rank leaps up and throws again, drops to its knee. . . . For the first time the Hunnish attack wavered, the forward lines again destroyed by the onslaught of javelins, and those behind confounded by the growing wall of thrashing horses on the ground before them. The rhythm had been broken—with corpses of both men and animals now carpeting the field, no longer could their comrades trace their complicated, weaving paths. Slowing to pick their way through the obstacles, sometimes stopping altogether, the attackers formed even better targets for the javelin hurlers, who increased the pace of their deadly throws.

But only for a moment—each man had but four spears, and these were soon depleted. There were no further orders from the king, and no need for any. Every man knew his place now, and every man drew his sword. For the Huns to continue the attack, they would have to engage man to man—but first they would have to leap their mounts across the barrier of thorny brush, through the ditch, and over the embankment of loose soil.

The attackers milled about angrily below the entrenchments, within easy javelin range had any remained to be thrown. A signal horn blew—a long, mournful tone, punctuated by a series of short blasts—and guttural shouts filled the air, relaying the orders conveyed by the Hunnish commanders in the rear. In an instant, a company of riders galloped forward, their short, compound bows drawn, arrow tips smoking from the flaming pitch into which they had dipped them, which in turn had been ignited from the earthenware jars of smoldering embers they had prepared that morning. With easy confidence, they cantered to the front of the line of attackers, their comrades giving way before them. Scarcely pausing to aim, the fire archers shot their flaming missiles directly into the base of the thickly coiled thorn brambles forming the core of the palisade. As if on command, as if a passing steppe god had been waiting for just such a cue, a gust of wind suddenly broke, raising dust from the feet of the defenders, fanning the nascent sparks of the fire arrows where they smoldered in the dry brush. Flames suddenly sprang up along the length of the line, licking at the thorns. Within moments, the entire defensive line lit up, and in a few moments more became a roaring inferno, the foul-smelling smoke from the green vines drifting into the defenders' faces, stinging their eyes and choking their breath. Guthlac looked questioningly at Vismar, who in turn peered anxiously through the smoke down the side of the hill, where he had last seen Odoacer and his men. The grove of woods was silent.

With the defenders' sight and attention temporarily diverted, another series of short blasts of the sheep horn suddenly pierced the tumult and shouting. From the Hunnish rear, a battalion of horsemen, three thousand men, burst from the formation and raced around the horde's left flank, skirting the lower base of the hill. In the smoke-filled confusion behind the trenches, not a man of the allied Germanic troops saw them depart.

From the copse of woods at the base of the hill, Odoacer's men impatiently observed the fighting above them. This new development they noted with interest—they had not in any way prepared for such a maneuver by the Hunnish squadron, but now the Scyri horsemen looked at Odoacer with questioning eyes. Without consultation or orders, he looked at his men and simply nodded his head.

The Huns thundered past the grove on their way around the hill, aiming to circle behind the entrenched defenders and enclose them in a pincer movement between themselves and the main body of Huns. Just as they swept by, Odoacer's men stormed from the woods where they had been concealed and, loosing a barrage of arrows at the Huns' unprotected backs, took up the chase.

The Huns had not even seen the Scyri cavalry emerge from the grove of trees behind them. Their first realization that their plan had gone awry was when the arrows hit. A hundred men—then two hundred—slumped gasping over their mounts, Scyri arrows emerging from their backs. Scores of horses, struck in the haunches by the attack from the rear, tumbled to their faces or skidded to a halt, wheeling in pain and rage. The Hunnish squadron fell into chaos, with those riders who were unhurt uncertain what had become of their fellows, craning their necks back to identify the source of the anguished screams. Men whose horses were hit leaped off their backs, tumbling to the ground and rolling to their feet in their light armor, just as the Scyri riders stormed into their midst, bows cast aside and cavalry swords drawn, slashing at the Hunnish riders ducking desperately for cover.

There was none. Huns who attempted to flee back to the safety of the horde were cut down by Scyri riders still racing from the woods, bows drawn and arrows nocked. Odoacer, finding himself in the thick of the fighting, dodged a sword slash by a footbound Hunnish rider whose horse had been shot from beneath him, and then brought his own blade down with the full force of his greater height, directly onto the Hun's head, cutting cleanly through the man's leather cavalry helmet and deep into the skull. The Hun dropped like a sack of barley. Jerking his blade free, Odoacer lifted his gaze before him.

What had a moment before been a pristine hillside meadow adjacent to the grove of trees was now a slaughtering ground. For hundreds of paces in every direction the ground was littered with dead men and horses, all Hunnish. By the same token, every living man he could see was Scyri. Not a single Hunnish horseman in the entire breakaway squadron had survived.

"Scout!" he shouted at a Scyri rider. The man trotted over to Odoacer triumphantly. "You have your signal gear?" Odoacer asked.

The man looked at him blankly.

"Your signal gear!" Odoacer shouted. "Pot of embers, pitch for the arrow? Answer me, man!"

With a start, the horseman understood, and hurriedly reached back to his saddlebag, whence he drew out a small jar stopped with a wooden plug.

"Go to the rear of the hill," Odoacer commanded. "Ride up close behind our own lines without being seen by the enemy in the front. Then shoot a fire arrow as high as you can, toward the enemy lines. That is the signal. He'll know what to do."

At last, the messenger found his voice.

"He . . . King Vismar? King Guthlac?"

"No, you dolt! Ellac the Hun! He doesn't know yet his ambush party has been destroyed. Now go!"

Blinking with confusion, the horseman sprinted away, pulling out the wooden plug with his teeth even as he rode. Odoacer watched with satisfaction.

With the last of the Hunnish riders dispatched, his men gathered expectantly around their leader. Odoacer wasted no time.

"Ride back on downhill toward the river!" he shouted. "Circle far around so the main body of Huns does not see you—let them continue to focus on the smoke and the trenches. Form rank on the gravel bank behind them. When you see the fire arrow from the top of the hill, behind the allied lines—charge the Huns with all your might!"

With a shout, the Scyri riders raced toward the Nedao, at a point half a mile upstream from the Huns' earlier crossing. At the bank they veered sharply left, following it to a point directly below the battle line, which they could see at the hilltop above them. Smoke still wafted in foul-smelling clouds over the field, and Odoacer could see that a number of large gaps had opened in the thorn barricade. The Hunnish forces, who since loosing the fire arrows had been milling restlessly along the battlefront, had now dismounted and deployed on foot, in a narrower, densely packed front directly across from one of the largest gaps in the barrier. Planks were being carried up, and readied to be thrown across the trenches.

"Watch for the signal!" Odoacer shouted to his men, and the order was passed down the line. Looking up just as he pointed, the men saw it in the afternoon sky, which had turned sickly and yellowish from the dissipating billows of smoke: the faint outline of a single fire arrow, its flaming-pitch warhead leaving a trail of greasy black smoke as it streaked up in a long arc, then fell to the ground behind the enemy lines.

The Hunnish sheep horn blew the signal for attack, and with a roar, the invaders surged forward toward the smoldering barricade, heaving planks across the trenches and scrambling up the embankment, fully expecting the embattled Germanic troops to be simultaneously attacked from the rear by their comrades who had circled behind the hill earlier. Meanwhile, Odoacer's Scyri horsemen on the riverbank emitted their own battle cries—and then, setting heels to flanks, stormed up the same hillside as the Hunnish horsemen themselves, only a few hours before, had charged up into the face of the Germanic barrage.

Yet as the Huns leaped forward across the embankment, they encountered not the distracted, rear-pressed Germanic forces they had expected, but rather a countercharge of furious tribesmen who themselves had just taken sight of Odoacer's troops far below on the riverbank, racing up the hill to hit the unwitting Huns from their own rear. The Scyri and Heruli, led by Guthlac himself wielding an enormous battle-axe, leaped over their own embankment, heavy blades easily swung by their massive arms, and the clash of metal and flesh as the two forces met on the soft soil of the embankment was deafening. The Huns, though expert swordsmen, were no match for their huge opponents, with their mail armor, heavier blades, and uphill position. The effect was like an oaken battering ram against a wicker horse fence. The front ranks of Huns were mowed down like grass, barely giving the rearward ranks time to turn and stagger back over the planks or drop into the ditch, fleeing by any means possible back to their original position, back to their waiting horses, back to . . .

The sheep horn frantically sounded the Hunnish retreat, but before the attackers could reverse their position, Odoacer's horsemen slammed into them from the rear, their blood still racing from the slaughter of the first Hunnish squadron only moments before. The Hunnish army was gutted. Terrified soldiers leaped and dodged where they could, ducking Scyri infantry who followed them across the trenches, tangling themselves in the legs of the Scyri horses that had just arrived. Wounded men fell screaming into smoldering palisades, while those still uninjured searched desperately for their own horses, which had scattered to the four winds in the confusion of the Scyri attack.

Racing through the melee, Odoacer found his target: in the rear of the Hunnish forces, still mounted yet wheeling to flee, was Ellac, distinguished by the fur trim edging his greased leather armor, and the pair of mounted Goth guards riding at his side. Odoacer thundered up, and with a single swipe of his blade sliced through the neck of the nearest Goth, whose trunk collapsed spewing over the back of his terrified horse. The second guard, though wielding a sword, glanced quickly at Odoacer's black expression and sprinted away, the wrong way, back into the smoke and carnage. It was only then that Ellac realized what was happening, and turned to look on the face of his victor for the first time. Though it had been nearly four years since they had last seen each other in the Great Hall of Attila's palace, he recognized Odoacer immediately.

"You!" Ellac snarled. "*You* are the man I want!" Standing high in his stirrups, he lunged forward, slamming his heavy cavalry sword down onto Odoacer with all the strength he could muster.

Odoacer countered with his own blade and felt the blow's metallic vibration shiver painfully through his arm. Before Ellac could slash again, he leaned back hard, pulling Fly-by-Night onto her rear legs, nearly off balance, and steering her forelegs down directly onto the haunches of Ellac's mount. The Hun's animal whinnied in surprise and pain, staggering as its rear knees collapsed and it nearly rolled to the ground, while Ellac sat back and jerked sharply on the reins to gain his own balance.

It was too late, for talk or for further fighting. Seizing the initiative, exulting in the confusion and missteps of his opponent, Odoacer reined his frightened horse down and, rising in his stirrups, brought his blade crashing down with all his might.

Ellac could see the blow coming, could see it even before Odoacer poised his blade, and tried to dodge, but with his horse still staggering beneath him, was only partially successful. The sword missed his head but sliced down into his neck, snapping through collarbone and scapula, driving deep into the middle of his chest, cleaving lengthwise down his torso, and then slipping back out easily above the pelvis. As Fly-by-Night spun away from the spray of blood, Odoacer turned to look, and for an instant saw Ellac still astride his horse, arms hanging loosely at his sides, eyes wide in surprise and glimmering lucidly, with nothing yet of the cloudiness of death. Then Ellac's own horse shifted to the side, and the gap fell open in Ellac's torso, exposing the clean-sliced clavicle and neck tendons. His face collapsed, and he slid off his saddle and into the red slurry churned up by his horse's hooves as it raced away to the safety of the river.

The noise of battle abated, and in a moment died completely. Wiping the perspiration from his eyes, Odoacer raised his head and looked about. His horsemen, still tense from their recent effort, began reining in their animals and walking them to patches of grass dry and free of cadavers. Toward the entrenchments, he could see the king's heavy infantry, some swaying softly in their fatigue, mute and stunned at the fury of the slaughter and the suddenness of its conclusion. Odoacer was struck by how utterly forlorn, even vulnerable, they looked, they the victors, in that futile, exhausted moment after the last foe had fallen, and before the realization of victory had set in. Around him stood men silent and withdrawn, almost unaware of one another's presence, their thoughts as void as those of the dead at their feet. Not a single Hun moved, not one stood or sat on the field, none even moaned in agony on the ground, awaiting death to overtake him. Not one had survived, and in the ferocity of the Germanic counterattack, not one had been able to flee. Ellac's army had been utterly destroyed.

A weak cheer rose from the entrenchments, floating over the field like a breeze, but after a moment that, too, died away, as men bent to retrieve their weapons and shields, tipped the helmets off their faces, and wearily trudged up the hill to begin the march to their homes. Still Odoacer did not move from where he silently sat his horse, and it was only after a long moment that he noticed Vismar approaching, his horse carefully picking its way through the mounds of dead.

The Scyri king stopped at Odoacer's side and stared down at the body of Ellac, whom he had never seen personally but whom he recognized for who he was, not by the fur trim on his armor, but because he lay at Odoacer's feet. The blood still trickled from the wound, seeping into the ground, and the dead eyes stared open and forthright at his conqueror, while Odoacer grasped his sword tightly in his hand, unsheathed and glimmering with a red sheen.

"This was a great victory," the king murmured. "More even than I had prayed for."

Odoacer nodded, feeling a crushing wave of fatigue roll over him. Fly-by-Night shuddered slightly as if she, too, felt it, transmitted from rider to animal and into the ground, like a lightning bolt through the length of a tree.

"A great victory," Odoacer repeated, his eyes still taking in the scope of the battlefield, the thirty thousand men dead, nearly that number of horses as well.

"You have achieved the vengeance you sought? You can live in peace now?" Vismar pressed.

Odoacer shook his head.

"Ellac was not the vengeance I sought," he replied. "I, perhaps, was his, and in seeking me out he did only what I would expect a Hun to do, and I bear him no rancor. Now that he is dead, my life is more secure, but I count that of little profit. My revenge remains unfulfilled."

"Ah." The king looked away, across the battlefield.

"You are surprised?"

Vismar shook his head.

"Surprised, no. I trusted your strategy and your strength, and I was right to do so. You have earned your legacy this day."

"But you are satisfied?"

The king paused long before answering. "Satisfied? For my own lifetime perhaps."

"Those do not sound like the words of a man who has just won a great victory."

"A victory over the Huns, true. This race will not torment us again, for though they remain numerous, their tribes and clans are too fragmented. A victory by Ellac this day would have sealed his reputation as a leader and unified their people. His loss will lead to their dispersal. We need never fear the Huns again."

"But . . ."

"But . . . their strength and their reputation have now passed to us—to the Scyri, the Heruli, the Rugi, and the other Germans. Other nations who previously had no cause to fear us, or even to notice us, will now look with new eyes upon the conquerors of the Huns."

"It is a good thing, no? To be noticed, to be feared, by other great peoples?"

The king shook his head.

"Perhaps," he replied quietly, turning his horse to begin its wary trek back toward the entrenchments. "As for myself—I preferred anonymity."

CHAPTER FOUR

Six Years Later, 463 A.D.

SOUTOK, CAPITAL OF THE SCYRI

I

The company of Roman soldiers marched down Soutok's main street in tight formation, eyes straight, expressions stern, though they had been carefully disarmed by the Scyri guards at the gates before being allowed to enter and approach the palace. The hobnailed sandals clattered noisily on the flagged paving, and their mailed tunics, swaying stiffly against the knees of their snug woolen leggings, had been polished to a high luster. Helmets remained down in battle position, rather than tipped back on the head for greater comfort and ventilation as when at ease. The troops were accompanied, in front and behind, by two squadrons of Scyri palace guards, and flanked by a company of Odoacer's horse troops. A pair of heralds advanced in front of the entire procession, clearing the streets with shouts and the occasional whack of a stick, while crowds of curious city-dwellers stepped out of the taverns and shops and stood in the doorways, watching the unaccustomed sight. Romans as a people were not strangers to the city, since traders, performers, and missionaries often passed through, generally on their way to another place more important. Never, however, had an official Roman military delegation entered Soutok, and few of the inhabitants had even seen a Roman soldier, other than the occasional tired veteran traveling with his wife and children to some uninhabited marshland to the north where he might make a home more cheaply than he could in the territory of Rome's own outer provinces.

Approaching the palace gates, which were now strengthened with cut stone and mortar rather than mere sharpened stakes, a result of the city's increased prosperity in recent years, they stepped into the courtyard. Marching up to the palace steps, the commander of the Scyri horse troops issued a call, and the party drew up in a halt. All eyes stared expectantly up to the portal of the new palace now under construction, the outer walls of which consisted of a confusing array of rough-cut stone, heavy timbers, and spidery scaffolding. An incipient roof of wooden planks covered only a portion of the structure, far off to one side. Within the portal stood Vismar, Odoacer, and a small group of officers and guards.

"What do you make of it?" Odoacer muttered to his grandfather.

The old king observed the spectacle in the courtyard. The years had been kind to him, but nonetheless he was not young, and had not been so even when Odoacer had first met him. Vismar was now bowed and stooped, his skin browner and more leathery than ever, his joints stiff and audibly creaking when he walked. He glanced at his grandson with piercing gray eyes, unclouded by cataracts or the vagueness of mind that also often comes with age.

"I do not see how it can be good," Vismar reasoned. "Roman military envoys rarely pay friendly calls. Especially accompanied by fifty legionaries. It is no small thing for them to venture across the Danuvius into our territory."

"They look prepared to do battle this very moment. It is good we disarmed them at the gate."

"They do indeed know how to dress before entering a city," the old king observed dryly.

An officer stepped forward from the company of Romans, removed his helmet, and approached to within a few paces of the king and Odoacer.

"Sovereign and citizens of the Scyri lands!" he said loudly in a guttural, German-inflected Latin. "Legate Paulus Domitius, of the Second Italica Legion at Lauriacum on the Danuvius, greets you! I bring tidings from the commander of the Roman legions—"

The king interrupted him, in equally labored Latin.

"Legate: I do not know which peoples you have visited with your 'tidings,' but the Scyri are civilized, and do not stand in the street shouting to one another. If you have traveled from Lauriacum across the river, then you have come far. Please allow your men to stand at ease, and come with me into the palace, where we might show you some hospitality, and discuss your mission in greater comfort."

The officer fell silent, somewhat taken aback, and Odoacer scrutinized him more closely. He was about Odoacer's own age, and similar in build—taller than the rest of his soldiers, with a hard stringiness about him and a cold cast to the eye that suggested his was no mere political appointment of a plump-handed city-dweller, but rather the position of an experienced soldier who had battled his way up to his current rank. His face was absolutely calm, indeed lacking in almost any defining features, with the inexpressiveness of a mask. His eyes showed obvious intelligence, but extreme caution as well, taciturn yet observant. But what most caught Odoacer's eye was the man's complexion: ruddy, despite the dust of the road and the weathering of the sun, with close-cropped, yellow hair, wide-spaced eyes, and a strong, fully developed face. A Germanic face.

After considering the king's words for a moment, the officer turned back to his troops and gave them a quick sign with his arm. They relaxed their postures and removed their helmets, chatting quietly with one another and glancing contemptuously at the Scyri guards around them. The officer then turned back toward the king, nodded, and walked calmly up the stairs, as two of the palace guards accompanied him into the large inner atrium, a mass of stone rubble and half-fitted timbers.

The king and his small party followed close behind.

"You will excuse, I hope, the palace's present condition," the old man said, with an expansive gesture of his arm. "We have lived here for some decades, but it is only in recent years, with the arrival of my grandson"—and he placed his hand on Odoacer's shoulder—"that our nation has become sufficiently prosperous to afford a true capital. Nothing like the buildings to which you are accustomed in Ravenna or Milan, of course—"

"I am not familiar with those cities," the officer interrupted curtly, "and I regret to say, Your Majesty, that I am unable to accept your hospitality. I have important news to impart, and then I must return to my men. If you please, we may stop and discuss the matter here, rather than entering your . . . palace."

The king was undismayed by the officer's rudeness or obvious rush, but rather peered at him closely, taking in the man's light hair and broad features.

"You are Germanic," the king concluded, "as am I. Therefore your people have the same blood as ours. No doubt our forefathers, yours and mine, fought together. I am curious— how is it you now command Romans? Assume a Roman name? Speak to us in the language of Rome, rather than in a Germanic tongue, which both of us would no doubt find easier to negotiate? Do you deny your father's and grandfather's heritage?"

Domitius opened his mouth to respond, and then shut it again, caught by surprise. The interview was not moving as he had intended. His face remained composed, but his eyes flickered briefly between the king and Odoacer as he considered his response.

"Your Highness," he said in a deliberate voice, as one might use on a slightly dense child, "I serve in Rome's Germanic auxiliary units, as did my father before me. Rome is a civilizing influence over the barbarian peoples it governs, and I am honored to serve it. You are correct: my father was of the Argentoratum clan of the Alamanni—but I am now proud to represent order, a new way of life, rather than the chaos and squalor of my German roots."

He then shut his mouth abruptly, as if he had said too much, and Vismar looked at him in grave silence.

"I speak to merchants," the king said softly. "I have ambassadors myself, to other nations, including Rome. Rome has its own chaos, and its cities their own squalor, moral if not physical. Its emperors are deposed every year—I could nearly set the seasons by it. I recall just a few years ago, when the great Roman general Aetius defeated Attila, he was rewarded by the emperor with a dagger in the belly. Shortly afterward, Gaiseric the Vandal entered Rome and sacked it with his horde."

Odoacer spoke up.

"This is true, Your Majesty. But when Gaiseric attacked, Rome was under the rule of a new emperor, Maximus, I believe. This emperor was hit in the head by a stone when fleeing the sacking, and then torn limb from limb by a mob of his own people."

The king shook his head sadly.

"Astonishing. No Germanic ruler I know would ever consider fleeing his city, nor would any tribesmen so basely murder their own ruler. You see, Legate—I bring up these sad topics because I see no attraction or advantage to an intelligent man like yourself from joining in league with a people like the Romans."

Domitius stiffened, though his face remained as expressionless as it had been a moment before. He gave a small nod, as if acknowledging the king's point.

"What Rome offers a man like me," he said calmly, "is opportunity and advancement, which I would not have had among the Alamanni. A man without wealth, or lacking noble blood, can hardly rise to a position of responsibility under a king, at least under my people's king. Yet in the legions he can. Indeed"—he looked pointedly at Odoacer—"the legions even now are seeking accomplished young officers to command its auxiliary troops. As you know, Rome has many Germans serving in its ranks—including entire cohorts of Scyri—but precious few trained officers from those nations—"

Vismar interrupted him.

"Odoacer is no mere 'officer,' Legate. He is my grandson and a prince of the realm."

"Ah." The legate gave a slight smile. "Regrettably, the legions have no need for princes."

Then stepping toward the king, he removed from his belt a parchment scroll, which he extended before him. Baldovic reached out to take it.

"I bear a message from my general," the legate continued. "As part of the Pannonian legions' policy of strengthening its borders along the Danuvius, it is requiring that all barbarians inhabiting within twenty miles of the river's northern banks abandon their positions and take up residence elsewhere."

The king looked at him in surprise.

"Do you mean to say that Rome intends to cross the Danuvius and occupy the northern bank with its own forces?"

"No," the legate replied. "Rome simply wishes to establish a buffer zone, to eliminate the border attacks and skirmishes against it which, regrettably, have become all too frequent in recent years. Our permanent garrisons will remain on the southern bank. We will patrol the northern region at will, to enforce our policy, but we will not occupy it. Neither, however, will the barbarians."

Odoacer had thus far considered these words in silence, but now he spoke up.

"Legate, the northern bank is populated by a number of villages and towns. Most are of other tribes who preceded us to this region, or even men of no tribe at all, but simply immigrant merchants and farmers who have settled there to trade with the river traffic and the Romans. What of these people?"

Domitius shrugged.

"That is their affair."

"Then why announce this policy to us? Soutok is well over twenty miles north of the river."

"Because," the legate replied, with a hint of testiness, "those people within the empty zone must retreat north. Since your kingdom, indeed this very 'city,' is just outside the zone, they will require resettlement on your lands. I am doing you the courtesy of forewarning you of the coming migration."

Vismar stared at the Roman for a moment, speechless. Finally, he found his voice.

"A courtesy?" the king murmured. "I'm afraid this will be impossible. The Scyri people are barely surviving as it is, on this bleak marshland they have been reclaiming over the years."

The Roman glanced around him at the ongoing construction of the palace, looking askance at the king's claim of poverty.

"You refuse to allow the river peoples to settle here, then?"

"We will make war on them if they do," Odoacer replied roughly. "This is our land. Those people are not our people; some are of tribes that opposed our own arrival here, and are therefore our enemies."

"They are Germanic, as am I, and you," Domitius replied, echoing the king's words to him of a moment before. "To me, you have offered hospitality, and concern at the state of my father's heritage. Yet to them you offer only death by starvation."

"It is not we who offer them death," Odoacer retorted, "but you. Their fate at Roman hands is not our concern. Our city is surrounded by marshes, and cannot be expanded. We cannot let others occupy our scarce lands, eat our scarce food. That would only prolong their dying, and cause ours as well."

The legate glanced toward the portal, listening to the restless murmur of the troops in the courtyard, and when he turned back his face betrayed his impatience to be done with this mission.

"If you make war on these people," he said coldly, "then I regret to inform you Rome will be forced to make war on you."

Vismar stared hard at the Roman.

"Those river tribes are your enemy, Rome's enemy, which is why you are driving them from the Danuvius in the first place. They are also our enemy, and have been for years. Yet you would make war on us for their sake? Since when has Rome attacked the enemies of its enemies? This is not a prudent policy, Legate—as even a 'barbarian' king like myself can see."

Domitius shrugged and stepped to the door. In his eyes, the interview was over.

"These are my orders, Your Highness. The river peoples are already preparing to move north, and will be here within two months. You will send us word of your consent to accept their presence, or face the consequences."

With a curt nod to the king, and another to Odoacer, he turned abruptly and strode out. The others stood in the doorway for a moment, and then Odoacer stepped forward, calling out to the officer as he strode down the palace steps toward his men, who rapidly formed ranks and began adjusting their helmets.

"Legate," he called out sharply. "What is the name of your general?"

The Roman stopped and turned halfway around to eye him.

"I serve under the *Dux Pannoniae Primae et Norici,* Supreme Military Commander of Pannonia and Noricum, who heads the Second Italica, the First Noricorum, the Tenth Vindobona, and the Fourteenth Carnuntum legions, as well as three naval squadrons of the armada of the Upper Danuvius, and all associated artillery cohorts and cavalry *alae:* General Orestes."

With a casual salute, Domitius turned and strode down to his troops, disappearing into the bustle of their preparations. In a moment, the only sound was the clinking of armor and the tramping of feet as they marched in rhythmic step out of the palace courtyard and into the city's main street. Odoacer turned back to the king, his eyes angry and face pale.

"Orestes," the old king muttered. "Orestes. That name is familiar. Does it mean anything to you?"

"A man I once knew," Odoacer said. "A very wealthy man."

"Germanic?" the king asked.

Odoacer nodded grimly.

"Germanic. But like the legate, he is not one of us."

II

They came as Romans come, without subtlety or hesitation, without dissimulation, like road builders ordered to remove a homestead so as to straighten the route of a thoroughfare. They came not as Huns would have come, with the fury of a winter blizzard, overwhelming in number, terrifying in speed and ruthlessness, leaving scarcely the memory of their victims behind; nor as Goths, in stealth behind trees, slipping silently and secretly through marshes, eliminating individual opponents like mute assassins and then, when victory was achieved, leaving the cities to molder and crumble, still standing, but bereft of wealth and inhabitants. Rather, they came as Romans, openly and without ruse, confident in their rightness and inevitability, forthright in their determination to accomplish their task.

After the legate's departure, there were no further warnings or negotiations, no cajoling or compromise. There were no recriminations—the Scyri had made their decision, and the Romans acted accordingly, as they said they would, as they had announced in advance. Roman fishwives might haggle in the marketplace, old men might debate in the Senate; indeed even Roman emperors, both east and west, might bluff and bluster and horse-trade with one another. But not Roman generals, not this Roman general. He had said what he would do, and now he was doing it. The only thing left was to announce, afterward, what he had done, and move on to the next assignment.

A pigeon brought first word, in a hastily scrawled message rolled into a tiny copper tube tied to its leg. The allied governor of a Rugi market town sixty miles to the southwest wrote he had been besieged by the vanguard of a Roman army, and could not mount a defense without reinforcements. Odoacer assembled five thousand light cavalry and raced off to assist, with instructions for the heavy cavalry and foot troops to follow as quickly as possible. The citizens remaining in Soutok, meanwhile, abandoned all other activities and set about strengthening their own town's fortifications.

The next day brought another pigeon, with word Vismar had already deduced from the columns of black smoke his wide-ranging scouts had spied on the horizon: the Rugi town had fallen, within hours after the initial Roman attack. Odoacer's mission, even as he led his horse troops west, would be changed from defensive, reinforcing a besieged ally, to offensive: attacking the approaching Roman column before it could strike Soutok. Vismar sent couriers racing west to catch up with his grandson, to inform him of the new circumstances and order him to await the arrival of the main Scyri army. Within a day of the second pigeon's arrival, the heavy troops had set off along the western paths toward the Danuvius, to the cheers of the populace. Their target was now almost in sight even from the ramparts of Soutok itself, for the columns of black smoke now originated from other burning towns and hamlets in the Romans' path, much closer to the Scyri capital.

At sunrise the next day, with Soutok's army already twenty miles distant, the early breeze brought to the people's ears not news of victory; nor even the clamor of river refugees wailing to be admitted through the gates; but rather the sound of Roman battle trumpets. Sentries on the walls turned in alarm at the distant bugling, for it came not from the west, whence the Roman attacks on the other river towns had originated, but from a completely unexpected quarter. The urgent horns were heard from the south, where the meandering waters of the Morava sloughed into a vast, fetid bog that drained only weakly into the Danuvius many miles distant— a dense, forested swampland which the Scyri, when settling here decades ago, had considered as impregnable a barrier against attack as a stone wall. When the sentries made their rounds on the city walls, nervously awaiting the distant approach of the Romans from the west, they had not even considered looking behind them toward the swamp. The bog was where no sane man went, and whence no danger was thought to approach.

The king, still rubbing his bleary eyes from his hurried awakening, rushed to the lightly manned defenses on the southern ramparts. From the dark observation tower, the smallest one on the walls, built to be staffed by only two sentries, he peered through the dawn penumbra. There, on the edge of the swamp only a mile from Soutok's unfinished walls, lay hundreds of river craft pulled up into the reeds. Many he recognized as the eel boats used by the clans of fisherman who, like generations of their ancestors in the Morava swamps, lived and raised their families on the shallow-bottomed vessels. Others, however, seemed to have been cobbled together clumsily, of mismatched lumber, but nevertheless were adequate to carry light-armed troops. His mind quickly grasped the trap into which Soutok had fallen: while one Roman army had been steadily marching from the west, luring Odoacer's cavalry to the defense of the Scyri allies, an even larger force had made its way up the Danuvius— or down the Danuvius, for the king was still unsure whether his enemy had originated from Noricum or Pannonia—in craft constructed by Rome's river armada. Additional troops had doubtless been transported along with them, in confiscated grain barges and other merchant vessels. At the boggy confluence of the Morava and the Danuvius, the troops had disassembled the larger craft and constructed smaller ones, more suitable to the shallow marshes, and then ferried their troops and supplies up the tributary, poling through the stagnant water and reeds in the dead of night, unseen by Scyri outposts or guards, who had all been deployed west to stem the attack perceived to be coming from that quarter. Even as he despaired, Vismar marveled at the Romans' ingenuity and daring, and at the sheer inevitability of their plan.

The captain of the guards peered at the distant troops with his keener vision, seeking out the pennants and banners.

"First Noricum and Tenth Vindobona," he muttered.

The king looked at him sharply.

"Two legions?" he said. "That many men?"

The guard captain nodded.

"Six or eight thousand troops, at least. And at least one full legion marching on us from the west, either the Second or the Fourteenth. That leaves a fourth legion still unaccounted for—it could be dispersed between the two fronts, or arriving from a different direction altogether."

There was little Vismar could do with the few troops left in the city, besides bar the main gate and send a pair of couriers racing west, to inform Odoacer before the Roman noose completely closed around the city. Defended only by the palace guard, Soutok would be unable to withstand a full assault. Its only hope was that Odoacer might return in time to break the siege—if he could avoid being caught between the pincers of the two attacking Roman forces. Should Odoacer fail, Soutok would be forced to surrender, or be destroyed.

The Romans would have ample time to complete the encirclement. Certainly it would be possible for them to storm the city and take it immediately if they wished, but this would be unlikely, Vismar reflected. With luck, the newly arrived Romans would have no idea that Soutok's army was actually far away outside the walls. They would learn this soon enough, for spies and leaks of information were inevitable in a siege. Nevertheless, as long as the Romans thought the city heavily defended, they would delay the final attack, giving the Scyri time, allowing them to hold out until Odoacer could return.

"Assemble the youths and young women!" the king ordered abruptly.

The guard captain turned away from his observation of the distant Romans and looked inquiringly at the king.

"Your Majesty?" he asked, doubt in his voice.

"The youths and young women," the king repeated. "Any person in the city who stands high enough to be seen over the ramparts, and who can walk without stooping."

The captain considered this, a slight smile appearing on his face.

"And then open the armory and issue them all helmets and spears, and set them to pacing the ramparts," the officer continued.

"Correct," Vismar concluded, turning to descend the

stone steps to the bottom of the wall. "From a distance the Romans will think our city fully defended. In the meantime, I go to prepare for siege."

With deliberation born of competence and confidence, the Romans began preparing a system of trenches around the entire city wall, just out of arrow range, supported by a high dirt embankment. They dug latrines behind the embankment, set up field kitchens, fenced in paddocks for the livestock they had seized from surrounding farms, and diverted a nearby stream to supply water stations, one for each cohort manning the siege trench. By the end of the day they had completed the encirclement, and on the dryer side of the city, away from the marshes, had constructed a complete headquarters camp, sufficient to shelter ten thousand troops, itself heavily fortified around its square perimeter by sharpened stakes and an elongation of the encirclement trench. All this Vismar observed from the ramparts, surrounded by weeping women marching doggedly in oversized helmets and heavy spears.

The first night of siege passed without incident, yet also without sleep. Rising several times, Vismar seized his walking stick and a lamp and hobbled slowly outside, past the scaffolding on the unfinished walls, and up the narrow stone steps of the nearest set of ramparts. Below, in the darkness, he saw the vast ranks of forces arrayed against him, represented by the tiny, uniform cooking fires burning low before each tent, the orange specks as incongruously cheerful as only inanimate, dead objects can be in the face of catastrophe, like the grin on the face of a corpse lying on a battlefield.

Each time, he slowly paced the wall tops, taking the measure of the enemy force, counting the number of troops, guessing at their level of readiness, musing on their morale, and knowing each time that the answer would not change. These were Romans, commanded by a general whose name, Orestes, had shaken even Odoacer, and they had no reason to be any less than what they appeared before him in the darkness to be: an immovable force who, within a day, should no miracle intervene, would be his masters. And each time he ended his circuit on the western walls by peering into the darkness, beyond the dim lights of the fires below him, across the rolling hills he knew lay in the distance, though it was impossible for him to see, toward his only hope of safety, however small.

On his fourth painstaking climb up to the high western watchtower, the sun had not yet edged over the horizon, yet the grayish pall cast across the eastern quadrant allowed him to make out the darkened hills to the west, to just distinguish the point where they melded with the distant blackness of the sky. And there, he saw a shadow that had not been there the night before, a shadow he knew would be invisible for some time to the Roman outposts in their lower position. Within half a watch it would take on its true form, a moving mass, which would then resolve into its individual components, men and horses, and when the sun's rays exploded over the eastern horizon, the riders, too, would shine in their individual details: polished armor and bridle bits, glinting spears and burnished shields. The king's first thought was fear as to which body this group of armed men might be—whether the Roman legion attacking from the west, or the horsemen Odoacer had taken to defend the river cities; but he soon comforted himself that the shadow was moving far too rapidly to be footbound Romans, and could only be the Scyri cavalry, and he knew that Odoacer had received his message.

His second reaction was dismay at how small the shadow appeared compared to the array of forces laying siege to him below, and how even smaller it would be once Rome's western legion had arrived to reinforce its comrades, and the difficulty Odoacer would face in breaking the siege without direct communication with the city; but the king perceived a dismal consolation in the fact that he had few troops within who could cooperate with Odoacer in any case, and Odoacer knew this, and so precious little communication was actually necessary. There is a certain comfort in being helpless, in utterly lacking decisions and authority, and therefore in having fate out of one's hands.

Sighing, Vismar descended the walls once again and hobbled to the palace chapel, where he knew the priest, a man as old as he, would soon be preparing for Mass. Kneeling on the packed-earth floor of the still unflagged and scaffolded structure, the barrel-vaulting of the apses open to the lightening dawn sky, he gave thanks for Odoacer's imminent arrival, and surprised the old presbyter, when he entered, with a look of contentment.

Orestes strode from the command tent into the pre-dawn gray, breathing in the cool air, absently scratching a rib and gazing toward the eastern sky, noting the roiling thunderheads and wondering idly whether the storm would arrive before they had taken the city that morning, or after, and whether his men would be able to take shelter in solid buildings or in their leaky canvas tents. It hardly mattered—his Germanic troops were inured to cold and wet, as tough as any men he had ever led. Nevertheless, he would be the first to admit he preferred commanding Huns because, though like all men they suffered from the weather, they were at least quiet about it.

He thought back to the day before, when his two legions had traversed the five miles of marshes to arrive at the gates of this benighted city—the only part of the expedition it had not been possible to plan in advance, for the eelmen's mobile village was difficult to reconnoiter and the number of available vessels hard to ascertain. Nevertheless, his scouts had done their job well, and the quantities of gold they had disbursed to the swamp-dwellers had greatly facilitated matters. Shows of strength are useful, he mused, but gold is better, and more easily procurable than good troops. He had long before learned the lesson that he would rather lose his entire war chest than even half a legion of veteran troops. Lost treasure might even be recovered the next day, if the conditions were right. But lost men—it might be years before the emperor replenished a depleted legion, if he ever did.

After Orestes' initial concerns about the eel-boats were

put to rest, he had even enjoyed the excursion through the marshes. Nearly five hundred vessels had collected at the meeting point—the eelmen were even more greedy for Roman gold than he had expected, or more resentful at the Scyri tribesmen who had taken over their lands a generation before. Not that there were five hundred eelmen even in existence in the entire marsh—he would be surprised if there were one-fifth that number. Nevertheless, the swamp men had brought with them every boat they could lay their hands on—sound or rotten, sturdy as a fixed dock, or tippy as a child's cradle. They had come in all sizes—from the substantial vessels on which entire families lived, to one- and two-man dugouts used to traverse the dark byways of the swamps and check the nets, to one huge flat-bottomed grain barge with old Greek markings, which the tribesmen had acquired from God knows where, and had used over the decades as a kind of floating meeting place for their annual councils. Orestes had loaded that ship alone with three hundred Roman troops and their supplies, along with several dozen skittish courier horses, and nearly fifty men had been needed to pole it through the marsh, preceded by a handful of dugouts manned by soldiers and eelmen with scythes to hack away at the overhanging trees to allow the monstrous craft to pass. A few hardy troopers, unwilling to sit crowded back to belly all day on a rotting craft with other men, tried to perch astride logs and propel themselves with contrived paddles, but they soon abandoned the idea and hailed the nearest vessel, clambering over the other grumbling soldiers and spending the rest of the day picking off the leeches that had attached themselves to their legs as they dangled in the water.

Yet despite the uncertainty, and the organization required for the short voyage, the eelmen had kept their promises: they had arrived at the meeting point, conveyed the Roman troops through the swamp, and, most important, kept the entire operation secret from the Scyri in Soutok. Not a word had leaked through to the outside, and when the Romans finally conquered the marsh and stepped back onto solid ground, within an easy jog of the city's walls, the population had been taken completely by surprise. If the Scyri had any defensive forces at all, they had rushed back inside and barred the gates, for there was not the remotest hint of threat at the moment that had most concerned Orestes: when his troops were establishing a beachhead on solid ground, and disembarking from the motley array of craft.

Now, this next morning, as he stared up at the dark city walls, savoring the silence in the moments before the dawn bugle would sound, his satisfaction was complete. A moment before, he had seen an elderly man standing on the highest part of the Scyri ramparts, gazing out over the Roman camp. He was undoubtedly a person of rank and wealth, for even in the pre-dawn light Orestes had discerned the luxuriant shimmer of his robes and the length of his white hair and beard. Perhaps the king of this misruled and doomed nation? Orestes did not know, nor did he have the curiosity to inquire, for that man, like every other inhabitant of the city, would within a few hours be either dead or his slave. This was the only fate that remained for such a people. The time for negotiations and conditions had passed two months earlier, on the day his legate had been rebuffed in Soutok.

The nobleman on the walls soon disappeared, and Orestes then heard the ringing of a bell inside the city walls. The call to Mass, no doubt, and he thought absently that the old man he had seen on the ramparts might have been on his way to that very Mass, and had simply paused to climb a watchtower and look out over the Roman camp. If that were so, he was undoubtedly, at that very moment, praying that the enemy's hands might be turned from the Scyri city. The enemy's hands: the Romans' hands; his—Orestes'—hands. He felt an odd thrill at this thought—that just behind these walls, he, Orestes, was the subject of prayers and supplications, that *he* was being identified to God as the oppressor of the Scyri, and therefore as being in opposition to God—for do not all men identify their oppressors as the enemies of God? If any man were to call Orestes evil or a demon to his face, he would take it as a mortal insult, and strike him down immediately. He had done so in the past. But the thought of a Mass being said not for his sake, but *against* his sake, of prayers rising to heaven equating him with an *enemy* of heaven—this was a turn he had never considered, a promotion in status. And though he, too, was a Christian, who trusted, in turn, that God was on his side and on Rome's, it was somehow perversely gratifying to be vicariously relegated to the depths of hell, to be cursed to God, however wrongly, to be condemned by earthly judges in hopes the Heavenly Judge would commiserate—in short, to be *feared*. It was at moments like these that Orestes understood the intoxication, the absolute headiness, that he had seen in Attila's eyes in the past, when the Hun knew a great conquest over a weaker people was within his grasp.

The nobleman on the ramparts had long disappeared and the bell had stopped ringing. Now a pair of sentries stood at the walls above, calmly watching the Roman camp spread before them, observing how Roman soldiers awoke, shat, ate their breakfasts, and organized themselves for an assault. On a whim, he ducked back into his tent, seized the conical bullhorn his herald used to magnify his voice, and strode to the edge of the Roman camp, just beyond the palisade, as near as he dared approach the city walls for fear of becoming a target of snipers. The Scyri were known for their good aim.

Lifting the horn toward the two sentries who stood watching him curiously, he gathered his breath and called out in Latin in as loud a voice as he could muster.

"*O Scyri fortissimi et nobilissimi:* You have been surrounded and your city is about to be annihilated. Do you understand me?"

The two guards gave no sign of comprehension, but neither did they turn away. Both stood stock-still, watching him with attention, and several other heads emerged behind them, though in the shadows Orestes could not discern whether they were soldiers, or merely observers from among the populace.

Orestes raised the horn again, deciding to assume his words had been understood. A number of Roman troops gathered behind him in silence, intently observing the reaction of the guards on the walls.

"Most noble and brave Scyri: Soutok is lost, your nation doomed. You have but one choice: to live or to die. Your fate is in my hands. The sun's rays will illumine your city in one hour's time. Before that moment, every person who leaves the city and walks peaceably to our lines will be spared. Wives and children will live, even men-at-arms will be allowed honorable surrender when they drop their weapons.

"But after that moment, no departure will be permitted, no surrender accepted. Every person within the city will be destroyed. You may resist, and you may even succeed in taking a Roman soldier down to hell with you. But you will not survive, and your effort will be in vain. It will be futile, a suicide, which is a great sin, and an even greater waste. My name is General Orestes, Commander of Rome's legions and fleets of Pannonia and Noricum. You have one hour's time. *Fiat voluntas Dei.*"

God's will be done.

He dropped the bullhorn to his side and stood watching, as the troops behind him crowded expectantly at the edge of the trenches. More people had gathered on the wall tops, and Orestes now could see they included both soldiers and common people, old men and women. The fact that civilians were on the ramparts indicated to him the city was only lightly defended, for a full complement of troops would never have allowed women to clamber about on the ramparts with them.

For a moment all was silence, as the watching Scyri stared down with as much expectation as the Roman troops below looking up at them. Orestes had the odd feeling the Scyri had understood nothing he had said, but had patiently let him prattle on as at a show or performance, and were now awaiting the punch line. Yet surely that could not be true. Soutok was a trading center of some regional importance—educated people inhabited it, Romans had passed through and done business there for years, Latin and Greek were surely understood, even by low-ranking palace guards. His offer had been generous enough—standard terms of surrender by Roman armies. Were the Scyri truly that perplexed at his words?

On the wall top, the observers seemed finally to decide there would be no further speech, and one by one they drifted away from the observation post until even the original two sentries, the last to remain at their positions, also turned and slowly began making their rounds of the ramparts. Orestes shrugged and walked back inside the palisades and to his campaign tent. He had done his duty, followed the book. As he entered the camp, he heard the morning bugle issue the official call to wake.

The order was needless. On the morning of battle, no man sleeps late.

Odoacer lay on his stomach at the crest of a small rise, a hillock barely high enough and distant enough to be out of sight of the Roman camp and its entrenchments below. Beside him, Baldovic also peered down through the shadows, while both sets of troops—Odoacer's cavalry and Baldovic's foot soldiers, who had joined forces on the rush back to the city—rested a half mile behind in a low swale. Odoacer smiled grimly. It was by pure chance they had returned by a northerly route. From here they would be in a good position to circle around to their left and come in at the enemy from the east—as the sun rose in the next few minutes, the low angle of its rays at their backs would prevent the Romans from noting the Scyri presence, even if they did happen to glance behind them.

"We have little time, my lord," Baldovic muttered. "The western legion will catch up with us as they advance on Soutok—or the main body below will discover our presence when they send out scouts to link up with the western troops. Either way, I'd guess we have an hour at most."

"It is him," Odoacer said, barely listening. "The bastard Orestes. If I had a dozen Hunnish archers with fast horses, I'd rush down now. He'd be dead before he had time to turn his head."

Baldovic turned and looked at him long and steadily.

"The city is under siege, and we have ten thousand armed troops behind us, who must be put into action immediately, or be lost. Perhaps you have a personal grudge against this man. But now is not the time to nurse it."

"Ten thousand troops . . . ," Odoacer repeated thoughtfully. "Not enough to defeat them, even with surprise. We'd be caught between their two armies before gaining victory. Already they outnumber us."

Baldovic looked back at the Roman deployment, his face expressionless.

"Therefore . . . ," Odoacer continued, "we don't fight them."

"We *must* fight them."

"Not yet, anyway. Our best chance is to get inside the city walls. *Then* we fight. The Romans would need at least triple our troops to overrun us behind the defenses—even then, it might take weeks or months. Time enough to organize resistance by allies outside the area. It could be done."

"We would still need to advance our troops past the Roman army, over their trenches, and through the closed city gates," Baldovic pointed out.

Odoacer considered this in silence for a moment, but his thoughts were interrupted by a third man, who crawled up behind them, careful to remain out of sight of the Romans below.

"Greetings, Prince," the man said breathlessly. Odoacer turned and recognized one of his cavalry scouts, his face still flushed and dusty from the road he had just ridden in on.

"The western legion is ten miles back, and seems to have joined up with a second. Their standards identify them as the Second Italica, out of Lauriacum, and the Fourteenth Carnuntum. They look to have marched the night through, and they're still moving quickly."

"Another legion?" Baldovic pondered. "That makes two behind us, and what looks like two besieging the city, plus the sailors of the naval fleet that brought them here from the river. Twenty thousand men or more. Double our numbers."

"And the road is good," said Odoacer. "The western legions

won't take long to arrive. Do you know if they've made contact with Orestes' troops below?"

I don't think so, my lord," the scout replied. "We killed three of their outriders, who may have been trying to bring word. Still, some others might have slipped past our men, by another route—"

"Baldovic," Odoacer cut in hastily. "We have no time for complicated maneuvers. Go back and ready the men, circling them around to the east, in line with the rising sun. Then bring them forward, all of them. Have the cavalry dismount, stay low, to delay the moment we are seen. The sun will soon edge over the horizon. The moment it rises completely, with the full light in the Romans' eyes, we go home."

"Home?" Baldovic looked at him questioningly.

"Home. We bull our way through. Straight into the Romans' backs. Storm through their lines, leap their trenches— they have boards and pathways for their own use, look for those—and head straight for the main gates. I'll lead the horsemen first, to soften up the enemy, and we'll remain in the Roman lines until your infantry catch up. But do not let the men stop to fight—if they do, we lose everything. Bull through. Bull through. Tell that to the men. Our strategy has two words: bull through."

Baldovic nodded, and began backing away on hands and knees with the scout. After descending the low hill, both men stood in a crouch and began trotting over to the troops, but Baldovic suddenly stopped and turned back, running partway up again, bent over at the waist.

"Prince! Prince!" he said in a loud whisper.

Odoacer, still on his belly, craned his neck back.

"What is it?"

"What happens when we get to the gate? Will the king know to open it to us? And not let the Romans in as well?"

Odoacer stared at him for a moment.

"That, my friend," he said, "is out of our hands."

As the Roman troops stood in loose formation atop their embankments, gazing at the city walls and awaiting the orders, the first thing they sensed was the sun's rays streaming across the plain behind them, lighting their backs with radiance. Though still too early for warmth to penetrate the morning chill and the heavy dew, the light nevertheless comforted by its mere presence, loosening the night-knotted muscles of their backs, illuminating the faces of their comrades, clarifying the obstacles before them, and the true height and construction of the city walls that were to be attacked. Orestes had positioned the bulk of the Roman forces on the eastern and southeastern sides of the city, such that at sunrise, when the rampart sentries looked out at the attackers in that direction, they would be blinded by the horizontal rays shining in their eyes. He knew this was only an incomplete aid—eyes could be at least partially shaded, and within an hour or so the sun would have risen to such an angle that it would not interfere with the defenders' line of sight toward the Romans—but for those few moments, at least, the effect on the city would be devastating. And if all went well, only a few moments would be necessary.

The second thing the Roman troops sensed was the thunder of hoofbeats behind them, which at first were nearly drowned by the cheerful banter of the men enjoying the sun's early rays, but which after a moment became louder and more powerful, a deep rumbling, felt as much in the gut as heard in the ears. The troopers assumed it was their own cavalry, deploying to the opposite side of the siege works or exercising in the fields behind the lines.

It was only when the rumble continued to grow and intensify that a few men idly turned to peer behind them, though their own vision was blinded by the shafts of light. They had no time to shade their eyes with a hand, nor to await the sun's rising to a more comfortable angle. With a furious crash of horseflesh on armor, the five thousand horse troops of Odoacer's armored cavalry slammed into the Roman siege troops from behind. In the space of a few breaths, a thousand terrified Romans had been trampled to the ground, or knocked into their own twelve-foot ditch, where they lay sodden and dazed in the marsh-seepage at the bottom. With shrill yips of excitement, the Scyri horse troops rampaged through the Roman lines, leaping across the plank bridges topping the entrenchments, chasing down individual legionaries who had dropped their weapons in their initial shock, flying through the deposits of spare weapons and water skins, scattering spear shafts and slashing open the containers of safe stream water. Within moments, the siege forces' eastern quadrant had erupted into chaos.

Mounted on his horse a quarter mile away, Orestes immediately comprehended the situation, though the suddenness of the attack from the sun's direction made his officers' jaws drop in astonishment.

"Which cohort is stationed on the southern end of the city, near the swamp—fifth, is it not?"

A tribune fumbled to identify the troops.

"Fifth, yes, sir—and the sixth, of the Tenth Vindobona."

"Pull them in, now, along the trenches, to reinforce the third cohort being attacked. The second and fourth cohorts—"

"Opposite us, sir, on the northern side—"

"Pull them in, too, and order an attack, immediately."

"Attack on what, sir—the barbarian horse troops, from behind?"

"No, idiot, the city itself, at the main gates!"

"The main gates?" The tribune hesitated for a moment. "Sir—the main gates are the strongest part of the city walls. We had agreed at the strategy meeting last night that the second and fourth cohorts would be posted opposite the weakest points, on the northern side."

"Are you questioning my judgment, Tribune?"

"No sir, I was just pointing out—"

"You're wasting my time, Tribune. Order the attack *now!*"

The officer wheeled and galloped to the crowd of waiting couriers who, after receiving his shouted instructions, immediately scattered. Observing the scene carefully from nearby, Paulus Domitius sidled his own horse to where Orestes stood impatiently peering through the sharp glare of the sunrise at the swirling dust of the battle.

"General, I overheard your orders, and just for the sake of clarification—an attack on the main gates? Shouldn't those cohorts be sent to repel the attack on our own forces?"

"It is not an attack, Legate," Orestes replied laconically.

"Not an attack? But, sir, barbarian cavalry have stormed into our troops' rear, and scouts report a large body of foot soldiers following close behind—"

"It is not an attack. The barbarians are not seeking to fight."

"But—"

"Damn. Are all my officers deaf? If you cannot hear what I say, at least see what I see."

Domitius fell into chagrined silence, and as the two men watched, a small number of Scyri horsemen broke through the Roman lines, clambered over the embankment, picked their way across the trench, and reined in on the flat ground at the other side. They were followed by others, and then with a shout, the entire body of horsemen broke through the lines, trampling and dodging the legionaries who opposed them, storming in a mass over the barriers. They gathered at the far side of the trench to redeploy their formation, while behind them their infantry comrades hit the enemy line, slamming into the already dazed legionaries, producing a cloud of dust and mist that again obscured the scene from the observing officers.

Domitius turned at the rumble of feet behind him, as the fifth and sixth cohorts passed in an urgent Roman trot, helmets pulled down, shields poised, swords gripped tightly, faces grim. They had seen and heard the attack from more than a mile away, sufficient distance as to let each man ponder, as he approached, whether this would be the last mile he would ever run, the last sunrise he would ever see. Now, as they approached the fighting, the battle could be smelled as well—the sharp piss-scent of panic-stricken men, the choking heaviness of the dust, the ferrous odor of blood, the sour latrine stench of bowels pierced—yet the running troops remained in perfect form and alignment, all eyes fixed before them on the scene they were approaching.

"They'll arrive in a moment," Domitius murmured.

"And they will have nothing to fight but the lice on their heads," Orestes replied. "Legate, find their cohort commanders, quickly. Order the fifth and sixth cohorts to attack the main gates as well."

Domitius turned and stared at his general sharply, but Orestes held his gaze.

"Now, Legate," Orestes growled menacingly.

Without a word, Domitius galloped off toward the newly arriving troops. A moment later the two cohorts veered left, across a hastily arranged plank bridge over the entrenchments, on a diagonal directly toward the city's gates. Their pace and cadence remained unchanged, their expressions as grim as before, for if anything, the walls of the city looked even more formidable than the chaos of the barbarians' attack.

On the ramparts above the city walls, Vismar peered down between the troops sheltering him with their shields. A murmur was beginning to spread among the men, to the townspeople clustered on the ground below inside the walls.

"They've broken through, my lord!" one of the troops said excitedly, pointing to the eastern embankment where the Scyri horse troops had emerged from the clash of fighting and were now forming up in the space between the Roman entrenchments and the city wall. "The cavalry have broken through, and the foot soldiers are engaging the enemy!"

The king squinted and raised his hand against the piercing rays of the sun on the horizon just behind the battle. How that sentry could see such a thing—that the cavalry had emerged from the clash at the entrenchments—was beyond him. Even without the sun, the thick cloud of dust and mist rising up from the plain before him was blinding. He would have to take the sentry's word for it. Now for his own task. The timing was delicate, and he had no way of communicating with Odoacer, or even of knowing whether his grandson was still alive after the clash at the entrenchments. For all Vismar knew, by guessing wrong he could be handing his city to Rome as a gift. . . .

"Open the gates!" the old king called.

Every man on the wall turned and gaped at their sovereign in astonishment. Had he gone mad?

"Open the gates!" the old man repeated, his voice rising in urgency.

"Sire," one of the men protested, "the battle is not yet won! Our troops have not yet defeated the Romans! If we open the gates now—"

"The battle—*this* battle—is not to be won," the king interrupted. "Not here, not now. There will be another day. Odoacer does not seek to defeat the Romans in their infernal trenches. He does not have the strength to do it. He wishes only to break through their lines and enter the city. Open the gates!"

"And if the Romans rush us?" one of the men challenged.

The king stared at him balefully. Nearly half a century he had been monarch over this small nation, and rarely had any man so openly defied an order, so blatantly questioned his authority. The man's gaze shifted and then dropped under Vismar's piercing stare, and he shrank back among the troops milling about on the viewing platform at the top of the wall. The others, too, looked away. The king's authority would not be challenged.

"If the Romans rush us," the king replied, his voice determined yet so soft the men edged forward to hear him better, "all the more reason to open the gates, for Odoacer will be rushing as well. Will you be the man to stand atop the ramparts and watch your comrades be slaughtered at their own city gates, crushed under the very walls they are defending, against the walls in which they were born—because you refused to open to them? By the Almighty God, I will not be that man. Open the gates!"

A half dozen men stepped out from the group observing the battle. Scrambling down the steep stone steps, they ducked their heads and entered the guard post built into a recess in the stone wall, at its thickest part, directly over the city's main gates. Normally, it was unmanned—since the walls had been completed several years before, rarely had the portals ever been opened, for they had rarely had occasion ever to be closed. As two of the men pulled the iron bar attached to the thick chain emerging from the wall, the catch embedded within the wall slid open, allowing the large stone counterweight snugged into its niche to swing free. The others seized a thick rope attached to a pulley, swinging the counterweight from its position and down to the ground, raising the huge bar securing the entrance into the city.

The massive oak-and-iron gate swung ponderously open.

Spying the nearest plank bridge laid across the trench, Odoacer raced his horse across and then wheeled her around on the other side, but Fly-by-Night fought the reins, jerking her head and angrily stamping the ground as if straining to race against the other horses. Odoacer pressed his knees tightly against her flanks, feeling her breath heaving and the muscles quivering in barely contained excitement, and he leaned over to pat her, reassuring her she had done well. The horse rolled her eyes frantically and pulled toward the battle at the embankment behind her, unable to understand why she had been reined in outside the fighting. The clamor was deafening as the other Scyri riders stormed over the earthen embankment and across the trenches. The near slope, fronting the ditch, had proven unexpectedly treacherous, constructed of loose soil that had not been tamped with boards and feet as had the other side, facing the camp. A number of horses, after clambering to the top of the embankment, had sunk into the dirt up to their knees, falling forward and pitching their riders into the trench. Odoacer could see a hundred men at the bottom, flat on their backs or struggling frantically to rise in their stiff armor before they could be crushed by other riders tumbling off the embankment.

Odoacer looked back, peering through the dust that had now become so thick as to almost blot out the sharpness of the newly risen sun's rays. Visibility fell to scarcely twenty yards on either side, but even then he could see that the number of horsemen cresting the top had slowed, and that most of his cavalry had now formed up at the base. The clamor and shouting of battle from beyond his view, on the other side of the embankment, would be the Scyri infantry, who had crashed into the Roman lines just as the horsemen had made their escape. Thus far all was well. Now pray to God that Vismar would read the situation properly, that he would open the city gates, and that the Scyri could slip through before the Romans recovered their senses. Already he could hear the Roman battle trumpets calling for reinforcements and redeployment. The Romans *would* recover their senses.

As he turned back toward the city walls, a searing pain shot across the side of his face. His view of the horses and riders in front of him flashed blinding white, and then gradually faded to gray, darkening as the weight of his body lightened, and he felt himself drifting, falling slowly through the air, like a feather dropped from a nest in a tree. . . .

Just as his view was closing in to black, the din of battle exploded again in his ears. He lifted his head and began to rise from the soft dirt in which he lay, but the pain made him gasp. He felt strong hands behind him, under his arms, lifting him to his feet, and he struggled to open his eyes and steady his legs. Heat flooded the left side of his body, and he felt welcome relief at this warmth, a comforting presence that afforded a sense of stability from the horror of the battle, and then he felt the warmth chill even on his body and grow sticky, and he realized it was his own flowing blood that warmed him, and he felt surprise even at his very lack of surprise that he could produce such a copious amount—he, who had never before been wounded in battle.

"Prince!" Baldovic shouted behind him, as he steadied Odoacer. "Prince, you've fallen from your horse. Can you ride? The infantry are beginning to break through the Roman lines. We must charge to the gate now! Prince, *Prince!* Can you hear me?!"

Odoacer struggled to stand and focus. Before him a

cluster of men watched wide-eyed, some on foot, chests heaving with the exertion of their rush over the ditch, some still astride skittish horses, casting nervous backward glances to where the clash of battle seemed to grow even louder.

"Prince," Baldovic said again, "the Romans are receiving reinforcements, they are consolidating. No more of our troops can cross the trenches. We must go, now—"

"Silence, Baldovic," Odoacer gasped, catching his breath at a new wave of pain. "What happened?"

"You caught a javelin. Glanced off the side of your neck, between the shoulder guard and helmet. It missed the artery, but knocked you off and you're bleeding like a pig. I tore a sleeve and tied it around the wound, but it's still bleeding and we don't have time. We must go—"

Another javelin whizzed past Odoacer's face and slammed into the ground in front of him, its butt end vibrating violently at the impact, like a serpent shaking its tail. Odoacer looked back. A row of legionaries stood atop the embankment not fifty feet behind them, red sleeves of their tunics glowing like beacons through the swirling dust. Suddenly, the air was filled with missiles and the wet, thwacking sounds of warheads slicing into flesh. A horse screamed in pain from its wound, an unnerving, womanlike sound that set Odoacer's teeth on edge and cleared his head.

"Help me on," Odoacer muttered, and immediately hands behind him lifted him onto his horse. Again he felt the reassuring quiver of Fly-by-Night's flanks beneath his knees. The wound at his neck burned now like a hot poker, but it no longer left him senseless; the worst was that his entire body ached from the impact of his fall and the loss of blood—but the city walls were before him, in plain sight, and as he shook his head to clear his vision he knew he was not imagining what he saw—one of the doors of the enormous main gate was lurching open. Vismar had understood!

"Baldovic!" he shouted. "Take the infantry! I'll hold it open for you!" Then he turned toward the horsemen impatiently awaiting his orders, the extent of their line disappearing into the roiling cloud of dust. "Men—no more fighting! Shields on your backs and don't look behind you. The gate!"

With a deafening roar, the horsemen bounded forward, leaping over the writhing bodies of the animals and men who had fallen in the dash across the trenches, out into the open ground before the city walls. There were no obstacles—years before, that ground had been cleared of trees and brush, to afford an unimpeded view for the sentries on the watchtowers, and to prevent hidden enemies from approaching within arrow range of the city. It was a quarter mile, no more, before the men would be able to charge through the yawning gate, a quarter mile, scarcely the time needed to say a single, calm paternoster, if one were able to say anything calm under such conditions; perhaps it would take a pair of *Credos* before all the infantry could make it in as well, but it could be done. His head spun, and he blinked his eyes to clear his vision. Once this distance was crossed there would be no more deaths, no more injuries, the blood could be stopped, the broken bones bound, the stench washed away. Though the Romans would remain in their infernal trenches around the city, still there was water and food inside the walls, enough for a pair of months at least, and beds, and feed for the horses, and comforting women with strong hands and soft breasts. The fast approaching walls faded to a blur, and he struggled to remain conscious. Women . . . a siege could be endured for a long time with women such as the Scyri had, now only two hundred paces, a hundred, if that . . .

Out of the dusty gloom in front of him a row of red beacons appeared, faintly at first, only a few, then brighter and bolder, and then the line of red tunic sleeves grew longer, fifty of them, a hundred, and then a thousand bobbing up and down, pumping in rhythm to the frantic sprint of the legionaries, the cohorts that had been pulled from the southern end of the encirclement and who were now arriving, simultaneously with the Scyri riders, at the open gate.

Odoacer peered up, through the dust cloud to the clear air above, the now blue sky illuminating all before him. The ramparts of the city wall were lined with sentries, each frantically loosing arrows at the approaching legionaries, but Odoacer knew these were not enough. There were not enough guards atop the walls. He had taken too many troops with him on his foray to the west a few days before, left too few inside the city to defend it against attack. Now he was paying the price—the entire city was paying the price for his stupidity. The few guards atop the ramparts would be unable to drive away the attacking legionaries, and his horsemen had not even arrived at the open gate—nor had Baldovic's foot troops, who were still at least a long *Credo* behind. He shook his head to clear the cobwebs, struggled, and then focus and clarity came rushing back to him, and he opened his eyes and regained his fury.

"Through the gate!" Odoacer shouted. "Do not stop to fight—bull through the gate!"

The order was needless. Every man knew what he had to do, to break his way through to the safety of the city, and only then turn and fight, for it would be easier to block the Romans at the gate, to confine them in the narrow passageway and then pick them off or drive them away, than to give them full maneuvering room on the flat clear ground outside the city, where they could spread their forces. Every man knew what he had to do.

The two forces met with a horrendous crash, metal on metal, punctuated by the shrill screams of dying horses and the roars of men thrown from their mounts or trampled underfoot. The Romans were breathless from their furious dash, but at the same time exhilarated, exulting that they had arrived at the gate in time to block the incoming Scyri riders. Two winded Roman cohorts alone could not hope to stop the frantic horsemen for long, but time was not a currency in which they were interested in trading. This was no battle to the death outside the walls. It was a race to enter the city.

Neither side sought to tarry outside the gate. The legionaries knew the Scyri infantry were fast approaching to reinforce their horse-mounted comrades, and Odoacer knew his footmen would be followed close behind by the Roman troops they had just overrun at the trenches. It was a race, not a race to victory over the opponent, but a race to enter the city first, while the gate stood open. Again he glanced up, and this time saw his grandfather, Vismar, eyes wide at the carnage he was witnessing below, mouth shouting orders he could not hear, in words carried away on the wind and over the din of battle. Men raced from the king to do his bidding, and looking back down, Odoacer saw precisely what it was. The gate had stopped its ponderous swing open, grinding to a halt with a great shudder, and now, just as ponderously, was beginning to swing back shut, into the very faces of the combatants just outside the walls.

"No!" he shouted and, with a desperate effort, ignoring the pain shooting up his face and down his arm, he viciously heeled his horse forward, slamming into a wide-eyed Roman stopped just in front of him with sword raised, trampling him savagely underfoot. A dozen other Scyri, also seeing the gate begin to close, surged forward with him, throwing their mounts into the sea of combatants as the gate swung closer and closer. Yet the Romans saw their intent and rushed, too, toward the narrowing gap, and before Odoacer had managed to fight his way through the dense throng, half a hundred Roman soldiers had plunged through the opening between the gate and the wall, and disappeared into the darkness behind. Odoacer nearly wept in pain and fury. He knew that few Scyri troops had remained behind within the city under Vismar's command, lightly armed sentries no less, unable to stand up to the Roman heavy infantry. As if divining his thoughts, the large gate again ground to a stop in its ponderous swing. He stared at it, in fascination and despair, urging it, willing it in his mind to continue to close, to block the incoming path of the Roman attackers, or to open, to allow his own exhausted men to rush past into the safety of the city, anything but this, anything but stopping . . .

A dozen more Roman troops forced through the gap, and then a dozen more, and before Odoacer could make his way through, the gate again began its swing, this time open again, and the entire body of legionaries rushed the gap, arriving in a solid block at the half-opened gate, pushing against it, hastening its swing. He looked up—the top of the ramparts now was empty, but for a single arm hanging limply over the edge. In a moment, a red tunic appeared at the top, peering down, and then another—and then the massive oaken door lurched completely open, and the floodgate burst, and two Roman cohorts swept inside, carrying many of the Scyri riders along with them in their momentum, leaving only a distraught and milling band of cavalry outside the gates behind them, heaps of writhing wounded, and the small column of Baldovic's foot soldiers, who now began arriving, limping and exhausted, from the distant trenches they had just crossed.

And then the remaining legions hit.

Fly-by-Night reared in panic, nearly throwing Odoacer, who struggled to clear his head and regain his balance. The air filled with the din of battle, and a hundred Roman archers suddenly appeared at the wall tops, firing iron-tipped arrows down upon the trapped Scyri. Odoacer looked about wildly, head spinning from loss of blood and the confusion of the attack. Most of his riders had fallen or been pulled off their mounts, and the remaining few wheeled their horses frantically, forcing them to rear and to kick out with their forehooves, while the riders slashed angrily with their curved cavalry swords or pounded at the helmets around them with the edges of their shields. As far as he could see, the Scyri infantry had been overwhelmed and fallen beneath the feet of the legionaries.

Glancing toward the gate, he knew all was lost. The opening was packed with Roman soldiers surging into the city, now that the main resistance had been broken and all that was left was to plunder. Looking past the entrance, Odoacer saw flames burst from windows and the rooftops of buildings inside, and the roar of battle was now augmented by the wailing of women, trapped in their burning houses or dragged into the streets. A wave of despair seized him as he realized that all he had fought for—his adopted city, his grandfather—all had been lost, all had been destroyed, just as the legate Domitius had threatened, just as Orestes had done to him once before, and in his hazy thinking he wondered how he himself—crown prince of the city, commander of the Scyri cavalry—had somehow been spared, even as enemy soldiers surged around him, pressing on him from all sides, even against his legs and the flanks of his horse. He looked down—his left side was soaked in blood, his clothes in tatters, his shield shattered, and his sword bent and useless. He was the very picture of the vanquished barbarian, as he knew the Romans saw him, and staring out at the sea of Roman helmets before him, all rushing madly toward the gate in a frantic bid to enter the city before the flames had consumed everything of value, he understood he was being allowed to survive not by any merit of his own, but merely by momentary neglect and confusion.

As Roman and Scyri alike surged around him, a wave of dizziness caused him to slump forward, and he dropped the reins. Fly-by-Night staggered, and Odoacer rolled off, tumbling beneath the feet of the legionaries crowding around him. Swearing guttural Germanic oaths, they kicked him brutally about the back and face before moving on, seeing such little importance in the bloodied, shattered figure in the dust that they did not even take the trouble to dirty their blades in his ribs. Odoacer rose to his feet and lurched into the clear, leaving broken sword and shield behind. He tossed away his helmet as well, to relieve the intolerable ache in his head, and then, almost as an afterthought, slipped off the shredded mail hanging in strips from his shoulders, of no further use as protection. Swaying in exhaustion, he looked around. From all parts of the field, legionaries were streaming toward the gate. Here and there, Scyri warriors could be seen, most lying immobile, others staggering like wraiths into the fields, or leaning against the shelter of the walls. In a brief moment of clarity, he realized he had only moments to live. Once the city had been destroyed, once all captives of value had been taken and all plunder seized, the conquerors would look to strip the dead—and the helpless living who still remained.

Scarcely thinking, his mind threatening at any moment to

shut down from the pain, he hobbled along the line of the outer wall south as far as he could, and then at its curve toward the west, he cut across the field toward the marshes. Glancing to either side he saw that other survivors, too, dozens, perhaps a hundred, had had the same idea, and were also stumbling along on legs stiff with pain, faces twisted, eyes like those of madmen. He did not know whether they had recognized him beneath his blood and grime and were following him as their leader; or whether instinctively, like injured dogs, they simply sought company in which to lick their wounds or die.

He heard a shout from behind, and at first his heart leaped at the thought there might still be resistance, some spark of defiance among the Scyri troops behind him, but when he turned, he saw the city engulfed in flames, smoke billowing into the cloudless sky, and he knew this was impossible. No, a shout could only betoken evil—someone had noticed that valuable prisoners were escaping. A moment later he heard distant hoofbeats, and stealing another glance back, he saw that a company of Roman cavalry had deployed and were rounding up Scyri survivors by lance point. He increased his pace as much as he was able: the tree line of the marsh was just ahead. If he could only make it . . .

An arrow hissed past his cheek, and then another. The shouts and hoofbeats behind him grew louder. Below him the ground grew suddenly soft, squelching wetness beneath his feet, and he almost stumbled at the unexpected change. In the years he had lived in Soutok, he had rarely ventured into the marshes, except for the occasional boar hunt, and then only with experienced guides at hand. There was never a reason to go in: nothing of value grew or lived there, trails were difficult to find, and the water stank, being unhealthy for drinking or swimming. No one dwelt there but a hermit or two and the eelmen, if you could call them men, no enemy even ventured to enter the morasses, but for the Romans . . .

He hobbled past an eelboat pulled up into a clump of reeds, and then another, boats that only the day before had transported the Romans from the great Danuvius miles beyond. Another arrow flew past him, slipping noiselessly into the knee-deep water before him and burying itself out of sight in the muck. He peered through the long shadows cast by the trees and overgrowth—he was not the first to arrive here—all around him men splashed through the shallows, some desperately tugging at flat-bottomed boats to drag them into deeper water, others already floating lifeless and bloody on the oily surface.

The shouts grew in volume, and he heard splashing near at hand, behind him. He glanced back and saw a dozen Roman horsemen, faces black with anger, hurriedly dismounting horses that had refused to venture into the treacherous terrain. The Romans, strong and uninjured, struck down the unarmed Scyri clustered around the boats, and then clambered aboard, pushing off from the reeds with their feet and hastily fitting arrows onto bowstrings.

Odoacer hesitated. He did not know these marshlands, was unfamiliar with the black waters or the creatures they might contain. He had never liked the eels drawn from these waters, not their taste, not their texture, and certainly not their appearance. Now, in the dim light, he could see an unctuous sheen on the surface, with strange bugs skittering through the riplets that ranged ahead of him as he floundered through the waist-deep water. All thought of pain in his neck and head had disappeared, all feelings of stiffness in his legs were gone—he was filled with a desperate desire to survive, and a frantic search for the means. The water? He was not a swimmer, no Hun was, yet the waters were not deep . . . yet. Surrender to his pursuers? Another arrow flew past his shoulder, followed by angry curses—there would be no surrender. A boat was almost upon him. A man nearby, splashing through the marshes in the same direction as he, emitted a yelp, almost doglike, stiffened at the impact of the arrow in his back, and then fell headfirst into the water, disappearing beneath the weight of his armor, and Odoacer was thankful he had stripped off his own. Yet disappearing . . . even in his haste Odoacer wondered how a man could so utterly disappear, though he was but a hand's-breath beneath the water's surface—the arrow in his back emerged and stood tall and straight, indistinguishable from the reeds surrounding him but for the incongruousness of the bright red feathers of the fletching. The man had disappeared beneath the surface. . . .

Hardly had the thought come to him than he knew what he must do. Taking a deep breath, Odoacer plunged into the water, closing his eyes against the scum on the surface, struggling to reach a bottom that he knew was only half a man's height down, but that would disguise his presence as effectively as if he had been buried that deep in the very ground. Even when submerged he could hear the swish and bubbles as arrows sliced into the surface, could feel the waves as men nearby thrashed in pain. On the bottom he seized a rotted log and pulled himself down to press flat against it; it broke off in his hands, and he groped frantically for a stronger piece. All seemed so calm and peaceful beneath the surface, only the muffled swishing of arrows as they skimmed past, like so many fish, like so many eels. . . .

His lungs were near bursting. Had the legionaries' boat passed yet? He had no way of knowing, yet no way of remaining where he was. Panic rose as his mind caught up to his body and he realized he was lying facedown *underwater*— had ever a Hun been in such a position and lived? He forced himself to open his eyes, to confront the horrors he might see around him—but saw nothing, save clouds of brown particles floating past him in a shaft of sunlight, the water as thick and sedimented as soup. Dust in the air had prevented him from seeing in the battle, and now dust in the water prevented him from seeing his pursuers. But he could hold no longer. Drawing his feet up beneath him, he pulled himself to a squatting position and then cautiously extended his legs until his head broke the surface.

Even before he had expelled his lungs and taken his first breath, his ears were assaulted by shouts. Other Romans had now arrived, seized other boats, and as he gazed about he saw the swamp was filled with them, standing in their tiny eel-barges, helmets off for greater visibility, guffawing as they took shots at the Scyri thrashing in the reeds. All around him men emerged from the water, took great gasping breaths and then plunged back in, followed by arrows and shouts of triumph or cursing. An object bumped into the back of his head and he turned, startled: a corpse floated past, facedown, riding high on the surface unburdened by the weight of helmet or armor, half a dozen arrows jutting jauntily from the shoulders and back like pennants on a boat. Odoacer shuddered, but his breath was cut short by another sharp pain, this time from his left shoulder. It was followed by a shout of triumph and he realized, without even looking around, that he had been spied, and hit.

Taking a deep breath he again dove to the bottom, grasping the log to pull him down, and then reaching behind with his right hand to break off the shaft close to the skin, to prevent it from emerging above the surface and giving away his position. He focused with all his might on the task at hand, at ignoring the pain from his injured shoulder, for he knew the legionaries above had marked his position, and would be waiting for him to surface. Just before slipping beneath, he had noted a broad cluster of reeds a short distance away. If he could make his way there underwater, perhaps he could wriggle into the clump, and then even raise his head for air inside their shelter, without being seen. The thought gave him new impetus, and he crabbed his way along the bottom, feeling for objects he could grasp to hold himself down while hugging to the muck as closely as possible.

As he scrambled along the bottom, eyes shut tight against the water and sediment, he became increasingly aware of an irritation along the skin of his legs, which he had thus far ignored. Now, however, the itching became more acute, even painful, rising to the fore of his thoughts and overriding even his other discomforts—the pain from his two wounds, his bursting lungs, the knowledge that a nearby eelboat filled with archers was scanning the water for him. Pausing, he grasped a log with his left hand as he cautiously reached his right hand back to his leg.

The limb was covered, from buttocks to toes, with small, fleshy bumps, which he took at first to be a rash. Squeezing one, however, he was surprised to feel it burst between his fingers, though with no sensation where it had broken. Wouldn't he have felt a sharp pain, or relief, at having broken a pustule of such size? Sliding his hand down his calf he grasped another, and this time, to his horror, felt it pull off his leg. Was his very flesh now falling off his bones? Was this miasma so poisonous, the water so acidic, that it was causing his body to decay even as he lived? He had not yet made his way to the clump of reeds he had been aiming for, but with the delay caused by the examination of his legs, he was running out of air. His lungs could hold out no longer, and again rotating to a vertical position, he raised his head above water.

Immediately, as before, his ears were assaulted by the shouts and screams of dying men around him, though he found he had surfaced in a small patch of shade cast by overhanging willows and, for the moment at least, none of the Romans nearby seemed to have spied him. He would allow himself time for three breaths before diving again. Meanwhile, he slowly brought his right hand up to his eyes to examine the lump of flesh he had pulled off his leg.

The knuckle-sized, grayish-black tumor in his fingers still oozed watery blood from where it had been torn from his leg, but it contained other parts as well, most obviously a round, sucker-like mouth. Odoacer stifled the retching that rose in his throat at the thought that his legs, and now his arms and other exposed skin of his body, were attracting these horrifying creatures. He crushed the leech in his fingers, bursting it as he had the first one, and then involuntarily dropped his hands down beneath the water to check that his loincloth was still intact. That, at least, would deter the monsters from his groin. Realizing he had taken the allotted three breaths, he silently ducked back beneath the surface and resumed his crabbing.

His strength was rapidly failing him, and he knew he could not move much longer. As if in answer to his prayers, he felt the muddy bottom beginning gradually to rise, and his hands and face began brushing against stiff stalks as he made his way up into the clump. Here, he knew, he must be careful—a rustling line of reeds as he moved through would betray his position. He crawled slowly, and grasped what he thought was a sunken branch, but then felt it twitch slightly and realized it was a human limb, and that another soldier had found, or drifted to, this place before him, and that whether the man was dead, alive, or unconscious, it would not do for him to clamber over him to share the same spot. He released the limb and swerved slightly, noting as he did how his head was now beginning to break the surface. The water was too shallow to hide him any longer—was he far enough into the reeds to hide from the Romans?

His head emerged, then his shoulders, while he pulled himself slowly along on his elbows, his legs trailing behind him as he made himself as flat as possible. The reeds rose above him to perhaps the height of an arm, but they were not leafy—anyone looking directly at him, he knew, would be able to see him. He carefully picked up his pace until his upper body had emerged from the water and now rested on the spongy ground, the reeds thick enough that he could no longer wriggle between them—rather, he flattened them beneath him as he slithered along, cutting his wrists and forearms on their sharp edges, dragging his legs behind through a thin trail of his own blood.

Shouts behind him caused him to pause, and he pressed his face flat into the humus, striving not to move a muscle. In the water behind he could hear an eelboat poling closer, the chuckling and chatter of the men inside it as they searched for survivors, even their excited breathing as here and there they discussed the armor, injuries, or weapons of the floating cadavers they pushed aside with their poles. He heard the soft twang of a bow, and at the same time felt an impact against the back of his thigh, like the punch of a small-fisted child, followed by a searing pain. He gritted his teeth and dug his fingernails into the soft earth, willing himself with all his failing strength to remain stone-still, even if the enemy were to nail him to the earth with their arrows. Another twang and another child's-punch—this time to the fleshy calf of his other leg, and he ground his teeth so hard against each other he feared they might break in his mouth. In an instant, the boat had poled its way closer, and he heard the occupants roughly poking at another object—he assumed it was the body of the soldier he had felt while still underwater—and then the slap of the hard wooden pole across the back of his legs.

He no longer had to force himself to lie still. His limbs had gone numb, and as he blearily opened his eyes he realized with vague surprise that everything in his vision seemed to be reduced, that blackness was closing in on the sides, tightening his view to a diminishing circle, small and distant, so that even the reeds just in front of his face seemed to recede to a point far away. The blackness grew, the circle of light that was his vision was now reduced to a mere pinprick. The pain, too, seemed to lessen as the numbness spread through his body, and he felt impossibly relaxed, impossibly sleepy, and then even his hearing began to fade. Sounds became distant and indistinct, and only the coolness of the water against his feet seemed to remain, a rhythmic tapping, a comforting caress, a lullaby that smothered even the prodding and slapping of the eelboat pole against his bleeding calves.

"Dead!" he heard one of the soldiers bark in a guttural Germanic accent, and then even the pinprick of light went out, and the soft lapping of the water faded, and Odoacer was left floating in sweet darkness.

III

Severinus made his home at the edge of the marsh, in a deep cleft in a rock rising incongruously from the swampland, which over the years he had gradually widened to become more than the simple shelter for rodents that it had been before his arrival. It was cramped, with a ceiling so low few men could stand up straight in it; and it was damp from the humid air of the miasma, and from the seepage that trickled down the walls in green streaks into crude hand-carved gutters. During the warm season, the sides and floor became carpeted with a mildew that sometimes caused sneezing among visitors. Nevertheless, this hollow in the rock had become a holy place, for he had *made* it a holy place, a place of devotion, and it was here, surrounded by moisture, insects, and the rot of the bog, that he felt closest to God and closest to nature.

He had recognized the shelter's promise from the very beginning, and had slowly and ingeniously converted it over the many years he had occupied it. Entire months, especially during the cold winters, he had spent absorbed in prayer and meditation as he slowly decorated the walls and ceiling with paints of his own manufacture concocted of plant juices, scrapings of rocks, and the blood of crushed insects whose name he did not know, but which the locals had long used to dye their clothing. A raised relief carved into the ceiling bore a depiction of Christ on the cross, while a stalagmite rising from a corner of the floor beneath the *corpus* was painted to form the centurion's lance aimed at His ribs. The centurion himself was painted on the wall in gray and red tones. A tiny natural airhole in the ceiling had been enhanced with translucent white shells to resemble the star of Bethlehem, and the first light that shone through it on Christmas day formed a shaft that fell on a wall painted with a manger scene, angels hovering above, wings iridescent with fish scales painstakingly affixed to the damp stone wall with drops of pitch. At the back of the cave, the solid stone had been hollowed into a kind of altar, on which burned a tiny lamp of fish oil, and the wall behind it was covered with holes from the nails that visiting penitents had used to hang clay votive offerings depicting various body parts, as pleas or as tokens of gratitude for the cures of their malaises. The stone floor in front of the altar was worn smooth from their knees and tears. Severinus himself slept on the ground at the foot of the altar, on a simple reed mat.

His kindness and devotion had made him greatly beloved of the eelmen and their families, who had adopted him as one of their own, though in fact he had come from elsewhere—no one knew whence, and no one knew when, for he had been there for the entire living memory of all but the very eldest of the marsh people. The children called him grandfather, vicious dogs licked his feet, and even the fish and frogs seemed to willingly allow themselves to be caught by his line on his weekly venture into the marsh to supplement his plant diet. His life was consecrated to God and to solitude, but in point of fact his solitude was rare, and the demands on his time great. He spent hours caring for the sick, cooling their heads of the swamp fever that all but he seemed to suffer, and praying for their recovery. His home was an open shrine, and many nights he returned to his humble cave after dark, exhausted from a day of ministering to patients, to find it already occupied by sleeping pilgrims, forcing him to take his rest in the shelter of a nearby stump, where he had taken the precaution of storing another reed mat for that purpose. His few needs were largely met by charity, sometimes in such abundance that he would spend days after receiving such gifts distributing his excess to the poor. He considered it a sin to keep more than a day's worth of food for himself, as this would demonstrate a lack of faith in God's ability to provide for him, and a lack of willingness to fast for penance on days his food bag came up empty. He gave away even the spare clothing that had been donated to him, and whether the season was warm or cold, no one ever saw him covered with anything other than the threadbare, patched tunic he was said to have been wearing when he had first arrived many years before.

It was one such charity case that he bent over now.

Odoacer slowly came to his senses. Every muscle in his body ached, and when he moved his left arm, sharp pains shot through his side from neck to hip. He moaned and then, without yet opening his eyes, deliberately took inventory of the rest of his bodily parts, carefully moving the toes of each foot, twitching his kneecaps, clenching his buttocks, and on up his body. Some movements caused him excruciating pain, and vivid memories came to him of arrows in the swamp, legionaries grinning at him from their eelboat, the triumphant calls of "Dead!" to their comrades. Other movements puzzled him, in that he could not even budge, or feel, the corresponding muscles, and he wondered vaguely whether it was because the limbs were bandaged tightly, or missing, or simply asleep. He focused on his shoulder blades: the surface beneath them was hard and cold. Indeed, the air itself was cool and rather damp, though he seemed to sense some sort of a covering draped over him, for it was his head and neck that felt the air currents most acutely—the rest of his body seemed either numb to all surrounding sensations, or overly, painfully aware. There was nothing in between, nothing that gave him comfort.

Sweat trickled off his brow and into his eyes, and with the dryness of his mouth and tongue he imagined the liquid to be some precious ichor, as if the very moisture of life were being wrung out of him; nevertheless, he continued on with his self-exploration. He moved mentally to his jaw and lips, then nostrils, and finally opened his eyes, peering through crusted lids at his dim surroundings, the slim shaft of light from the airhole, the shadowy pictures crudely etched into the walls, the stalagmite rising from the corner of the floor beside him, seemingly the only angular, well-defined object in the entire room of rounded shapes, green-filtered light, and hazy shadows. He turned his head slightly to find the hermit seated on a low ledge shaped painstakingly into the rock wall, holding an earthen cup of steaming liquid in his hand as if it were ambrosia. Severinus eyed him curiously.

"Ah," the old man said, with a hint of a smile in his voice. "He awakes. I was told he was the prince of the Scyri nation, but I suspected he might have been the eighth sleeper of Ephesus instead."

Odoacer fixed his eye on the strange being, unsure how to react. Finally, from a voice that came from deep within, from his chest, but seemed to originate from even farther away, so labored and quiet it was, he spoke hoarsely through dry lips.

"What?"

Severinus smiled delightedly.

"And he speaks! Though lacking in eloquence. The sleepers of Ephesus! Surely you must have heard the wondrous news, you, a prince with your networks of traders, ambassadors, and informants. Only recently discovered! Seven young Christian noblemen, not unlike yourself, condemned to martyrdom by the Roman Emperor Decius two centuries ago. They were thrown into a cave near Ephesus that was sealed with a boulder, and abandoned to asphyxiation. They were forgotten until recently, when a landowner moved the boulder, thinking to use the cave as a cattle-stall. One of the young men, Diomedes by name, woke and wandered into the city to buy food for his companions. When he tried to pay, the people marveled that he offered coins of great antiquity, and arrested him for having stolen hidden treasure. During the interrogation he expressed amazement at seeing churches, and crosses on doors, and other evidence of open Christianity. The bishop was summoned, and Diomedes led the townspeople to the cave, where the other young men were also found, very hungry, I'm sure. After great praising of God for this marvel, the young men finally lay down and died once and for all, as is wont for men of such advanced age. For the three days you had been sleeping, I thought you might have been one of Diomedes' comrades."

"Diomedes?"

Severinus looked at him with slight exasperation.

"Yes, Diomedes, as I just said. Hmm. The lamp is lit but the oil is stale. Perhaps you might have been a vision of Saint Sebastian."

"I—I know of Sebastian." Odoacer's alarm at the mad dialog was increasing.

"*Saint* Sebastian. He of the many arrow wounds and the pained expression. The latter, of course, being the natural consequence of the former."

Odoacer's eyes drooped in fatigue. Without noticing, however, the old man continued on with his chatter.

"Of course, as his healer, that would have made me the sainted Irene, otherwise known as Innocentia." He scratched at his long beard, plucking an object that he held up to his eyes for examination, then crushed between dirty fingernails. "Which I'm obviously not. Take some broth."

The old man squatted down and held out the chipped bowl. Odoacer lifted his head and sipped at the clear soup, which had a surprisingly strong, fishy flavor. After taking a mouthful he closed his eyes and dropped his head back to the stone floor. He allowed the broth to linger in his mouth for a moment, wetting his palate and throat, before swallowing it with effort, savoring the warmth as it spread into his belly. He then opened one eye and again raised his head slightly.

Severinus fed him sip after sip and watched the color slowly return to Odoacer's face, and the light of intelligence to his eyes. The bowl was soon empty and the hermit ducked through a hide-covered doorway, letting a stray wisp of smoke enter from the cooking fire outside. When he returned, Odoacer struggled onto one elbow, wincing at the pain, and held out his hand to take the bowl for himself.

The old man chuckled delightedly, carefully handing him the bowl of hot liquid.

"An ancient recipe of my own distant tribe," he said, "a broth of leeches and soporific herbs that has nourished many an injured man in troubled times . . ."

Odoacer blew a mouthful of broth over the floor.

"Broth of leeches!" he sputtered. "You consume creatures that have been feasting on another man's blood?"

"*I* do not consume them," Severinus replied, offended, "as I am healthy. *You,* however, are consuming creatures that have been feasting on your own blood, which in addition to being an amusing irony, is surely an effective means of regaining the strength they have stolen from you, is it not?"

Odoacer's hand wavered, the contents of the bowl sloshing. If he had the strength, he thought, he might dash it to the floor. As it was, he struggled merely to hold it up. The old man eyed the vessel warily, sensing Odoacer's intent.

"Please do not break my bowl. It is the only one I have, and I shall then be forced to serve you broth from my cupped hands, which I doubt will improve the flavor."

With great effort, Odoacer set the bowl down onto the stone floor. He stared at Severinus, defiance flashing in his eyes, and the old man stared back, a smile creasing the beard around his mouth. Then a wave of fatigue came over Odoacer, covering his eyes like a woolen blanket, and he let his head drop back to the cold stone floor, and the sound of the old hermit's prattling faded from his ears, and he fell once more into blissful sleep.

For two days he struggled thus between waking and sleeping, and then on the day the hermit withheld the broth of medicinal herbs, the narcotic effect wore off, and Odoacer awoke as if from a dream. His body screamed pain, and he moaned in agony, opening his eyes and slowly lifting himself up onto an elbow. The first thing he saw was Severinus, illuminated in the single beam of light, smiling approvingly.

"Ah," the old man said. "Pain. I know it is unpleasant, Prince, but it proves you are alive, your fever has broken, and you are healing. Muscles are not pierced by arrows without great pain, and torn fibers are not knit again without an identical quantity of pain. Six wounds do not heal effortlessly."

"Six? I remember only three . . ."

"Your Roman friends sought to make sure you were truly dead. And they nearly succeeded, but for dragging yourself onto dry ground before you passed out, where I found you."

"The Romans—they are gone?"

Severinus sighed.

"Yes, gone. Everyone is gone, Scyri, Romans, and fishermen. Only the mad remain, still wandering the woods at night calling for their lost ones. You will hear them. Broth?"

Odoacer took the bowl shakily as he pondered these extraordinary words. Six arrows? The region deserted? *Broth?* He looked suspiciously at the soup.

The old man smiled.

"No leeches. They do not keep, and you slept long. Soup of roots and mushrooms I myself have collected."

Odoacer sipped it, carefully at first, and then with increased gusto as he felt the strength returning to his limbs, though the pain made him wish to cry out with every movement. He looked at the old man.

"Who are you? What do you do here?"

"I?" The hermit smiled. "I am no one. An old man who lives alone. I am Severinus."

"Severinus—I have heard of you." Odoacer paused, recalling stories he had heard in the past. "You are the holy one the priests are unsure of. They say you attract pilgrims to your dwelling here."

He nodded at the altar and the wall behind it, covered with clay depictions of legs, hands, breasts, even unidentifiable internal organs, which visitors claimed Severinus had cured by laying hands upon them.

"Ah," Severinus said sadly. "There will be no more pilgrims. The tribesmen are in hiding or have vanished entirely."

Odoacer looked at him closely.

"You relied upon these pilgrims for your food, did you not? For your livelihood."

The hermit shot him a sharp glance.

"I rely upon God alone. What He wills to send me, I accept, and what He withdraws, I yield. God forbid I should blame my problems on pilgrims who do not come."

Odoacer considered this notion.

"I suppose a pilgrim who does not come is not actually a pilgrim," he ventured.

Severinus shrugged, plucking a crudely fashioned clay foot from the wall and examining it.

"Then perhaps," he replied with a wry smile, "I have no problem."

"You still must eat. People must still find healing, mental and physical."

"Perhaps they will find another way to heal. Perhaps they will find another way to move beyond this world, beyond sleeping and eating, beyond damp caves and watery broth."

"What can there be beyond this world? What can possibly merit our pain and suffering here?"

The old man eyed him.

"Did you not just spend five days there, beyond? What did you see?"

Severinus was looking at him with such intensity, all rheumy eyes and tangled beard and skinny arms emerging from the ancient tattered tunic, that despite Odoacer's own pain and grief and fatigue, it was all he could do to keep from laughing. The five days he had spent sleeping were like days vanished. He had seen nothing of the beyond, he remembered nothing, and for now, his whole world was simply that—sleeping and eating, a damp cave and watery broth. He could imagine nothing more, nothing in the world, nor could he even imagine wanting more than that. The old man prodded him with the clay foot.

"You saw nothing?" he asked. "Do you also desire nothing?"

Odoacer shook his head. He had been born into the world with nothing. He had left his first nation, the Huns, with nothing. And now—the realization hit him, but did not stagger him, for he felt almost comfortable with the idea—for the third time in his life, he again had nothing.

"Nothing," Odoacer repeated, "except . . ."

"Yes?" the hermit said, leaning forward at this chance, perhaps the last chance he would have in his life to restore a man's soul, to perform his commission. "Except?"

Odoacer looked at him.

"Except more broth," he said, extending his bowl.

The hermit stared for a moment, speechless, then smiled and, taking the bowl, ducked out the door flap. Odoacer could hear him chuckling to himself outside as he stirred the pot over the cook fire.

After three weeks, Odoacer stood for the first time, hunched over to be sure, but nonetheless standing. Truth be told, he would have been unable to raise his head to his full height even had he not been encumbered by the low ceiling, for as he moved he could feel the just-healing wounds throughout his body stretching, threatening to tear at any moment if he reached too far, if he allowed himself too long a stride. The hermit had sewn the punctures and gashes with thread fashioned of the intestines of a dead water rodent he had found, and had changed them several times during the course of the healing process as the edges of the wounds had knitted together. Now, Odoacer took care not to undo the old man's handiwork, and the results of his own painful and quiet suffering.

After shuffling warily about the small room for a few moments, enjoying, as he never expected to enjoy, the view of his surroundings from a higher vantage point, he made his way back down to the floor with a grunt. Altogether a satisfactory experience. Severinus watched him in silence throughout the exercise and now eyed him approvingly.

"You heal well," he said. "Soon you will be able to walk comfortably. I will remove the remaining stitches after you have rested."

"I have had great incentive," Odoacer replied. "Desire for vengeance is an effective healer. And determining how one is to go about achieving it—that keeps one's mind occupied during the healing."

The old man raised an eyebrow.

"What an odd thing to say."

"What? That I desire vengeance?"

"No, no, but that your desire for it is what heals you. An odd thing for a prince to say, with all the knowledge and resources at your disposal since you arrived among the Scyri. One would almost think it was you living alone in the cave, rather than me."

"What do you mean?" Odoacer growled.

"Vengeance is worthwhile only against a crime aimed personally at you. You would not take revenge on the weather for a lightning strike on your house, would you? Or revenge on a bear that invaded your camp while you were away and ate¯ your food? Those things are not personal offenses against you. Lightning strikes randomly, or perhaps only at high points. Bears go where their noses lead them, to food, whether it be a field of berries or your own store of meat. If anything, the fault lies with the victim—for building a tower so high as to attract lightning, or for leaving meat unguarded."

"This was an attack on my city, on my grandfather, on my people. Is that not personal?"

"Not to Rome. Rome is like a bear taking food where it is available. It had no personal animosity to you, it was merely following the path it perceived as its destiny, and removing objects standing in its way. There is only one earthly power: Rome. It crushes all rivals, yet there is nothing personal about it, and railing against its injustice is like railing against the weather. There is one other power, but it is not of earth, and it is that heavenly power with which I myself have chosen to ally. But for you—if you seek not to ally yourself with heaven, if you seek to remain earthbound, and to live up to your potential as prince and leader—for you, your only path to success is to ally yourself with the earthly power, with the *only* earthly power. With Rome."

Odoacer stared at him.

"Ally myself with Rome? With *Orestes*? How can I join with the man who has destroyed my tribe and my family, not once, but *twice*?"

Severinus shook his head.

"You still do not understand. Did this Orestes know you were with the Scyri before he attacked?"

"Possibly—he must have known of a Scyri prince by my name . . ."

"And even if he knew that, would he have recognized your name as that of the young son of a rival whom he betrayed years ago in a distant land and whom he must surely have thought dead? Would he even have cared? Are you truly so vain as to believe the earth turns, the sun shines, and Orestes strikes for you alone? Then you are like an ant cursing God from the top of a blade of grass. Orestes was not taking personal action against you. The legions are not his proprietary instrument, nor the instrument of any man but the emperor's, or Ricimer's, and even then there is the question of who is the instrument of whom. Vengeance on Rome, even vengeance on Orestes, is useless. They would not understand. And of what good is vengeance if its recipient does not understand, or even remember, the offense he committed against you?"

Odoacer mulled this over. The plans he had so carefully laid in his mind over the past weeks of painful healing now dissolved. Without revenge, without the hope of that satisfaction, what was there for him to even live for? Severinus watched him carefully, observing his turmoil and confusion, and then after a moment interrupted his thoughts.

"I would not counsel vengeance even if its recipient did understand your motive. For as the Scriptures say, vengeance is the Lord's. It is pure vanity, a needless risk. The worst thing is that you will find it unsatisfying. Yet there is still much you can do."

"Like begin looking for my own cave?"

The hermit chuckled.

"Perhaps. But you would be betraying nothing, least of all your grandfather, by allying your wits and strength with any remaining Scyri survivors you might find . . ."

"There are some?"

"Oh, yes," the old man replied vaguely. "The woods are full of them, those who have not yet wandered away. But not enough of them to wreak the vengeance you seek, to oppose Rome."

"What are you saying, then?"

"Make the best of the situation. Improve your lot, use your talents, which are considerable. Go where they can be used. Go to Italia, become a new man. Remember who you were, understand who you are; but anticipate what you might become."

Odoacer remained silent, and for some days afterward

spoke little. Each day he stood in the cave, stretched his wounds a bit further, paced about and felt his strength returning. There was nothing more to say, only a great deal to think about. After two weeks, he hobbled to the cave entrance, pulled aside the tattered skin covering, and stepped outside.

Severinus remained patiently inside by the altar, eyes closed, lips moving in prayer. There was no sound. Many hours later Odoacer returned, a dead hare under his arm, the remains of a vine snare still hanging from its foot. He dropped the animal on the ground at the entrance to the cave, then ducked and entered. He was exhausted, his face pale, tensed in a rictus of pain, and in his fatigue he failed to duck far enough, slamming his forehead painfully against the low threshold of the entrance. He paused for a moment, knees flexed, hands outstretched to catch himself should he fall, eyes closed against the throbbing pain. Then he slowly ducked again, lower this time, and walked up to the old man as the scrape on his forehead swelled painfully.

Severinus peered at him. "You go to Italia, then?"

"I leave now. I wish only I could return your kindness with something other than a rabbit, which I know you will not eat. But I have nothing else."

"The poor will eat it, and be nourished by it, and that is gift enough. But you—you wear only a tattered piece of leather about your waist. A poor way to enter the center of earthly power, is it not?"

Odoacer offered a thin smile. "It is more than I had when I entered the earthly realm itself, and less than I had when I entered my grandfather's kingdom. I will make do. Thank you. I hope to repay your good works."

Severinus struggled to his feet, and standing before the tall young man stooping before him, placed his hand on his head, ignoring the blood matting the front of his hair.

"Go on to Italia," he said. "Go, you who are now clad in paltry skins. For you will soon be able to give great gifts to many."

Odoacer stood motionless as the hermit's hand rested on his head. Then he nodded slightly, turned in silence, and stepped out the door, ducking low. Severinus stood still, listening, until the sound of the shuffling steps faded into silence.

PART
II

In times of peace, individuals and states follow higher standards. . . . But war is a stern teacher.

—THUCYDIDES

CHAPTER FIVE

Four Years Later, 467 A.D.

ROME

I

The Decumanus Maximus, Rome's magnificent main east-west thoroughfare, was a riot of colors, with gaily tinted banners fashioned of costly silks strung across the broad boulevard in such profusion as to resemble the shade awnings of the Colosseum. The pavement had been swept and scrubbed of grime, and the buildings and monuments on either side had received fresh coats of paint in a gaudy rainbow of hues to mark the occasion. The vast shantytowns that had sprung up in the alleyways and sidewalks, housing those whose homes had been destroyed in the Vandal invasion a dozen years before, had been cleared away. Public buildings whose stones and columns had been smashed by the invaders, or stolen for use in illegal housing projects, had been hastily repaired; and side streets whose flagstones had been torn up by squatters to gain access to the city's sewers and water mains had been patched, and remained guarded by hastily assembled companies of *vigiles,* the city's police force and fire brigades, who patrolled the most sensitive sites.

East of the city center, at the starting point of the grand procession, stood a towering bronze statue, the Colossus of Nero, depicting the body of that formidable emperor garbed as the sun god Apollo. The figure's head had been replaced several times over the past four centuries by the visages of later rulers, and though the current version had been battered beyond recognition during the invasions, the venerable *corpus* itself had now been polished to its original brilliant luster. Nearby, the statue's namesake, the massive Colosseum, was festooned with banners and ribbons fluttering gaily from its four galleries. From the height of the distant Capitolium, at the western end of the Via Sacra, the lavishly decorated stadium resembled not so much a formidable monument to pleasure and death as a massive bird's nest, or a child's kite, wavering and airy, shimmering with every breeze, as if it might lift into the air on a gust of wind and be blown away.

Crowds gathered eight and ten deep along both sides, and a half mile away, where the avenue crossed the threshold of the Regia and entered the Forum Romanum, good order broke down entirely, and the broad space teemed with swarming, celebrating, and drunken humanity, awaiting the arrival of the royal column. Cohorts of *vigiles,* who had been urgently mobilized to control the crowds, warily eyed the boisterous revelers as the wine sold by strolling vendors at the street corners flowed freely. All legitimate businesses in the city had been shuttered for the grand celebration. The Senate had been suspended, the courts of justice closed. Only those areas that hosted activities of leisure and festivity—the theaters, the baths, the brothels, and of course the greatest stage of all, the public street—remained open, and indeed for the past week had resounded at all hours of the day and night with cavorting, revelry, songs both bawdy and sober, and prayers to God and to the ancient deities.

Beyond the Forum, order began to be restored again only at the start of the Via Sacra, which led to the summit of the Capitolium. Along the route, four resident legions of the urban cohorts, the emperor's personal military guard, had been stationed in full armor, riot shields at the ready, restraining the surging crowds and protecting the lives of the senators, foreign ambassadors, and magistrates who had taken up their places along the sides of the monumental street to view the procession. During the months of planning for the event, rank had been carefully calculated, and the positions of the dignitaries assigned flagstone by flagstone in order of increasing merit, up to the steps of the Temple of Jupiter Capitoline, the political heart of Rome. The careful preparations had thus far been successful in preventing unseemly disputes between Rome's leading citizens as to precisely who was entitled to stand on which crumbling marble step to view the coronation. Many senators, their fortunes still precarious from the losses suffered by their estates and investments from the Vandal invasions, completed their ruin on this day with the silks and jewelry in which they bedecked themselves and their wives, to disguise the very poverty into which they had just thrown themselves by purchasing such luxuries.

It was the *calends* of January, the first day of the new year, and Rome had much to celebrate, not least of which its new emperor, Anthemius, who was just arriving after his long march west from Constantinople to assume the position left vacant by his murdered predecessor Libius Severus. In the triumphal chariot, used by every ruler since Julius Caesar half a millennium before and carefully preserved and restored, Anthemius was accompanied by Count Ricimer, who had presented himself scarcely a few hours earlier, at the third milestone outside the city. Several other leading generals rode in other ostentatious cars behind them, and preceding them were the carriages occupied by members of Anthemius's household, Rome's new royal family: his wife, Euphemia, daughter of the Eastern Roman Emperor Leo and now an empress herself; his grown sons, Marcian, Romulus, and Procopius; and his daughter, Alypia, surrounded by a body of armed guards who had also marched from Constantinople. The route of the Triumph, from the Colosseum up the Via Sacra to the Capitol, was the final leg of the long journey, but this short distance, scarcely a mile, was taking the huge procession nearly a full day to wend through the unruly crowds. The inauguration would be culminated by Anthemius's formal confirmation by the waiting senators, on behalf of the people of Rome and their barbarian *confoederati,* and would be followed immediately afterward by the nuptials of Alypia and General Ricimer in the Basilica of St. Peter. This would be another cause for celebration—the happy union of the Western Empire's civil and military administrations, and at the same time, a joining of the wealth and fortunes of the two sister empires, East and West, which had so often been estranged.

Yet despite the festivities, Anthemius was not content. Indeed, he seethed with impatience at the procession's stalled progress, as the legions before him and alongside strove to force back the surging crowds, pressing and pushing at his men's shields from all sides. For a quarter of an hour his horses had made no progress whatever. Peering up through the thick haze of smoke from the food vendors, and the flower petals descending like snow from the rooftop terraces of the Basilica Aemelia and the Basilica Julia, he could see the steps of the Capitol scarcely half a mile ahead. As close as he was, he despaired of arriving before his temper exploded or his bladder gave way, both of which, after six hours of standing at attention in the creaky, ancient vehicle, were in an advanced state of crisis. With a superhuman effort he maintained the smile into which his facial muscles had been frozen for the greater part of the day, lifted his arms in a weary wave, and muttered angrily out of the corner of his mouth to Ricimer, beside him, whose reddened, perspiring face indicated that he, too, was suffering.

"Have you no control over this godforsaken slum? These people are not subjects—they are a mob! Utter rabble!"

Ricimer's smile, too, was frozen in a grimace of impatience and discomfort.

"With all due respect, my emperor and father-in-law—"

"I am not your father-in-law yet. The wedding does not take place until after we arrive at the Capitol. *If* we arrive—"

"My *future* father-in-law. It was perhaps a mistake for your staff to schedule the procession, *and* the wedding, *and* the distribution of donatives to the troops, all on the same day as your very arrival, which caused quite a stir in itself."

"Only in Rome would the arrival of a mere two legions cause a stir. In any decent city of the *Eastern* Empire, where the populace is accustomed to a certain grandeur, this would be of no more notice than the arrival of a merchant caravan. Though I doubt any caravans of note have arrived here in quite some time," he sniffed, glancing around at the by-standers' shabby clothing and the tawdry quality of the vendors' wares.

"Westerners differ from easterners," Ricimer replied evenly, as the chariot lurched forward another few yards before again grinding to a stop. "They are perhaps more effusive, less wealthy—"

"And less disciplined," Anthemius muttered, swatting at an overenthusiastic citizen who had squirmed his way between the shields of the guards surrounding the chariot and lunged at the emperor with a toothless grin and outstretched hand, crying for alms. "Incidentally, while I was passing through Tuscany, the local bishops requested an audience."

"Really," said Ricimer, vaguely interested. His mind was already ranging ahead to the speech he would offer upon their arrival, his formal presentation to the emperor's daughter, and the wedding that was to take place shortly thereafter. The scope of his good fortune was extraordinary, even for him, Ricimer, the most ambitious man in the empire, beginning with this sudden marriage to a woman whom he had not yet even seen, but for whose sake he had divorced his wife of twenty years when the union had been proposed to him by Anthemius's ambassadors just a few weeks earlier. Nevertheless, what was of more immediate concern was this new emperor himself: would he be a weakling like the previous three, capable of easy molding and maneuvering by Ricimer and the palace eunuchs? Or a man of more fortitude, as he suspected might be the case with Anthemius, a military commander handpicked by the Eastern Roman Emperor Leo? The impending wedding was a good sign of future cooperation and prosperity; but Anthemius's stony attitude toward him since their introduction was not. What would be Ricimer's own role in the new administration? Would he remain supreme military commander of the West? Or be relegated to a figurehead position? Would he rule? Or be ruled?

"As you know, Count," Anthemius continued, and Ricimer's wandering thoughts were abruptly brought back to the present situation, "the bishops have strongly supported my ascension to the throne. They are aware of my devotion to the Church. Yet they inform me that strong vestiges of superstition remain present in Rome, and indeed that preparations are already being made for the Lupercalia to be celebrated here next month."

"That is possible," Ricimer responded, wondering why the emperor should be concerned about this minor religious festival. "The tradition has been celebrated here since before Rome's foundation. Its roots go deep."

"It is a savagery, a profanation, which would never be tolerated in Constantinople," Anthemius spat. "The bishops are right to deplore it. I'm told that live goats are sacrificed, and that young men make themselves up as Pan and run naked through the streets, carrying leather thongs in their hands with which they whip passing women, and worse, 'bestowing' on them the gift of fertility. It sounds to me like organized rape."

"An exaggeration, my lord, without a doubt."

"Indeed? The bishops have been eager to suppress this barbaric custom for years, apparently, but have received no support from the chief civil magistrate, who—"

"The magistrate is not Christian, my lord—"

"Who himself was witnessed running naked through the streets last year, hirsute and obese as he is, without so much as a wink or a reprimand from his superiors."

"His superiors?"

"I am referring to you."

"My lord," Ricimer replied with studied patience, "I am the military commander, and the magistrate is—"

"The civil authority, I know," Anthemius interrupted. "Do not play stupid with me, Ricimer. We both know who wields true power in the city. I lay responsibility at your feet for any disturbances to the public order."

Ricimer seethed, but with great effort suppressed his reaction as the cart again lurched forward. The procession was now well past the Forum and in *plena Via Sacra,* and the crowds on either side, now comprising mainly the nobility, the senatorial class, and their families, were here considerably more restrained. Progress was finally being made—they had nearly arrived at the base of the Capitol's steps.

Anthemius turned and coldly eyed his chariot companion.

"We have much to discuss about the current state of Rome. Her morals and economy are far inferior to her sister cities in the East, which I intend to remedy at once."

Ricimer grimaced.

"This is the day of your investiture, my lord, and of my wedding to your daughter. Is this the appropriate occasion to be discussing such matters?"

At the foot of the broad marble steps, the advance troops fanned into a colorful array, armor gleaming brightly in the sun. The chariot rolled to a halt, and an attendant dressed as a Syrian prince, swathed in silks and with his face daubed with kohl and rouge, stepped forward to assist the emperor and the count. The two men, however, practically leaped from the vehicle in their eagerness to descend.

Taking the shallow steps two at a time, Anthemius nodded perfunctorily to the nobles and dignitaries standing on either side of him, as Ricimer kept pace. At the top Alypia, who with her mother had already arrived, was waiting with her attendants to greet her father and her future husband. She was a tall, slender woman of perhaps half Ricimer's age, clothed magnificently in silken robes and wearing a splendid jeweled tiara, in anticipation of the wedding to take place immediately after the investiture. Her face was largely obscured by a saffron-colored silk veil, but with the gust of a slight breeze, Ricimer caught a glance of white skin on a fine, delicate jaw, full lips, and a row of pearly, even teeth. He was pleased with his prospects, at least from the mouth down.

Rushing up to her, the emperor gave her a quick kiss on the veil, and muttered the briefest of introductions.

"Alypia—Count Ricimer."

He then brushed past, Ricimer striding at his heels, with

merely the briefest of glances at his astonished bride and her maids.

Ordering the bewildered guard to open one of the massive doors, which had been crudely covered with bronze plate to replace the exquisite gold foil that Gaiseric's Vandals had pried off, the emperor swept majestically into the atrium of the empty temple, the political heart of Rome itself, where the Senate met on important occasions, in solemn assembly. For a moment he stood and looked around impatiently, but saw no indication as to where the latrines might be located, nor any servants or even senators to ask, as all had remained outside the doors. He refused even to look to Ricimer for guidance—six hours of jostling against him in the chariot was all he could tolerate. Crossing to the nearest column, a tall, fluted specimen of purest white marble that had been deftly repaired from the damage caused by the Vandals' axes, Anthemius stepped behind it, yanked his robes up to his belly, and began pissing onto the veined marble floor. Almost light-headed with relief, it was only moments later, after the flow had slowed, that he heard a faint rush and sigh echoing from the other side of the vast room, and he opened his eyes to see Ricimer standing in an identical posture against an opposite pillar, a similarly relieved expression on his face. Finally dropping their garments back down, the two men stepped gingerly over the twin streams, which meandered lazily from the bases of the columns into the center of the atrium.

"This is how I am greeted in Rome," Anthemius said, striding into the gallery and looking about critically. "No forethought. No courtesy. Like two alley dogs marking their territory."

"On the contrary," Ricimer mused, also gazing about at the Senate's historic ceremonial meeting place, and then glancing down at the dampened column from which he had just stepped. "Many a man throughout the centuries has dreamed of doing precisely this. It is a singular accomplishment."

Anthemius looked at him with disgust, and pulled a scroll from the sleeve of his robe.

"I am also greeted, I find in this report from the procurator, with the imminent military collapse and financial bankruptcy of the Western Empire, and repeated attacks from Vandals around the entire western Mediterranean. Under your watch, Count Ricimer!"

Ricimer stared intently at Anthemius and walked toward him, his hard-soled military boots echoing in the vast, empty room.

"Yes, let us talk of this, my *lord*," he said menacingly, all pretense at civility gone now that the crowd and the nobles were safely at bay behind the massive bronze doors. "Let us discuss how, under my supervision six years ago, an entire navy was built in a matter of sixty days—*sixty days!*—to launch against Gaiseric and his pirate raiders—"

"And the plan failed. Your vaunted fleet was sunk, thousands of men killed—"

"Not under my watch. Control of the fleet was given to the Emperor Majorian."

"Whom *you* appointed—"

"Under pressure from *your* predecessors in the east, Aspar and your patron Leo!"

"Would you now be insulting the emperor? An insult to Leo is an insult to me. Oh, I am quite aware of my three predecessors' fates at your hands. Rest assured, I do not intend to be your fourth victim of imperial assassination, my future son-in-law. The thousands of witnesses who saw us enter this august chamber just now, and my guards standing just outside the door, will see to that. Not to mention the fact that my will provides specifically for my assets to be distributed *outside* the hands of any family members who might seek my life."

"What are you suggesting?" Ricimer inquired coldly.

"I am suggesting that Majorian destroyed the Roman navy; that you appointed Majorian; and that you should therefore be sufficiently honorable as to accept the blame for the debacle."

"Majorian," Ricimer snarled, "was the most militarily competent emperor in generations, yet when he failed in his duties, I ensured his removal—as I did with both his predecessor and his successor. I also facilitated your own rise to this office. I wonder—should I accept blame for that as well?"

"That is outrageous! You had nothing to do with my appointment! I rose to the position through my own merits. My father was a general and patrician of the Eastern Empire, and my grandfather a prefect. My wife is the daughter of the Eastern Emperor. I myself am a count, consul, and patrician. If anyone in this room is in his position through a sinecure, it is you, Ricimer, for it is only through your fortunate marriage to my daughter that you retain your exalted position, and are not hanged for insubordination."

"Ah, yes, that. My marriage to your precious daughter. And my support by all the western legions."

"So. Now the game is clear. Why do you not simply name yourself emperor?"

"You know as well as I, that I lack the august bloodline that runs so abundantly in your own veins, father-in-law. My own barbarian blood would be too uncouth for the Roman population to stomach. For better or for worse, I fear we are stuck with each other, for reasons of both family and state. I suggest you play your role in this farce, and allow me to play mine."

Anthemius glared at him, and Ricimer held his gaze. Finally, the emperor looked away.

"In this you are right. We must face our public, and your wedding and festivities, and there will be no further opportunity for conferencing for some time. However, there is an urgent matter to discuss: the defense of the empire. Rome is nearly bankrupt. There is nothing in the treasury with which to mount a defense against the Vandals."

"Funds can be borrowed. Perhaps from your benefactor Leo."

"What a brilliant idea, Count. In fact, I have already arranged precisely this. As an investiture gift to me, Emperor Leo will assist the West in the defenses it appears unable to assume on its own. You, as commander of the western legions, will provide what land, troops, and resources you are able, and will assume joint command for invading the Vandals on their home territory, Africa. I had hoped, when we came to know each other, that you and I would be able to arrive at a common understanding of the military's needs. But now I rather doubt this will be possible."

Ricimer gaped at him.

"You have arranged for an invasion of Africa? Under *joint* command?"

Anthemius watched him closely, enjoying the moment.

"Oh, I understand the western legions and generals are loyal to you, Ricimer, and so your position and title will remain intact. Nevertheless, you will work together with Fleet Admiral Basiliscus, who will assume responsibility for all day-to-day military operations, both western and eastern, commencing with command over the forces that will reconquer Africa from the Vandals."

"Basiliscus—Leo's brother-in-law? You expect me to serve under the eastern emperor's *brother-in-law*?"

"You can hardly complain. You are marrying my own daughter. The two empires are now joined. Basiliscus will be the combined legions' commanding officer."

Ricimer was silent for a long moment, considering this unexpected turn.

"So you are withdrawing my overall command of the western legions, and yet you still wish me to provide troops for this venture."

"And command them in the invasion—*under* Basiliscus. Presumably from your forces of eastern Gaul, Noricum, and Pannonia, as the legions stationed around the Mediterranean will be needed to defend against the reprisals Gaiseric's Vandals are certain to launch against us. I do not doubt your ability to fight battles, Ricimer. It is your judgment in governing empires I question."

"And when do you anticipate commencing this operation?"

"The new fleet is being prepared even as we speak. Funds are being raised, additional troops levied. Consolidating a force of this size will take perhaps a year. You have that much time to develop your own role in this effort, whether to actively participate, or to remove yourself entirely. I would not dissuade you from the latter. I will admit I cannot forcibly remove you from office, Count. But I can ensure that your governance will not further endanger the empire. Your formal title remains intact—but your command will be under the authority, and the watchful eye, of Basiliscus."

Ricimer's eyes narrowed in fury. There was little left to say, and outside, the noise of the crowd was already rising, in repeated chants for the new emperor to present himself. Anthemius began walking toward the door, which was now ajar as one of the guards outside cautiously poked his head in to investigate the delay.

"Come," Anthemius said peremptorily over his shoulder as he nodded and smiled casually. "The Senate and people of Rome—and your new bride, Alypia—await us."

Striding out the door to the portico at the top of the marble steps, he left Ricimer fuming in the center of the empty atrium, as the two tiny rivulets conjoined and formed a small pool at his feet.

II

Ricimer stood on the bridge of the Roman flagship, anchored just offshore of the tiny North African port of Mercurion, the site of a crumbling temple to Hermes, forty miles southeast of Gaiseric's capital, mighty Carthage. Low brown hills extended as far as he could see, patched here and there with the fields of wheat and olive groves that had at one time made this one of the wealthiest of Roman provinces. Yet history here was fickle. For nearly a millennium Carthage had been a threat; thrice Rome had conquered and destroyed it, and each time it had found the resources to revive, and eventually to threaten again. This time, however, the danger came not from the Carthaginians, who were, at best, a dying race of slaves and peasants, no longer the proud warriors of Hannibal's time. Now it was from the Vandals, a Germanic people utterly incongruous in these hot desert climes with their reddened skin and large bodies, who had conquered Carthage several decades before. Driven from eastern Europe by the Huns, they had stormed Rome's legions at the Rhine and crossed Europe as far as Hispania, where they were at last stopped by running out of land—they had met the sea, the end of the world, and could go no further. Rome, in an effort to remove the Vandals from the rich Iberian trading ports and silver mines on which they squatted, convinced them to set sail across the narrow strait dividing Europe from Africa, and to take the long empty coastline of Mauretania, as far down the western coast as the tribe might care to go. Rome then happily regained its wealthy legacy of Hispania and Lusitania.

Abysmal foresight, thought Ricimer. Unbeknownst to Rome, the Vandals had no intention of remaining on the dry, worthless territories to which they had been pointed. Within months of the landing, Vandal settlements had already sprung up far to the east of the Pillars of Hercules. Their progress was inexorable, and like an aqueduct slowly collapsing in an earthquake, column by column, the African provinces fell.

One after another, the beautiful cities along Africa's northern coast, Tripolis, Caesarea, Rusguniae, a string of Roman pearls with centuries of trading and cultural ties with the mother country, were conquered in an orgy of fire and blood. Even the great bishop Augustine was unable to hold back the slaughter and, besieged in the fortified town of Hippo, had died of a combination of old age, starvation, and sheer fury. Eventually the Vandals seized Carthage itself, along with all the agricultural territories and wealth of Numidia. With that, the entire southern Mediterranean lay open to their grasp. Originally a forest people, the Vandals now took to the sea like porpoises. Every port sprouted new shipworks and became bastions of Vandal sea operations. Extortion and looting became the norm, and Rome's Mediterranean islands—Sardinia, Corsica, and Sicily—were reduced to Vandal pirate strongholds. The coasts of Hispania and Gaul were laid waste, and not even Rome was spared, as witnessed by the Vandal attack just fourteen years earlier, from which the city's wealth and confidence had still not recovered.

Behind it all was Gaiseric, a cripple, deep of thought and few of words, contemptuous of luxury yet greedy for wealth, given to mad fits of rage, a master of intrigue among the Vandal clans, and shrewd in sowing the seeds of division, in conjuring up new hatreds. This was the very man who had led his wandering tribe out of Hispania, across the hot beaches of Mauretania, and into his present glory of Carthage. He was now old—very old, though Ricimer was not sure that mattered, for there are some races of people who seem to become enfeebled with age, and others—like the Vandals, apparently—who only become stronger. It was Gaiseric who had led the attack on Rome, bellowing obscenities from the prow of a blood-spattered pirate ship ramming the wharves of Ostia. It was Gaiseric who had taunted Ricimer for the last decade, appearing at the head of his naval squadrons just where Rome least expected him, devastating shipping lanes, enriching himself with the wealth of senators and wives he captured and held for ransom, openly mocking Rome's attempts to destroy him. It was Gaiseric who had driven Augustine to grief at seeing whole cities sacked, villas razed, their owners killed, churches deprived of priests, and holy virgins and ascetics dispersed; some tortured to death, some killed outright, others, as prisoners, reduced to losing their integrity, in soul and body, to serve an evil and brutal enemy. . . .

But it was Gaiseric who was now besieged inside starving Carthage.

How the wheels turned. The Eastern Emperor Leo was no idiot; he had proven that with his financing of this campaign. For as Ricimer stood on the bridge of the warship and gazed around the harbor, he could not help but be impressed.

A thousand ships, most of them constructed in only the past year at massive shipyards Leo had specially erected along the heavily wooded coasts of Asia Minor and northern Greece. They were manned by a hundred thousand troops, many of them veteran eastern legionaries pulled from garrison duty after the final defeat of the Huns above the Danuvius. But Leo's greatest contribution had been what Ricimer had least been able to provide from the West's resources: money. One hundred thirty thousand pounds' weight of gold, an enormous sum, had been collected by Constantinople, most of it at sword point. Entire cities had been forced into penury, rich men had been beggared, poor men made corpses. In the end, however, the money had been collected, the armada built, the troops levied. Despite Ricimer's initial misgivings, he now admitted that the effort was truly astonishing, far greater than he himself could have arranged. Yet to his mind, all had been ruined by Leo's choice of commander: Basiliscus.

Basiliscus, the twin brother of the emperor's wife Verina and the greatest annoyance to Ricimer since . . . well, since the emperor himself. The man's reputation was adequate, even impressive in some regards, though hardly what one might expect of a man assigned to command the combined legions of the Eastern and Western Empires in the reconquest of all Africa. A short, pudgy man of middle age, with firm jowls and broad, fleshy lips, he reminded Ricimer of nothing so much as a rug merchant in an Egyptian bazaar, satisfied at having bilked his last customer and avidly awaiting the next. Indeed, his toadying to Anthemius and his lust to one day wear the imperial crown himself were so badly concealed as to make him the laughingstock of the imperial court. Nevertheless, Basiliscus had acquired skills, in politics or extortion, that had allowed him to prevail over his other shortcomings.

Ricimer shook his head—he had enough concerns without being distracted by Basiliscus's scheming. Again he looked across the harbor and, almost despite himself, felt a surge of pride at the sight of the thousand Roman warships gathered that spring day, pennants fluttering in the eastern breeze that had brought them here, a mere day's sail from the undefended harbor of Carthage itself.

"Orestes?" he said aloud, without turning from his vantage point on the bridge. Ricimer had always had a keen ear for footsteps, and had recognized the tread he heard approaching behind him.

"Here, sir," the general replied, and then Ricimer heard a second step, lighter and more tentative, like that of a woman—unlikely here on the viewing bridge of the Roman fleet's command ship. He turned and found, to his surprise, Orestes accompanied by a boy perhaps eight years old, dressed in a tiny version of a Roman general's parade armor, accurate in every detail down to the miniature links in the mailed tunic and the polished leather cavalry boots. The customized kit must have cost a fortune, but the effect, particularly with the solemn, wide-eyed expression on the little boy's face, was impressive. A slight smile played upon Ricimer's otherwise stern features.

"And who might this be?" he asked. "Hold, let me guess. I call for General Orestes, and I find myself facing two Orestes, for the smaller is the very image of the larger. My friend, I was unaware you had a son."

Orestes remained stern, his jaw set firmly, but his eye softened slightly at his commander's compliment.

"Indeed, sir, he is the eldest of my three children, the other two being females. Son, bow to your commanding officer, and mine. Count Ricimer, I present to you my son, Romulus Augustus."

Ricimer raised his eyebrows.

" 'Romulus Augustus?' Combining the names of the founder of the city, and the founder of the empire. Almost as if you intended him for the imperial diadem. Most propitious, Orestes, even provocative, for a Germanic chieftain like you, is it not?"

Orestes remained expressionless.

"My lord, my late wife, the boy's mother, was Lavinia Aureliana, of an ancient family of consuls and senators, making my son's blood as Roman and as royal as many others who have worn the purple. Yet I would be loath to aspire to such a position for him. His destiny is to be a military commander, is that not right, boy?"

Romulus nodded silently, without diverting his eyes from the face of Ricimer, about whom he had heard many legends and stories.

"So I gathered from his clothing," Ricimer replied. "Most impressive. But I did not know you had brought him with you on the fleet. Rather irregular, is it not? Not to mention dangerous, for both you and your only heir to be traveling on the same vessel during an invasion of hostile territory?"

Orestes did not flinch.

"Not at all, my lord. While the fleet has been here in the harbor for a week now, Romulus has just arrived from Sicily, on a pleasure yacht I hired in advance to convey him and his tutors. They will remain a day only, perhaps two, and then return by tacking to the southeast to avoid any encounters with Vandal ships out of Carthage. Indeed, reports have it that the carcass of a whale has washed up on a beach a day's sail east of here, whose skeleton is large enough to shelter twelve men, and Romulus is eager to examine it. I'm sure you will agree, sir, there is no better education than to experience the world firsthand—which I am most eager for my son to do."

Ricimer nodded.

"I commend your effort," he replied. "And I hope that within . . . what, ten years? . . ."—he lifted the lad's chin with his thumb and forefinger, to get a better view of his face and gauge his age—"I hope to give him an opportunity to join my staff. Perhaps under his own father." He laughed, releasing the boy's chin. "Perhaps *over* his father!"

Orestes proudly placed his hand on his son's shoulder.

"Sir, you wished to speak with me?"

"Only a status report, General. Our vaunted Admiral Basiliscus refuses to have anything to do with me, and conveniently 'forgets' to invite me to his staff meetings, which I know you attend, so I am forced to obtain my information secondhand. Where do we stand with the invasion?"

"Very little new, sir. As you know, General Marcellinus recently sailed on Sardinia and came upon the Vandal pirate fleet there unawares, sinking many of their ships and expelling the remainder from that island. We have received word by smoke that General Heraclius, who landed a large contingent of marines outside Tripolis in Libya several weeks ago, easily defeated Gaiseric's troops there, and is now marching west on Carthage—we expect him to be camped outside the walls by tomorrow. With the reinforcements we sent him after he took the beachhead, that gives us nearly thirty-five thousand men on the ground, landward of the city, blockading all roads into the port, while the winds still remain favorable for us to drive the fleet toward it from the sea side. Marcellinus will prevent the city from being supplied by Gaiseric's remaining pirates. Admiral Basiliscus only awaits word that Heraclius's land forces have secured their position, and then the order will be given for the fleet to weigh anchor. With luck, by this time in two days, we will be dining on ostrich meat in Gaiseric's own palace."

Ricimer grimaced. He was not sure that such a complete and total victory by Basiliscus over Gaiseric, who had been Rome's nemesis for four decades, could be considered luck, at least to him personally. Yet he had to admit that after the victory, once the legions had returned and Carthage was again a safe Roman provincial capital, it would be good to focus his attentions on what most concerned him: movements in the court, and pressures on the Western Empire's borders. Against all likelihood, Basiliscus thus far had proved himself quite capable—not necessarily at warfare, but at maneuvering himself into the right place, at the right time, in such a way that he would be able to declare a stunning, massive victory over the Vandals *without* warfare. Truly an enviable position, and Ricimer made a mental note to study the man's methods over the next few months, to discern where he himself might be able to learn, and what he must ascribe to pure, dumb luck.

"The next general staff meeting is this afternoon, at the ninth hour," Orestes continued. "And, I might add, General Basiliscus made a point of asking me to invite you. It appears he genuinely wishes you to attend this time."

"Oh?" Ricimer looked up with some surprise. He was uncertain whether Basiliscus's unforeseen interest in his presence boded good or ill. "What do you make of it, Orestes?"

The German shrugged.

"Hard to know, sir," he replied. "But I'm told Gaiseric's ambassador is arriving shortly. Scouts say his train has been spotted already, moving quickly, as if on an urgent mission. Basiliscus is even now being rowed to the beach to meet with him."

"Interesting," Ricimer mused. "Old Gaiseric is surrounded and no doubt realizes he is defeated, and is requesting terms of surrender. No wonder Basiliscus wishes me to attend the meeting. He intends to formally announce his victory."

"Possibly," Orestes confirmed, inwardly pleased that his superior, on his own, had drawn the conclusion that he himself had been unwilling to point out for him. "Sir, if there is nothing else, I would like to show my son the ship, and then return him to his own vessel."

"Of course." Ricimer looked down. "Romulus Augustus," he said. "You cut a fine figure, young man. Like a little emperor. An *Augustulus*. Remember, a tribune's position on my own staff awaits you in ten years' time."

The boy grinned, and he and his father strode off, while Ricimer turned again to his view from the railing. On the distant beach, he saw a cluster of colored pennants dancing in the breeze, and the glint of armor in the sun. Gaiseric's ambassador appeared to have arrived. Well and good. The sooner this whole farce was over, the sooner he could get back to the real governance of the empire.

"Gentlemen," Basiliscus said, smacking his fleshy lips slightly as he spoke and peering up with his small eyes as Ricimer and Orestes entered the cramped admiral's quarters. Basiliscus's aide, Joannis, a hulking yet competent Greek who had worked his way up through the ranks, was already seated uncomfortably on a stool pulled up to the conference table, and several other senior officials were also present. The room was close and humid, stinking of men confined too long on a ship, and Ricimer hoped the meeting would be short. Looking around the room, however, he was surprised to see no sign of Gaiseric's ambassador.

"General." Ricimer greeted his rival with an amiable nod.

"I was under the impression we would be meeting with the Vandal representative today."

Basiliscus stared at him coldly, perturbed at Ricimer's obvious effort to seize control of the meeting.

"You will be pleased to know, Count, that I have already met with the good Ambassador Velsimic, and we have come to complete agreement on the Vandals' terms."

"So quickly, then? In only one short meeting on the beach?"

"The Vandals recognized, rightly, that they are in no position to haggle with me."

"And what, precisely, are the terms to which you agreed?"

Basiliscus smiled, savoring the moment.

"Complete and unconditional surrender of Carthage, with all its weaponry, though the civilian population, their personal goods, and the city's food stocks are to remain unharmed. Complete surrender of the Vandal naval fleet and merchant marine, including those vessels we term pirates, and withdrawal from their foreign bases to Carthage, with Rome to then take possession of all ships outfitted for plunder or warfare. Dispersal of the Vandal land forces, return of all Roman and foreign prisoners they hold hostage, and surrender and exile of Gaiseric and his senior officers to a third nation outside the Roman Empire, where they will be prohibited from ever again exercising the military arts."

"Exile of Gaiseric and his officers? Not arrest and trial?"

Basiliscus shrugged.

"Not without a battle. The old man is sick and will likely be dead within the year. I made an executive decision, that it is not worth engaging our troops and losing lives to arrest a man who will not live long enough to be brought to trial."

Ricimer pursed his lips for a moment, and then stood.

"My congratulations, Admiral. An equitable arrangement. I will prepare my troops for the occupation."

Basiliscus leaned back to consider him, again making a slight smacking noise as if rolling an olive inside his mouth.

"No hurry," he said simply.

Ricimer paused.

"Excuse me?"

"I said, there is no hurry. The occupation is not to begin yet."

Ricimer stared at him blankly.

"Ambassador Velsimic tells me," Basiliscus continued calmly, "that Gaiseric's senior commanders have registered some opposition to the surrender, though he is certain to prevail over them, by arresting them, if need be. He requires five days to put his internal affairs in order before our troops enter the city."

Ricimer stared incredulously.

"Five days? *Five days!* Five days for the Vandals to hide and disperse their weaponry? To empty their harbor of all their vessels? To abscond with the entire treasury, or to distribute it to Gaiseric's relatives in the provinces? Five days for Gaiseric and his officers to walk out of the city disguised as mule-drivers because *there are no Roman troops within the walls to stop them*?"

Basiliscus fixed his eyes on him calmly. "Are you finished, Ricimer?"

"*Count* Ricimer, you fool. I am still military commander in chief, and your superior officer. You gave them *five days* to surrender?!"

Basiliscus glowered, fighting inwardly to contain himself.

"Velsimic is a fair and honest man whom I have known and dealt with in the past, when he was assigned to Constantinople. I trust him implicitly, as nobleman to nobleman, and I see no reason why you should not as well, as I'm told you also come from noble stock. Though perhaps I am wrong . . ."—he looked the furious Ricimer up and down—"about your trusting him, I mean."

"You are taking the word of a Vandal, with no surety, no hostages, no guarantee, when Rome's victory and the success of its entire African campaign is at stake?" Ricimer roared, heedless of the presence of the other men in the room. "This is not mere stupidity, Basiliscus, this is lunacy!"

"You are calling me a lunatic?" Basiliscus asked calmly.

"Or a traitor!" Ricimer exploded. "Rome is not a merchant, to accept the surrender of subject nations on installment. I go to prepare the land troops. The occupation begins immediately."

Basiliscus stood up abruptly, his face flushing red, and the others at the table also rose.

"I am overjoyed," the admiral said calmly, though his eyes flashed fire, "that my staff was present to witness your outburst. 'Lunatic,' you called me. 'Traitor.' I am the emperor's representative. Indeed on this ship, in this armada, I *am* the emperor. Count Ricimer, you are under arrest, for high treason."

Ricimer stood dumbfounded as Joannis, sword drawn, seized his arm. At the same time, two armed guards who had been waiting outside burst into the cabin, taking position just behind him.

"Orestes," Ricimer said calmly. "Go now to the legions and tell my officers what you have just seen. This is gross insubordination . . ."

Orestes, however, did not move. All eyes in the room turned to the German, who stood immobile by his stool, watching. After a moment he turned and took two steps to stand beside Basiliscus, who gave him a slight nod of assent, without taking his eyes off of Ricimer.

"Times have changed," Orestes said, the corner of his mouth turning up slightly in mocking acknowledgement of his former commander's disgrace.

Ricimer could barely speak in his fury.

"You have no authority to arrest me, Basiliscus! I am your commanding officer. I am beholden to no man but the emperor himself!"

"Ah, and this time you are correct," Basiliscus rejoined, with a slight smile of contempt. "And in anticipation of just such an eventuality, the emperor prepared your arrest warrant in advance, for me to use at my discretion." Thumbing through a sheaf of parchments in front of him, he removed one which, even from across the table and upside down, Ricimer could see contained the emperor's seal and signature. "Here it is. Joannis, show this to the prisoner, out of his reach, please."

Ricimer spat.

"Why don't you just save yourself the trouble and assassinate me?"

"A good question," said Basiliscus. "That is indeed precisely what I had proposed to the emperor before we departed on this expedition. It appears, however, that your new wife has taken a genuine liking to you, despite everything. It would be awkward for the emperor, as her father, to put you to death. And the emperor also recognizes that you control the western legions which, though incompetent, do carry a certain weight, and it would be uncomfortable for them to revolt in the middle of the African campaign. No, Ricimer, you need not fear death, for the present."

"What then . . . ?"

"Ah, you have Orestes to thank for this, for he has devised the ideal solution."

"Orestes . . . you knew all this in advance? You Hunnish mongrel, you German traitor, damn you to hell."

Orestes observed Ricimer with silent amusement, until Basiliscus interrupted the outburst.

"Count, you will be sent back to your estates in Milan, escorted by a body of my personal guards, for a much needed rest following your sudden 'nervous breakdown.' In the interim, the western legions will come under my command. As soon as their loyalty is solidified, your retirement will be announced."

"You are endangering the empire!"

"And only *you* can save it, I suppose?" Basiliscus sneered. "Your transport vessel awaits, Ricimer, and your baggage has already been packed. That will be all, gentlemen—good day."

Cursing, Ricimer was escorted out onto the deck, where he saw that, during the conference, Basiliscus's own vessel, the fleet commander's yacht used to transport officers between the various sectors of the squadron, had been brought up alongside the command ship.

"Onulf!" Basiliscus called out to one of the sentries on the yacht. "Bind his wrists and gag him until you are safely out to sea."

The guard leaped off the yacht and onto the command ship, where he cinched the count's wrists behind his back to prevent him from flailing or struggling as he crossed the narrow gangplank between the two vessels. Before the crewmen on deck could even remark on the astonishing sight of the commander of the Western Empire's legions being led away in ropes, the yacht had pushed off.

Basiliscus and Orestes watched from the upper deck where Ricimer had stood only hours before, as the yacht's oarsmen skillfully maneuvered among the anchored vessels to the far edge of the harbor and then to the open sea beyond.

"That was regrettable, but necessary," Basiliscus commented, more to himself than to Orestes. "I trust you understood the need for that intervention—for a change of command, as it were."

Orestes nodded, avidly observing the departure of his former commander.

"Still," he replied, "it was unfortunate Ricimer could not see the need to spare the legions unnecessary battle by granting a mere five days' respite."

Basiliscus smiled.

"And so we have made corrections for the benefit of the empire."

Suddenly, a word from Basiliscus's order of a few moments before cut through Orestes' thoughts.

"Did I hear your guard's name was Onulf?" he asked casually.

"Onulf, yes, an eastern barbarian, a loyal man. I brought him with me from Constantinople. Why, do you know him?"

"I once knew an Onulf, many years ago. It couldn't possibly be . . ."

"Of course not, the man's never been to Germania."

"No, of course not."

"Come. Even with five days' reprieve, there is much to

prepare in order to receive a vanquished city. You will ride at my right hand in the Triumph—*Count* Orestes."

Orestes looked at his new commander in surprise, but Basiliscus had already stepped away to descend to the lower decks. With a last glance out over the vast fleet's bobbing ships, Orestes turned to follow.

III

On the fourth night after Orestes' departure, the Roman fleet, its sailors, and its soldiers, were sleeping the dreamless sleep of imminent victors. The initial celebrations had already been held, and there now remained only the formality of actually receiving the city the next morning. All had been prepared, carefully coordinated with Heraclius's land forces outside Carthage's walls. At first dawn, the massive fleet would hoist anchor and sail with the eastern breeze the easy forty-mile journey to the vanquished city. The lead ships' arrival was estimated for noon that day. Already the lines of every vessel had been strung with pennants and colored bunting, the hulls scrubbed of mildew down to the waterline by agile seamen hanging from knotted ropes, the sails bleached to a blinding white that would reflect the Roman navy's newfound magnificence. The soldiers on board the vessels had for the past four days drilled incessantly in the limited space, and spent every free moment polishing their arms, their mail, and their helmets, to present a lustrous reflection of Rome's military strength. When the vessels paraded into the harbor of Carthage the next day, every marine on board would stand at stiff attention, polished shields and javelins poised, lining the long decks from stem to stern, demonstrating to the Vandals the futility of resisting Rome's might, convincing them of the wisdom of their timely surrender.

Camped on the ground outside Carthage's walls, Heraclius's troops had been engaged in much the same activity, drilling on dusty, makeshift parade grounds in full view of the Vandal observers atop the city walls, polishing armor, and sharpening weaponry, while the staff officers spent their days mapping the route of the impending triumphal march through the city, dividing the urb and the suburbs into manageable quarters for more systematic looting or, as Heraclius preferred, "requisition of enemy assets." Junior officers coordinated with the fleet's naval liaisons the time of each party's departure so that the land and sea forces might arrive at the city's harbor at precisely the same time. On the docks, it had been agreed, Gaiseric and his senior officers would be waiting to surrender their weapons, and to place their lives and fortunes officially into the hands of their conquerors, submitting, as vanquished barbarians had submitted for twelve centuries, to the superior military, intellectual, and moral power of Rome.

All was in readiness for the events of the next day, and even the moon itself seemed to have found the preparations in order, and had retired early. Though midnight had scarcely been called by the watches, their cries echoing from ship to ship across the vast fleet, *Luna* had already dipped below the horizon, her work done, leaving the night dark but for the feeble sparks of the sentries' lamps on the deck of each ship, and the vague phosphorescent line marking the distant beach, where the foam bubbled and hissed from the tiny breakers lapping gently at the sand.

All was in readiness, as it had been for the past four hours, as it had been for the past four days, and Basiliscus, satisfied, had also retired early, scarcely after the sun had set, with orders not to wake him until an hour before sunrise. And from the moment he had closed the door on his cabin, nothing had changed that might cause the watchmen alarm, for even the early setting of the moon had been foreseen and accounted for, and found to be inconsequential to the defense of the fleet. Nothing had changed, and the night had progressed slowly, the hours dragging by as they do for men on watch duty, pacing the same line across the deck, nodding to their fellow guards as they meet at the bridge, and turning to walk slowly back the same route. Nothing had changed.

Except the wind, which had, at sunset, shifted to the northwest.

The helmsman on the flagship had noticed the shift, even in his sleep, for the sounds of a ship's own resting change with the wind. The creak of the hull planking increased in pitch as the vessel swung slowly around against its anchor ropes; sails that had been furled tight against the eastern breeze suddenly loosened their stray flaps and corners against a western blow. Grommets and lines, secured on one side of the vessel, began rattling lightly on the other side. Other helmsmen, on other ships of the fleet, awoke at the change in sounds, at the shift in the wind. They, too, considered the implications for a moment, calculating whether a storm might be in the offing, but decided with a shrug that the past four days of clear skies could but offer at least another two days of the same, after which the fleet would all be safely anchored in Carthage's port. The only inconvenience of the wind's new direction might be the additional tacking required to bring the fleet the forty miles. Arrival would be delayed, the flagship's helmsman concluded: by four hours, perhaps six. He made a mental note to inform the general upon his waking, in order for the requisite couriers to be sent to General Heraclius, to time the land army's entry into the city accordingly. And then he, too, shifted in his hammock and fell back to sleep.

Days earlier, the veteran Vandal seamen and seers of Carthage had predicted the change in wind nearly to the hour, and the previous evening a strange squadron of thirty ships had departed the city. Each mysterious, blackened vessel towed behind it an equally mysterious longboat. Roman scouts from Heraclius's legions spied the maneuver and reported the news to the general, who was awakened in irritation to hear it. Within an hour, three companies of horse couriers were dispatched, at quarter-hour intervals and taking separate routes, to bring news of the black ships to the Roman fleet. None of the couriers arrived, though three boxes of amputated thumbs were the next day delivered to Heraclius as a gesture of mockery.

At two hours before dawn, the first tar-blackened ship exploded into a roaring ball of flames scarcely a hundred yards from the leading edge of the Roman armada anchored serenely at Mercurion.

Within the space of a few heartbeats, the western breeze, which had now stiffened to a substantial wind that chopped the waters and fanned the flames, drove the vessel careening into a Roman troop carrier before the watchman was even able to wake from his drowsiness and sound an astonished alarm. The Vandal vessel's bronzed prow slammed the Roman ship broadside, slicing it through nearly to the oaken keel. The fire-ship's masts, which had been chopped halfway through at the base before being ignited, toppled with a shriek of cracking wood, and fell with the weight of tarred timbers and oil-soaked sails directly onto the Roman ship's deck, just as the troops were rushing up from below at the watchman's panicked cries. Within moments, the troopship was a conflagration, as screaming soldiers leaped off the decks on all sides, only to be smothered by the flaming sails that fell on them from above, or knocked senseless by the falling yardarms of the splintered vessels. The anchor rope securing the Roman vessel's stern burned through, and the ship swung around, ripping the bowlines from their moorings and allowing the vessel to drift the short distance to the next ship in the line. There, the men were already awake and standing by with gaffing hooks and poles to push the burning hulk away from their vessel—but it was impossible. Barrels of naphtha and pitch stacked on the decks exploded, splattering their flaming contents for yards in every direction. As the burning Roman ship approached, the heat became too intense for defenders armed with mere poles to remain in position. They were forced back to the far side of their deck—and their own ship became the next drifting inferno.

Along the entire line of the harbor other Vandal fire-ships were ignited, and as each set of new flames leaped to the sky, the Vandal marines on board jumped off their fiery vessels and swam to the longboats towed behind, where they were hoisted aboard by comrades and handed oars for maneuvering.

The fire-ships lighted the night sky like blazing banners, as burning scraps of oil-impregnated sail streamed behind them in the cutting wind, and flames soon engulfed the entire seaward side of the Roman armada and began raging into the center of the huge fleet. The water churned with screaming figures, white faces gleaming in terror in the light of the roaring flames. Men dove off the blistering decks of their ships, flailing in their armor, fighting one another to seize splintered beams floating nearby. Some held fast even to flaming pitch barrels, preferring possible burning over certain drowning, while others chanced the long swim to the beach through the rain of flaming timbers, rather than face immolation from the roaring fires on their ships. The close, orderly deployment of the Roman fleet, in which Basiliscus had taken great pride, assisted the progress of the fire, which spread quickly and irresistibly; and the whistling of the wind, the crackling of the flames, the shouts of the sailors and soldiers who could neither hear nor obey, the strokes of the poles with which they strove to push off the fire-ships or their own burning companions, created vast chaos.

As the flames spread, the Vandals in their longboats rowed into the midst of the splashing survivors, hurling javelins, slicing with swords through the arms of those who seized their oars in desperation, clubbing over the heads those who attempted to swim away. Romans who miraculously escaped the fury of their ships' flames were beaten to death or drowned by the boat-mounted Vandals, who cheered with every blow they struck.

Meanwhile, the Romans in vessels on the far side of the harbor were still only vaguely aware of the danger they faced. In the position nearest the beach, isolated from the rest of the ships and remotest from danger, Basiliscus's vessel remained unharmed. Indeed the fleet commander lay soundly sleeping for long moments after the initial attack, before the officer on watch realized the source of the flames he had been observing, and hastened to rouse his leader. Basiliscus took stock and, seeing in the graying light of dawn that a full five hundred of his ships were in the process of being destroyed, ordered his captain to strike oars immediately and row out of the harbor. The maneuver was successful, and he was followed by other ships nearby, which in turn opened up space for the remaining vessels that still survived after the conflagration, to distance themselves from the burning hulks around them, deploy their forces, and engage the enemy sailors.

With the arrival of dawn, the outnumbered Vandals retreated, though not without showering upon the Romans a lengthy litany of obscene catcalls and taunts. The Romans spent the remainder of the day rescuing shocked survivors, who with the increase in the wind and the change in tides were in danger of being swept out to sea if not quickly plucked from the water.

The bodies of the dead were left to be retrieved later by salvage crews in lifeboats, though their efforts soon had to be abandoned, for the small boats were set upon by hundreds of sharks that swept into the harbor, like a plague on the tide, attracted by the smell of blood and the stench of burnt flesh. The rescue crews hastily turned and rowed their besieged craft up onto the beaches, and then spent the rest of the day watching in a mix of morbid fascination and despair as the water of the harbor churned with teeth and fins, and the foam of the surf left a glistening red line upon the sand.

IV

"I admit," Ricimer said, putting his feet on the table in his study and reaching for a bowl of nuts, "that as incompetent as Basiliscus was, he had a talent for picking guards. Do you not agree, Onulf?"

Onulf stood stiffly at the entrance to the room, eyes straight ahead, expressionless. Six months previously, the yacht bearing Ricimer had arrived at the port of Genua, and Onulf had flashed a letter from Basiliscus to requisition military horses and carts from the garrison there to transport the prisoner to Milan. Since then, he and his fellow guards had dutifully watched over the count with strict, even extravagant rigor. Indeed, for the first several weeks Ricimer's wrists had remained bound, except when he ate, or wrote at his desk. Though that precaution had been abandoned when the sentries realized Ricimer had no desire to escape from his own house, they nevertheless did not leave him alone for an instant, even when he slept. The thirty-odd guards in the squadron were highly disciplined, had organized a tight schedule of duty shifts and, unless ordered otherwise by Basiliscus, intended to watch over their prisoner indefinitely. Ricimer, after a month or two, had seemed to resign himself to this state of affairs, and indeed had even occasionally attempted conversation with his keepers, though without great success, as the eastern guards claimed to speak little Latin, and the count had never been fluent in Greek. This time, however, he made a more serious effort than usual—speaking slowly and clearly, and sprinkling his sentences with as many Greek words as he could call to mind.

"I'm complimenting you, idiot, though you don't understand a word I say."

Onulf's scowl indicated he did indeed understand.

"I said you and your squadron are fine guards. I can't even take a piss without you peering over my shoulder to check my progress. Six months we've been here, and your attention never flags, does it Onulf?"

His words were met with stony silence.

"You never let your guard down, do you, Onulf?"

More silence.

"Allow me to ask you a question. You needn't answer, I won't be offended. How much does Basiliscus pay you for your duties?"

Onulf remained silent, but the brief flicker of his expression told Ricimer he had at last struck a nerve. He pressed on.

"Let me put it this way: the question is not 'how much,' but rather 'when.' *When* does he pay you, Onulf? Have you and your men been paid since we arrived here from Africa?"

Onulf shifted uneasily on his feet.

"Be sure to tell me if I cross the line, will you? I do not

wish to pry into affairs where I have no business. But I am curious. If the eastern court is organized like the western, you and your men are not regular army, but rather Basiliscus's personal guards. You are on his staff payroll, budgeted from his discretionary account allocated by the emperor himself. You do not receive funds from the legions' paymaster, but from Basiliscus's own hands, is that not so?"

Onulf remained silent, but blinked in consent.

"And from these wages, which I imagine are considerably higher than regular army wages, you support your family, correct? A wife, perhaps a child or two?"

No reaction.

"Or three?"

Onulf's lip twitched.

Ricimer sighed. It was difficult to make progress, to know whether the barbarian understood anything. He was clearly no brute, or he would not have been chosen as the captain of Basiliscus's personal guard. Yet he was either completely ignorant, or else extremely, almost inhumanly disciplined. Ricimer was inclined to bet on the latter.

"My friend, I just received a letter from a colleague who had been traveling recently in your former land, in Constantinople. He writes of extraordinary things, which you might find interesting. May I relate some of them to you? Whether you consent or not, I will do so, for I find lately that talking to myself is the most agreeable company I can muster these days.

"My friend writes me that after the disaster at Mercurion—at which your master lost more than half his fleet and upwards of thirty thousand men, though I'm sure you have already heard this through your own sources—Basiliscus fled in disgrace back to Constantinople. There he was met on the docks not by an honor guard, but by a company of urban cohorts seeking to arrest him, whom he somehow evaded. He fled through the city, followed by the soldiers and a jeering mob, and sought sanctuary at the Basilica of St. Sophia, wrapping himself around the altar support with arms and legs and prehensile tail until his weeping sister was able to obtain a pardon, of sorts, from Emperor Leo. Leo is said to have rebuked him with the words 'Better an army of deer led by lions, than an army of lions led by a deer.' "

Onulf still remained staring straight ahead, but a flush of red was rising up his neck and face. Ricimer was certain his words were being understood, and very clearly.

"But that is not all, Onulf. After the fire-ship incident, General Heraclius and the Roman land forces were left stranded below Carthage's walls, and had to retreat to the surviving fleet still anchored at Mercurion. Thirty miles of desert. Along the way, the Vandals harassed them unmercifully, and Heraclius, too, lost more than half his men, and then was arrested by the acting fleet commander upon his arrival, for being in league with Basiliscus. Marcellinus, who had supposedly defeated the pirates and recaptured Sardinia, was attacked by a Vandal fleet he had neglected to destroy, and was driven to Sicily, where he was assassinated by one of his own captains. And old king Gaiseric—are you listening, Onulf?"

Onulf remained staunchly at attention, and even the reddening of his face had subsided. The only sign he had understood Ricimer's words was the twitching of the muscle in his jaw as he furiously clenched and unclenched his teeth. Inwardly, Ricimer smiled, for by this sign he knew his stony-faced guard was a man beaten as thoroughly as if he had been captured in battle.

"King Gaiseric held a massive victory celebration in Carthage, in which he himself—though allegedly old and decrepit—led the dancing and took three new wives, one of them the captive daughter of Valentinian. That girl is now, apparently, with child, Gaiseric's own bastard, his blood mingling with that of a former Roman emperor. When Gaiseric heard the fate of Marcellinus, Heraclius, and Basiliscus, he apparently expressed great satisfaction that the Romans themselves had removed from his path his three greatest antagonists. Reportedly, Sicily is once more under Vandal control, and the entire Mediterranean is now his again for the plundering."

Ricimer watched Onulf in silence for a long moment,

sensing the guard's turmoil. At length, Onulf turned his gaze and looked Ricimer straight in the eye—something he had never before done.

"It is for this reason," Ricimer continued quietly, "that I asked about your pay—yours and your squadron's. You are not going to be paid, Onulf—you are forgotten men. You have no way of returning home, short of walking, and the minute you abandon my estate and set foot outside the city I will set my legions upon you, for they remain loyal to me, and I know this with a certainty through my correspondence. You cannot kill me, or plunder my household, for the same reason, the loyalty of my own troops, which will mean death to you should any harm come to me. And from this day forward, I forbid you to sleep in my house and eat of my stores, at least in your capacity as guards holding me prisoner. You may, however, remain on my property as guests. Challenge me on this if you will, Onulf, but I see in your eyes that your heart is no longer in it."

Onulf lowered his gaze. He was intelligent after all, Ricimer thought, not simple-minded, but possibly only simple-hearted, as only a man who makes a living as a guard can be. Still—Onulf had dropped his defenses, he had listened to Ricimer, with his heart as well as his ears. Ricimer's words had penetrated. And now he would need time to consider what he had heard.

Ricimer turned away as if concluding an interview, though Onulf was scheduled to remain on duty for several hours more. The count picked up a folded parchment, sealed with his wax insignia.

"I wish this letter to be delivered to the assistant commander of the Milan garrison. As you leave, give it to the courier at the guard post outside my gates. He will know to whom to deliver it."

Onulf glanced at the paper, but made no move to take it.

"General Bonifacio is away from the city," he said, in rough but serviceable Latin, "consulting with the emperor." Ricimer smiled amiably at these first words uttered to him by Onulf.

"I am aware of that. Which is why I have addressed this letter to the *assistant* commander. I wish to meet at sundown with this man, a tribune, who is—at least technically—still under my command. As you are my guard, or rather my guest, you may be present at the meeting. Indeed, I wish you would attend, as this tribune is an easterner like yourself. Now leave me, and order the letter delivered. I will see you this evening."

Onulf hesitated a moment, then took the letter, spun on his heel, and strode out the door.

At sundown, Onulf walked back into Ricimer's office without knocking, followed an instant later by the house's steward, an ancient Tuscan eunuch.

"Lord Ricimer," the old man announced, "the interim garrison commander has arrived. Shall I show him in?"

"By all means," said the count.

Onulf, unsure of his role at this meeting, took his customary position near the door, standing straight as a spear shaft, his eyes focused on the middle distance.

"By God," said Ricimer, "you are no longer my guard, Onulf. Find yourself a chair and—ah, the garrison commander." Ricimer rose from his seat and strode forward in greeting.

"The *interim* commander, sir," the man corrected him. "As you know, my rank is tribune only."

"Of course," Ricimer replied, smiling. "Tribune Odoacer, allow me to present to you a compatriot of yours, my former guard Onulf."

Ricimer then fell silent, looking from Odoacer to Onulf and back again. Onulf, too, had frozen. Only Odoacer seemed puzzled, for he had not noticed Onulf standing in the shadows against the wall when he had entered the room. Now, glancing back at the target of Ricimer's gaze, he started, and then staggered back a step in shock.

"More Huns than I have seen in one place since Catalaunici," Ricimer said softly. "And the resemblance is remarkable . . ."

Without a word, the two brothers fell into each other's

arms, pounding one another on the back. After a moment they both burst into surprised exclamations, the guttural words of their ancient language tripping from their mouths, their broad Hunnish faces wreathed in smiles. Ricimer stood in silent amusement, then strode to the side table and poured out three goblets of wine, handing two to the pair of soldiers who stood grasping each other's forearms and exclaiming eagerly.

"I had no idea you were known to each other"—Ricimer interrupted them—"but I would like to offer this in token of my congratulations. Your reunion, I think, bodes well for us all. Drink up, and then, Tribune Odoacer, a short explanation might be in order."

The men took the goblets and tossed back the uncut wine in a single gulp, and Ricimer marveled at how their timing and gestures were nearly identical, as if they were twins, and how they both flushed an identical shade of red as the uncustomary strength of the liquor immediately went to their faces. Odoacer burst out laughing.

"Pardon, my lord," he said in lightly accented Latin, "for it is certainly improper to have a private reunion in your very office, and in your presence."

Ricimer shrugged.

"Brothers, I assume? Long separated?"

"Many years—two decades I think, though I've lost count. We last saw one another in Hunnia—"

"When we were Huns," Onulf said hoarsely.

Ricimer smiled.

"Yes, I gathered from your faces you had once been that. Go on."

"Sir, that's all I know," Odoacer continued. "We fled Hunnia together and went our separate ways. Onulf went east. I wandered south and west, to my ancestral tribe, the Scyri, where I was named a prince and commander."

"The Scyri," Ricimer mused, looking at him slyly. "Did Rome not defeat them some time back?"

Odoacer scowled.

"Yes, we were defeated, by a jackal named . . . no matter. The tribe was destroyed. I was wounded, but after my recovery I gathered the survivors, a thousand or so men, and we traveled west, to Italia, on foot. There we encountered Bonifacio, who was a tribune at the time. His troops challenged us, but we assured him of our peaceful intent, and he was impressed that we had penetrated the Roman border garrisons. Realizing that we were warriors, lacking only in arms, he offered to take us under his command, as his legion had seen a great deal of action along the Rhine and was desperately undermanned. We—the Scyri—joined his legion as a body. In due time, Bonifacio was promoted to general, and placed me in charge of the two Scyri cohorts. We served along the Rhine for some years and then were transferred here. I have been stationed in Milan for two years."

"And I have been away from Milan for nearly the same length of time," Ricimer mused. "I remember this transaction involving the renegades, as I signed the approvals for it at the time, but had forgotten about it until recently. I have heard favorable things of your Scyri cohorts. They have a reputation for great bravery. And your brother here, who went east, fell into the ranks of the personal bodyguard of our friend Admiral Basiliscus, and—well, I'll let Onulf explain that to you later. Come, gentlemen, another cup of wine—and then to business, for we have much to discuss."

The goblets were refilled, and Ricimer invited the brothers to sit at the table.

"My friends," Ricimer began, "the Western Empire is in great danger."

Odoacer nodded.

"I am aware of that, sir."

"Are you? And what do you know?"

Odoacer paused to collect his thoughts.

"Many of our comrades did not return from Africa, and General Bonifacio has been absent a great deal, in conference with the emperor and other senior officers. The garrison here is disciplined, but becoming less so, and I do not have the rank or authority to maintain order for long, except among my own cohorts. If all the western legions are facing similar difficulties, then I am not optimistic."

"Which is why we are meeting tonight. Tribune, I see in your eyes what you believe, even if you are reluctant to speak of it openly. With the defeat in Africa, Emperor Anthemius has lost all credibility among the nobility, but more important, among the troops. The Vandals continue to run rampant, cutting the shipping lanes, and within a matter of months trade goods and even food will become scarce. The emperor will then lose credibility among the common people as well. Many people have seen this, and anticipate it."

"But nothing has been done?"

"No one has the ability to do anything. Except me. Except *us*. For this I need your support—the support of the Scyri cohorts, and of the Milan garrison. You are the largest cohesive body of troops in Italia, larger even than the urban cohorts in Rome, larger than any other city garrison. If we march together, the others will be sure to join us."

"March?" The brothers looked at each other in puzzlement. "March where?"

Ricimer gazed at them long, with a hard expression in his eyes. Leaning over, he removed the jug of wine from the table and set it on the cabinet behind him.

"Enough wine for you. Where will we march? Rome, of course. Where did you think?"

"I will go," grunted Onulf. "Immediately, with my men."

Ricimer smiled.

"Thank you," he said. "That makes thirty troops. I need about a thousand times that number." He looked pointedly at Odoacer.

Odoacer gazed thoughtfully down at the table.

"The Scyri will follow me where I lead them. They are loyal to Rome—so long as Rome pays . . ."

"But . . . ?" Ricimer waited patiently, until Odoacer looked up.

"But Rome has not paid in several months, and—"

Ricimer pounded his fist on the table, making the cups jump.

"I knew it!" he roared. "Even the legionary pay is withheld! Onulf, you are not the only man whose children are going hungry tonight."

Odoacer looked at his brother with interest.

"You have children?"

"Damn it, Tribune, this is not the time," Ricimer interrupted. "You say the Scyri are loyal as long as Rome pays—but Rome is not paying. So the Scyri follow the money, is that it? And the other troops in the legion, is it the same?"

Odoacer looked at him evenly.

"The same, sir. The men must eat, their families must be shod. Without pay, they will desert."

Standing, Ricimer walked to a corner of the room, knelt down, traced with his finger in the mortar around a floor tile, and found the tiny finger hole he was seeking. Prying up the tile, he exposed a small hollow, just large enough to insert his hand up to the elbow. As the two brothers watched, he withdrew a cloth sack about the size of his fist, and then another. Leaving the tile off, he brought the two bags to the table and dropped them, one in front of each brother. Each made a metallic thump as it hit the table.

Both men stared in silence at the bags, but neither moved to open them. After a long moment, Odoacer looked up.

"You are asking me to commit betrayal. You are seeking to bribe me."

"Who is your commander?" Ricimer asked.

"General Bonifacio—"

"No. Who is your supreme commander? Above him?"

"You, sir. But—"

"Correct. And following the orders of your own commander is certainly not treachery."

"But this money—"

"Is simply the pay to which you are entitled for services legitimately rendered to the empire."

Odoacer considered this a long moment. Finally he shook his head.

"I cannot do this. You are asking me to rebel against the emperor."

Ricimer remained expressionless.

"Open the bag," he said.

"I know what it contains."

"Open the bag!" Ricimer roared, drawing his dagger suddenly and stabbing it into the sack on the table in front of the startled Odoacer. The tightly wrapped cloth split open and gold coins scattered in every direction, spilling onto the floor and the men's laps. Ricimer withdrew his blade and held it in front of Odoacer's eyes. Impaled on the tip was a thin gold coin, the soft metal neatly pierced by the sharp point of Ricimer's steel.

Odoacer slowly brought his gaze up from the spilled money before him, to the pierced coin in front of his face, and his eyes grew wide in amazement.

"This coin," he said, almost choking. "Eastern—from many years ago. Where did you get it?"

Onulf tore into his own cloth bag, pouring the coins into a small heap on the table in front of him. They were the same—ancient gold, from a distant civilization. Both brothers stood slowly and faced Ricimer, who set the dagger down on the table in front of them.

"Rome is now defended," said Ricimer, "by a man whom the emperor has appointed his new commander in chief. Perhaps you have heard of General Orestes?"

The silence was absolute as both brothers stared avidly. Then, scarcely glancing at one another, both bent and simultaneously pushed the gold coins on the table back to Ricimer.

"I need no bribe," Odoacer said, "to do this for my people—and for Rome. I will keep only this."

Picking up the dagger, he plucked the pierced coin off the tip and tucked it into the pouch at his belt. "As a reminder. When do we march against Orestes?"

Ricimer smiled. "Patience, my friends. There is still months of work to prepare for such a march. And do not reject my gold too hastily. There is much more where that came from, and the men—*your* men—may need convincing by more than mere thoughts of revenge."

"And will you name yourself emperor?" Onulf asked.

Ricimer looked at him with surprise, and then smiled wryly.

"No, my friend, the Roman people would not stand for a 'barbarian' such as myself claiming the crown—there are plenty of malleable Roman officers and senators who can capably fill that role. You will not be the mere bodyguard of an emperor. However, under me, you may become a commander of a legion; and you, loyal Odoacer"—he clapped the latter on the shoulder—"will be my second-in-command, in our quest to restore the empire, and its legions, to their former glory."

The two brothers glanced at one another, their faces still expressing amazement.

"And now, gentlemen," Ricimer continued, "pick up the gold, or leave it on the table, as you will. We agree as to our future. Go, for you two have a great deal to talk about, I suspect."

"Yes, sir," said Onulf. "And you . . . ?"

"I?" Ricimer smiled. "Onulf, you and your men may have the night off."

With that, Ricimer strode out of the room, down the corridor, and out the front door of his house, unchallenged by soldier or guard, a free man for the first time in many months.

CHAPTER SIX

Five Years Later, 472 A.D.

ROME

I

For months, Emperor Anthemius had barely moved from the dark room. In happier days, it had been his private *triclinium,* a sparkling jewel of a dining salon on the far end of the wing of the *palatium* hosting the royal family's private apartments. Anthemius was particularly fond of the room's floor: a stunning mosaic that he had designed himself, and that had been laid by Ravenna's finest artisans. It featured a startlingly lifelike depiction of the great poet Virgil, with two muses hovering languorously but discreetly in the air behind him. The poet was kneeling, head bowed, holding a thick sheaf of manuscripts offered in homage to a godlike personage sitting before him on a golden throne embossed with the wolf-and-suckling emblem of Rome. What pleased Anthemius most about the magnificent mosaic was that the face of the heroic ruler representing the Roman state bore a none too subtle resemblance to himself, a fact that delighted him when pointed out by dining guests, at which he always feigned polite surprise and skepticism. Nevertheless, the furniture had been arranged in such a way that no guest's seat or feet would ever be placed over the portrait's head.

Three of the walls were covered with marvelous frescoes, employing a modern Greek technique of exactly replicating the colors of the floor and adjoining walls, extending the room's natural lines and angles directly into the painting. The effect was such that when seen in dim light, or by the flickering of lamps, the room appeared to run *through* the walls to an amazing distance beyond, or to be lined on all sides with perfectly clear mirrors that reflected one another into infinity. To complete the wondrous illusion, the murals had been painted with furniture and decorations that exactly matched those actually existing in the room, even down to the floor mosaic. In the frescoes, guests lounged casually on couches and plucked fruit from tables, imitating the behavior of the real guests at the emperor's dinner parties, and flattering their flesh-and-blood companions by their very presence, for the painted guests peering into the room from the walls, from beyond time and beyond space, were none whom any living Roman had met: Cicero smilingly inspecting a chickpea between thumb and forefinger, Socrates looking askance at a goblet set before him, Cleopatra in eastern finery depicted with an asp peering from behind her doelike neck. As an illusion, it was the finest Anthemius had ever seen, and on days when he was alone he delighted in passing through the hidden door leading from his adjacent bedchamber, walking into the darkened room, and using a small taper to light the mirrored wall sconces, all with his eyes half closed and without daring to look about him. Then, when the reflective candles had been lit, he would stand in the middle of the room, open his eyes wide, and take in the dazzling company around him.

Yet it had been many months since he had played this little trick on himself, and now, without emotion, he glanced around the darkened room from his seat, a single candle barely illuminating Plautus's gap-toothed grin from an upper corner of one of the murals. The faceted crystal skylight, which had once showered the room with sparkling beams, both magnifying and diffusing the sun's rays and illuminating the portraits even on cloudy days, had been covered with a shoddily tacked piece of coarse burlap, drooping lazily on one side like the slatternly tunic of a Roman street whore. He noted vacantly that cobwebs had begun forming at the angle of the ceiling, and that the beautiful mosaic had not been swabbed and polished, and now bore the dull patina of neglect. He had long forbidden the palace staff and servants to enter the room, for he had converted it from a center of private entertainment to a mere workroom, as it had the advantage of being adjacent to his sleeping quarters, and he felt incapable of walking any further each morning in the depression and lethargy that had settled upon him.

Now, the floor was littered with parchment scraps and notes, a random commingling of military maps, and diverse jottings of his own feverish invention. The long dining table was covered with dusty scrolls and codices, but for the small space at the very end that he kept clear of debris for his own writing, which he performed in a tiny, cramped hand at the very edge of the mitered marble slab. Books and papers spilled onto the chairs and into the dusty corners of the room, where they mingled with trays of half-eaten food and discarded articles of clothing he had neglected to send out for laundering, as he forbade his valets to dress him, or indeed even to approach or touch him.

In the years since he had ascended to the purple, all had rotted, all had gone sour. He glanced up at King Midas, one of the painted guests on his wall, who in ancient legend had turned all at his touch to gold, and the thought occurred to him that he, Anthemius, was perhaps the mirror image of that mythical king, the *anti*-Midas, whose every touch yielded dross. Yet even as he reflected on the analogy, he found it absurd, for if the ancient king had eventually come to suffering and downfall because of his miraculous gift, then Anthemius, as his opposite, should eventually arrive at blessing and glory by his touch of decay. Yet decay is all he caused, and it was small consolation to him that, in fact, decay was all he had found upon his arrival. Rome was like a lovely fruit with flawless skin, an exquisite apple sought after by princes who longed to sample its sweetness, but which, when acquired and tasted, was found to be maggoty; and it was of no consequence which prince finally won the prize—in the end, the worm would out, and the fruit would wither and rot in his hands.

With a quiet click the door opened, and without announcement or introduction Orestes stepped into the room, closing the door behind him and warily picking his way over the rubbish-strewn floor to stand before the emperor. Even by the light of the single candle, and the pinpricks of rays that seemed to force their way through the dusty air from the loosely woven burlap above, Anthemius could see from his general's face that he was deeply worried.

"It is true, then?" the emperor asked in a monotone barely audible to Orestes, though there was no other sound in the abandoned wing of the *palatium*. The empress, their children and their families, and their attendants had long since fled for the safety of Napolis, and the murmurs of courtiers had been replaced by the measured tread of the urban cohorts who, along with the emperor, were now the only residents of the palace.

"They have arrived?" the emperor persisted. "Ricimer has arrived?"

Orestes looked at him a long moment in silence.

"Do you wish my official report, then?"

Anthemius rose suddenly to his feet and exploded.

"Damn you, General! Has he arrived or hasn't he? Is Ricimer at the walls?"

Orestes met the emperor's outburst with a stony gaze.

"It is as you heard. Ricimer arrived last night with the legions of the Milan garrison, and an army of Germanic auxiliaries. By diverting troops here, from the Burgundian region, he has completely depleted the northern garrisons, leaving the Rhine borders virtually undefended. It is only a matter of time before the northern barbarians begin pouring across the river. Indeed, the Burgundian garrisons have been abandoned for some time now, nearly half a year, and therefore the barbarian invasion may have already begun. As you know, however, we have received no communications from those regions for some time—"

"You blather, General. No situation on the Rhine is as critical as it is here in Rome, for Rome is Rome. What of Ricimer's troops *here*?"

"They are camped north of the city, on the banks of the Aniente, at the bridge known as the Pons Salarius. Our

Second Parthica legion, which was temporarily garrisoned at Ostia, intercepted them at that point, supported by half the urban cohorts. Our forces retain complete control of the Tiber, both north and south of the city."

"And I am told that his band of rebels includes a number of cohorts of Scyri tribesmen, under the command of a certain Odoacer. Is this true?"

Orestes stared at the emperor, mildly surprised at the extent of his intelligence. He himself had only recently learned this fact, and the name *Odoacer*, floating up from his past life like a piece of flotsam from a ship he had long thought sunk, had caused him several sleepless nights of late. Could this be the same Odoacer whom he had known years before in Hunnia? Logic at first told him no, the coincidence was simply too great—yet further inquiries had removed all doubt. This half-Hunnish mongrel, son of his old rival Edeco, a reminder of his own past as a traitor and a grave-robber, had somehow resurfaced, seemingly from the dead, undoubtedly seeking a vengeance nursed for many years. Orestes would not permit him that satisfaction. He almost welcomed the fact that Odoacer was leading this Scyri crew—it would allow Orestes to deal with him once and for all, as he would an annoying pest, a mosquito or a horsefly, which he had finally trapped in a corner.

"General," the emperor insisted more vehemently, "is this true?"

"It is true, Augustus."

"Were you not the officer responsible for annihilating this tribe some years ago, General? Fierce fighters, so I am told. Deadly archers. How, then, do we now have entire cohorts of these barbarians at our very doorstep, fighting in the armor of Roman legionaries no less?"

"They are rabble and deserters, nothing more, Augustus. They tied their fortunes to Ricimer some years ago, and now they are squatting on a muddy tributary miles up the Tiber. They are of no concern to us."

"And there they will stay, correct? Ricimer will be unable to broach our defenses? Rome's walls on the east and the south are twenty-one miles long, and impervious to rams or undermining—true? And your urban cohorts have bottled them up on the north and west—is this not so?"

"Correct."

"Then Ricimer and Odoacer and their band of rebels can stay until they rot."

Orestes paused a moment, then spoke up again.

"Ricimer has a great many troops. Our urban cohorts and the Ostian legion are strong and well-trained, but stretched very thin. Twenty-one miles of wall, plus the city's northern quarters across the Tiber, is too much to defend permanently—"

Anthemius stood and cut him off savagely.

"Idiot! You failed once to quell the disobedience of our barbarian subjects, and now those same barbarians have returned to attack us. Need I find another commander to repel this uprising? Bonifacio is in the city, and the urban cohort commander Gilimer . . ."

Orestes' eyes flashed anger.

"I am reporting the situation, Augustus. I cannot long hold twenty-one miles of wall, as well as the northern quarters. Gilimer would face the same problem."

"And what would you do?" Anthemius sneered. "Capitulate now? Invite Ricimer into the city for a cup of wine, ask him not to play so rough with your boys?"

"I will not be mocked."

"You have no choice. At the snap of my fingers, I will happily dismiss you and appoint another in your place."

"In the middle of a siege? That would be madness."

"What is madness, perhaps, is to trust a Goth general to conduct a defense against another Goth general."

"No more so than for a Roman emperor to order his urban cohorts into battle against his own Roman auxiliary legions."

"Do not tempt me, Orestes . . ."

The two men stood silently, facing each other, Orestes breathing slowly and heavily in an effort to control his anger, Anthemius's head trembling slightly, like one so fatigued he could scarcely stand. After a moment, the emperor reached back, felt for his chair, and sat down heavily.

"Forgive me, General. I can scarcely think these days, or determine who is my friend and who my enemy. Has any man ever been so hounded as me, by my own son-in-law, no less? What favors have I ever refused Ricimer? What provocations have I not endured! I gave my own daughter to a Goth, sacrificed my own blood to the safety of Rome."

Orestes composed his expression.

"There is nothing to say, Augustus. The man is a traitor and a scoundrel, and he will be punished as such."

Anthemius looked up at him with interest.

"And what is your plan of action?"

"A simple one. We still control the western seacoast and access to Ostia with the Misenum Fleet, and therefore Rome is protected. Moreover, the cities to the east and south are loyal, and will soon be sending militia to our aid, and the Ravenna Fleet remains under our control. Ricimer is isolated. Time is on our side. We need only starve him out, and overwhelm him at the appropriate time."

"Then do so. Rome's fate is in your hands. Go attend to the defenses."

Orestes saluted, spun sharply on his heel, and walked out the door, leaving the emperor once again alone, slumped with exhaustion in the gloom of the single candle.

Outside, he found awaiting him the commander of the urban cohorts, the Goth veteran Gilimer, who had distinguished himself in many battles and bore three missing fingers on his sword hand, cut off by a Vandal blade in the invasion two decades before. Legend among his men held that the wound had so infuriated Gilimer that, unable to grasp his blade, he had leaped upon his attacker and strangled him with his left hand alone, using the blood pouring from his other to blind the man. When Orestes observed his fellow Goth's icy demeanor and absolute control over his men, he had no doubt but that the story was true.

"Tribune Gilimer," he called, gesturing for the officer to approach.

Gilimer saluted laconically with his maimed right hand.

"I want the guard on the emperor's quarters doubled, tonight, and for the remainder of the siege," Orestes said in a low tone, glancing sharply at the door to the *triclinium*.

Gilimer looked at the guards.

"Sir, I already have eight-man shifts posted at all times. And we are short of troops as it is, with so many attending to the siege. Do you fear an attack on the emperor?"

Orestes studied the tribune's face closely, but the grizzled officer's gray eyes betrayed no challenge—merely a question.

"No, it is for quite another reason. Inform your guards that the emperor is not to leave his quarters. He is to be forcibly prevented, if necessary, from doing so."

"And if the emperor orders my men to release him?"

"*My* orders are that he stays, and you will obey *my* orders, Tribune, not the emperor's."

At this, Gilimer raised his eyebrows slightly. He made no move to protest, but neither did he step away to execute the order. The urban cohorts were a powerful force in Rome—indeed, the *only* force in Rome—and Orestes suddenly realized he would need to give their commander greater justification for disobeying the emperor.

"The emperor is unwell, Tribune. He does not realize the danger Rome faces, and for his own safety, he must not be told. You will allow him no visitors, nor is he to be allowed out of his rooms."

Gilimer considered this for a moment, then nodded.

"And where will I find the additional men I need for this guard? Would you have me reduce the forces at the Aniente, or the patrols along the walls?"

"We will pull the urban cohorts back from the Aniente, to this side of the Tiber. The defense will be waged from within the walls and the river."

"*This* side of the river? Then we are abandoning the suburbs across the Tiber?"

"It is our only chance of holding the city. I will cede to the rebels the Vaticanus and Janiculum hills north of the Tiber. Ricimer can take possession of them as he sees fit."

"So our troops—"

"Will then only need to hold two crossings: the Pons Milvius, across the Tiber to the north, and the Pons Aelius, connecting to Hadrian's Mausoleum and the Vaticanus. Two bridges are much easier to hold than eight miles of open suburbs. Let Ricimer take the Vaticanus—it is of no tactical benefit to us. He can confess his sins at the basilica. May the bishop assign him fasting as a penance, because that will at least give meaning to his starvation. I still hold the city, and the port of Ostia."

The corner of Gilimer's mouth twitched in what Orestes felt must pass for a smile, and the cohort commander saluted again before turning and striding away. Glancing out a window of the corridor, Orestes could look down on a section of the ramparts in the near distance, and confirm that the walls were heavily patrolled, for their entire length.

"So, Odoacer," he muttered, peering into the distance toward where he knew the enemy legions were assembling. "You have been foolish enough to take me on again. This time, I shall finish what I failed to do before."

"I would not have believed it had I not seen it for myself," Odoacer said as he clung to the rungs of the watchtower hastily constructed by his men. Just that morning, reports had come to Ricimer in the command tent that Rome's urban cohorts were withdrawing from their entrenchments north of the city, anchored by the Tiber on the right, and the walls of the Janiculum's estates on the left. At first he had dismissed the news as wishful thinking, or perhaps a ruse or drill by the city's troops—valuable properties, like those on the Janiculum, are not usually yielded so easily. But when additional scouting reports confirmed that the pullback was being executed not in haste or abandonment, but in slow, disciplined order, Odoacer felt it time to reconnoiter the position for himself. Ricimer concurred but, wary of a trap, refrained from accompanying him, remaining instead in the main rebel camp on the banks of the Aniente, the small stream that flowed west into the nearby Tiber.

Odoacer climbed higher into the flimsy scaffolding, feeling the structure sway slightly beneath his weight, but gave it no notice as he craned his neck to peer over the low ridge toward the city in the distance. The scouts were right, of course; just the day before, the very ground on which the watchtower was perched had been patrolled by the emperor's troops. All around him were the broken garden walls, sheds, and houses of the suburban neighborhoods that had been occupied and partially dismantled by Anthemius's soldiers when building their fortifications. Just below the tower he spied what he knew from maps to be the Pons Milvius—the Milvian Bridge, the white limestone facing of its high arches gleaming brilliantly in the sunlight as the placid Tiber rolled slowly beneath it, scarcely two miles upstream of Rome's center.

The river shone clear and blue, a deceptively beautiful stream from which Ricimer had forbade his army to drink for fear of contracting disease. Even here, far upstream of the city, he warned, though the waters appear clean and refreshing, they conceal mysterious humors that sicken any who are not Roman, and therefore inured to its poisons. Some miles downstream, after the river emerges from Rome's southern ramparts and flows into the suburbs and the port of Ostia, and thence into the sea, not even the Romans will drink it, for upon passing through the city the water becomes visibly fouled by the trash and sewage of the million people inhabiting its banks. For centuries, the river had been a source of life; now, for those who drink of it, it becomes a cause of death, and for the dead themselves it becomes even more, for cemetery plots and monument stones are expensive, while the river disposes of its victims without charge. It was not for nothing that the largest cemetery in Italia was the sandbar of Ostia, where every day a score of corpses washed up, bodies of the old and forgotten, or of the newborn and rejected, who were buried there in the ever-lengthening trench maintained by the municipal sanitation authorities.

But Odoacer's eyes were focused on the Milvian Bridge itself. A century and a half earlier, the rebel Constantine had fought a mighty battle at that site, under a fiery banner held by angels in the heavens announcing his victory over the forces of Rome. Odoacer could imagine exactly how the bloody tumult on the bridge must have looked: then, it was packed with frantic, fleeing soldiers; now, he could see, it was jammed with a mob of wailing refugees. Their cries wafted to him on the faint breeze, and by squinting and staring hard enough, he thought he could even make out individuals—women and children mostly, many with large, cloth-wrapped bundles on their heads, some trundling slowly over the crossing pushing wheelbarrows stacked with household items and elderly grandparents. Here and there he could see the glint of metal and a flash of crimson—imperial troops straining to pass through the crowds, or perhaps driving them forward like cattle. After a moment he concluded it was the latter, for he could discern that the guards had stationed themselves at regular intervals along the roads leading to the bridge, and among the crowds fanning out on the far side of the crossing, and that they themselves were not moving, but rather hastening the fugitives along.

Odoacer glanced at the Scyri scout accompanying him on the scaffolding.

"What do you make of it?" he asked, in their old language.

The scout shrugged and spat. "Who can tell what these Roman dogs do to their own people? The urban cohorts attack us, we attack the urban cohorts, and the urban cohorts now attack their peasants. Orestes served Ricimer, now he serves the emperor, whom Ricimer attacks, while Orestes—"

"Silence," Odoacer growled. "I do not seek your opinion on strategy. I ask about this bridge."

The scout clamped his jaw shut, offended at the rebuke, but his silence did not last long.

"It is not just here," he said.

"What do you mean?"

"Another two miles downstream at the next bridge—the Pons Aelius. Same thing. Refugees pouring over it as well."

"The Pons Aelius?" Odoacer closed his eyes and tried to envision the map of Rome at which he had stared for so many hours in the command tent. "That's the bridge leading from the Vaticanus into the city itself. Do you mean Anthemius's troops are abandoning the Vaticanus as well?"

"So it seems." The scout looked around him at the abandoned fortifications and rubble that had so recently been occupied by the imperial troops. "Why would they do that, sir? They had a good strong position atop this ridge. Satan's own bitch couldn't have broken through their lines. Not easily, anyway."

Odoacer stared at the Milvian Bridge and then downstream as far as he could see, to the oxbow bend in the river. His mind was working furiously. What did the maps show at the head of the Pons Aelius, on the Vatican side? The Mausoleum—Hadrian's Mausoleum. He had heard of it— one of the great structures of Rome, a massive, thick tower higher than any other building in the vicinity, a fortress that could be held by only a few men against an entire army.

"What did you say?"

"I said, why would they have abandoned these walls here? We would have been hard-pressed—"

"Not as hard-pressed as we will be now. They've just pulled back behind the greatest wall of all—four hundred feet of river. With only two crossing points into the city, the Milvius and the Aelius."

"But they've just given us the hills of the Janiculum and the Vaticanus," the scout argued, "with all the suburbs. That's worth something, if only for the plunder. If only for the food!" He looked furtively at the half-ruined houses, and his hands gripped the scaffolding so tight his knuckles turned white. "It's been a week since I've eaten anything but biscuit."

Odoacer nodded. He knew the minute he turned away the man would be racing back to his company, calling for his comrades to help him forage through the homes and warehouses of the abandoned suburbs.

"Don't bother," he said.

"Don't bother what?" the scout asked guiltily.

"Looting. There's nothing left."

"How . . . ?"

"This was a planned withdrawal. The Romans have already taken every scrap of food they could find this side of the Tiber before they retreated. And they can still receive supplies from the south, from the port of Ostia. The city will be able to hold out for months, if not years."

"And we're stuck with biscuit, and living in half-rotted tents."

"Well, at least your luck has improved there. They may have taken all the food, but they didn't burn all the buildings. The men will be able to sleep in houses tonight, rather than in the open air."

The scout began sulkily climbing down the scaffolding.

"I'd take a good hock of mutton any day, over a dry floor to sleep on."

Odoacer climbed down the shaky structure after him.

"You take what you can get, soldier. Be thankful you are not one of the refugees."

The scout leaped the last few feet to the ground and glared up.

"I was a refugee," he replied. "I know how it feels to be herded by Romans."

"As do I," Odoacer said as he, too, jumped to the ground. "And Orestes cracks a harsh whip. Either he will be dead, or I will, before I will live those days again."

Ricimer slouched in a chair in the spare apartments of the bishop of Rome, adjacent to the great Basilica of St. Peter at the summit of the Vatican hill. His eyes were deep-set and weary. As Odoacer looked at him, he sensed that Ricimer had aged ten years in the past few days of the siege, though nevertheless there was a trace of a smile on his lips.

"You are feeling better?" Odoacer asked as he dropped wearily onto a wooden bench across the room from his commander. He wondered idly whether he himself looked as bad as he felt, and if he did, why Ricimer didn't send him to the medical tent for a rest. His body complained as though he had not eaten in two weeks, or slept in three—or was it the other way around?—and what was most irritating was to hear the sounds of carousing that wafted from the city, just across the river, and to smell the odors of cooking, and the smoke of the fires, though he knew Rome was not altogether on a good footing—spies had also brought word of extreme hardship, of disease and starvation running rampant, even of cases of cannibalism, though what was true, and what was mere rumor, and what was rumor invented by Romans specifically for the purpose of demoralizing the attackers, was impossible to determine.

"You are feeling better?" he asked again. "The doctors have given you a cure?"

"The pain comes and goes," Ricimer said grimly. "Stones, they tell me—in the kidney, or the bladder, or some such organ. A rich man's ailment, like gout. Feels like a spearhead broken off in my back, and now I'm pissing it out."

Odoacer frowned.

"Stones? Is that possible?"

"Very possible, I assure you. I'll set one for you in a commander's ring, to remind you of me when I'm dead."

Odoacer winced.

"What do you need for a cure?"

"Gravel root, parsley—the doctors mix it with milk. Vile, but they say it helps. And fasting, of course . . ."

Odoacer shrugged. "Milk is difficult to find, but fasting—that's the one thing we are not short of in this army."

"How are the men's spirits?"

"Good, considering. They are warm and dry, most of them sleeping on the floors of churches, with the officers lodged in private homes. I have been drilling the troops every day, and we have erected artillery along the entire right bank of the Tiber between the two bridges. At night we lob fireballs into the city's river quarters. By now, most of the buildings along the left bank have been abandoned or burned. It keeps the populace on edge, and forces them away from the river and toward the city center, which increases their hardship."

"You have accomplished a great deal." Ricimer winced as

another wave of pain gripped him. Odoacer paused for a moment to observe him, then continued with his report.

"Not enough."

"What do we lack?"

"You know what we lack. The enemy still controls both key bridges over the Tiber, and especially the Mausoleum on our side of the Pons Aelius. There is apparently a spacious garden on the top of that tower, where the enemy has erected a number of artillery weapons—wolves, ballistae. The one time we attempted to storm it, they dropped building stones on our men. Killed or wounded fifty. The fortress is impregnable."

"Can we surround them and starve them?"

"That tower may hold years of supplies. And it is connected to the head of the bridge, the Pons Aelius, so the defenders can be supplied from the city. As long as Rome eats, the tower eats."

"And is Rome eating?"

"We have not been able to seal all routes into the city. Some shipments still arrive from Ostia. The suffering in the city is great, we hear, but not fatal."

"And our men?"

"That is another question. We have requisitioned all supplies and food within a fifty-mile radius. Beyond that, the populace has hidden their stores, and we cannot divert enough men to attack stubborn towns without weakening the siege here."

Odoacer fell silent. Ricimer waited expectantly for a moment, then wearily stood and faced him.

"Is that all?" Ricimer said.

"Perhaps I have not made myself clear, sir. We are stymied in our advance, blocked by the Tiber and the two bridges. The men are exhausted, and we hear reports of a hostile force marching against us from Gaul in support of the emperor. Worst of all—"

"Worst of all is the food problem. We are starving. Correct?"

"Yes. Yet the city continues to eat. Count Ricimer, we cannot hold out much longer."

"The food problem, my friend, I have resolved, through a visit I received this morning."

Odoacer looked at him skeptically. "A visit? You mean from Olybrius?"

"You know of him?"

"Bah. He arrived from Ravenna yesterday, and my men escorted him down from the Via Salaria. Nothing but a disgraced old Roman senator. He has no control over food supplies."

The corner of Ricimer's mouth turned up in a hint of a smile.

"You are a stranger to Roman politics, and I would not expect you to know the full story."

"And what might that be?"

"That he is married to Placidia, the daughter of the former emperor Valentinian . . ."

"Ah, well," said Odoacer dismissively. "That would make him a reasonable heir to the throne, which I know you've been seeking. After Anthemius is overthrown, the people will need someone they can rally behind."

Ricimer nodded.

"Very perceptive. We will have our troops acclaim him emperor tomorrow, as a rival to Anthemius, and we will send messages to the city to announce this to the urban cohorts and the people. We will also announce that Olybrius is prepared to pay a generous donative, *if* he is allowed to enter the city and assume the throne."

Odoacer stared at Ricimer a moment, then strode across the room and looked out the window.

"I'm not sure you understand the true situation."

"And you do? Pray, enlighten me."

Odoacer ignored the sarcasm in Ricimer's voice.

"There will be no difficulty convincing *our troops* to acclaim Senator Olybrius. They need someone to rally to as emperor."

"Correct. Go on."

"Yet getting the people of Rome to do so will be impossible. Conditions are bad in Rome, but not bad enough, even after three months of siege. Very few citizens are deserting to our lines, and no urban cohorts. Anthemius retains tight control, through Orestes, and the people will not flock to Olybrius's banner, even if he is a popular local politician. And despite the offer of a donative."

"Is that all?"

"Is it not enough?"

"You have not allowed me to finish telling you the full story."

"Pray tell me, then," Odoacer replied, mimicking Ricimer's own mocking tone earlier.

"More important than Placidia's parentage is her family. Placidia, you see, was once held captive by Gaiseric the Vandal himself, and indeed the old bastard still holds her sister, Eudoxia, whom I believe he has gifted to his son, along with the child she bore him. When Senator Olybrius fell out with Anthemius a few years ago, Gaiseric returned Placidia to him simply to tweak the emperor's nose. Now Olybrius, if he is made emperor, has offered to call on the Vandal's aid as a kind of family favor."

Odoacer's eyes opened wide. "Senator Olybrius is Gaiseric's brother-in-law?"

Ricimer thought about this for a moment. "Well, yes, an in-law of sorts."

"So by acclaiming Olybrius emperor, we are actually calling upon an alliance with . . ."

Ricimer nodded.

"Assemble the troops for this afternoon. No need to delay for tomorrow. Find a site on the riverbank, within earshot of the city, and out of ballista range of that damned Mausoleum. The acclamation will be heard far and wide, and Olybrius has already brought enough gold in his traveling chest for a down payment on the donative."

Odoacer turned to go, but as he reached the door another thought occurred to him.

"The senator might as well delay distributing the funds. There is nothing to buy in the camp in any case. The men will merely gamble it away, and cause dissension in the ranks."

"Nothing to buy?" Ricimer replied. "That reminds me. Announce to the troops a celebration in four days' time."

"A celebration?" Odoacer looked startled. "Is this wise?"

"More than wise, it is necessary. And Odoacer . . ."

Odoacer turned back, puzzled, to see the count's face twisted in pain.

"Reserve some milk for me."

"The Vandals have *what*?!" Anthemius repeated, stunned.

"They have captured the port of Ostia," Orestes replied, maintaining his calm with great effort, even as his body fairly trembled with rage. "Our naval squadron from the Misemum Fleet, which had been guarding it, has been destroyed."

"Have you no control over Gaiseric?!" Anthemius exclaimed. "Is the man a Hercules, or a Mithridates? Is there not a soldier in Rome who can stand up to a ninety-year-old Vandal scavenger?"

"I would remind you, Augustus, that I had no authority over the fleet—"

"Your authority was the defense of Rome! Clearly that included its only source of provisioning by sea. And that meant commanding the fleet! Are you a traitor, or merely an idiot?!"

Orestes' eyes narrowed in fury.

"You pathetic invalid!" he snarled. "You lie here in your filthy, darkened room, staring at your paintings and gobbling fruit brought in on silver platters by my soldiers, while your city's streets fill with trash and your people starve."

"And whose fault is *that*, General? Whose fault is it that Rome's urban cohorts cower behind walls, that the river quarters have been burnt to ashes, that the bishop of Rome is encamped in my very atrium because a troop of rebel auxiliaries have occupied his basilica at the Vatican? *I* did not lose this siege! I placed my trust in my generals, who assured me of their competence—"

"I have already informed you, the Gallic legions are on

the march in our support. My scouts inform me they are now traversing the Alps. Three weeks only, and they will be arriving—"

"*Three weeks! We have been under siege for three months*! Look out the window, at the river—*look*!"

The emperor ripped away the heavy woolen drapes covering the window of the tower, and light flooded the room. Orestes blinked, and the emperor shrank back like an owl, but immediately recovered and lunged toward the window.

"*Look at the river!*" he screamed. "Corpses! Have you ever seen the Tiber in such a state? Corpses!"

Orestes knew full well what he would see. The river was littered with corpses. In a city the size of Rome, hundreds die each day of normal causes, but in times of siege, with the accompanying disease and starvation, the death figures double and treble, especially among the very old and the very young. And with the city's shrinking perimeter and crowded conditions, there was no place to dispose of the bodies. The time-honored expedient of allowing them to float to Ostia for burial no longer held; their sheer quantities meant that cadavers washed up against the city walls and piers, spinning lazily in eddies, clogging at the breakwater of the Tiberina, the boat-shaped island in the middle of the river, as if seeking comrades in their fate, raising a horrific stench and contributing even further to the people's fear. Some weeks ago, Orestes had assigned a company of men on barges to fish the swollen corpses from the waters, but the job had become increasingly burdensome and demoralizing, and men could no longer be diverted from patrolling the walls. In recent days, cadavers had accumulated beyond all their efforts to prevent it, at some points nearly choking the river with their volume, and the people with their stench.

"*Look at it!*" the emperor shouted, his voice becoming increasingly shrill. "Whose side are you killing, general?! I'll have you arrested for treachery! I'll have you arrested! Guards! Guards!"

Orestes had had enough. Though the guards outside were under his own command, it would not do for them to suspect the emperor's support of him was failing. As Anthemius screamed in his hoarse old man's voice, Orestes stepped up calmly and placed his hand on the emperor's neck, so thin and bony his fingers nearly encircled it. The voice and breath were immediately cut off, and the emperor's eyes bulged in shock, his mouth still open and lips moving as if he were continuing to scream or gasp for breath. Half dragging and half carrying him across the room, Orestes deposited him on the couch where he habitually sat in meditative silence. The old man curled his body in a fetal position, panting and groaning, clutching his neck, while Orestes stepped to the window and flung the drapes back across the opening, again submerging the room in darkness. *Damn this crazy old man*, he thought. *Damn Odoacer, who is the cause of all these troubles*. Taking a last glance around, he strode to the door and stepped out.

Sliding the lock-bolt in the door behind him, he glanced around, and found the guards clustered nearby, staring at him wide-eyed.

"We thought we heard something, General," one of them said. "We thought we heard the emperor call out . . ."

"Thank you for your concern, gentlemen," Orestes said calmly. "The emperor is a very sick man, *very* sick, and he was shouting in pain and hallucination. You"—he pointed at the oldest guard, the one who looked most reliable—"go and seek the palace physician. Inform him that the emperor is feverish again, and requires a sedative."

The man saluted and began to turn, but Orestes stopped him.

"Soldier," he said. "Henceforth all of you will be assigned to the wall. We have no men to spare to guard the emperor. Therefore, inform the physician *he* is to remain with the emperor, and that the sedative is to be a strong one. Very strong. I do not wish the emperor to be troubled with news from outside until the physician and I have jointly determined he is well enough to hear it. Now go."

The soldier walked down a corridor toward the servants' quarters, where the palace physician stayed, while Orestes set out in the opposite direction, leaving the guards staring after him open-mouthed, amid complete silence from behind the doors to the emperor's chamber.

II

"We have been waiting for a morning such as this for weeks," Ricimer said, still reclining on his bench in the bishop's apartments, gazing out the window into the pre-dawn darkness. His face was wan and his eyes hollow, but a spark of excitement gleamed from them in the dim light.

"Yes, my lord," Odoacer concurred, leaning out the window and peering down the side of the Vatican hill.

Nearby, in the faint light of the stars and the cold quarter moon, all was clear and sparkling, all as visible as a charcoal sketch on white parchment. In the distance, however, where the elevation dropped to the river, conditions were different. At the base of the hill, the lower reaches of the suburbs were swathed in a thick layer of mist, hanging low and dense the entire length of the Tiber for as far as the eye could see in both directions, marking the river as a long, woolly strip of cloud drifting between the city's hills. The mist hung thickly over the boardwalks and swampy areas of the right bank, obscuring even the view of the braziers Odoacer had ordered burning every fifty paces along the river's edge, to brighten the dismal nights passed by the guards patrolling the riverbank, and allow them to warm their hands during their cold shifts. Tiberina Island to the south, and the Aelian Bridge just below, which ordinarily were perfectly visible from the windows of the bishop's house high on the Vatican hill, were also completely enveloped in the dense fog. Only the great circular tower, the Mausoleum, was visible to mark the crossing point. Its lower floors were buried in the cloud, but its upper stories rose from the mist like a boulder from the snows of the Alps, and Odoacer could see Orestes' soldiers patrolling its rooftop terrace as clearly as if it were daylight, nervously fingering the winches on their ballistae, looking for signs of danger below.

"Conditions such as this do not happen every day," Odoacer mused again. "I will order the men awakened quietly, without bugles, and to eat a full breakfast. Cold meat, eggs, biscuit, everything they can find."

Ricimer looked at him with impatience.

"Breakfast? It is a luxury we cannot afford. The Vandals have set up a supply route, it is true, but there is still little food to be spared. And by the time the men have eaten, the conditions may have changed. No, we must do it now."

"You placed me in command of the attack, and this will be my first order. We need full bellies. Not only will we surprise the enemy, but we will surprise them on empty stomachs. The advantage will not be apparent at first—but if a battle takes more than two hours, it is the army that ate breakfast that wins."

"Learned that from Attila, did you?" Ricimer grumbled.

"If there is anything I learned as a Hun it was that."

"And as a Hun, did you not learn to negotiate with other barbarians? You cannot convince the Vandals to fight alongside us?"

Odoacer faced his commander squarely.

"Gaiseric is adamant. He insists that the city holds nothing of interest that his troops did not plunder the first time, and he will not risk them. He was happy to break the Roman fleet at Ostia as a favor to Olybrius, and to send us supplies, but he will go no further. We are on our own."

"Then be quick about it. And tell the steward to throw out this damned milk."

"It doesn't agree with you? The physician ordered—"

"To hell with the physician," Ricimer barked. Throwing aside the coverlet he stood and staggered over to the window, seizing an army canteen lying on a table as he made his way past. Odoacer stood aside and let him hobble up to the sill, where he placed his hands on the edge and leaned out, looking from side to side, up and down the river as far as he could see.

"Go!" Ricimer ordered. "And remember—Anthemius is to be taken alive, and brought to me."

"I remember."

"And tell the troops . . ."

He raised the canteen to his mouth and swilled the contents, relishing the heavily cut soldier's wine as it flowed down his throat, a few drops dribbling out the side of his mouth and hanging in the weeks-old beard like drops of blood. At length he set the canteen down with a thud onto the thick window ledge and smiled, then grimaced and shuddered as his left hand clutched at his belly.

"Tell the troops . . . I drink to their success!"

With a loud *CRACK!* and a muffled whoosh, a dozen onagers loosed their payloads toward the middle of the Milvian Bridge, as best as the artillerymen could guess its location under the layer of fog blanketing the river and swirling serenely over the walls on either bank. The fiery missiles— barrels of naphtha—tore through the air, and the clatter of their impact on solid stone, followed by the bright flash of orange flames that exploded through the fog cover, showed that at least some of the shots had found their mark. At Onulf's measured orders, the onager-men adjusted the positions of their weapons, which had been knocked askew in the kickback, cranked down the long insectlike arms, and loaded new barrels into the slings. Working mechanically, every muscle focused solely on the task at hand, ignoring the distant screams of pain wafting through the fog from their invisible targets, the men rocked the machinery into place, cranked the arms, and loaded; and again, rocked, cranked, and loaded.

The rhythm broke only when each arm had been winched fully down, when aim had been adjusted, and firing was imminent. Then, with an almost synchronized movement, twelve torchbearers stepped from the pre-dawn darkness, touched flames to their payloads, and waited a measured count for the fire to spread around the entire perimeter of the tar-coated naphtha barrels. Not too little, lest the flames be extinguished in the missile's flight through the moisture-laden air, nor yet too much, lest the thin wooden staves of the barrels' sides—planed far thinner than a normal wine or oil barrel—be burnt through, spilling the fiery contents over the sling of the launching device and disabling the entire weapon. After waiting the proper count, the package would be fiercely blazing, and its launch through the air would fan the fire's ferocity. Upon impact, the barrel would burst, spattering the contents, and covering men, animals, and structures in the vicinity with inextinguishable droplets: burning beads of molten fire that clung to skin and hair and could not be put out or wiped away until it had cooled and hardened, causing unutterable suffering among its victims.

As the artillerymen settled into their task, Onulf wheeled his horse and raced downriver a short distance, where he had deployed three companies of archers on the right bank above the near foot of the bridge, at the edge of the drifting fog. At his command, the bowmen took aim through the cloud cover, along what they guessed to be the foot of the bridge, one hundred yards away, near the upper limit of their range. A thousand iron-tipped shafts hissed through the air, tearing through the fog yet leaving no trace behind, clattering into the stones and barricades, caroming with a ringing tone off solid iron helmets, yielding muffled thuds as the warheads bit into mailed armor, burrowing through iron links or biting into the oak-and-bronze layers of the shields.

The sounds were distinct and menacing, even from far up the hill on the right bank, for as the ancients knew, sound carries well over water, and even more efficiently through fog. Yet it was the arrows that made *no* sound that caused Onulf's archers to rejoice, and the Romans on the bridge to hunker lower behind their barricades. Those were the arrows that had landed in soft flesh, the ones that had slammed into an unprotected face, pinned an unlucky hand to a support post, or fallen from a high arc onto a man's instep, and through into the mud beneath. Within moments, the night air was rent by screams of pain, and the weeping of civilians caught in the cross fire between the attacking artillerymen; and fiery glows from burning missiles illuminated the darkness along the length of the bridge.

Across the Tiber, the Roman defenders soon overcame their initial surprise and deployed a stiff resistance, in the form of similarly equipped archers and artillery pieces. As the two sides stepped up the intensity of their firing into the fog, the bridge and its barriers at both ends became a maelstrom of flames and hissing arrows. The Roman commander on the bridge, determined to bar access across the river, ordered bugles to sound, and their frantic blaring rose above the screams of the dying, summoning the guards on the wall to the aid of the bridge defenders. Troops hastened from the eastern and southern perimeters of the city, where they had been patrolling against a feint or attack on those quarters, and the *vigiles,* the fire and police brigades, mobilized to lend additional assistance.

Rushing to the scene himself, Orestes was at first taken aback at the fierceness of the attack, though at the same time he was relieved: such an assault could only mean the end of the long siege. It was now, he knew, that the battle—and his score with the Hun, Odoacer—would be decided. From what he could glean through the fog, the attackers were throwing all their forces at the Milvian Bridge, and like Constantine a century and a half earlier, were seeking a decisive victory at this spot. Orestes' mind raced. Odoacer, he imagined, would attempt to soften up the defenders with devastating fire and arrows, before pouring his army over the ancient structure and overwhelming the crippled defenses; and Orestes knew his men would then be the only barrier against the ultimate destruction of the city. He smiled to himself; for having guessed his enemy's plan, this was where he, Orestes, would make his own stand, where his own name would be emblazoned among the roll calls of history's giants. This was where he would save Rome from the brutality and barbarism of this rebel horde. Orestes turned and issued rapid orders to send heralds into the streets, to mobilize every able-bodied man in the city, to hasten to the site of the impending battle, to defend Rome from destruction. So long as he lived, Odoacer the Hun would not set foot in the city. The Milvian Bridge was where Orestes would join in fame with the great Constantine, one the defender, the other the attacker, and where he would earn immortality.

Yet on the west side of the Tiber, where the firestorm from the rebel onagers continued without respite, Odoacer stopped his horse and stood stone-still. Poised on the hillside just above the sharply delineated fog line, he observed the artillery crews as they fired round after flaming round at the location of the bridge. Between volleys, he peered through the fog, listening carefully over the oaths and grunts of the onager-men as they struggled with their ungainly weapons. And over the clamor of the artillery, he could hear just what he hoped to from the other side of the river: the frantic call of bugles, the shouts of men deploying their defenses, the clatter of horses, and finally, the tramp of feet as the urban cohorts that had been frantically summoned from other quarters of the city began to arrive. And then he, too, smiled, knowing the measures Orestes was taking to concentrate his forces—for this was not where Odoacer intended to make *his* stand.

He nodded to a tribune standing nearby, in command of a cohort of new recruits assembled at this spot the night before.

"Now," Odoacer said, and the tribune leaped onto his horse.

"To the bridge!" the officer cried, and with a roar, the unit of greenhorns fell into position and trotted off toward the near base of the Milvian Bridge. In a moment they had disappeared into the fog, leaving no trace of their presence but for the sound of their hobnailed sandals thumping out the tattoo of five hundred men marching to their goal. Again, Odoacer paused to listen, counting silently to himself, picturing in his mind the cobbled street that descended to the river, envisioning every intersection and building they would encounter before arriving at the barriers barring access to the bridge. In his imagination he ticked off the streets they would cross, the alleyways they would pass, until the road narrowed in its approach, and the first arrows began to fly from the defending archers—arrows, Odoacer knew, that would be shot in panic into the gloomy fog, with only a blind chance of injuring his men. *There*, he said in his mind as he imagined the scene, *there are the forward defenders, just where we had spied their positions from the surrounding buildings yesterday. They look strong, but they are few—no great challenge, nor were they meant to be; they are deployed there merely to delay us, if only for a few moments, to allow the main body of defenders time to assemble on the bridge and beyond, to lure us into a trap from which we will not be able to extricate ourselves. There—the arrows are starting to fly, and my troops will react—now!*

And just as he had planned, a clamor floated up from the point in the fog he knew his troops had reached. It was a roar of a mere five hundred voices, but so breathtakingly loud and deliberate they sounded like five thousand, accompanied by the rumble of marching and running feet, again so loud they sounded as if another five thousand troops were coming to the bridge's attack. In the distance, he could hear the urban cohorts' reaction.

"More troops!" He faintly heard the enemy's orders, floating back to him across the river and through the fog. "More troops—a legion attacking the bridge! Send up the reserves on the walls! More troops!"

Odoacer nodded in satisfaction. The ruse was working, the green soldiers were stopping just short of the danger point, feigning just enough of an attack to send the enemy's outposts retreating in panic, and not pursuing them, but rather stopping—stopping short, right there in the street, in the dense fog, unseen by enemy and friends alike, and raising the greatest ruckus of which they were capable: clanging shields on javelin shafts, stomping loudly on the flagstones, shouting commands and soldiers' oaths to one another, creating the noise and chaos of an entire legion in the fog and darkness.

Having confirmed the effect, he wheeled his horse and raced down the river road, nearly blind in the mist that enveloped the river promenade, praying his horse would be sure-footed on the deeply rutted flagstones; but praying, most of all, to arrive in time at the position where he had deployed the bulk of his troops—just short of the Pons Aelius, that wide three-arched bridge connecting the Vaticanus with the heart of Rome itself, overshadowed by the glowering circular tower of Hadrian's Mausoleum.

Arriving at the first lines of the deployment, he reined in his horse. Around him, the mist remained thick as mud, though the air would soon begin to lighten and gray as the pallid sun rose on his left, beyond the city. He knew there was little time—the fog cover would dissipate within an hour, and then the guards in the tower above, already alarmed by the shouting and commotion they could hear from upriver at the Milvian, would be able to see what was taking place directly below them, at the base of the Mausoleum, where Odoacer's troops had gathered silently under cover of the dark and mist. Even now, the defenders atop the massive circular building suspected a ruse—missiles and bricks lobbed from the heights above crashed to the ground among the troops, startling men and horses alike and occasionally dropping a man to the cobbles, crushed by a building stone or pierced vertically by the acute angle of a blindly shot arrow; nevertheless, thus far all had remained nearly silent, and neither the defenders in the tower, nor those still remaining on the Aelian Bridge and beyond, could have any idea of what faced them in the mist—the ten thousand veteran troops preparing to storm the bridge.

By silent gestures, Odoacer sought out Gundobar, the Burgundian commander, Ricimer's nephew, whom he had never seen in action but whom Ricimer had assured him was the equal of a Roman-bred general. He found him astride his horse, peering anxiously east, where the sky was becoming visibly light. Odoacer observed him for a moment, gauging the man's presence, his state of mind. For a German he was small—short and wiry, with the long, dangling mustaches typical of men of his tribe, but wearing a full complement of a Roman general's chain mail. Most of the German auxiliaries Gundobar had brought also wore Roman kit, of greater or lesser completeness. Odoacer knew that these troops, having been trained under Ricimer's command, would lack for nothing in bravery or skill.

Gundobar conferred quietly with a pair of foot officers and then, as if sensing he was observed, turned in his saddle and looked hard at Odoacer for a moment before recognizing him. One of his mustaches twitched in faint acknowledgment, and the beads of water that had formed in it from the surrounding mist trickled onto his chest.

"Onulf has begun the diversion?" Gundobar whispered impatiently.

"He has," Odoacer confirmed. "You can hear the commotion at the Milvian. We will give Orestes a moment longer to sound the alarm. He is pulling troops there from all over the city."

"We cannot wait any longer," Gundobar said, jerking his head toward the whitening sky and sending another tiny shower of droplets onto the sodden tunic over his chest mail. "The tower guards above will soon see our deployment."

"Do not forget your orders. Orestes is to be taken alive. I will deal with him personally. The emperor, too, for Count Ricimer has a score with him. But above all, Orestes."

"I know. The troops have been instructed. But remember—anything can happen in battle."

Odoacer glared at him. "Orestes is to be taken alive— without fail! You have arrayed all the men? Two full legions?"

Gundobar shrugged. "I have given *orders* to array them, but in this soup, who can tell? I trust my officers. As you must trust yours."

"We discussed this last night. Array is all-important. The men must storm the bridge in a narrow front. The crossing is only thirty feet wide. If they attack it like a mob, they will bottleneck and crush each other, and the defenders will cut them down like slaves in a galley. We have only one chance at this, Gundobar. It must be done right the first time."

"We have drilled it. We set up a mock bridge on the far side of the Vaticanus and stormed it."

"I know."

"Then you must trust the men to know what to do."

"That is what I hope," replied Odoacer. "But I cannot see it to confirm it."

"The fog—you cannot have it both ways. It blinds the enemy, it blinds us as well."

Odoacer considered this for a moment in silence.

"In the end, we officers are of little use, no?"

Gundobar shrugged again.

"You trust the men or you don't, and they will know if you don't. Trust them, and let them know you trust them."

"I don't send into battle men I don't trust."

"Then let's get on with it."

Odoacer nodded.

"It is in our hands now."

Gundobar shook his head and gestured toward the troops. "No. It is in theirs."

From the *triclinium,* where he lived now day and night, Anthemius pulled back the heavy woolen tapestry covering the window and peered into the darkness. His light sleep had been interrupted by the sounds of fighting north of the city—bugle commands, shouts of men. They were sounds to which he should, by now, have been accustomed, for every night the rebels deployed some such attack, somewhere along the extensive lines. Prodding, seeking—the emperor knew they were constantly searching the defensive lines for a weakness, looking for a lapse of attention, a gap in the wall through which they might storm. It exhausted him—he had not had a solid nights' sleep in months—and it kept the entire city on edge. How could Rome rest, knowing that an invading army was encamped just across the river, occupying what had formerly been its own wealthy suburbs?

Yet Anthemius was not dismayed, for the one benefit of the enemy's constant probing was that it kept his urban cohorts alert and disciplined. There was no time for the politics and machinations that so seemed to obsess their officers during times of peace; the men had no occasion to become bored, to lower their guard. Though the mere width of a river separated Rome from destruction, never did Anthemius feel more secure than he had during the months of the siege—for never had his own troops been in such a heightened state of preparedness.

Yet this night was different. He could sense it.

The sounds of distant fighting were the same, as was the tumult of men racing through the streets to converge on the point of the enemy attack. The moon shone weakly, casting a narrow, stingy light. Only the thin, black outline of its bulk was visible, the barest suggestion that this horned sliver would once again, in two weeks' time, return to its glowing, sensual roundness.

What was it that had awakened him? Why did he tremble merely at pulling aside the draperies to peer out the window overlooking the peaceful Tiber?

The Tiber . . . where *was* the Tiber? He craned his head farther, to see past the thick windowsill. There, below, were the familiar streets and forums on which he had gazed daily for the past months. Rubbing his eyes he turned back into the room and looked about him. By the light of the dim candle he spied the familiar painted illusions on the walls, Horace's mischievous grin, the flexing of Hercules' vast shoulders. All was intact, all was as it should be. He turned back to the window. The streets, the buildings, the massive walls of the nearby Circus Maximus rising on its arcades just below his tower, dominating all within the casting of its shadow. Squinting into the blackness, he cast his mind's eye farther to the north, to the oxbow bend of the river, where he knew stood the ancient and lovely Aelian Bridge, the only crossing into the city center. He pictured the bridge in his imagination, meditating on the gentle slope it employed to traverse the width of the river over the three arches comprising its span. Three, he knew there were three, for many times in the past he had stood on the walls overlooking the bridge, marveling at their stolid Roman symmetry, at their timeless classical proportions, even if, this time, he could scarcely even see the river . . .

Could not see?! He leaned out further, straining to reach,

his toes lifting from the delicate mosaic of the floor as he balanced his chest on the broad sill. Struggling, he willed himself to focus his mind, to filter out the competing stimuli, the sounds of distant battle, the men and horses racing through the street below him, the flickering lights of thousands of tiny lanterns, as men—soldiers, onlookers, scoffers, and looters—streamed through the streets like swarms of fireflies blown in currents by the gusting wind, all racing to the city's northern quarters to the impending battle. Carefully, he slowed his breathing, ground his knuckles into his ears to stanch the noise, and peered at the river . . . where the river was . . . where the river *should be* . . . nothing. It was gone. No water could be seen. He stopped to think. The Milvian Bridge, a good two miles to the north, was the source of the commotion, from what he could understand of the chaotic shouts and commands that drifted to him from the streets below. It was to there that all the troops were hastening, and if he listened carefully, he could even make out the faint sounds of the distant battle, carried to his ears on the still night air—the screams of horses, the crashing of missiles on stone. And yet the Aelian Bridge, which was much closer to his window than the Milvian, and far more vulnerable, was attracting no notice at all—no sounds of battle, no orders for reinforcements. And suddenly he knew, knew with more certainty than his own name, what Odoacer was doing. He pushed away from the window and stood trembling, staring wildly about, until his breathing calmed enough for him gain his voice.

"Fog!" he screamed. "Fog over the river! Orestes! It's an ambush! Guards . . . !"

Racing to the far end of the room he seized the handle of the stout oaken door and attempted to fling it open, yet produced only a grunt of pain as he nearly pulled his shoulders from their sockets. The door did not budge.

"Orestes!" he screamed again, jerking madly on the door handle until he was panting and hoarse. Recognizing that the door was impassably barred from the outside, he reasoned that a terrible mistake had been made. Raising his fist, he pounded at the door with all his strength, yet his feeble efforts on the thick wood sounded pitiful even to him, and within a moment he was kneeling in despair against the walls, shoulders trembling in frustration as he sucked on his bleeding knuckles. Suddenly an idea came to his head—the benches! The heavy, wooden dining benches!

"Guards!" he called out again, yet his voice was now so weakened that he knew they would be unable to hear him. Seizing hold of a bench, he dragged it to the door, tipped it onto its end, and adjusted its position so the hard ball on the foot, held by a carved animal claw, was just at the same height as the upper hinge. With a grunt, he rocked the bench back and then pushed it, hard, onto the hinge. The impact of metal on metal produced a satisfying clang, much louder than his feeble shouts. He inspected the hinge. Slightly bent, as if its nails had been knocked askew within the doorframe. He again lifted the bench and slammed it onto the hinge. Again it moved, and this time a gap appeared between door and frame, as the heavy wooden boards sagged. Again and again he pounded until finally, with a creak of straining wood and failing metal, the hinge pulled free and the door leaned in, supported awkwardly by the lower hinge alone and whatever was barring it shut.

Slipping his bloodied hands into the crack, he pulled, and the door budged. The bar across it must not have been strong—the room was not designed as a stronghold, the bar was merely a later addition, installed at Orestes' orders. Another tug, and the door came free, falling inward with a resounding bang, uprooted hinges still hanging forlornly from the jamb.

Anthemius felt a surge of strength and anger. "Guards!" he called, his voice stronger. "Guards!" He stepped over the door and into the corridor. He was surprised to see no one there, nor even a light—all the torches had been removed, and a single oil lamp in a corner was nearly guttered out. He leaned against the damaged doorframe and gazed into the dark.

"Guards!" he called one more time, and then lifting his

hands to his neck, he seized the intricately embroidered but filthy silk dressing gown he wore. In a spasm of frustration he tore it, reveling in the satisfying whine of the ripping fabric and the rush of cold air on his body as he rent the garment in short, desperate bursts from neck to feet.

"The fog!" he cried. "Ambush!" But there was no one to hear, and only he was aware of the enemy's plan. Stepping out of the ruined gown he glided forward, sensing the smooth stone floor beneath his bare feet. Eyes straight ahead into the darkness, hands outstretched to prevent collision with a wall or column, he edged forward, step by step, inadvertently kicking the tiny lamp beneath his toes, though the oil in the reservoir was so depleted the flame did not spread, but merely died out.

"Guards!" he sobbed, but there was no one to hear, and the emperor of Rome stumbled through the corridor, naked and blind, summoning his legions.

III

By plan, deep-barreled Gallic drums were used to signal the attack, rather than military bugles whose high, brassy pitch would have carried more easily over the river and alerted the defenders more quickly. As the drums sprang to life, their low throbbing was perceived by the waiting troops as a visceral thudding in their bellies. At the deep pulse, the attack line formed up, centuries of ten men deep and eight abreast, the width of the Aelian Bridge. The first unit was followed by a squadron of a dozen horsemen, deployed in ranks of four, then another unit of foot soldiers and accompanying cavalry, fifty centuries in all, a legion, arrayed in a long line that snaked through the fog along the bank of the river. It was the first phalanx in which the men had fought, perhaps the first one formed since this bloody formation had fallen out of favor centuries before. It was a human battering ram; yet far from terrifying the troops who served at its front, in its lethal vanguard, it exhilarated them, and they vied for the honor of being the first across the bridge. Of the eight men in the leading line, four were centurions, and a dozen others of that rank followed closely behind. If any man was to set an example in the fearsome deployment, no centurion in the army would admit to trailing in the rear.

The lead unit marched forward, warily following the broad avenue that passed through the gardens surrounding the circular mausoleum, its massive bronze doors closed and barricaded from the inside. Utter silence prevailed from its upper windows and rooftop, which disappeared above them in the fog, but which the troops knew were manned by a large company of defenders. Keeping step with the rapid yet measured cadence of the Gallic drums, they compressed their ranks until their shoulders nearly touched, and then, feeling a sudden rush of chill air as they ascended the short incline where the street narrowed, they stepped onto the bridge, and into the thickest part of the fog. Visibility dropped so low a man could barely discern the backs of the troopers two ranks ahead of him. The leading ranks took their first dozen steps on the bridge in eerie silence, without a hint of opposition from any defenders, and for a moment, hope rose that the distraction of the decoy attack upstream at the Milvian had been so successful as to draw all the enemy's strength away from the Aelian, that they might pass unimpeded over the bridge and into the city.

Without warning, without so much as an officer's distant command, the still air was rent by a sharp hissing sound, as if the phalanx had stumbled into a nest of vipers. The soupy fog was cut by a barrage of arrows from archers at the head of the bridge, unseen and unheard. The impact of the missiles, unaccompanied by any orders to fire, caused the lead marchers to slow their pace, some dropping to one knee behind the shelter of their rectangular shields, as they had been trained to do for so many years, and as they had trained their men to do, drilling the maneuver so many times it had become automatic, a reflex.

Yet it was not a reflex compatible with a phalanx. Behind the lead marchers, the second and third rankers continued to advance, shield bosses pushing into the backs of the men in front of them. At the pressure from behind, the leaders stumbled back to their feet, shields bristling with arrows, and more missiles flew past in an ominous, buzzing cloud. A pair of men in the center sustained leg wounds, fell, and were trampled by the soldiers behind, who were unable to pause or veer from their predestined path, pressured by the ranks that followed them in turn. Another two lead marchers were struck: one, skewered in the throat, staggered and then pitched silently forward onto his face; the other, pierced through the sword arm and realizing he could not fight, lurched to the stone balustrade at the side of the bridge, rolled over the barrier, and dropped into the water. In the brief instant when he lifted his shield, exposing himself to the lethal cloud of arrows, his body was pierced a half-dozen times, and though his momentum carried him over the side, he was dead before he hit the river.

The attackers continued stubbornly onward, into the very maw of the defenders' barrage. Odoacer, sitting his horse at the rear of the first century and himself feeling the pressure of the archers as arrows skittered off his helmet and sank into his shield, realized the difficulty, and that his men would have only seconds to overcome the hail of arrows, or be overcome themselves. No longer was there need for silence or surprise. Turning in his saddle, he bellowed back into the fog to his corps of waiting officers.

"Buglers! Sound the charge!"

As the shrill notes pierced the darkness and hit the ears of the marching soldiers, some paused and turned in surprise. The line of men advancing on the bridge, already visibly wavering, seemed to hesitate further, and Odoacer sensed the forward progress of his own horse slow. Turning forward, he lifted his voice and bellowed into the gloom.

"Charge the bridge! Forward to victory!"

The men ahead of him picked up the pace, but so, too, did the volume of arrows increase. Leaping off his mount, Odoacer's feet slipped in a stream of blood trickling down the slope of the bridge, and he dropped briefly to one knee. Immediately regaining his balance, he slapped his horse's haunches to drive it away, then began shouldering his way through the troops stalled ahead of him.

"Forward, men!" he roared. "Run! Run!"

The pace increased, and as Odoacer pushed forward he tripped again, this time over a body lying on the paving stones at his feet. Ignoring the obstacle, he continued forcing his way through, stepping over increasing numbers of arrow-riddled corpses until he realized he was no longer stepping on flagstones at all, but rather on a solid, sodden carpet of flesh. This could not happen—after advancing so far in their quest, they could not be defeated at this point, by a mere bridge.

"Run, *run!*" Odoacer bellowed again.

Only by advancing into the very barrage of arrows, running roughshod over the enemy archers and into the mass of footmen he knew would be deployed behind them, did his troops stand any chance of taking the bridge. Those archers, too, would be hampered by the narrow space—no more than ten or a dozen could squat in a row at the far base of the bridge, a dozen more standing above them, perhaps a third dozen firing from risers beyond that. Thirty, forty archers, no more—yet if skilled, each could fire continuously, an arrow every two breaths, into his attacking troops, who could field a front of only eight men—it was formidable odds, he knew, but surely the enemy bowmen would be tiring as much as his own troops, their aim blind in the fog, their stamina flagging, their fear increasing . . .

Their fear! He could not see the defenders, but neither could they see him. In the fog, they could not know who was attacking, how many men were advancing toward them, whether their deadly barrage of arrows was having any effect. The enemy knew only that something was coming, from the thud of the drums and the blare of the trumpets. But what exactly? A hundred men? Five hundred? Five legions? Was this the main attack, or a diversion from the attack occurring up-river at the Milvian, which for all they knew might entail an even larger force? Their fear must be increasing, even more than his own men's. Their fear must be exploited . . .

Suddenly, behind him Odoacer heard a loud crash, then several more, like large objects toppling. He paused for an instant—should he continue pressing forward, rallying his troops into the artillery barrage? Another crash interrupted his thoughts, this time accompanied by bellows of rage and pain from men and horses. His mind raced—could it be an attack on his flanks, or on the rear of his troops? How could the enemy have maneuvered past him, given the paucity of crossing points over the Tiber, and in the thick night fog, no less? Yet as the cries of terror rose behind him, Odoacer knew this was something he could not ignore—he must turn back.

The men around him eyed him sidelong—aware of the terrific slaughter their comrades in the front were enduring, and now they themselves would soon be caught up in it. The number of arrow-ridden corpses on which they were treading increased, and then they found themselves not merely treading on them, but *climbing* them. Progress slowed and bodies began stacking before them, their own comrades forming an unwilling barricade. From left and right came the sounds of splashing in the waters, as injured soldiers leaped over the balustrade so as not to impede the charging troops behind them, and perhaps to save themselves from death by trampling. From the corner of his eye Odoacer could see even un-injured soldiers drop formation and stumble toward the side of the bridge, preparing to leap over even *before* they became injured. All the while they remained hunkered behind their shields, darting swift glances over the rims, straining to peer through the fog, to divine the source and distance of the murderous hail of arrows decimating their ranks, yet fearful of exposing their faces too long lest a missile find its way over the shield-top and into their eyes . . .

In rage and frustration, unable to advance forward through the faltering ranks of foot soldiers ahead of him, and knowing he must return to the rear to investigate the increasing chaos he could sense, Odoacer raised his voice in a wordless bellow, a throaty roar that seemed to echo off the surrounding stone, the street, the bridge walls, even the distant buildings somewhere far ahead in the fog. At the sound, the men around him physically jumped in surprise and then, as if prodded into action by an ox driver's goad, surged forward, again jamming their shields into the backs of the troops in front of them, fitting their shoulders and faces into the hollow inside, and pushing with their feet in the thick leather sandals, straining to gain purchase against the bloody surface beneath them, to grip with their soles and push forward, preventing retreat or sideways drifting by those before them.

At the same time, even before his own cry had died away, the men around him took up the challenge—and an identical bellow was raised by the troops nearby, and then by the troops beyond them, and even further beyond, forward and back, until the deafening roar filled the air around him and had spread, he knew, as far back as the end of the legion train, off the bridge and into the invisible darkness, and would soon be heard by the entire city, but most important, by the half a hundred archers at the far end of the bridge. Those archers would now know that, far from quenching the attack, their murderous arrow barrage had, rather, enraged the beast, increased the determination of the attackers racing across the bridge, and that no matter how many enemy were cut down by arrows hurtling blindly through the mist, no matter how many were slaughtered underfoot by their own comrades and messmates, for every man who fell, ten would take his place, fifty or a hundred would step into the breach, and the archers' volleys, for all their murderous intent, would ultimately be futile.

As the improvised war cry rose into the air, men surged forward, with impetus and momentum that carried them on their path as surely as the sound of their cry was carried over the Tiber, skipping and skimming the surface like the thrown stone of a boy. The pace increased—indeed, no longer was it the slow, slogging trudge of a moment before, of men who knew they were walking cadavers; rather, it now became true progress, a full trot, as men hastened to fill the gaps that had opened in the ranks ahead of them. Even beneath his feet Odoacer could sense the change: the number of fallen, which in some places had built to layers of three or four, now thinned and decreased. Footholds even existed where none had fallen, at first simply a step or two here or there, but then increasing in distance, until the men could trot forward several paces without trampling a single limb or splashing through puddles of blood.

The effect was mesmerizing. The harsh cry that had ripped from the men's throats emboldened them, and now that they sensed greater forward progress, and a decreasing number of casualties, they raised their voices even higher in volume, and seemed almost to leap forward. At the same time, the volley of arrows dropped and, after a moment, died away completely. Had the defenders run out of missiles? Not likely, Odoacer thought—they had had months of inactivity, confined within the city walls, to be fashioning arrows. Food among the enemy might be in short supply, sleep and rest even shorter—but there would be no shortage of weaponry. He knew the answer: fear. It was the enemy's *fear* that had overcome them, fear of the unknown force attacking them from the foggy darkness, fear exacerbated by the enormous cry that had welled up from the void, that audible embodiment of pent-up ferocity storming over the bridge. It was fear that had prevailed, not clouds of arrows, nor the attackers' brute determination to advance into the thick of them. The army most afraid had lost. Odoacer knew, without even setting eyes on the enemy, unable to see even farther than the helmet of the man in front of him, he knew the archers defending the far end of the bridge had thrown away their bows and turned tail, leaving the field of battle to their comrades, foot soldiers who would be massing for the defense behind them, spreading in the street like a solid wall, several yards back from the end of the bridge, and he knew that in at least this initial clash, in this first challenge to overcome sheer *fear,* his own men had prevailed.

Lowering his shield, Odoacer stepped to the side, pressing himself against the wall and letting the men and horses behind him surge past, until a gap opened in the lines and he was able to drop back. In doing so, he was surprised at how far he himself had advanced in such a short time—the action had been so intense, so fast-moving, that he was already at nearly the middle of the bridge. The first several units swept past him, followed by their accompanying cavalry squadrons, then another gap appeared in which he stopped to look back, and then several more centuries trotted past—but now a third gap opened, one wide enough that he could not discern through the fog how far the next ranks of troops might be, though the air was rent with the sound of clashes and angry men both in front of him and behind. The lead troops, he knew, had now come in direct contact with the defenders at the far end of the bridge, and were battling furiously to break through the defenses and into the city proper—yet their efforts would only be successful to the extent that supporting troops could continue to pour over the bridge, to add to the weight being brought to bear against the defensive lines. Volumes of troops—*thousands* of troops—would have to make it over the bridge if the attack was to prevail; yet here he was standing in no-man's-land in the middle of the bridge, a thousand men having passed by him, perhaps a thousand more lying dead at his feet or floating in the waters below—and no support troops appearing from the darkness. Taking a deep breath, he rushed back down the ramp toward the near end of the bridge, hurdling the dead, ignoring the cries of the wounded.

Rushing blindly through the fog, he followed the sound of the trumpets, which were still blaring the attack in increasingly ragged tempo, interrupted by the shouts of men and the sounds of chaos and crashing. Leaping off the ramp at the bottom of the bridge, he raced onto the broad avenue running parallel to the river, below the front wall of the Mausoleum gardens, and nearly slipped again on the water- and blood-slickened cobblestones beneath him. Recovering, he paused for a moment—the avenue should have been thick with soldiers, pressing forward and up the bridge ramp in phalanx formation to bolster the attack on the city—yet here only scattered units remained, as confused as himself, separated from their centuries and uncertain whether to advance onto the bridge or retreat in search of their stalled comrades. The longer the gap between the troops remained, the greater the likelihood his troops in the vanguard would be overwhelmed by the powerful defenses on the far side of the bridge. Worse: dawn was now approaching, and though fog still obscured everything beyond a few paces' distance, vague shapes were beginning to appear. The sun would soon rise, and then the mist would burn off. There was little time. Odoacer shouldered through the confused troops, still following the sounds of the trumpets. Catching sight of a horse, he seized the reins and hailed the officer.

"Where is the phalanx?!" he shouted. "Where is Gundobar?"

The officer peered at Odoacer in confusion, not recognizing him at first, and looking down at himself, Odoacer realized he was covered with blood from the corpses over which he had stumbled, his shield heavy with embedded arrows, and his officer's insignia effaced—in the chaos of the battle there was no telling who the man thought he was. Whipping off his helmet, he shouted again to the man.

"What is happening here?" he roared. "Where is Gundobar?"

Suddenly recognizing him, the man pointed vaguely back.

"To the rear," he shouted. "The troops have retreated. Gundobar was caught in the sand!"

"Sand!" Odoacer bellowed. "What the hell—"

"Molten sand!" called the officer. "The enemy is throwing it in barrels from the rooftop! They hit the street red-hot and explode onto our troops . . . they—"

Odoacer instantly understood.

"Get off your horse and help form up the troops!"

"But sir!" the officer shouted as he hastily dismounted. "The men cannot get past the Mausoleum! The enemy is launching—"

"The men get past by getting past!" Odoacer roared. "The enemy are as blind as we. Now go!"

Slapping aside the horse, the two men raced down the street along the long garden wall, toward the sounds of trumpeting and shouting. Just as they reached the corner, a bright flame appeared out of the darkness above them. Instinctively, Odoacer threw himself into the gutter, sliding painfully on the rough cobbles as he hit the blood-tinged stream of effluent trickling against the high curb like a filthy brook. The officer accompanying him did not react as quickly. The flaming object heaved from the Mausoleum roof crashed directly into his path, and his momentum kept him running forward even as the naphtha-soaked barrel burst into fragments, spewing red-hot sand and metal filings directly into his face, and for thirty paces in every direction.

At the officer's scream of agony, Odoacer glanced up briefly, but immediately ducked back, submerging his head in the effluent as a shower of red sparks descended upon him. Those areas of his body not protected by mail—his upper arms, his calves, the back of his neck—exploded in pain as the tiny grains burrowed into his skin with a sizzling hiss. He writhed as he lay facedown, forcing himself not to raise his head until the rain of particles had slowed, and then covering his face with his hands against stray pieces still falling as he rolled onto his back to quell the pain by wetting the other side of his body in the stream. Yet there was no time—no time to dodge bombs from the darkness, to wallow in the filthy water. Rising to his feet, he glanced to where the barrel had landed, the wooden staves now guttering in a puddle of flaming liquid. The officer lay beside it on his back, limbs twitching in death throes, his face scarcely more than pulverized meat with a gaping hole where his mouth had been. Odoacer paused to stifle the nausea in his belly and the pain in his limbs, before resuming his slow trot around the Mausoleum wall.

Turning the corner, he plunged without warning into a vast crowd of men, still deployed in close formation as if preparing a charge—the missing rear half of the phalanx. The men nearest him, able to see him clearly in the now whitening fog, gaped at him in surprise, at the bloodied face and the body soaked in the gutter filth in which he had lain.

"Gundobar!" Odoacer bellowed. "Where is Gundobar!?"

The men stared for a moment, and then pointed to the side, where a number of wounded soldiers had collected in various states of injury, some prostrate as if dead, others swaying unsteadily on their feet, the various parts of their bodies that had been hit by the flying sand and metal looking much like the destroyed face of the officer who had accompanied Odoacer a moment before. One of them stepped forward, face and arms sheeted with blood, gray eyes peering out in a piercing stare. The long mustaches, sticky with red, were unmistakable.

"My God . . . ," Odoacer exclaimed. "Gundobar?"

The German strode up, grimacing in pain but still able to walk.

"It is only on the surface," he grunted. "The attack—did it succeed?"

"Not yet," Odoacer replied, "and it will fail unless we reinforce the phalanx."

"Then we go!" the German bellowed, and turning stiffly toward the lead ranks of the column behind him he raised his bloody sword arm. "Men—to the attack!"

The column surged forward, nearly engulfing and knocking down Odoacer and Gundobar before they themselves could turn and begin their trot alongside the men, back around the circular walls of the Mausoleum to the foot of the bridge. Alerted by the war cry, the guards on the rooftop began heaving down their infernal barrels with renewed vigor, and here and there along the length of the column of soldiers, horrific crashes could be heard, though the men continued to trot stolidly past. Agonizing screams again filled the air, accompanied by the calls of the surrounding troops to fill the gaps left by the wounded. The rooftop guards were limited by both the numbers of barrels they could prepare, and their blindness in the fog, and many missiles overshot their marks, exploding harmlessly against the sides of neighboring buildings or falling into the gutters, where their effects were muted by the effluent stream. The long column of men skirted the Mausoleum perimeter and advanced to the bridge's entry ramp, where the sounds of fierce fighting on the far end assaulted their ears.

"Gundobar!" Odoacer shouted, seizing his comrade by the shoulder. "The bridge is covered with casualties! The men will not be able to maintain the phalanx . . ."

"Then they break formation! It is not needed, so long as they do not bottleneck."

"I will lead them across and form them up the other side, to reinforce the beachhead. You—"

"No! You have seen your glory today, and are needed to command the rest of the army," Gundobar responded, eyes flashing. "*I* will lead the men across!"

"You are in no condition to—"

But before Odoacer could finish, Gundobar had whirled and sprinted toward the bridge, sword high above his head, mouth twisted in a scream that resounded over the stones and carried to all the troops, both those behind awaiting their moment, and those in front whose moment had already come.

"Attack!"

The troops loosed a deafening roar and surged past Odoacer, who again pressed against the balustrade at the side of the bridge to avoid being swept on, or trampled underfoot.

Exploding onto the bridge, the troops stumbled over the mounds of bodies, the living groaning in despair at being trampled once again by comrades, the dead solicitously providing secure footing for the men charging over the blood-slickened stones. Stepping into a gap in the files, Odoacer merged smoothly into the flow of attackers, increasing his pace with theirs, as their fury swelled at the growing sounds of battle at the far end of the bridge.

And suddenly, just as he crested the arch, the clamor stopped. The men's momentum carried him at a breathtaking pace down the far ramp to the massive gate piercing the thick city wall, the Murus Aurelianus, which served as the left bank's breakwater. In the graying mist Odoacer could sense the dark, shadowy structures of the two defensive towers looming above him, but was unable to raise his eyes for fear of losing his footing in the frantic sprint, of being trampled beneath the feet of the men behind him. No longer was he their commanding officer, no longer did his voice carry weight, for indeed his voice could scarcely be heard above the roars of the men around him. Darkness, fear, and greed— especially greed—are no respecters of age or rank.

His feet stumbled against an obstacle, and then another, and in a moment he was leaning forward, shield rim dragging clumsily, right hand scrabbling on the wet, sticky pavement as if he were an ape or a cripple, groping in confusion under the towers' dark shadows. In their mad sprint, Odoacer and his men had careened headlong into a mound of bodies at the gates of the city wall, some not yet even dead but rather living men too wounded to rise, and they grasped at his hand, his ankles, his shield, as he struggled through the narrow confines of the gate. He forced himself to lift his face, like a swimmer threatened with drowning, straining to see light ahead, to keep from falling underfoot, to avoid joining those over whom he himself was blindly trampling.

And then Odoacer emerged through the gates and into the clear, and here, with the river mist blocked by the high city wall through which he had just passed, the view suddenly opened up before him. He could see down entire streets, lit by torches not of night watchmen, but of mobs that had suddenly poured from buildings on all sides, joining his army's rampaging soldiers as they ran roughshod over the overwhelmed defenders. The remnants of the urban cohorts scattered into the streets, abandoning their shields and arms, fleeing for safety. Odoacer stopped and gazed about, the first rays of the sun lighting up the eastern sky and exposing the broad avenue before him, the great Porticus Maximae that skirted the southern quarters of the city; then he turned and cast his gaze north up the elegant Via Recta, still shrouded in the morning shadows where it ran along the city walls toward the great Baths of Nero. Behind him, men poured through the gap in the walls, running rampant into the streets, but his task was now over. There was nothing more to be done, even had he wished it; after five months of siege outside the greatest city on earth, men cannot be controlled once they break through.

Suddenly, unaccountably, he felt an overwhelming sadness. Though he had never set foot in Rome, nor had ever considered himself Roman, he now realized that all sackings are the same, whether of an insignificant, wood-palisaded Scyri village in Noricum, or of the Eternal City of marble. Without need to look further, he knew the result, and he knew the suffering that would come.

Standing in the middle of the great intersection, with the sun rising in his face, he dropped his shield and lowered his sword, even as men rushed by him on all sides, frantic with greed, desperate to gain what had so long been denied them, what they were afraid of losing should they not arrive even before their comrades. And even as thousands rushed by him on all sides, he stood utterly alone.

But then the thought came to him that his task was not, after all, completed. Not so long as Ricimer's orders remained unfilled. *And not so long as Orestes remained free.*

Raising his sword above his head, he mustered his last strength, and roared to the men who sprinted past, though he knew they could not hear him.

"The Emperor is to be taken alive! Anthemius must be taken alive!"

He dropped the blade and seized the arm of a soldier running past.

"Did you hear me?" Odoacer bellowed into the man's face. "Anthemius must be kept alive!"

The soldier stared stupidly into Odoacer's eyes, not recognizing him as his commanding officer, possibly not even as a comrade, and roughly jerked his arm away.

"Let go, fool," he growled rudely. "And move on, before you miss your share."

With that, the soldier guffawed loudly and rambled toward a door on the street, which he began kicking in.

Odoacer slumped in exhaustion before looking up once

again and staring defiantly at the men whom, a moment before, he had led, but who now were nothing but a mob. He had a fear—one fear only, greater than any he had yet felt on a day that, for most men, had been full of fears. His fear—his obsession—was that in the confusion, in the murderous chaos that was even now engulfing his troops, the greatest prize of all would be lost. He mustered his remaining strength and strode into the street, an island of purposeful determination surrounded by a river of pandemonium, frantic soldiers and terrified citizens rushing past on all sides. The greatest prize of all must be claimed by no man but himself. Squaring his shoulders, he pushed his way through the conquerors—Romans, Germanics, and Scyri—who a moment before had been his troops, his allies, his own men, but whom he now viewed as his greatest threat.

The palace, he must make his way to the palace.

"Orestes!" he called, his hoarse voice rising above the fray. "Orestes is mine!"

IV

Ricimer glanced in disgust at the object on the table, then let his head drop back to the pillow, his eyes glistening with fever, his lips dry and cracked.

"Water," he croaked.

Odoacer handed him his own canteen, which Ricimer grasped with trembling hands and lifted to his lips. He drank in long, greedy swallows, a steady stream trickling down the side of his face, though he did not seem to notice. Odoacer waited patiently until he lowered the container and handed it back.

Ricimer's face expressed no comfort or relief, and again he turned toward the table, and this time his eyes filled with rage.

"Yes, that's him," he said, his voice stronger now. "A week of searching for the emperor, and this is what you bring me? This . . . this decayed head? Take it away. It reeks."

Odoacer nodded to the guard, who stepped forward,

grasped the cranium by its blood-matted hair, and thrust it back into the rough sack in which it had been brought.

"I thought I made it clear Anthemius was to be taken alive," Ricimer continued.

"He was under our noses the entire time, and we did not know it," Odoacer replied quietly. "When Gundobar first brought a cohort here to the *palatium* to search the premises, he expected to find the emperor, Orestes, their families, and their senior staff and officers. He found nothing but a few terrified servants. We interrogated them, and they claimed the noble families had slipped out of Rome weeks earlier, and that Orestes and his staff had abandoned the palace the night of our attack. Nobody had seen the emperor in weeks. He was said to have been ill in his private apartments, but Gundobar's search turned up nothing."

"Why would you believe this story? The servants were obviously put up to it—"

"We interrogated them separately, and . . . applied pressure. Their stories were consistent."

"And you did not search further?"

"We did, but it was a question of manpower," Odoacer said. "Rome had to be secured—our troops were running rampant, and the city would have been reduced to rubble, and the population to corpses, if discipline were not restored. This took some days."

"Our troops are *Romans,* restoring Rome to Roman rule—why would they wreak havoc?"

"The men had been starving and pent up on the Vaticanus for many months—they were blinded by greed and by victory. They were taking out their rage on civilians and on public facilities. Orestes' troops had removed their uniforms and melted into the crowds, or simply slipped out through the walls in the chaos."

"Asses," spit Ricimer, shooting a resentful glance at Odoacer. "I'm surrounded by asses. I fall bedridden for a few days, and the siege goes to hell."

Odoacer stiffened.

"The attack was successful. It was flawless."

"But the occupation was no better than that of the Vandals. Go on—where did you eventually find him?"

Odoacer stepped to the window for some air. He was exhausted—he had hardly slept in the last two days, and over the entire week since his troops had first entered the city he had rested no more than three hours straight. Victory was secure, control over the city consolidated at last—yet now he was being reprimanded by a sick man who had contributed nothing, who was obsessed over a personal feud. Anthemius had not been the only fugitive still at large—Orestes, too, had fled, and Odoacer's own quest for revenge remain unfulfilled. Ricimer's complaints were trying his patience.

"We had nearly given up finding the emperor, thinking he had slipped away," Odoacer said. "Then three days ago, when Gundobar was performing a final search in the lower foundations of the palace, a naked madman leaped at him from the shadows, wielding a rusty old sword, and screaming 'Death to Ricimer.' Gundobar reacted instinctively, and ran the old bastard through the stomach. Apparently that did not stop him. The man leaped at him again, and this time Gundobar swiped with his blade and took off his head. After securing the area, Gundobar went upstairs and told one of the captured servants to descend and clean up the mess. The servant recognized the attacker as the emperor."

"Yet it took you three days to confirm this and come to me?"

"The servant spent the night with the body and attempted to smuggle it out of the palace the next day. He was caught, of course. Then he had to be re-interrogated, and it took us this long to wring the story out of him. We brought the head to you for final confirmation."

"And a good thing you did, or we might still be searching. I knew Anthemius was mad. But not so mad."

Odoacer swayed on his feet in fatigue. If the count did not release him soon, he felt he himself might go mad.

Ricimer mused for a moment, then again turned his fever-bright eyes to Odoacer.

"And order has been restored, you say?"

Odoacer nodded.

"Olybrius was formally acclaimed emperor, paid the donative he had promised the troops, and announced a general amnesty to the civilian population. The city's administration is now beginning to function again, and celebratory games have been decreed. Within a few weeks all will be back to normal, with a native Roman as emperor. The Greek is dead, the siege will be forgotten. The troops have taken over the old praetorian barracks, and will soon be back in a routine."

"And Orestes—what do you hear of him?"

Odoacer grimaced at this reminder of his failure.

"Holed up to the north, with a small body of troops," he spat. "He has already sent ambassadors to Olybrius, pledging his loyalty and offering his services—"

"*Offering his services!*" roared Ricimer in an unexpectedly strong voice, struggling to sit up. "As long as I am alive, that son of a whore will not set foot within these walls! You tell Olybrius—"

"I did," Odoacer interrupted. "Olybrius knows who runs things. He is emperor of Rome because of you, and he has proclaimed his gratitude to you. He mentioned you in his acclamation speech."

"Ungrateful son of a bitch," Ricimer muttered. "Has he once been here to visit me? My bed is at the other end of the same hall as his apartments! Has he once come to seek my counsel?"

"He will," Odoacer replied. "The situation until now has been . . . fluid. Olybrius simply wishes you to rest. You are his chief military officer. Military actions, however, are now far from his mind. He has the games to arrange, new appointments to the magistracy, the restoration of city services—"

Ricimer sank into his pillows, exhausted.

"You tell Olybrius . . . tell him . . . he may wear the purple, but this empire is mine. You tell him . . . Orestes will not . . . he will not . . . you tell him . . ."

The words trailed off as Ricimer closed his eyes. Odoacer eyed his commander a moment longer, then turned and left the room, without saluting or even closing the door behind him. He nodded at the guards and physicians waiting outside, then strode down the corridor, light-headed with fatigue, though taking extraordinary care not to show it, not to stumble or trip, like a man who knows he is drunk and seeks so hard to hide the evidence that he demonstrates precisely his drunkenness, by his overly careful manner of walking.

Emerging into the bright sunlight outside the palace's main gate, he blinked, collecting his bearings, then turned toward the military barracks by the palace entrance, where he had arranged his quarters near those of his senior officers.

Nodding to the guards as he passed, he slowly climbed the stairs, demurring to a scribe who wished him to sign some property-transfer documents, and shrugging off a pair of officers asking where to quarter the enemy's confiscated horses. Entering his apartments, he bolted the door behind him to prevent interruption. Then he breathed a sigh of relief that he was alone, stumbled into the next room, no longer caring for appearances, and dropped onto the bare military cot he used as a bed. He slept twenty hours, without interruption.

In the week to come, Ricimer's condition worsened. He passed a stone, then another, but the fever continued and he lost weight. After two weeks he began to bleed, and the doctors were helpless to stop the flow. After three weeks he fell unconscious. In the fourth week he died.

That week, Emperor Olybrius came to terms with Orestes' ambassadors, and a vast sum of money changed hands. For the second time in his life, Orestes was appointed Supreme Military Commander of the Western Roman Empire. On the day he entered Rome with his collected troops, he followed the same route as had Anthemius years before. Olybrius formally welcomed him on the steps of the Capitol, proclaiming there was no man in the empire better qualified than Orestes to assume command of the legions. In his acceptance speech, Orestes pronounced an end to hostilities between the two military factions, and announced that the two bodies of troops, which scarcely a month before had been mortal enemies, would be consolidated into a new, rejuvenated legionary force based in Italia.

Odoacer was not present to watch the ceremony. The day before, disgusted at his enemy's vindication and return to power, he had summoned Onulf and the few centuries of Scyri troops that remained under his own command, and slipped out of Rome by the eastern gate. Twenty years after the first time, the two brothers once again found themselves on the run.

They led their troops in an eastward circuit far beyond the city bounds to avoid encountering Orestes' incoming legions, and headed north.

PART

III

If Rome can perish, what can be safe?

—SAINT JEROME

PART
III

CHAPTER SEVEN

Three Years Later, 475 A.D.

ROME AND THE DANUVIUS CAMPS

I

"Father, who is Julius Nepos?"

Orestes put down his pen and looked up, blinking at the lamplight that flooded the office when his son had walked in. As his eyes adjusted, he gazed fondly at Romulus—a tall, handsome lad with the light complexion and blond hair of his mother, a Roman noblewoman from northern Italia who had died some time before, and the long limbs and strong frame of his father. Appearances were everything in the Roman court, and therefore Orestes knew that his son was a born leader of the empire, and had groomed him as such. His training in military craft, rhetoric, and history had begun when he was but a very small boy, and his knowledge of weaponry and horsemanship was second to none. Nevertheless, Orestes had not felt it prudent to rush matters, and had therefore kept the boy isolated as much as he could from the machinations of the inner court, and had refrained even from allowing him to accompany him on most of his military campaigns, with the exception of the naval invasion of Africa several years before.

He smiled. Romulus would soon come of age; perhaps it was time to end his sheltered lifestyle.

"It is a complicated matter, son—"

"I'm fifteen now, no longer a boy. Everyone talks of him—the tutors, the slaves, even the slaves' children. It is not right for me to appear ignorant."

Orestes rubbed his eyes and nodded.

"Indeed it is not. You've finished your homework, completed your fencing practice? You have no further chores?"

"I've finished everything. Now—Julius Nepos?"

"Julius Nepos. Very well. As you know, when we returned to Rome after the rebellion, Senator Olybrius was emperor. He did not remain in power long—"

"I once heard a eunuch say *you* had him killed. Is that true?"

Orestes blinked in surprise, then laughed.

"I? Kill Olybrius? Not I, son. No, a great many emperors have come and gone in the past few years, mostly gone, at the hands of their military commanders—but Olybrius was not one of them. He died of natural causes, a sudden apoplexy, the doctors said. Undoubtedly brought on by unhealthy living. He was very fat, as you recall . . ."

"And very wealthy."

Orestes laughed again. "That, too—"

"How did he become so rich? I've heard rumors—"

"Don't listen to the eunuchs," Orestes interrupted. "They talk much, but know nothing. Olybrius had a . . . sudden bit of good financial luck shortly after he was made emperor."

"But you fought against him, did you not?" Romulus asked, confused.

"A tragic misunderstanding," his father replied, "brought about by a power-hungry barbarian who escaped in the confusion of the siege."

"So you reconciled with Olybrius, then?"

Orestes nodded.

"It was actually in our interest that Olybrius remained in power," he said. "Though he was not originally on our side, he turned out to be very much . . . of like mind. He always accepted my suggestions for governance."

"And then, when he died, General Glycerius came to power."

"Yes, Olybrius reigned for less than a year. Glycerius was also a good ruler for us. That was as it should be, he was a patron of Gilimer, who suggested him. Of course the Senate quickly acclaimed him emperor, at my recommendation, for he was a Roman patrician, and a senator himself."

"Then why did he leave?"

"Ah, that is a great mystery, son. He underwent a religious conversion while in office, and apparently expressed his dissatisfaction with secular politics to the Holy Father, who then offered him the Bishopric of Salona—"

"He preferred to be a bishop to emperor?"

Orestes shook his head.

"Who knows what goes through the minds of Christians when once they find religion? As if he didn't have a greater opportunity to serve people by being emperor than as a mere bishop."

"But he announced his abdication months ago, yet only left for Salona a few days ago."

"I pressed him to remain longer, to allow the Senate and me time to identify a new candidate for emperor. It is a difficult thing these days: to find a Roman of noble birth, acceptable to all parties, and who at the same time actually *wants* the position . . ."

"And so this Julius Nepos is the man you chose?"

"*No!*" Orestes snapped, startling his son. "Nepos is *not* the man Rome wants. At least not the man Western Rome wants. He was appointed to the position by that meddler in Constantinople, Leo, who thinks it his prerogative to fill every vacancy that appears in our half of the empire. That's how we ended up with that madman Anthemius some years ago."

"So Nepos is an eastern Roman?"

"A Greek, through and through. Nephew to Emperor Leo, by marriage to his niece Verina, who has always been eager to promote her family, even at our expense. Thus far, the Senate has not approved Nepos's appointment. And as long as I am in command, it will not."

"But the servants say Nepos is coming to claim his title. Is he coming? What will you do?"

"He is indeed coming," Orestes responded, "but not here, not to Rome, the great coward. He and his uncle Leo have again named Ravenna the capital of the empire, and he is marching only that far, with a force of eastern troops. He may even have already arrived, as far as I know. It matters not a whit, for I know he dares not take a step beyond that city. And even there, he will have to barricade himself within the palace for his own safety. I am certain the people of Ravenna will tolerate his presence even less than the people of Rome."

"But this cannot last," the boy pressed. "Rome cannot have an emperor who is not acclaimed by its people, a prisoner in his own palace. You must arrange for a true emperor!"

"That I have done, lad," Orestes replied, regaining his calm.

"But who? This is what I wish to know—I'm fifteen, it is time for you to keep *me* better informed than the palace staff, Father."

Orestes looked at his son thoughtfully.

"You are right. I am glad you came to me. I leave tomorrow."

The boy looked at him quizzically.

"Tomorrow? Where are you going?"

Orestes picked up his pen and returned to his papers.

"To Ravenna, obviously."

"Alone?"

"I am taking three legions of urban cohorts, their artillery, and three cavalry *alae*. I am preparing a greeting for Julius Nepos."

"And . . . ?" Romulus peered at him hopefully.

"And?" Orestes kept a straight face as he looked back up with feigned impatience. "What more have you to tell me?"

"Father!" the boy protested.

Orestes grinned.

"Pack your bags, boy. This time you come with me."

II

It seemed to Odoacer that the last three years had passed as in a dream: the months and seasons running into one another, a blur of time, a frenzy of activity. The commission with the

Tenth Vindobona he had hastily arranged for himself and his men before leaving Olybrius's court had brought him safely into the anonymity of the vast ranks of *confoederati,* the foreign-born legions posted sullenly on the empire's crumbling northern and eastern borders. Here, they were beyond the immediate notice or interest of Orestes, who had assumed supreme command of all Western Roman military forces after Ricimer's death—though Odoacer was unable to escape the irony that the legion he now commanded was one of those that had destroyed his own Scyri kingdom scarcely a dozen years before. Here, on the windswept plains of the Danuvius River valley, almost at the very site of his former home, he patrolled a region comprising a number of minor trading posts and border garrisons, with an undermanned legion of ill-trained Germans and veteran Scyri at his command, and a handful of horse troops conscripted from—God knows where, he could scarcely understand the heavily accented Latin of these small, dark-skinned riders who claimed provenance from some remote region of Asia Minor, and whom he had inherited upon arriving at this familiar, but forlorn land.

His troops' fighting strength was low—the Scyri were the only experienced soldiers in the lot, though they were loyal to Odoacer in the extreme, utterly devoted to him as the commander who had first made them an effective fighting force for their tribe long ago. Yet these men were comparatively few, several hundred only, a small proportion of the Tenth, and most were now approaching retirement age. Of Odoacer's other troops, the Germans were young and strong, but seemingly drunk more often than sober, and uninterested in the discipline and drills Odoacer had attempted to impose upon them. And the horsemen of Galatia—or Pisidia, or Bithynia, or wherever it was they claimed to be from—were content to train on their own, with their own ragged but enduring ponies, and as long as they remained loyal and competent, Odoacer left them to their methods. Onulf was responsible for a mixed cohort of Scyri and Germanics, whom he handled well; and Odoacer's three other cohort commanders all exhibited varying, but adequate skills.

Yet the lack of competence among the *confoederati* seemed to raise no alarms among Odoacer's superiors, either in the Danuvius command center at Lauriacum, nor much less at headquarters in Rome, for in recent years the Danuvius region had become so bleak and unpopulated that even northern invaders—unabsorbed Germanic tribes, dispirited remnants of the Huns, Slav raiding parties—seemed to avoid the area. The river villages were of no interest to attackers, the farms and estates were scarcely more wealthy than the villages, and what little there was of worth in the region was adequately, if desultorily, protected by Odoacer's legion. And so, despite the unit's overall lack of experience and capacity, it was in little danger of attack, unlike the beleaguered units on the Rhine; and it consequently escaped the notice of senior officials.

And with the lack of challenge, from either enemies or the senior command in Rome, the Tenth quietly and unobtrusively ran itself, much to Odoacer's preference. For despite his hard work, and the loyal support of Onulf and his fellow Scyri, his heart was heavy. His mind was filled with ghosts that harried him, the voices of his Hunnish nation, of his Scyri subjects buried in the swamp and woods practically at his doorstep, of the Roman troops he had most recently led into battle—all of whom were lost now, dead to him. In Odoacer's forty-five years, he had accomplished nothing but survival, and survival lacked meaning when it had been at the cost of so many deaths, of the loss of friends and family, of entire cities that depended upon him. Twenty years ago he had been a Hunnish prince and commander of a crack unit of plains riders. Now, tired and scarred, he had lost nearly every man with whom he had ridden; though he was still a commander, it was over a ragtag band of foreigners and mercenaries in a land that had once been his, but now was foreign; and the man who was the cause of these misfortunes, of the shambles of his ambitions, of the death of his very father and grandfather—this man, Orestes, still lived, and from all accounts, happily thrived. Odoacer knew the demon of bitterness and vengeance was eating him alive;

indeed, he often recalled the conversation he had once had with Severinus on this very topic, many years ago. But surely the old holy man was, by now, long dead; at least, Odoacer had heard no word of him since his return to these parts, though he had to admit he had made no real effort to seek the hermit out, for that would have involved once again venturing into the dismal regions of both the swamp and his own memories.

Onulf observed his brother's actions in silence, knowing that his attitude could only but harm any future prospects Odoacer might still hold. Indeed, Onulf often spoke of his concerns to Odoacer. His worries had taken on a new impetus in recent months, however, as news had filtered through to them from Rome, news that did not bode well for the brothers. The circus of new leadership in Rome since Olybrius's death and Glycerius's abdication seemed to have finally stabilized. This meant that the distractions among the army's senior echelons would soon end, and the high command would again begin attending to border threats and deployments. Moreover, word had it that Orestes had assembled most of the urban cohorts and Italian legions and marched on Ravenna, a bald-faced challenge to the pretender Julius Nepos, who had fled into exile. It did not take a military genius to realize that with the home garrisons thus occupied defending against possible reprisals, outlying units would soon be called in and redeployed, to secure the wavering loyalties of other Italian cities and ensure Orestes' protection from the insulted Leo.

It was only a matter of time, Onulf told his brother, before even their own ill-regarded *confoederati* units on the Danuvius would be ordered to move, and Orestes and his senior command would begin planning and evaluating troop capabilities, not only in terms of manpower and weaponry, but in terms of their commanders' leadership capacity. And then Odoacer's name would once again spring to the fore of the count's mind. If there was no place on earth so anonymous as the Roman legions when the high command was distracted by power plays in the capital, there was no place equally so exposed in wartime. And the signs that this was happening, that Leo would send his own army to the West to restore Nepos, were becoming increasingly clear. As if anticipating this very act, as if to force Leo's hand, taunting him over Nepos's speedy fall, Orestes had immediately placed his own man in power. No sooner had the urban cohorts marched into Ravenna and taken over the emperor's palace and government facilities than Orestes had called an assembly of the people in the city's massive forum and announced the name of the new emperor of the Western Roman Empire, the descendant of a long and distinguished line of Roman noblemen and consuls:

Romulus Augustus, Orestes' bewildered fifteen-year-old son.

The boy's appointment as emperor stunned the troops; it was a stroke of such unvarnished greed and nepotism that every man in the ranks, even those previously loyal to Orestes and the Roman senior command, was outraged.

In Ravenna, Orestes moved quickly to mollify his powerful urban cohorts with an enormous donative of gold raised from the coffers of Nepos, who upon fleeing the city had left behind the treasure he had brought with him as a gift from Leo only a few weeks before. With money in their hands, the troops in the capital sullenly acquiesced. Orestes settled into the emperor's palace in Ravenna to secure the permanence and safety of his son's new position, and of his own historical legacy, and to plan for the attack he felt certain would be forthcoming from Constantinople.

However, no donatives had been offered to the Germanic *confoederati* in the remote garrisons of the Danuvius. Traditionally, an emperor's donative was meant for all troops, whether of Scyri, or Syrian, or full-blooded Roman origin, not merely for the units most visible by dint of their posting in the capital city. Romulus's rise to power was bad enough; but the skewed distribution of the donative—vast amounts to some units, and none to others—was further outrage.

Vague threats of rebellion passed among the troops, plans hovered ominously in the air, but none seemed to truly coalesce, no single man seemed capable of channeling rage into action. As Odoacer walked among the cooking fires and winter huts in the evenings, the men fell silent at his approach; conversations seemed suddenly to become interrupted at his presence, unanswered questions hung pregnant in the air. With the distant appointment of a boy emperor, the link between Odoacer and his men, the bond of loyalty and devotion dating back years, became strained—the tie of trust had become tenuous, a barrier had arisen between them. The men looked at Odoacer questioningly—was he still one of them? Did he share their anger at the appointment of Romulus as their commander in chief? Or was he, their general, one with Orestes? A supporter of the boy emperor? Had he betrayed them—no, betrayal was too strong a word—deceived them, shown himself to be a man who, for the sake of his own ambition, was willing to countenance a fraud against the prestige of the legions, indeed against their very safety and survival?

The questions begged to be answered, but Odoacer, in his distraction, seemed incapable of doing so. Onulf could not draw an answer from him, could scarcely even convince his brother to stand still for a moment to engage conversation. Odoacer continued his work, night and day, as if nothing was amiss. That which had, in the past, cemented the troops' loyalty to him—his untiring efforts on their behalf, his willingness to take on any task, however menial, his eagerness to lead from the front and assume any danger in battle—these things now became a barrier, an impediment to thinking, to planning, to answering. Odoacer seemed possessed by a demon of incessancy, so frenetic were his efforts, his physical movements, his travels. The troops' questions increased and their morale dropped, seemingly in direct proportion to the very quantity of his labors. Men who had faithfully followed him for years, whose own lives they would have sacrificed at the merest hint of a threat to his, now doubted. And still, Odoacer offered no answers.

And with Odoacer's refusal even to listen to his brother's warnings, Onulf was forced to begin considering options on his own. His brain began doing the work of two, and he became the reverse image of his brother, silent, brooding, fearful of the night, spurning sleep rather than welcoming it. Men began to talk of the strange behavior of the two brothers, of the differences that had seemed to rise between them, of how perhaps the internal strife and tensions they were witnessing from a distance among the senior command in Rome were here being reflected in a microcosm, in this local conflict between the two leaders of their own legion.

The men watched and wondered, and began losing confidence in their commanders, in the wisdom of their orders, in their demands and challenges. And as Odoacer lost the trust of his legion, the legion began losing its way.

On his latest inspection of the border outposts, Odoacer completed his rounds early, and almost without thinking, directed his horse on a detour off the main river road, to the ruins of his former Scyri capital. It was a trip he had long avoided, haunted, as he was, by his youthful memories of the place. The site was now a mound of rubble and charred logs, cold and lifeless, inhabited only by wild pigs and the encroaching forest. He knew immediately the visit had been a mistake; no sooner had he arrived than his mind had filled with visions of the past, regrets for what he might have done, what he had failed to do. The ruins were empty, yet inhabited, with spirits, with half-formed memories; everywhere he turned he sensed eyes upon him, though none were visible, and voices calling to him, though none were heard. Directing his horse toward the great swamp, he stopped at the edge, reluctant to go farther, to lose his way or, perhaps, to find what he did not wish to see. Then he turned away, willing himself to think no more on these things, and never to visit this site again.

The next morning, just as the bugles aroused the troops, a knocking at the door startled him from his sleep and he woke groggily, in ill humor. Sitting up with a grunt, he rubbed his eyes and ran a quick hand through his hair.

"What is it?" he growled.

Onulf opened the door, stood a moment in the entrance to adjust his eyes to the darkness, and then spoke softly.

"Brother," he said, glancing curiously behind him into the lighted area of the vestibule, "there is a visitor who wishes to speak to you. An old man. He says he knows you."

Odoacer dropped back onto his pillow with a groan, throwing his arm over his eyes. Every stranger seeking an audience with him claimed to "know" him, and it was possibly true; this man might have exchanged salutations with Odoacer during a procession in Rome, or sold him an orange during a march through a provincial city; a simple glance might have become inflated, in the stranger's eyes, to a personal relationship. Or perhaps it was merely some local official seeking safe passage through the garrison's territory. Odoacer sighed and sat up, then looked at Onulf impatiently.

"Well, send him in."

"I cannot," Onulf replied. "He stands at the edge of the camp, refusing to enter, nor to go away until you agree to see him."

"Then let him rot there, for all I care."

Onulf nodded and began to leave, but Odoacer suddenly stopped him.

"Onulf."

His brother turned around.

Odoacer paused before continuing, observing his frosty breath in the chill air, even inside the hut.

"It is very cold outside."

"It is bitter. I have given the sentries permission to light warming fires."

"Why does the old man refuse to enter the camp?"

Onulf shook his head.

"He claims he is unaccustomed to people. That he has lived alone for many years, and that people, especially soldiers, make him uneasy. In his favor, I can say he looks very holy."

Odoacer mulled this over, as an idea began forming in his head.

"What is his appearance?" he asked.

Onulf shrugged. "Sparse hair, long beard. His tunic is so rotted and patched it is beyond description. I will give him some bread and tell him to move on. He may be a lunatic."

"No," Odoacer replied, "I will go myself."

Still fully clothed from the night before, he stood and slipped his feet into the boots set neatly at the foot of his bed, then threw on the cloak he had draped over a chair the previous night.

"Shall I go with you?" Onulf asked.

"No. I'll return before breakfast." Odoacer blinked into the light, then strode through the vestibule and out the door.

He shivered as the cold wind bit through his woolen soldier's cloak, and to warm himself he swung his arms briskly and picked up his pace. The walk to the gate took but a few moments, and he passed through without pausing, nodding at the guards huddled by fires at either side of the entry. Looking about, however, he saw no other person and, puzzled, turned back to the guards.

"Did you see an old man here, asking for me?"

One of the guards pointed to a nearby grove of trees.

"Said he would wait for you there. He looked tired—I figured his camp is in there."

Odoacer crunched over the frosty ground toward the trees, which he knew surrounded a boggy creek where the man would certainly be camped, if the water had not frozen solid. At the bank of the stream, however, he found no sign of life, and stood puzzled, wondering where to look next.

"Your wounds have healed well?"

Odoacer turned. The voice seemed to have come from just beside him, and despite its hoarseness, he would have recognized it anywhere.

"Severinus? Where are you? No games with me."

A low chuckle emerged from the base of a tree at his right, and approaching nearer he saw the old man squatting in exactly the same pose in which he had seen him so many times in the cave near the old Scyri city, open and alert, yet invisible, like some forest animal. His clothes, even his exposed skin, were the color of the dirt or the tree bark at his back, and his hair and beard seemed to melt into the surrounding leaves and twigs. Only his bright eyes stood out from his surroundings, but if he closed them, in sleep or in meditation, he would be nearly invisible. Odoacer observed him for a moment.

"You refuse to enter my camp, old friend? You hide from me?"

Severinus smiled, toothless and weary, but his eyes gleamed.

"Hide? Do I hide? My cave is but a few miles from here. I saw you yesterday, on your patrol, but you turned away, unwilling to show yourself to me. It is not *I* who hide. I am always present to those who seek me."

"I am glad to see you; but I do not seek you."

"Ah, do you not? Once before you sought me, unknowingly. I healed you when you were sick, but that was nothing. What was greater was that I set you on the path to your destiny."

"My destiny?" Odoacer smiled bitterly. "Is that what this is? Forgive me if I do not weep for gratitude."

Severinus's smile faded.

"You are still lost. Word has it you are still lost."

"Where do you hear such things?" Odoacer asked, in irritation.

"Do you imagine that just because *you* do not visit me, no one visits me? How presumptuous."

"Pilgrims?" Odoacer asked in surprise. "Have the pilgrims returned to you?"

"Aye," the old man replied, "and from your own camp, too. Some I knew as young men, as I knew you. They tell me of your troubles, of your movement in a questionable direction."

"And so you reproach me for not seeking you out to set me straight on my path again? Is that it? I am too busy for this, my friend. And you will freeze to death if you do not come inside and warm yourself."

"I do not reproach you. I commend you. You *did* seek me out."

"I what?"

"You did not have to leave your duties just now, come out here to a frozen wood, to search for an old hermit; yet you did, and I am grateful for it. You are not completely lost. As far as a man may have strayed from his destiny, as far as he may have wandered from his path, if he still seeks to find it again, then he is not completely lost."

Odoacer peered at the cold and sterile sun, still low on the horizon but filtering weakly through the trees. He had no patience to converse in riddles, to humor an old man.

"The news you have of me is wrong," he replied, sighing. "I am not moving in a questionable direction. I have no direction at all. I tread water, as I did in the swamp that day you found me, and I prefer it that way. I have lost—battles, comrades, opportunities for vengeance, all but life itself. What direction would you expect me to take?"

Severinus stared at him, expressionless, then looked away and shivered in his thin cloak.

"Come with me to the garrison," Odoacer continued. "You shall have a hot bath and a breakfast, and my quartermaster will fill your bag with biscuit for your return journey—"

"Do you remember the parable of the servants and the talents?" Severinus interrupted him.

Odoacer stared at him.

"Parable? Forgive me, but I do not recall it. You know I am not a religious man. When you've seen what I've seen, it is difficult to believe in God."

"Ah." The old man nodded and fell silent, as Odoacer continued to look at him.

"Severinus?"

He looked up with a befuddled expression, as if he had just been awakened. Focusing his gaze on Odoacer, he smiled.

"Speak, my son."

Odoacer sighed, ill-put to hide his exasperation.

"You have walked miles in the cold to see me, and now you wish to recite Scripture? The servants and the talents, you said?"

Severinus's eyes clouded in confusion for a moment, and then he smiled as he recalled the reference.

"Yes, the book of the sainted Matthew! Wonderful parable, wonderful. Thank you for reminding me of it! The four servants and the talents of gold."

Odoacer nodded resignedly. In truth, he had little to do back at the garrison, and the old man had once saved his life; the least Odoacer could do was to hear him out for an hour. He squatted down, drawing a small flint from his cloak pocket, with a wad of tinder. Sparking it against his dagger, he tossed a handful of twigs and bark on the small flame, and as it grew, stepped away for a moment to collect some larger branches. Within moments he had built a crackling fire, and Severinus sighed happily, rubbing his hands to warm them, and leaning comfortably back against the tree. Odoacer prodded the fire with a stick, and then settled back himself, leaning on his elbow on the frozen ground, facing the old man.

"Tell me the parable, my friend, or remind me of it, for surely you have told it to me before. So much of those days I recall as a dream. The pain, the drugs you gave me, I can scarcely discern between what you said to me, and what is imagination."

The old man nodded.

"And perhaps in the end there is little distinction between the two, for much of what I say is of my own imagination. Many years of living alone does make it difficult to distinguish between imagination and fact, between need and desire, sometimes even between life and death. At times I thought you were dead, so still did you lie; and yet an eyelid flickered, or a wound bled, and I felt you cross from one side to the other."

"I myself feel as if I have died many times. Or better yet, lived many times. I lived once as a Hun, then as a Scyri prince. Lately I have been a Roman, but I no longer feel that. I cannot say what I am. There is much I lack in myself, from the days when I was a Hun and felt I ruled the world. There are things I miss of those days—the confidence, the certainty of knowing my path. All was clear, and even death held no fear for me. Now, it seems, the world moves on, regardless of what a man might do or fail to do, and there is little point in his doing anything at all, for in the end, he only increases his suffering, and then to culminate his life, he dies. Ironic, no? That death be the very climax of life? I should perhaps become a hermit, too. I have no doubt I would be a better one than you, Severinus."

At this, the old man raised his eyebrows.

"I wish you the best, then, for it is not a path to be taken lightly. Please explain for this dense old man—how would you become such a good hermit?"

Odoacer smiled.

"Ah, it is nothing you have done, old friend, for your actions surely are blameless. Rather, it is your motives, for although they, too, are blameless, perhaps even blessed, I fear they are too innocent. Innocent to the point of futility. Despite your great age, Severinus, you still have not learned the lesson of futility. You made great effort to see me on this cold morning, so clearly you do not understand how futile and paltry a man's efforts truly are."

Severinus stared at him in silence for a moment, then directed his gaze to the horizon, to the cold sunlight, and his face relaxed, filled with joy, and Odoacer thought, looking at him, that if saints truly existed on earth, they must somehow look like Severinus.

"For even as a man going into a far country called his servants and delivered to them his goods," the old man said, and he closed his eyes in pleasure as the centuries-old words rolled off his tongue, as effortlessly as a song from the lips of a child.

"And to one he gave five talents, and to another two, and to another one, to each according to his proper ability: and immediately he took his journey. And he that had received the five talents went his way and traded, and gained another five. And in like manner he that had received the two gained another two. But he that had received the one, digged into the earth and hid his lord's money.

"But after a long time the lord of those servants came and reckoned with them. And he that had received the five talents, coming, brought another five talents, saying: 'Lord,

thou didst deliver to me five talents. Behold I have gained another five over and above.'

"His lord said to him: *Well done, good and faithful servant, because thou hast been faithful over a few things, I will place thee over many things. Enter thou into the joy of thy lord.'*

"And he also that had received the two talents came and said: *'Lord, thou deliveredst two talents to me. Behold, I have gained another two.'*

"His lord said to him: *'Well done, good and faithful servant: because thou hast been faithful over a few things, I will place thee over many things. Enter thou into the joy of thy lord.'*

"But he that had received the one talent came and said: *'Lord, I know that thou art a hard man; and being afraid, I went and hid thy talent in the earth. Behold, here thou hast that which is thine.'*

"And his lord, answering, said to him: *'Wicked and slothful servant, thou oughtest to have committed my money to the bankers: and at my coming I should have received my own with interest. Take ye away therefore the talent from him and give it him that hath ten talents. And the unprofitable servant, cast ye out into the exterior darkness. There, shall be weeping and gnashing of teeth.'* "

Severinus once again fell silent, eyes closed, a half smile on his lips, as Odoacer waited patiently. Finally, thinking the old man had fallen asleep, he prodded him gently.

"Severinus. Did you not say there were *four* servants? What of the fourth servant?"

Severinus opened one eye and peered at Odoacer.

"Ah," he said. "Have you considered the fate of the fourth servant?"

"Severinus, there was no fourth servant in that parable."

The old man chewed his lip a moment in silence.

"But what if there had been?" he said finally. "What if he had been given, say, three talents, which he invested diligently like the first two servants, but lost all the money, yielding him nothing to return to the master? Then he would be even worse off than the servant who had buried the money. What would the master have done to him?"

Odoacer mulled this over.

"I suppose that, since the man who had buried the talent was condemned by the master, this fourth servant would have been killed on the spot."

"No," Severinus replied. "I do not believe he would have been killed, nor even condemned, like the third servant. I suspect—no, I *believe*, given what I know of the Master—that he would have been praised, and given another chance, to learn from his mistakes and make things right."

Odoacer looked at him in puzzlement.

"What is your point?" he asked finally. "God does not reward poor investors."

Severinus shook his head.

"No, my son. God favors those who take the opportunities given them. Opportunities are blessings, like good health, or a faithful wife, or wine to make us glad. Accepting opportunities implies failure occasionally, perhaps often, because men are fallible and faith is weak. But they are blessings nonetheless."

"I cannot believe that God rejoices in failure."

"It is not failure in which He rejoices, but the *attempt*. Accepting an opportunity implies a faith in God, in the bounty of His gifts. It implies gratitude for His generosity, love for His mercy. But *failing* to accept an opportunity, failing even to try, signifies the opposite: a lack of faith, a separation from God, ultimately an arrogance and pride that says we do not trust the gifts God drops in our laps; we, as men, know better than Him, we trust in ourselves rather than rely on Him. Hence the punishment of the third servant, who did not even try. Despite his seemingly humble apology and return of the single talent, that servant was the most arrogant and defiant of all. He was timid and timorous with his gifts, and therefore squandered them. That servant merited punishment."

"But," Odoacer interjected, "the fourth servant lost his master's resources—"

"But he did not squander them," the old man continued. "He accepted the opportunity, took his chance, invested in good faith—and *then* he lost them."

"Perhaps he was merely stupid."

"Perhaps; but that is no sin. God does not punish stupidity—He punishes pride, and lack of resolution, and timidity. Pride and fear, you see, are often one and the same."

Odoacer pondered this.

"And you came all this way to tell me this? Old man, whether or not your words are true, you cheer me greatly by your devotion. Come. You mustn't stay here, camped in the cold, without food. I will give you a cot in my own room this night, and tomorrow we will discuss where you can safely settle. There will be still more cold days. I will send some men now to your cave, to collect your things."

Severinus shook his head.

"I do not wish to disturb your men."

Odoacer stood and brushed off his cloak.

"Then I myself will go there in the evening, with supper."

Severinus shrugged.

"As you wish," he said simply.

That evening, Odoacer picked his way along the familiar old path at the marsh edge, leading a pair of men and a mule. He knew that all of Severinus's possessions could have fit into a single pocket of his tunic, and that the old man himself could easily be carried on one of the mules back to the legionary garrison. Yet it would have been rude to demonstrate his knowledge of the old man's poverty and feebleness, and so he brought the extra men. When they arrived at the cave, however, Severinus was not there. A pair of startled pilgrims resting and praying in the rustic shelter claimed not to have seen him since early that morning—but remarked that he often disappeared for days at a time when making his rounds of the nearby villages.

Odoacer and his men waited a few hours at the cave without sign of the old hermit, and then, disappointed, returned to the garrison. Odoacer resolved to shrug off Severinus and his eccentric movements and speech as simply the vague wanderings of a possibly holy, but undeniably half-mad old man. Yet he could not shake Severinus's words from his mind, and he spent that night awake, pondering them.

Talents—what were Odoacer's talents? What were his risks? Where were his resources to be invested, where the losses to be avoided? Sitting in his room, considering his actions over the past several years, the changes and events that had been wrought, his head spun, yet for once it was not spinning into chaos, or inertia—now it was into focus, into a coalescing clarity. Words and thoughts solidified, options began to stand out from vague presentiments. The increasingly hostile mood in the garrison, Onulf's warnings, the men's mutterings, rumors from Ravenna of redeployment—all were beginning to fall into a pattern, one that for many months he had neglected but that now, he realized, required him to act. Severinus's words pierced him—where were his talents, what had he been hiding in the earth these past years?

Emerging from his thoughts after many hours, he stepped to the window of his command hut, and looked out. By the angle of the moon and the sounds of the camp, he knew it was well past midnight. Oddly, however, he felt refreshed, even invigorated, and as he turned back toward the room his spirit was light, as if a great weight had been lifted from his shoulders, as if the ghosts that had been weighing upon him since his arrival in this haunted land no longer had the power to oppress him. He smiled, but it was not the smile of a decision made, for none had been made. He did not know what he was to do, indeed he had not even had time to consider or identify all his options, to analyze the situation, to discuss events in Rome and in the garrison with his brother. His smile was not of a thing done, for it was far too early for that.

His smile was from the knowledge that he had an opportunity, and that God would bless his attempt at seizing it. He scarcely knew what it was—indeed it was more a vague sense than true knowledge—but the opportunity, he knew, was there, it required action, and he would take that action. It was not the knowledge that he would do a *certain* thing that lifted his heart, for that was far too advanced a stage for him at this point in his thinking—rather, it was that he would do *some*thing.

Unable to sleep, he spurned the bed and returned to his chair, confident now that his impasse had been broken. Whether he presented to his Master a doubling of his investment, or a complete loss, his efforts, whatever they might be, would be blessed.

III

"What now, Gilimer? What is it the men want now?"

Orestes glared balefully at his second-in-command, the tribune with whom he had led the legions from Rome to the northern Italian capital of Ravenna to overthrow Julius Nepos. The march here had taken scarcely two weeks, and no siege was needed, for Nepos had fled like a dog across the Adriatic, to the protection of Leo's troops. It should have been cause for great celebration among Orestes' forces. Yet since the occupation of Ravenna, the army had been simmering with discontent.

Gilimer peered into the vast, empty hall of the emperor's courtroom. Orestes had declared himself chief magistrate and had met with Ravenna's leading officials, citizens, and merchants to enforce his authority, ensuring the appointment to critical positions of men on whose loyalty he could rely. Now Orestes' first week in Ravenna was done, and he had dismissed the last petitioner just minutes before. The room was deserted, the light from the vast skylights above had waned, and no torches or candles had been lit within. Gilimer could scarcely see in the gloomy room, but he entered and walked with slow, measured steps down the aisle to the magnificent dais at the front, where he knew Orestes was seated.

"I have been seeking for three days to meet with you,

Count," Gilimer said calmly, his voice echoing against the marble columns and mosaic walls as if he were in a cave. The thick-soled military boots resounded loudly on the floor as he strode. "The men are impatient."

"And why is that?" Orestes' voice snapped from the shadows ahead of him. "The very day we entered Ravenna, the very *hour*, I announced a donative to the men larger than they had ever received from previous emperors, and in the past few years, the men have received many. Five pounds of gold pledged per centurion. Five pounds! And half that for each common soldier! In generations past, if a soldier received a fraction of such a bonus, even once in his career, he would die happy! Now what have we? Legions of illiterate German mercenaries demanding Herculean ransoms every six months, or threatening riot. The only people happy in Ravenna are the whores. Did I not place you in charge of the urban cohorts, Tribune?"

"You did, Count," Gilimer replied, continuing to walk slowly forward.

"That includes discipline, does it not?"

"It does, my lord."

"So where is their discipline? Stop there. You may sit on the jurors' bench."

The echoing beat of Gilimer's steps ceased. Glancing to the side, he found the straight-backed marble bench in the front row of the amphitheater-shaped courtroom, each seat separated by an ornately carved armrest. Stepping from the aisle, Gilimer coolly sat down, propped one leg on the armrest, and looked at his leader's furious face, which he could now see glaring at him from the dais in the dim light.

"You are of Germanic blood," Gilimer said calmly, "as am I, and though you married Roman nobility, I suggest that does not change your ancestry."

"Go on."

"I also suggest that discipline goes both ways, Count."

There was a long silence as Orestes stared down at the veteran soldier lounging insolently on the bench before him.

"You realize, Tribune Gilimer, that your words border on

treason? Perhaps a year or two in the brig would improve your attitude. My guards are just outside this door."

"As are *mine*, General. Perhaps your guards might obey you, but perhaps mine might obey me. Or vice versa. I suggest we not involve them in our discussion. The outcome would be unclear. That is my third suggestion already this evening. It is time we move on in this conversation."

Again Orestes stared at his subordinate with a long silence. Finally he spoke again.

"It is not I who is stalling. My first words to you were, 'What do the men want?'"

Gilimer calmly returned the stare.

"The men do not feel they are being treated fairly."

"Not being treated fairly!" Orestes roared. "They had a pleasant two-week march up from Rome, entered Ravenna without a single casualty, and then were given the largest donative in the history of the Roman Empire! The treasury is empty—it is *I* who am not being treated fairly! I am poorer now than Nepos, who was driven into exile!"

Gilimer nodded.

"Possibly. But all is relative. The troops have noted that their comrades elsewhere in the empire, particularly the *confoederati* in Africa and Hispania, have been given land grants. *Vast* land grants, in some cases entire districts and provinces, which they are then allowed to administer autonomously. It is this—"

"Don't be thick, Gilimer," Orestes interrupted. "Did you not explain to the men that land grants were used in those places rather than cash simply because Roman administrators in those distant provinces do not have access to large sums of gold and silver? Land is plentiful, specie is not."

"Nevertheless," Gilimer continued, "the troops have decided they value land over cash. Particularly our troops of barbarian origin, for whom wealth has traditionally been counted in the form of land and estates, rather than coin. They have little use for gold."

"Confound it, Gilimer, if they don't want coin, then have them buy their own land with it!"

"It is not so simple, General. Such purchases would by necessity be piecemeal and expensive. A plot here, a farm there, without connection. That is not what the men seek."

"What is it, precisely, they seek?" Orestes repeated, exasperated.

"Rewards such as their distant comrades have received. Territory. Autonomy."

Orestes' face darkened in rage.

"*Autonomy?* Only barbarians would even think of such a thing. Do they realize where they are? In Italia—the heart of the empire, Rome's territory for a thousand years! This is not some abandoned sand dune in Africa that can be as easily deeded to a retired centurion as it can be abandoned, or left to the enemy. This is Italia! And they want—"

"One third," Gilimer calmly continued.

Another long pause ensued, followed by Orestes' stunned reply.

"What did you say?"

"One third of Italia," Gilimer repeated. "The troops feel it fair recompense for serving under—"

"For serving under me?" Orestes growled menacingly. "A German, like them, who has risen to the pinnacle of power in the Roman Empire! They protest serving under *me*?"

"No, sir. It is not you they protest serving under, but rather the new emperor."

"My son? Romulus Augustus is the most qualified emperor in a generation, far more worthy than was Anthemius, or that ape Olybrius that Ricimer appointed, or the coward Nepos. I would not have placed my son on the throne if I did not think him utterly deserving. He is—"

"Fifteen years old . . ."

"Damn you, do I not know the age of my own son?"

"He is a mere puppet, General. You know it, and the troops know it. The men view it as an insult and a disgrace to serve under such an emperor. Your donative may have been the largest in history, but it was not enough to convince the troops to willingly serve under a boy whose cheeks are still smooth. They demand more."

"One third of Italia."

Gilimer nodded.

"One third. To be administered independently by officers they will elect from among themselves for the purpose."

Orestes stared at him, his eyes cold and expressionless.

"In return for which they will serve obediently under their new emperor, Romulus Augustus?"

Gilimer nodded, and Orestes leaned back in his chair.

"One third of Italia, merely to serve the emperor as they vowed when first sworn into the legions? One third of Italia, to keep a promise they have already sworn to uphold?"

Gilimer did not nod now, knowing by the strain in Orestes' voice, and the long, skeptical pauses, the outcome of the discussion. He stood and stepped back into the center aisle.

"You do not wait to hear my answer?" Orestes asked, as Gilimer began striding out of the room. "You would leave without listening to my own proposals for dealing with these complainers, with these softened, emasculated fools who would seek to rape and plunder Italia as their compatriots have already done in Africa and Hispania? You do not wish to hear—"

"I do not need to hear your answer. I already know it."

"Damn right you do!" Orestes roared, standing up from the ornate magistrate's throne on which he had been seated. "Damn right you do!"

Gilimer strode to the back of the room and out the door, without looking back.

"You tell them to go to the devil!" Orestes bellowed after him. "That is my answer! I will not be cowed by a mob. In the name of the Emperor Romulus Augustus, you tell those craven blackmailers, those Germanic thugs, to go to hell!"

The door slammed behind Gilimer, leaving Orestes again in the darkness and silence of the empty chamber.

IV

"The men have gathered, Brother. They are asking for you."

Odoacer looked up from the chair where he had been

sitting in the darkness in front of the brazier. The window had been unshuttered just enough to draw the charcoal's fumes, without letting in too much of the bitter cold. Though the night was far into the second watch, he had scarcely noticed the time pass, and indeed had not emerged for hours, even for the evening dismissal of the troops. Few of the officers remarked upon this, as Odoacer often worked in his room, but Onulf had noticed, as his brother had been unusually thoughtful since his visit with Severinus the day before. Now, when Onulf entered the room, he noted that Odoacer had failed even to light a lamp. Stepping back out the door, Onulf took a small tallow from a sentry, and returned.

"The men have gathered," he repeated. "They are expecting you."

Odoacer blinked into the light.

"This is the rebellion that has been rumored for weeks, is it not? Since Orestes named his son emperor? What do they expect of me?"

"You are their commander."

"I command a Roman legion, and I therefore represent the hierarchy of leadership, the emperor they rebel against. If they rebel, I will be lucky to keep my head intact. As will you."

Onulf paused for a moment.

"That is not true. They see you as one of them, not one of those miscreants in Ravenna. At least they *want* to see you that way. For the Scyri among them, you were their prince, their hereditary ruler. For the others, you are a respected soldier whose honor and career have been insulted as much as theirs by this appointment of a boy emperor. These men have followed you into hell, and they have followed you out into this wilderness. They will continue to follow you, if you only give them the word. That is what they are waiting for."

"And so they expect me to lead them? Lead a half-assed troop of *confoederati* on a rebellion against the empire?"

"They will do as they will do. The decision is out of your hands."

"Ah. But we must do something, correct?" Odoacer

replied. "Refuse them or accept them. But will it matter either way? Are their minds already set? It would hardly seem I am needed at this grand meeting."

Onulf looked at him hard.

"You may not be needed. But you are *wanted*. Refuse them if you like, or accept them. But you can no longer ignore them."

Odoacer paused for a long moment, considering his brother's words.

"So you, too, would forbid me from hiding these things in the earth."

Onulf looked at him, puzzled.

"What did you say?"

Odoacer stared at him a moment longer, then a thin smile came to his lips.

"Nothing," he replied.

Standing quickly, he reached for the heavy woolen officer's cloak he had draped over a nearby chair, and then, after a moment's consideration, walked to the small chest on the floor in the corner, where he kept his insignia of rank. Opening it, he immediately found what he was looking for—the heavy gold chain bearing the torque, the ornately wrought medal of valor he had been awarded by Ricimer and Olybrius after the siege of Rome.

As he draped it over his neck, Onulf watched with curiosity.

"You have never worn that before. Why now?"

"It is an important meeting, or so you say. Perhaps it is best I show my authority. Lead on."

The brothers strode out the door together, and immediately saw the massive bonfire that had been built in the central square of the camp. Without a word, they began walking toward it.

Already, nearly the entire garrison was gathered around the blaze, and Odoacer noted that troops from some of the outlying border posts had also ridden in for the occasion. This was strictly against military regulation; when off-duty, men attached to the forts were prohibited from leaving them, except for dire cause. In his current mood, however, Odoacer could work up no anger, and so he ignored the infraction; indeed, the truant soldiers themselves made no effort to hide their presence, and some even nodded and grinned at him, as if already assuming his complicity.

One man was just concluding his speech, while a new one stood to take his place. This second man Odoacer recognized as Pelleus, one of his senior centurions—the legion's *primus pilus,* a Dacian by tribe, who had always had a reputation for quiet competence and unquestioning loyalty. Odoacer now wondered to whom, when it came down to it, was the Dacian's loyalty attached. To the empire? To the legion? To Odoacer himself, as its commander? He and Onulf watched with interest from the fringe of the circle of firelight, as Pelleus stood and cleared his throat.

"Men," the centurion called out, raising his voice to be heard over the crackling and spitting of the flames, which had risen so high that the men in the front row around the fire were red and sweating from the heat, despite the cold around them.

"Men, you all know me. I've fought with the legions for twenty-four years, and I'm of the age when I'm counting the days to my retirement. I've given the empire the best of myself—lost an ear for it one year"—here he turned slowly in the firelight so all could see the angry scar at the side of his head, running wormlike and white across a smooth, hairless spot where the ear had once been—"and got a hole in my lung here—" He unabashedly lifted his tunic to his neck to show the red welt just below his right nipple, where an arrow or a blade had once entered.

The crowd of men fell silent, the younger recruits' eyes wide at this display of what they had to look forward to over the next two decades of their careers in the legion. Before dropping his tunic back down, the old soldier slowly turned in the firelight to show his back to the troops.

"And you'll take care to notice," he called out, "that there are no scars on my back, except from the fingernails of the whore I bedded in Virunum last month!"

At this, the solemn moment was broken, and the men roared out their laughter and catcalls. Even Odoacer and Onulf grinned. Pelleus raised his hands for silence, which he was able to restore only after some difficulty, for a number of canteens and wineskins had appeared, and were now being passed avidly among the men.

"As I said," the soldier resumed, "I've come to the age when I'm counting the days to my retirement. And this is what I think: I've given the best of what I've got—my ear, my lung, more than twenty years of my youth—and Rome owes me. It *owes* me!"

The low muttering grew as the men voiced their agreement.

"And what does it owe me? What is a man's life worth? If I had died early, Rome would have given me a burial, and that's it. A burial. As it stands, it got two decades of labor and a few body parts out of me, so now it owes me! I put my X on a contract when I enlisted—a contract I wager is one-sided, but a twenty-two-year-old recruit don't know any better, don't know what two decades of life is worth, so he puts his mark on a contract and then he's owned, blood, body, and soul, for the rest of his life, or if he's lucky, for just the twenty-five years. Yes, I did it, and I'll stick to my bargain, and I wager Rome will come through. When I retire, Rome will find me six acres of farmland somewhere in the provinces and a little shack in a neighboring village, and I'll sit there shelling beans I grew in my own dirt and telling my grandchildren lies about the scar on my head and those ten scratches on my back.

"But you know, men—those six acres are nothing. To my mind they ain't worth the parchment I signed. Yes, Rome owes it to me, but it's worth *shit*!"

The men now had fallen dead silent, and Odoacer sat stone-still on a log where he and Onulf had found space. He was oblivious to all around him, except the words from the centurion, words he had never heard spoken by a centurion before, and for which the man could be arrested and flogged, and drummed out of the legions without a copper to his name.

"When I signed on to fight for Rome," the veteran continued, "was I thinking about six acres in Noricum a quarter century later? *Hell, no!* Does any young man sign up for the legions for such a thing as that? Does any man sign up thinking of his own mortality, thinking he might be—he'll *probably* be—dead of battle or disease in the next year, or ten years? That if he makes it to twenty-five years in the legion, he'll be one of the precious few who actually do? And if he does survive, those six acres will be damn paltry compensation for all the shit he's had to put up with over the years. Does any man think of that? Did *you*"—the old soldier pointed directly at a young trooper in the front row, scarcely more than eighteen or twenty years old, undoubtedly recruited just recently—"did *you* sign up just to earn a poverty-stricken retirement in your old age?"

The boy looked at him with wide eyes.

"Did you, boy?!" Pelleus bellowed. "Did any of you?"

Scattered shouts of "No!" emerged from the vast crowd of men, and the centurion let them rise and develop their own rhythm and cadence, until a thunderous chant of "No! No! No!" filled the air around him. He raised his hands in the air and threw his chin back, looking up to the heavens, for all the world like an ancient seer or priest divining the meaning of the stars. When the chant became raucous and ragged, he dropped his head and his hands, and again began pacing before the fire, glaring into the rows of troops, until all had again fallen silent.

"No!" he repeated. "That ain't why you joined the legions, and that sure as hell ain't why *I* joined the legions. I went to battle for the same reason as Achilles—that my name would not be forgotten, that I would earn my own bit of immortality by doing immortal deeds. That I would sacrifice a happy but anonymous old age, surrounded by my grandchildren, in favor of a brilliant career fighting for the empire. That if I died young, my death would be all the more glorious.

"Well." He paused, and every eye looked at him avidly. "I can't say as to whether my career was glorious, or whether I gained immortality. I rather think the contrary—that if I died now, my name would be forgotten as fast as if I had died in my sleep in a farm hut, surrounded by bean shells. But know this: no matter how glorious my life, everything I did, I did for Rome. I fought for her, bled for her, whored for her, prayed for her. Every memory I have is of her, though I've been to the city of Rome only once in my entire life. And what the legions have given me, what Rome has given me, is my honor as a legionary. My title, as a *primus pilus,* the senior centurion of this legion. When I retire and walk down a street, whether a gold-cobbled street in Constantinople or a muddy track in the most pathetic little shit-hole town in Dalmatia, I will be able to hold my head high because I served in, and survived in, the Roman legions. I have *honor* . . . ! And that, my friends, is worth more than six *thousand* acres of bottomland in the heart of Italia, and is worth more than all the gold and mansions of any Roman patrician who inherited his wealth from his daddy or stole it from the people through taxes. I have *honor*—and *that,* they cannot take away from me!"

He stared around fiercely, peering into individual eyes. Every man had fallen silent as the dead, scarcely breathing as he listened to the veteran's words.

"Or can they?" he asked softly. "Can they take away my honor? What if they change emperors every six months, in a competition of the least qualified to rule? What if they throw massive donatives to you each time, buying you off to shut your hole and stop complaining? What if they run short on money and give the gold only to the pretty-boy cohorts in the city, and conveniently forget the legions out on the borders, sleeping in the mud every night and getting shot at by Germanic river-swimmers every day? And then, just when you think things can't get any more senseless down in the golden palaces in Ravenna, what if they name your new emperor, your new commander, and you find he's a pimple-faced fifteen-year-old who boasts he can lead troops because he is accomplished with the wooden sword?

"Then where's my honor?

"When I walk down that gold-cobbled street with my head held high, will people bow to me in reverence and respect?"

"No, no!" came again the scattered shouts of the troops.

"Hell, no!" Pelleus spat bitterly. "They'll laugh at me. 'He served under the *Augustulus*,' they'll say, and they'll shuttle their little boys away lest they get it into their heads to join the legions, too. When I walk down that muddy street of the shit-hole in Dacia, will people approach me with awe, ask me to stay in their humble village, become a leading citizen?"

"No!" the voices roared more loudly.

"Damn right!" the old soldier bellowed. "The boys will throw dirt clods at me, and boast about growing up to become bandits, or border smugglers. 'Where's the honor in that?' I ask them, but I already know the answer. 'Where's the honor in serving the *Augustulus*,' they'll call back to me, laughing, and then they'll run away to pelt me with more clods."

"No! No! No!" the shouts resumed, and now every man was on his feet, and their wave of anger carried far beyond the circle of men around the roaring blaze, out of the camp itself, and even echoed across the placid, flowing waters of the river, to the camps of squatters and hunters on the other side, who woke in the darkness and peered toward the glow of the Roman camp opposite them, and wondered.

Most important, however, the chant carried itself into the darkness within the camp, within the men, and within Odoacer's own heart, and he suddenly knew the meaning of Severinus's parable, that the man who fails to act is truly the man who is most damned, even more than the man who acts yet fails; and he knew that whether his fate be failure or success, the time had come to act.

Odoacer stood, and the men around him fell silent as he stepped forward. Others, too, dropped their voices, and as the shouts and chanting died raggedly around him, Odoacer strode to the fire.

Standing before the flames, he could feel the heat at his back, and he suddenly felt lightheaded, though whether it was from the lack of food in his stomach, or the intensity of the emotions he was feeling at that moment, he did not speculate. All around him was silence but for the roaring and crackling of the flames, and he gazed at the men before him with vacant eyes, eyes without seeing, for his thoughts had turned inward, meditating on what the old soldier had just said, and on what Severinus had told him the day before. He stood still, but for the slight sway in his stance, staring at the faces in front of him, hundreds of faces, whose features, flickering and wavering in the firelight, blurred and ran together like the fading lines of a chalk portrait in the rain, adding to the feeling of dreamlike weightlessness he was experiencing. He closed his eyes to think, to focus, yet his mind was empty. He had planned nothing before he had stood and walked into the firelight.

But suddenly, as sure as he knew his name, as sure as knew he was the son of Edeco and the brother of Onulf, and that Orestes was the enemy that stood between him and vengeance for his father's blood, as sure as he knew this, Odoacer knew what he had to do. At that very instant he felt the fire's heat surge behind him, an impetus, lending him an energy and a clarity he had not experienced for many months, and when he opened his eyes again, all was in focus—every man's face became clear, down to the individual scars on their cheeks, the rough stubble on their heads, the coarse weave of the fabric of the cloaks draped over their shoulders. Suddenly, all became clear.

"My friends," Odoacer spoke, his voice raspy, and every man unconsciously craned his neck and inched forward so as not to miss the commander's words.

"My friends, Pelleus here has spoken true, with as much wisdom and philosophy as we should expect from a man who has given far more than mere muscle and sweat to the legions over many years. And I, for one, am not unmoved by his plea, that Rome owes him first and foremost not his meager retirement, but rather those intangible rewards for which we all fight, every day, without which no money or acreage or possessions has any value. I am speaking of honor, of dignity, and of the good name of a Roman soldier.

"You cheered Pelleus, and rightfully so, for by naming a boy as emperor, Orestes has mocked and insulted us. He has told us our loyalty and efforts are worth no more than a slave's forced obedience to a capricious master. By appointing an urchin to command the empire, Orestes has told us we are an empire of slaves or simpletons, who can be commanded by that urchin. He has debased the only currency we truly value, the only currency we thought could never be taken away from us: our honor. And though I would ignore the insult were it directed only against me, now that I have seen the grave injury it has inflicted on my men, I can ignore it no longer. Whether you cheer me or condemn me, I care not. I do not ask that any man follow me, nor will I punish any man who does not. I act on my own, without persuasion or coercion, nor will I apply any to any man. But on this night . . ."

Odoacer carefully unfastened the *fibula* of the woolen officer's cloak at his neck, and draped it over one arm. Slowly, with intense focus, he removed the heavy gold chain and torque from his neck, placed it carefully on the cloak, and then folded the entire package into a compact bundle.

"As of this night, my friends, I can no longer serve in an army ruled by Orestes. I relinquish my command in the Roman legions."

Odoacer turned, took a step toward the bonfire, and tossed the folded cloak, with the *torque* inside, into the crackling flames.

There was an audible gasp from the men before him, but then, with a roar of approval, every man leaped to his feet and surged forward, and for a brief instant Odoacer stepped back, fearing a riot, that he would be thrown into the very flames into which he had disposed of his command. A dozen hands reached out to seize him, gripping him and lifting him into the air, where he was placed on the shoulders of a pair of burly legionaries from the front row. The cheering was deafening, as disconcerting and disorienting as the stifling silence of but a moment before, and Odoacer again felt himself swaying and lightheaded, though this time supported by grasping hands, and by the broken-toothed grins of a thousand eager faces, some of whom, he saw, were weeping in the emotion of what they had just seen. Suddenly he felt a hand upon his shoulder, even at the height at which he was sitting, on the shoulders of two giants, and twisting his head, he saw the veteran centurion whose speech had preceded his, and who had also been hoisted up by his comrades, a fellow hero, though one far more eloquent in his speech, and deserving of his honors, Odoacer thought, than himself.

Pelleus seized his commander's forearm, grasping it in his fist as Odoacer seized the centurion's arm in turn. The two men locked eyes for a moment, and then grinned, and as the cheers washed over them, they released each other and held hands straight up, in the manner of champions in an Olympic race. The tumult was overwhelming, until the centurion finally gestured to be allowed to speak once again. For a long moment, the men ignored him, but then gradually the cheering died down enough that the centurion, his voice as harsh and as clear as a gong, honed from years of shouting orders on parade ground and battlefield, could be heard.

"Men," Pelleus bellowed. "Men, you heard the commander. Our names, our very honor as soldiers of Rome are at stake. And tomorrow we redeem it—tomorrow we take it back!"

This was met with confusion and silence as the men stared in puzzlement at the veteran.

"How?" came scattered shouts from all around. "Where, Pelleus? Where do we redeem it?"

Pelleus sat swaying on the shoulders of the men who carried him, looking about proudly, a grin locked on his face.

"Where?" he called out. "How can you ask me that? You know where!"

"Where? Where?" came the chorus of calls around him, and other smiles, too, began appearing throughout the crowd, and individual cheers again began rising into the air.

"Where?" he shouted, egging on the crowd. "You ask me *where*?"

"WHERE?" came the unified response, a combination of question and approval, of concern and celebration.

"We follow our commander!" Pelleus shouted. "We follow Odoacer—to *Ravenna*!"

Before he had even uttered the final syllable, the men's cry of exultation drowned him out, and they again surged forward, engulfing all those in the middle, commander, centurion, and carriers. Peering over the crowd, Odoacer saw Onulf standing near the back, arms crossed in front of his chest, silent but smiling. When he caught his eye, Onulf stepped forward and began shouldering through the crowd toward Odoacer. After a few moments he made his way in close, and grasping the shoulder of one of the legionaries carrying Odoacer, pulled himself the final few feet to his brother's side, where he gestured to him urgently. Odoacer leaned over as far as he could from his position.

"Brother!" Onulf shouted in Hunnish. Odoacer could barely hear over the roaring of the troops, but he knew that in any case, no one around them would be able to understand the foreign words.

"Odoacer!" he shouted. "You will do this thing? You will take these few men, this single legion, and challenge Rome itself?"

Odoacer frowned and sat up tall again on the men's shoulders, but Onulf pulled him back down, so that he was practically shouting in his ear.

"Odoacer!" he continued. "There must be no hesitation—you must commit, once and for all! You still command these men, and they will follow you, where you lead them, to their deaths if necessary! You would go against Orestes?"

At mention of the hated name, Odoacer knew that his decision, though seemingly spontaneous, was one to which his life had been leading for two decades; without a moment's hesitation he knew—*he knew!*—his decision was the right one. If he succeeded, he had the world to gain, his honor to gain, satisfaction for his father's blood to gain—and if he failed, he lost nothing but his life.

And even then, even if he failed, his name, Odoacer, son of Edeco, hereditary prince of the Scyri, would be redeemed, for he would have at least *tried*.

He turned toward his brother and, as if prompted by an invisible signal, both men's faces split into grins.

"Onulf—are you with me?" he shouted.

"To the end!"

"Then—to Ravenna!" Odoacer bellowed over the cheering.

And he sat back up again as the legionaries moved forward, carrying him on their joyful parade around the garrison perimeter. Before they advanced out of sight, he looked back toward Onulf, who was no longer struggling to hold his place in the mob but rather stood alone at the edge of the firelight. They caught each other's eyes once again, and as Onulf raised his fist in salute, both men knew what the other was thinking. No longer were they the prey, the quarry. For the first time in twenty years, they would be the hunters.

V

"The word we received a week ago by fire signal from the Upper Danuvius appears to be true, my lord," Gilimer said, reporting to Orestes. The count continued his rapid walk through the garrison camp outside Ravenna toward the parade ground. Romulus, matching his father's rapid pace stride for stride, glanced at the old veteran quizzically, then fixed his gray eyes on his father.

"What, the mutiny among the border troops?" Orestes replied. "Malcontents, nothing more. A few cohorts whose tribunes were a bit rough on them in discipline, or who are bored with the winter."

"No, sir," Gilimer continued. "A courier from the Noricum and Pannonian command just arrived. It appears to be more than that. An entire legion, the Tenth Vindobona, Germanic and Scyri *confoederati*."

Orestes' step faltered for a moment, almost imperceptibly, and then he renewed his rapid pace.

"Scyri?" he inquired. "Every time I think I have effaced that tribe from the earth, more seem to appear. And this time in my own employment, no less. Commanded by . . . ?"

Gilimer glanced down at a scrap of parchment he was carrying.

"Commanded by General Odoacer, sir. As you recall, he arranged a transfer to the northern borders for himself and his men just before you returned to power."

"Yes, I recall him," Orestes replied seething, "and I had every intention of dealing with him after my reorganization of the legions before I was distracted with this Ravenna affair. Now it appears the matter is a bit more complicated."

"Father?" Romulus interrupted. "There is a rebellion? As emperor, I should not hesitate to lead a detachment north to quell it—"

"Now is not the time," Orestes snapped impatiently. "You have much to learn about command. If you respond to every minor provocation, you will not only dissipate your troops' strength, but also dilute your authority, and try your men's patience. An affair like this will evaporate like ice in the spring melt. Rebellions do not last long if they require the soldiers to trudge many weeks through bitter cold, especially when deprived of food and shelter."

"So we do nothing?"

"Correct. Odoacer deludes himself. He is a madman, ignorant of his folly, reaching for things beyond his grasp. You see lunatics like him every day on the street corners: weaklings boasting of burdens they can lift, poor men of treasures they spend, cowards of giants they can defeat. And now this Hunnish peasant, Odoacer, calling himself Mars. Gilimer, send word to the Noricum and Pannonian command to cut off supplies to its outlying garrisons. Let these Scyri taste a few weeks of famine while squatting on their frozen river mud. That will quickly cure them of their little mutiny."

Gilimer looked sidelong at his commander.

"Beg pardon, sir, but we fought Odoacer and his troops at Rome. They are hard men, not easily intimidated. Cutting off their food may not be enough. We may need additional—"

Orestes abruptly halted, forcing the others to stop short as well. He glared at Gilimer.

"You would contradict me, countermand my orders, in the very presence of my son?"

Gilimer held his commander's gaze evenly.

"I seek only the best course of action in the face of this rebellion."

"You forget your place, Gilimer. This is a mere mutiny, as occurs every week somewhere in the empire, among ill-trained and undisciplined border forces. There is no 'rebellion,' except by you, against my authority, and if it rears up again, I will quash it as quickly as I will this little mutiny on the Danuvius. Do I make myself clear?"

Gilimer's eyes flashed in anger, and he opened his mouth as if to speak, but then held his tongue. With a quick salute, he turned and strode off back toward the governor's palace, which Orestes had set up upon his arrival in Ravenna some months ago as the staff headquarters for himself and his officers. Orestes glanced back as he and Romulus resumed their path toward the drill grounds, where they could now hear the sounds of the men assembling in formation.

"A competent officer, Gilimer," Orestes said to Romulus, "but prone to second-guessing his superiors, in front of others, which is not to be tolerated. He must be treated with a firm hand, Romulus, as you witnessed. You must treat all men under you with just such a firm hand, including myself."

"Even you?" Romulus asked in surprise.

"Even me, at least in public. It is a matter of exerting your authority—which you must do in exaggerated fashion, at least at first. Gilimer simply happened to be a convenient subject for illustration. As you know, there are hesitations and doubts among the troops as to your fitness to command—"

"My fitness?! I've trained with the army's own drill instructors! They tell me I'm a better swordsman than most of the veterans!"

"That may be, but it does not make up for your lack of age or experience. The only way you will be able to gain the men's confidence is by demonstrating your authority over them, as a male wolf over the others in the pack. And that will require some harsh measures at the beginning, until the men realize that even at your age, you are not to be trifled with. Today will be a good opportunity."

Romulus pondered this for a moment.

"I didn't think any doubts still remained about my accession to the throne. It has been some weeks now, and there have been no complaints."

Orestes scoffed.

"Oh, complaints there have been, in plenty, though not loud ones. Mutterings. At your presentation today, you will put them to rest."

"I was told this was merely my formal introduction to the troops. The presentation of a vine-staff of command, a formal acclamation."

"It will be that, but this little mutiny casts a new imperative on the event, which we have not had time to discuss. An emperor must be adept on his feet, not only in the sword ring, but in the lecture hall as well. I have seen you declaim. You have adequate skills—as good as most emperors I have seen, and better than many."

"Declaim? You are expecting me to give a speech?"

"Not a long one, merely something to assure the troops you are aware of the situation in the north, that you have it under control—and that they had best not be tempted to join in this mutiny."

Rounding a corner they came in view of the parade ground, where the two legions of Rome's urban cohorts in Ravenna were assembled. Romulus stopped short as he saw the large body of troops, formed up in full armor, crimson cloaks beneath polished mail lending a bright, festive atmosphere to the scene. Orestes continued on a few steps, then stopped and turned to look at his son expectantly.

"I have not even been presented to the men," Romulus said calmly, though his voice quavered slightly. "Yet now you expect me to create a speech out of thin air, and exert my authority over ten thousand veterans."

Orestes glanced at his son without expression.

"You will do as I order you to do," he replied evenly, "or your reign as emperor will be a very short one."

A week of marching through snow and ice, even on the well-packed roads paralleling the right bank of the Danuvius, had taken its toll on the men. Odoacer had long since dismounted from his cavalry horse and ordered his officers to dismount as well, not only as an example to the footbound troops, but because such travel was difficult for the animals—the way was slippery, and so pitted that several horses had already broken their forelegs and had had to be put down. Now, as he trudged along the road, listening idly to the crunching of ice beneath his military boots, he could not help but notice the red streaks staining the snow here and there. Though none of the men complained, some, he knew, suffered from poorly shod feet, or frostbite, or any number of difficulties a soldier might endure when on a long march. Pain and injuries were to be expected—but the effect was multiplied when the temperature was so low a man's piss froze almost before it hit the ground, and when flesh turned an ominous white and began peeling after only a few hours of exposure.

Inwardly, Odoacer raged at Orestes and at the maneuverings from Ravenna that had forced him to this extreme. For the past several weeks, all supplies to the rebels had been cut by the Pannonia and Noricum central command. Worn footwear had to be endured, moth-eaten cloaks and blankets patched, and belts tightened around stomachs. Neighboring cities had been forbidden from supplying food to the rebels, and the troops' meager stores in the camp on the evening of the great bonfire were all they had on which to live. The choice was either to hunker down in their quarters and starve, or venture onto the road and freeze. For Odoacer, the choice had been simple: better to die standing, as a true warrior should, than starving and bedridden.

Thus far, the troops had supported him wholeheartedly in his decision, and Odoacer marveled at their fortitude. For the first time in his life, he had taken command of an army at his own initiative. In the past, battle had always been at the orders of another: Edeco in his youth, his grandfather during his sojourn in the Scyri lands, and later Ricimer. Every man must eventually assume responsibility for his own life, for his own decisions, even if it is on his deathbed. In this rebellion, Odoacer had taken up the challenge the heavens had offered him, and the men gratefully followed his lead. Nevertheless, Odoacer reflected, his glance again distracted by a long pink streak in the road and a depression in the snowbank beside it, where a body had reclined in exhaustion—nevertheless, God could have afforded him better weather for his initiation.

His thoughts were interrupted by the soft crunching of hooves up ahead, and before even looking into the cold, gray dusk that was fast descending, he knew it was the courier he had sent out several hours before, the only man in the force he permitted to continue riding, in the interest of covering greater distance. The hoofbeats slowed as they approached, the rider searching for his commander among the numbers of bundled troops, officers as ragged as the men. Odoacer raised his hand and whistled, summoning the young rider.

"You have sighted Virunum?" Odoacer asked, careful not to betray the fatigue and impatience in his voice. "The mileposts have all been buried or destroyed—I feared you had lost your way."

"The town is near," the courier announced, dismounting and walking his horse beside Odoacer. "Two or three miles."

"That is good. But . . . ?"

"But what, sir?"

"That is what I ask you. The news cannot be all good, or you would have already announced it to the forward troops, and have a smile on your face. What is the bad news, courier?"

The courier paused a moment before answering.

"The bad news is that the gates are closed. All residents of the countryside have been evacuated into the city walls, and the guard outposts forbade me riding nearer to talk or even identify myself, on threat of receiving a volley of arrows. By orders of Arderic, their commanding officer, they said. I could see the walls in the distance, but could not approach, so I returned."

"You did well," Odoacer said. "Give me your horse. I will see walled-up Virunum for myself."

Odoacer took the reins and hoisted himself smoothly into the saddle. He wheeled and threaded the animal carefully through the troops toward the front of the long column.

He arrived an hour later, just as darkness was falling. Through the swirls of tiny, dustlike snowflakes that were beginning to fill the air, he could make out the winking lights of the sentries' lanterns on the city walls.

"We have arrived," he announced with satisfaction to the first troops who staggered up shortly after, who loosed a tired but enthusiastic cheer. "Wait here, until the rest of the legion has arrived. We will approach as a unit."

The men dropped their packs and collapsed into the snowbanks at the side of the road. In the time it took for the full column to arrive, complete darkness overtook them, and the men lit pine torches, broken off from dead trees in the surrounding forest.

"Form up, men!" Odoacer called out. "Virunum's outposts have been pulled back into the city, and none have challenged us."

"Caution, Brother," Onulf said in Hunnish. Odoacer had not noticed him sidle up during the formation of the troops. "The town may be hostile. Our men are not fit to engage tonight."

Without looking back, Odoacer acknowledged his brother's warning.

"I know the garrison commander, Arderic," he said. "Met him at the staff conference in Lauriacum last fall. He's a good man, not prone to rash action."

"All the more reason to beware," Onulf replied. "A man like that does not shift loyalties lightly."

"You are right," Odoacer agreed, setting his mouth in a thin line. "Arderic must be won over." Lifting his face, he called out to the troops:

"We approach in peace, but are prepared to fight."

The men nodded and adjusted their gear, tightening armor and removing the leather covers from their shields.

"Now," Odoacer called out after a few moments. "In files of centuries until we approach the town, and then assemble in parade formation below the walls, just beyond arrow range. Officers!"

Shouted commands were given and the bass beat of a drum struck a brisk rhythm. The legion took up the march, and within moments had assembled below the walls, two hundred yards distant.

Odoacer approached warily, inspecting the gates, which were closed tightly. Armed sentries patrolled the ramparts, which he could barely discern through the thickening snow swirling about his face. It occurred to him that perhaps the guards on the wall had been unable to identify him and his men in the darkness, thinking perhaps they were a crowd of farmers or refugees from the countryside. It is not every day that five thousand armed men arrive out of the forest, in the night, through a driving snowstorm. Scarcely had this thought crossed his mind, however, when a flash of orange on the wall top told him that the guards were indeed alert, and the whistle of the fire arrow past his ear told him he was not welcome to approach farther.

"Hail!" Odoacer shouted in Latin to the wall top, uncertain whether his words could even be heard over the hissing of the wind. "Extend your welcome to the Tenth Vindobona, which seeks shelter behind your walls!"

The sound of voices carried to him on the wind, though the words could not be understood.

"I say," he repeated, "the Tenth Vindobona! Our men are freezing! We seek shelter!"

A voice came back, clearer yet still indistinct.

"Tenth Vindobona, acknowledged! And who is your commander, Tenth?"

Odoacer paused, certain now that news of the rebellion had preceded them, and that whether or not his troops would receive shelter for the night in the bitter snowstorm was dependent upon his name. There was nothing to be done. He turned his face toward the wall, into the cutting wind.

"The Tenth is commanded by General Odoacer!"

Again there was a pause, and indistinct voices from the top, before the same brassy herald's voice drifted back down to him.

"Odoacer, the Hun—he who calls for rebellion against Rome?"

Odoacer paused for a moment, his heart pounding. He cleared his throat. "That is he!"

At these words, all went silent on the wall top, or the wind shifted and carried the response away. All Odoacer knew was that he was left standing in silence, that without permission he could not advance another step forward, and that without the promise of safety within the walls, he could not return to his troops in the darkness behind him. Dropping his face back down, inspecting the ice that was beginning to coat the perspiring back of his horse like hoarfrost, he pulled his cloak up over his head in shelter from the driving snow, and waited.

"Valiant men of the urban cohorts," Orestes shouted to the assembled troops on the parade ground outside Ravenna. "I present to you the Emperor and Commander of the Western Roman Empire, Restorer of the World, Ever-Victorious, our own Romulus Augustus!"

Scattered cheers rose from the throng, punctuated by shouts of "Augustulus! Augustulus!" and derisive laughter from those nearby. The shouts were immediately taken up as a mocking chant, which threatened to grow louder, until Orestes cast a glowering expression at his lead centurions, ordering them by a quick chopping gesture to stifle the men's outburst, which they did by a series of well-placed fists and pummels with sword handles. The troops fell into a desultory silence as Romulus stepped forward.

"Friends and comrades," the boy called out, in a voice surprisingly strong and sure, though his choice of epithet caused some tittering among the veteran troops, disdainful that a fifteen-year-old boy would refer to himself as their "comrade."

"I come before you this day to thank you for your acclamation, and to praise your determination and valor in expelling from our sacred shores that false emperor, Julius Nepos, that Greek imposed upon us from the eastern court, who would usurp authority, abrogate power to himself, make us slaves of the eunuch-led tyrant of Constantinople! I assure you, by the authority of my father, your military commander and a veteran of many battles for the cause of the Western Empire, that we will not allow such foreigners to rule us! By acclaiming me Augustus, you maintain the patrician stock of the noble emperors of Rome, through the senatorial bloodlines of my mother's family. Further, you have—"

"The donative!" came a cry from the back of the crowd, as the centurions craned their necks and peered into the ranks to identify the culprit. "Where is our reward?" rose another voice. "Our territories? Are we less than the African legions?" A third voice emerged, nearer this time to the front. "They received territories!"

Shouts rose up, and this time the centurions were powerless to stop them. From all sides came the disjointed refrain.

"Where is our reward? Where the territories? To hell with your bloodline!"

Romulus raised his hands above his head, to no avail, for the troops began shouting all the louder, though this time without semblance of coordination or even a unified chant. The acclamation was degenerating into a mob action.

The boy glanced helplessly at his father standing just behind, in a small knot of officers. Orestes stepped forward, raising his own hands for silence. After a moment, the troops grudgingly obeyed, and their shouts and catcalls subsided to a low rumbling. Orestes glared furiously, face red with emotion.

"Your reward!" he shouted. "Your reward! Have I not promised you your reward? Of all the emperors that have sat on the throne since I have commanded you, have you ever failed to receive your bloody reward?"

Some of the men in the front ranks dropped their gaze.

"Never have you been denied your just reward!" Orestes continued. "Nor will you be now, on my honor as your commanding officer, and my son's honor as your emperor. Yet can I pull territories from my pocket? Does even the emperor have the authority to simply transfer vast tracts of land and peoples to new owners?"

A low muttering rose from the men before him.

"He does not!" Orestes roared. "Your rewards were not earned instantly, nor may they be given instantly. You have fought many years in Rome's service, in the service of her emperors, and your deserved rewards must be carefully devised, lest they lose value and insult your efforts. Therefore—"

"When?" came an angry cry from the back, echoed by further calls. *"When?"*

"Arrangements are being made," Orestes bluffed. "Assignments are being given. Magistrates and surveyors will be sent throughout northern Italia after the roads dry this spring, to survey the terrain and negotiate a change in rule over selected areas. Moreover, we are facing a minor uprising, a mutiny, if you will, by certain ungrateful border troops in the north, which is proof to you that our *confoederati* and other distant legions are *not* being better treated than yourselves. This uprising must be put down before your territories can be identified in peace and calm; only then can an effective transfer take place."

More muttering rose from the troops, a mix of outrage and confusion. Orestes, however, did not give them time to calculate their gains and losses.

"That is my offer," he called out immediately, "the most generous donative the legions have ever received. In return for which you will unconditionally acclaim my son, Romulus Augustus, as your emperor and supreme commander. Take it or leave it—you who leave it, will leave the legions and the city of Ravenna this very day, and will not be prosecuted for desertion. Your shadow will never again darken a legionary tent, whether you have twenty years' or two months' service. However, if after nightfall I hear of treachery or of disrespect for the emperor among the ranks, you will be arrested and tried by the military tribunal. That is my offer!"

A silence fell as the troops considered this extraordinary exchange; at first individually, then in growing unison, the cries of acclamation arose.

"Romulus Augustus! Romulus Augustus!" came the shouts.

Orestes glanced at his son, who stepped forward at the cue and raised his hands in the air, acknowledging their decision.

"Romulus Augustus! Romulus Augustus!"

No further words were needed. After a moment, Orestes and Romulus turned and, accompanied by the small group of officers, strode back through the city streets to the staff headquarters at the governor's palace, as the urban cohorts scattered to their assigned tasks.

An unintelligible command floated to his ears over the howl of the wind. Odoacer peered toward the garrison palisades, and saw the gate swing slowly open. Before he could react, a company of armed men on horseback cantered out of the enclosure, riding swiftly toward him through the driving snow. In a moment, two of them fell in alongside his own mount, extending lanterns to illuminate the surrounding area, while the others continued their canter toward his troops waiting in the cold darkness behind him.

"Hail, Odoacer, Commander of the Tenth Vindobona!" said one of the men in flawless German, and when Odoacer peered at him through the dim light, he saw him saluting smartly.

"Arderic?" Odoacer asked in some surprise, thinking he recognized the face of the garrison commander.

"The same," the man replied as he reached out to grip Odoacer's forearm. "And you are welcome to my garrison."

"My men . . . ," said Odoacer, nearly dead of fatigue and confusion. "My men are still back at the tree line . . ."

"My riders will escort them in. Scouts warned of your approach this morning, though we could not be certain whether it was your troops, or imperial legions sent from Italia or Dacia to stop you—hence our reluctance to open the gates, until we were certain of your identity."

Arderic clucked to his horse, and the three men started forward on a trot toward the walls.

"You know, then, of our 'movement'?" Odoacer asked warily.

Arderic loosed a sharp burst of laughter.

"*Know* of it? Word has flown through the provinces. The only news that has excited the men more was what preceded it—when we heard Count Orestes had appointed his brat as our emperor and supreme commander. It was all I could do to keep the troops from rioting."

"Yes, mine as well," Odoacer muttered.

"But you had the balls to take action. You channeled the men's rage into this rebellion. You alone, Odoacer, of all the commanders in the empire, have taken control of the situation."

"I have my own reasons," Odoacer replied wearily, "unrelated to affairs of state or politics. Orestes and I go back many years. But if I am the only commander in the empire to rebel, then I will be the only one to lose my head when we are caught."

Arderic laughed again.

"Do not be too sure," he said, as the horses passed through Virunum's walls.

Inside, the city was lit with hundreds of torches, as if for a festival or a feast, though the streets were virtually empty. The three men passed down the main avenue toward the small forum, where Odoacer was surprised to see the entire garrison, a full legion, assembled in parade formation, despite the lateness of the hour and the driving snow.

"What is this?" Odoacer asked in astonishment. "Are the men being punished . . . ?"

Before he could finish, his words were drowned by a deafening cheer, as the troops roared out their welcome to him, rhythmically thumping their shields with spears.

"On the contrary, friend," Arderic replied, smiling. "They are acclaiming you defender of the legions. Your men will stay here with us—when we heard your supplies had been cut, we began ordering extra food and rationing our own, knowing the future would hold the same for us. Our store-houses are bursting, and will tide over both our legions for many weeks, even months, until the roads dry and we begin the march."

"Begin the march?" Odoacer asked, wondering whether he had heard Arderic correctly over the troops' cheering. "Begin the march? You would join us? I must warn you, friend, even with our forces combined, our troops are very few, compared to those the emperor could muster against us . . ."

Arderic stared at him.

"How long have you been hiking here from your own garrison?"

"A week, in the snow."

"And you have heard no news that entire time?"

"What are you talking about? How could I hear news in those godforsaken hills?"

Arderic leaned over on his horse and shouted into Odoacer's ear to make sure he was heard over the tumult around him.

"General—you have thrown the empire into chaos! Couriers are running by the dozens between all the garrisons to exchange information. Every unit along the Danuvius and the Rhine has declared its support for you! It is only a matter of time before we hear from the legions of Gaul and northern Italia as well. Even those of Dacia and Dalmatia are wavering, their loyalties divided."

Odoacer stared, thunderstruck, and then heard a shouted command behind him, and the tramping of feet. He looked back and saw that his own men—bedraggled, unshaven, bone-weary, limping in pain—had just passed through the main gate, led by Arderic's horsemen. The local troops broke rank and milled around Odoacer's astonished men, thumping them on the shoulders and thrusting wineskins and chunks of dried meat at them. Within moments, the newcomers had recovered from their amazement, and were mingling freely with their Virunum comrades as if celebrating a great victory.

Odoacer turned back toward Arderic.

"I have brought my entire legion. That makes two legions in total, here in a camp built to house but one."

"My men will make room in their own huts, and tomorrow we will send parties out to cut logs to build more. It is not just your legion we must make room for, General. All the northern legions are converging, and when word spreads that you are in Virunum, then all will come here. Your moment has arrived, General."

"You exaggerate."

"Can you doubt it? You are the man the troops will acclaim as commander. You are the man who will lead the march to Ravenna. It is you who will restore the good name of the legions, after years of the emperors' buying us off and insulting us with the incompetence of their appointments."

"And what will happen then? What will happen once we arrive at Ravenna, with five or six or ten legions in tow? Who will the troops follow? Where will their loyalties lie, when Orestes begins throwing gold and land at them, and I have nothing to offer but a name? What kind of a movement do you suppose I am leading here, Arderic?"

A shadow passed over the garrison commander's face, but only for a moment, as he gazed out at the sea of men thronging the streets and forum around him.

"Your motives," he said, "your issues with Orestes, are for you and him to resolve, and God, too, if you wish to bring Him into it. As for the troops, there is no hesitation. The men will follow *you*."

The two men sat the horses silently for a long while, watching as the troops surged around them, celebrating, in the falling snow.

VI

The late August sun beat down mercilessly on the Germanic troops who, unaccustomed to such heat, had thrown away most of the clothing with which they had marched south from their consolidation points along the Danuvius. Rough woolens, they discovered, were unbearable under the hot sun, particularly with the mail armor Odoacer insisted they wear at all times as they entered Italia. The effect was magnified by the concave shields they carried on their shoulders, and the heavy packs with corded shoulder straps, which seemed to cut all the more harshly into their skin when padded by the itchy wool. Before the sun had even reached its meridian on the first day out of the Alps, the ditches at the side of the road filled with the soldiers' discarded clothing, and for several days afterward it was a source of great hilarity among the men to observe the frightened expressions of the local inhabitants as twenty thousand men marched through their villages wearing little more than loincloths and battle armor.

With the inevitable onset of sunburn and blistering of the northerners' fair skin, augmented by discomfort from the swarms of mosquitoes and flies that tormented them as they descended into the northern Italian lowlands, many of the troops regretted having so hastily discarded their woolens, scratchy as they were. The sweltering Germans seized bewildered passersby and villagers, stripped them of their clothing, especially linen or other soft fabrics, and used it to cover their own sunburnt bodies. After Odoacer forbade such plundering, however, there was little the suffering troops could do but coat themselves with oil and sprinkle themselves with the reddish dust that accumulated at the roadside, in a poor effort to protect their burning skin. The results were not ineffective: because of both the dirt and the color of their skin beneath, the northern troops became known as the "red men," and all but the stoutest or most curious of onlookers fled at their approach.

On their fifth day out of the foothills, before commencing their final trek across the spine of Italia west to Ravenna, they approached the military garrison of Ticinum Papiae. Here, Odoacer issued the command to halt and set up camp just beyond missile range of the fortified walls. Puzzled, as it was still early in the afternoon, yet not questioning the opportunity to shorten the day's march from the usual twenty miles, the men fell out of formation, though keeping close to their arms and supplies in case the Roman garrison hunkered inside the walls should launch a sudden attack. As the centurions paced out the plan of the camp to be constructed, the men rested in the shade of a sparse grove of trees nearby, and Odoacer ordered an awning erected in a clearing some distance away. Here, he called a meeting of his chief officers, Arderic, Gundobar, Onulf, and a handful of others who had joined him since his call to arms the previous spring.

As the officers arrived moments later, they looked questioningly at Odoacer, for it had been several days since they had held a general staff meeting. Foremost on their minds was to know the reason for the halt, as close as they were to Ravenna and to the final confrontation they knew awaited them there. Ticinum was an odd place to stop, for they had passed by several such armed cities since descending out of the Alps, including the great administrative center of Milan just two days before, but none had tempted Odoacer to stop and fight, nor had any posed a threat to the progress of their march. Ticinum would appear to be no different.

"This city, we take," Odoacer announced after the officers had gathered, foregoing a greeting or preliminary discussion. "We will not leave Ticinum Papiae behind us without capitulation."

The officers looked at one another in surprise, and Gundobar spoke up first.

"Odoacer, we did not even stop to take Milan two days ago, but rather diverted the troops far around its walls. This city is much smaller, an unimportant garrison, yet besieging it could cost us days. That would extend our troops' time away from the Danuvius and Rhine, where the borders are already weakened against invasion. Remember, the legions we left behind are loyal, but they are at half strength; it will be only a matter of time before the tribes beyond the river realize their opportunity."

"And," Arderic continued, "it allows Orestes greater time to strengthen his defenses against us at Ravenna. The longer we stay here, the more difficult our task when we finally arrive at the goal. We are less than a week's march from the capital. Let us continue on."

Odoacer looked at his officers.

"Sound reasoning," he responded, "but for one thing. Orestes is no longer in Ravenna. He is here."

His men looked at him in surprise.

"In Ticinum?" Onulf asked. "You know this for a fact?"

"We have a guest. Some of you may even know him. Though not of our army, he is one of us, by language and by intent."

Turning around, Odoacer loosed a whistle. Four guards nearby looked up and, when Odoacer gestured to them, commenced walking toward the awning at which the officers were meeting. As they approached, Onulf and the others saw they escorted a fifth man among them, a Roman officer in full battle regalia but for the crimson tunic Romans typically wore beneath their mail. He, too, had apparently succumbed to the heat, and wore only a light linen shift, such as one might sleep in.

"Gentlemen, I present to you Tribune Gilimer, commander of the urban cohorts under Orestes, and an Ostrogoth by birth. He arrived at my command tent this morning before we departed, after talking his way past our outposts and even killing one who apparently did not agree to be talked past. He claims to have accompanied Orestes here to Ticinum a week ago, and the urban cohorts he brought with him have tripled the normal size of the garrison stationed here. The civil authorities have cooperated with them, and have furnished Orestes' troops with food, spare weaponry, and provisions. The walls of Ticinum now shelter a powerful and well-armed force, and Orestes intends to attack us from the rear as we pass by—*if* we pass by."

The officers stared at the newcomer for a moment in stunned silence, before all erupted at once into shouts and arguments. Odoacer gestured with his hands for silence, and after they had quieted, Gundobar raised his voice.

"Why would you believe this absurd claim?" he blurted. "Look to the top of the city walls—there is no evidence of a triple garrison. Orestes sent this man to stall us here, to delay our arrival at Ravenna, to gain additional time to prepare his defenses."

Odoacer nodded.

"Perhaps. I, too, thought of this. I have informed Gilimer that if we find his claim to be untrue, he will be killed, which of course he knew before coming to me. Yet still he came to me, knowing I would investigate and discover the truth, which I suspect to be as he says. If he is merely stalling for Orestes, he would be sacrificing his life to do so. I find it hard to believe any man would voluntarily martyr himself for Orestes."

Arderic looked at the prisoner skeptically.

"Men are often willing to die for a cause, or for other incentives. Orestes may be holding his family hostage, or in some other way compelling him."

Gilimer spoke up for the first time.

"Perhaps my motives are not so noble as protecting my family, General," he said contemptuously. "Perhaps I had a simple falling-out with my commander. Men often do that as well."

"If you cannot convince us of your motives, why should we believe you?"

"Because you have much to gain by doing so, and little to lose."

"How is that?" Onulf queried.

Gilimer sighed, looking askance at Odoacer, who answered for him.

"Gilimer is correct," Odoacer said. "If Orestes did indeed

remain in Ravenna, he would have called in most of his garrison troops there as well, to reinforce his urban cohorts. Garrisons such as Ticinum here would be staffed with only skeleton units. If we attack here and find it easily overcome— within, say, a day or two—then we know that is indeed the case, that its men have been diverted to Ravenna. An understaffed garrison here will confirm that Orestes remains in Ravenna with the emperor and the urban cohorts, and we can then strike our friend Gilimer, here, from the list of those receiving food rations—"

"But," continued Onulf, understanding dawning in his eyes, "if Ticinum puts up stiff resistance, stronger than we would have expected from an undermanned garrison, then we know it has something important to protect—or an ambush to plan."

"Correct," Odoacer confirmed.

"No," Arderic said, as all eyes turned to him. "It still makes no sense. Why would Orestes leave the emperor unprotected, in a capital city stripped of half its forces? If we knew he had done that, why would we not skirt past Ticinum Papiae as quickly as we could, and fall on Ravenna immediately? Beware, Odoacer, that you have not let your mind be clouded by your private feud with Orestes. You are responsible for twenty thousand men, your men, *my* men, and their lives are not to be taken lightly. Your task is not to conquer your personal enemy. It is to capture Ravenna, and then to seize the boy emperor."

"No, idiot," Gilimer snarled, and every man turned to him, surprised that a prisoner would so audaciously interrupt a field commander. "The Augustulus is *not* your target. He may be the emperor, and Orestes' son, but he is a mere puppet. True power in the empire resides with Orestes, and if his son is deposed, he will merely appoint another figurehead. Without Orestes, Ravenna is of no consequence. It is an empty palace, frivolous mosaics, nothing more. Listen to me, Odoacer: your target is not a city. It is a *man*. And that man is here."

The others fell silent, looking from Odoacer to Gilimer and back again.

"So we besiege Ticinum Papiae?" Odoacer asked his officers.

One by one, the men conceded, reluctantly at first and then more decisively, and Odoacer turned back to the guards who had brought Gilimer.

"Take him back to the brig," he ordered.

"We have no brig, sir," one of the guards responded.

"Then make one," Odoacer snapped, "out of sharpened stakes, or whatever you find. This man is to be chained and kept in confinement. If Ticinum is taken on our first assault, he is to be put to death, as punishment for delaying us here needlessly. If the siege is more difficult, then bring him to me. Understood?"

The guards nodded and, seizing the prisoner roughly by the arms, marched him back to the site of the main camp, where the troops, now rested, had already begun digging in.

One time, years before, Odoacer had stood on a low rise and contemplated with trepidation the fearsome siege works that the invaders, commanded by Orestes, had constructed around his benighted city of Soutok. Now, he took grim pleasure in their reversal of fortune.

Over the next two days, Odoacer's troops dug the exact counterpart of the ditches, mounds, and palisaded barriers that had once surrounded the Scyri capital. Hearkening back in his memory to those fortifications, he commanded that trees be felled, and planks hewed from their logs and planed, to serve as bridges over the barriers when it came time to storm the town's walls. Some of the men grumbled that such measures were unnecessary if the town were to be taken in a rapid attack, as they anticipated, but Odoacer would not take the risk that a large enemy force might suddenly dash from the walls and storm his own encampment, at some weak point identified from their watchtowers. His twenty thousand troops were barely sufficient for the invasion as it was. One wrong move could cost him half his men. Even losing a quarter of them would make the venture untenable.

As the trench works grew, the more certain he became that

Gilimer's story was true. Placing himself in the shoes of the sentinels on the city walls, or in the position of the garrison commander, or of Orestes himself, he realized that if the town truly were as undermanned as he had originally expected, it would be suicidal for it not to surrender when its commanders saw the extent of the fortifications and the number of troops laying siege to it. Indeed, the town walls were not even particularly well-constructed—relatively low, and of undressed stone—and there was therefore no possibility of escaping the defeat the defenders must know would be coming. Unless Gilimer *was* right, and there truly was such an enormous body of troops within, that the garrison could repel the assault and inflict fatal losses on the attackers.

On the fourth day came a blare of trumpets from the town, the gate opened a crack, and a herald emerged, alone and mounted, in full dress uniform of the emperor's urban cohorts and with the insignia of a tribune of horse. With a white pennant snapping decisively over his head on a cavalry lance, he began walking his animal carefully toward the invaders' lines. At his approach, all activity on the siege works ceased; from a hundred yards in either direction, men began trotting along the palisade toward the point at which the lone rider was directing his mount. Odoacer, too, working with a squadron of Raetian bowmen to erect sniper scaffolding upon a low rise, turned and began walking over with the archers. Within moments, the palisades were crowded with men. Twenty paces distant from the trench, the tribune stopped, butted his lance against the ground, and produced a bullhorn from a strap at his belt.

"Fellow Romans!" the officer shouted through the bullhorn, and the quizzical murmuring among the Germanic troops fell silent.

"Soldiers of Rome! Though you come from distant lands—from Noricum and Pannonia, from Dalmatia and Raetia, and even beyond, from Gaul and Hispania—you are soldiers of Rome, as am I, as are my comrades within the walls behind me. In our common identity, my friends, we are brothers, with no quarrel between us, between you and ourselves.

"I come forward to speak with you, to ask that you look to your commander—there, for I see your commander standing just before me, arms crossed defiantly, like a property owner overseeing his slaves—that you look to your commander, and ask why he has dragged you from your cool and green lands, why he has brought you to this sweltering and dusty country, turned you into half-clad 'red men,' forced you to eat dry biscuit and dig ditches in the hot sun?"

The troops listened in silence, and from here and there among the crowd of naked men, coated in dirt, chests still heaving from the exertion of their shoveling, murmurs of indignation rose, though it was impossible to tell whether they protested the herald's audacious words, or shared his resentment at their hardships. All eyes turned to Odoacer, who stood unmoving, arms crossed, just as the herald had mocked him for doing, staring with fury at the tribune facing him under the white pennant of truce.

"Look to your commander!" the herald bellowed again, "and ask him—ask him now, before you lift your shovels again, before you hoist another log to the palisades—ask him why he has brought you here? What does he offer you? What gain can you hope to accomplish by this madness, by this attack on your own comrades in arms? *Whom* are you fighting, and *for whom* are you fighting?"

The murmuring among the Germans increased, and a pair of stones were thrown in the direction of the herald, which fell short, though they caused his horse to dance skittishly. The Roman gained control of his mount and raised his bull-horn once again.

"You have marched this entire distance to Italia for *nothing*! For *nothing*, I tell you, if you follow this man! Years ago as a Scyri princeling, he refused to recognize General Orestes' authority, and his people paid the ultimate price for his folly. Now once again he commits the same tragic error! Yet all is not lost for you. My commander has authorized me to tell you that you, too, will share in the donative to be awarded to the urban cohorts on the occasion of the Emperor Romulus's accession. You, too, and all the legions, even the *confoederati,* will be granted a share in the vast territories to be redistributed to those men—to *us!*—who have so valiantly shed our blood and sacrificed the best years of our lives for the sake of the empire. Magistrates and surveyors are even now traveling the length and breadth of the Italian peninsula, requisitioning one third of the land of the noble families, one third of their estates. You men will be the recipients of this land, of these rich and bountiful territories! You men will be favored beneficiaries of the new Emperor Romulus Augustus!"

At this, dead silence encompassed the watching troops, and again all looked to Odoacer, who as before, stood stonestill, teeth clenched, face dark with fury at the herald's words.

"You men," the herald continued, "will be wealthy, if you will but lay down your arms and join with your Roman brethren in the garrison! But by the living God," he roared, rising on his horse and heaving the lance before him, burying its white pennant in the soft, dry earth, "by the living God, you will be *dead* men, lacking not only your donative, but anything else you possess as well, if you insist on this insane undertaking, this attack on your fellows, this treacherous betrayal of the Emperor Romulus Augustus himse—"

His words were cut short by an arrow flying with such power and speed that scarcely anyone even saw it hurtling toward him before it slammed into his mouth in a spray of blood, the iron-tipped warhead emerging for half the length of the shaft from the back of his head, as if the skull and the metal helmet presented no more resistance than the skin of an unripe melon. The arrow's momentum lifted the man bodily off his saddle and into the air, flipping him backward off the horse's crup, into a crumpled heap in the dirt behind the animal, dead before he hit the ground. The horse whinnied in terror and sprinted away.

Stunned, the men traced back the arrow's path, until their eyes again met with Odoacer, who stood with a bow, still vibrating, he had seized from one of the archers accompanying him. Looking fiercely about him, he stepped forward to address the men.

"The herald spoke true in one thing, and one thing only," Odoacer called out. The troops fell silent, necks craned forward in tense expectation.

"The donative of which he spoke, still stands. The magistrates and surveyors, if they truly are performing their tasks, will continue to do so, and if they have not yet begun, *I* will ensure they do so. You men, you legionaries, faithful to Rome, will inherit not only its wealth, but its ideals, which are not to be corrupted by such as this tribune and his ilk. But most important, by defeating these men, you will gain what Orestes cannot offer you. You who have marched far from the empire's distant, cold boundaries, you will gain the name and the honor, the untarnished, *uncorrupted* honor, of true Romans!"

The troops exploded in a cheer that spread in circular ripples to the men at the far end of the trench works, echoing against the city walls and into the fields and groves beyond. At first a mere incoherent roar that drowned all words, a pure expression of the men's support for their commander, it soon devolved into the rhythmic chant for which Odoacer had been waiting.

"Roma! Roma! Roma!"

As the chant resounded, Onulf stepped up to his brother's side.

"Gilimer's information was correct, I am sure of it," he said flatly, in Hunnish.

Odoacer peered over Onulf's shoulder, past the cheering men, to the forlorn figure lying dead in the grass beyond the trenches, the feathery shaft of the arrow emerging from his face and vibrating softly at the breeze.

"I knew that man," he said grimly. "Paulus Domitius. His words were poison to the troops. A herald he may have been, but he threw away his flag of truce, Orestes' flag of truce. He declared war, and now he is its first casualty. Orestes will be the next."

Odoacer turned away and bent to seize a pine sapling that had recently been bucked and debarked. Placing one end on his shoulder, he began dragging it to the archery scaffolding, to add another piece of material to the increasing height of the sniper tower.

VII

In the darkest part of the night, just before dawn, half the urban cohort within the garrison, some two thousand men, slipped single file through the main gate of Ticinum and along the outside walls, crouching low and remaining close to the structure. Two hundred yards away, at the first line of the newly dug siege fortifications, all was quiet, and from the watchtowers at the tops of the city walls, the garrison sentries could confirm that the cooking fires in the invaders' camp had died down to coals. The only movement was the occasional flash of a torch or field lamp through the picketed walls of the palisades behind the trench, as the invaders' own sentries slowly made their rounds of the camp.

The crack garrison troops, faces and clothing greased black for disguise, crept low and assembled below the south wall, opposite the point where, their observations had told them, the invaders' presence behind the trenches was the weakest, and the furthest in distance from Odoacer's headquarters on the north side. On the south end, though the trenches had been dug to their full depth, the complete palisade had not yet been erected, and only a thin line of Germanic infantry troops had been stationed behind it, supported by a small archery squadron and some mounted cavalry. By day, this presence was sufficient to serve as an initial buffer, to hold off any sally by the garrison troops until a larger force could be summoned from the main camp a half mile distant; yet Odoacer had considered such an attack unlikely, as Ticinum's walls bore no gates on that side. All signs indicated that any movement by the urban cohorts outside the walls would have to be initiated from the north, which would give Odoacer's troops ample warning before the weak sections of the entrenchments could be breached.

By night, however, Odoacer's troops were unable to see the maneuverings taking place a mere two hundred yards from their trenches, against the dark shadow of the city walls. The undermanned south end represented the weak spot the urban cohorts needed to breach the forces arrayed against them. And they were armed with their most formidable weapons:

Wooden planks.

A hundred of them, ripped from houses and sheds in Ticinum the previous day, split from roof beams, torn from the walls and shacks of the city's poor. Most of the boards were sufficiently narrow and light that they could be carried by one man with some difficulty, or two men with ease. Some were short, and were precariously lashed or nailed together to make longer boards. Some were mere ladders. All were at least twelve feet long—sufficient to allow the garrison troops to cross over the newly dug trench.

At a low whistle, they picked up their boards and sprinted across the dark clearing toward where they knew the trenches lay. Moving in a tight mass and carrying no lights, the black-painted attackers arrived at the ditch unnoticed until the last moment, when the sounds of the planks dropping into position roused the guards on top of the unfinished palisades, who raised their torches and peered into the darkness. It was too late. As they strained their eyes toward the town, a dozen arrows pierced each sentry before he could call a signal, arrows loosed from point-blank range just below them. The urban cohorts poured across the thin defenses protecting Odoacer's south camp.

It was only then, as the attackers scrambled up the wall of dirt heaped on the far side of the ditch, and began breaking through the half-erected wooden stakes, that the alarm was sounded, and the few Germanic troops camped on that end of the siege works were awakened by the noise. Centurions and officers raced from their tents, hurriedly strapping on armor and donning helmets as they shouted for the troops to assemble and defend themselves. Within moments, the lead garrison troops had fought their way over the trenches and through the palisades, and were furiously rampaging through the camp, clearing the way for the men behind them and, if

the attack were successful, for the remainder of their comrades waiting expectantly within the city walls.

Half a mile away, on the eastern side of the trench works
just at the edge of the main camp, Odoacer awoke with a start,
listened for a moment to the distant shouting that drifted to his
ears on the still night air, and leaped from his cot.

"Onulf!" he bellowed, quickly donning his mail and seizing the helmet and sword belt where they hung on a post. He
rushed out the door of the tent and saw the camp was already
in chaos.

"Onulf!" he roared again, and this time his brother appeared, racing from an adjacent officers' tent, with Gundobar
arriving from the opposite direction, grimacing and limping
heavily, still suffering the effects of his burns at the siege of
Rome.

"The enemy has breached our trenches!" Gundobar
shouted, gesturing toward the clamor which, by now, was
nearly drowned by the shouting of the men around them.
"On the southern flank!"

"Assemble the troops, quickly!" ordered Odoacer. "The
Noricum and Pannonian legions, now! Orestes is trying to
break through our lines and escape! Onulf, take the two legions to the southern trenches, and Gundobar, assemble your
Burgundians!"

The two officers nodded and began racing toward the
troops' billets when suddenly Odoacer leaped after them.

"Wait!"

They spun back to Odoacer, who was looking at them
with eyes wide, a sudden realization dawning on his face.

"No! Do not take those forces to the south side! Orestes is
not seeking to escape!"

"What are you saying!" exclaimed Onulf. "Brother, let
me assemble the troops—"

"No—that is what he wants us to do! If he wanted to escape, he would have done so already, since we have so few
troops at the southern end. No, listen—they are still fighting
there—the urban cohort stopped to fight! That can mean
only one thing . . ."

Gundobar jumped in. "Orestes *wants* to fight—wants us to send troops there from the main camp, divide our forces—"

"So he can attack us here at the main camp with the rest of his garrison," Onulf continued. "Here, against our strongest point—we would not expect it . . ."

"But it would no longer *be* our strongest point if we sent half our forces to his feint," Odoacer said. "He would divide us, with the advantage of surprise and darkness, circle behind, rout us—"

"Sir!" gasped a winded sentry who had just sprinted up to the command tent in the dark. "Sir! The companies on the southern line have been attacked. My centurion begs you for reinforcements."

"How many attackers, soldier?" Onulf queried.

"More than us, and we are a full cohort—*were* a full cohort . . ."

Odoacer had heard enough.

"There may be a thousand or more. Gundobar, your Burgundians."

"I have only five hundred . . . ," Gundobar replied.

"It is enough. They are good troops. We do not need to defeat the garrison soldiers, just stop them. Not even that, merely delay them. Set up a blockade. Prevent them from reaching the main camp. Take cavalry as well, a hundred horse, harass them from the flanks, contain them . . ."

Gundobar nodded and raced off before Odoacer could even finish, and Onulf looked at his brother.

"You do not wish me to reinforce him, to counter the attack?"

"We need every man we can spare, here. What is ready, Onulf? The siege engines, the catapults? Onagers or other artillery? What do we have?"

"Nothing yet—for the past two days, every man has been assigned to the trenches and palisades, and a few to building the sniper towers. The onagers are not yet assembled—we have only the ladders, as they were the easiest and quickest to build, and we needed them for the tower. We—"

"Ready an attack, *now,*" Odoacer interrupted. "We will

turn Orestes' game against him, attack his own stronghold
while his own troops are divided. Ladders, you said?"

"Forty, maybe fifty, and more can be made quickly, from
the stakes used in the palisades."

"Call for volunteers. First man up each ladder will receive a year's wages, and first man over the top of the wall,
five years' wages."

Onulf smiled grimly.

"Five years' wages? You know the troops are not moti-
vated by gold. You have not paid them all year as it is, yet
still they fight."

"The troops know I'm good for it," Odoacer growled.
"Especially after we take Ravenna."

Within moments, Onulf had mobilized a large squadron of
archers, marched them over the trenches into the open space
near the city's eastern walls, and commenced a devastating
barrage of arrows that cleared the enemy ramparts of sentries and defenders. The archers had been formed up and
positioned so hastily that even after the lead ranks had begun loosing their arrows, many of their comrades were still
sprinting down the paths over the trenches to join them.
Regular infantry were ordered to begin hauling spare arrows and even the armor and shields of bowmen who had
not had time to don them before rushing to the walls. There
was no time for perfection. Chaos was the rule, speed the
requirement.

Scarcely had the first arrows been released than the infantry began forming up behind the archers, at first organized by century and cohort, but when that proved too
time-consuming in the confusion, simply by blocks of a
hundred men, any hundred men, regardless of the units to
which they were officially assigned. Odoacer, spurning a
horse because of the danger of the animal's tripping in the
darkness, trotted back and forth across the rapidly forming
lines. In a voice gravelly from thirst, he called to his troops
as they raced out of the camp, struggling to strap on armor

and helmets even as they ran, staggering into the makeshift formations his officers were organizing.

"Into ranks, men, fall in!" he roared, swatting a laggard with the flat of his sword, and cursing under his breath as he nearly tripped over a soldier who had stumbled at one of the makeshift trench bridges. "Into formation! Our archers have pinned down the wall tops. Who will be first up the ladders?"

A chorus of shouts greeted his demand, and a handful of ladders appeared among the ranks, carried from the assembly station in the main camp, tossed over the palisade to avoid blocking the infantry pouring over the plank bridges, and caught by willing hands on the other side. Within moments, four other ladders appeared.

"Onulf!" Odoacer bellowed. His brother, doing much the same work a hundred paces farther up the main trench, raced over.

"How many men have assembled?"

Onulf peered into the darkness and shook his head.

"Hard to say—the situation is confused. Two thousand, maybe more. But they're forming up quickly. Count to a hundred and the numbers will be doubled."

"Not enough time. Ladders?"

"I saw six or eight thrown over the barricades on my end."

"And I saw a dozen here. That makes twenty. Call the charge, now!"

"The buglers and couriers have not arrived, the officers are scattered, the formation is chaos—"

"Everything hinges on the ladders. More men would do us no good, they would not fit on the ladders. Run back up the trenches, and order the assault—I'll do the same here. Ladders, man—call for more ladders!"

Onulf raced back up the line, bellowing for ladders as he went, and saw another three passed hand to hand over the trench even as he ran. Odoacer, meanwhile, seized a soldier running past him by the arm, and spun him around.

"The Burgundians, soldier," he shouted. "What do you hear of the Burgundians?"

The trooper paused a moment, peering at his questioner, and then snapped to attention.

"I know nothing, sir—their squadron was tented next to my own, they were summoned by their commander, and ran off like deer to the south fortifications."

"But none have returned? Have there been assaults on the main camp from that side?"

"None, sir, not since I left, a few moments before."

"Good man. Are you afraid of heights?"

"Heights, sir?"

"Heights! See the ladders?"

Glancing at a ladder being carried past, the soldier quickly understood, and turned to Odoacer with a grin.

"I will see you behind the walls, sir!"

Racing after the ladder-bearers, he disappeared into the chaos.

Odoacer trotted down to the archery position.

"Bowmen, keep up the tempo! Do not stop for an instant, not even to aim! Fire as fast as you can, as fast as the arrow supplies come to you. Do not let the enemy sentries stand on the ramparts!"

Without waiting for a reply, he ran toward the lead ranks of infantry, who were impatiently jogging in place in the darkness.

"Move the ladders up to the front—there! Fifty men behind each ladder; ready! *Charge!*"

Immediately, the first three ladders, each carried by half a dozen men along their thirty-foot length, swung out of the crush and careened toward the walls. Behind each one, fifty men hurriedly formed and sprinted after them. Odoacer could see no further in the darkness than the men in his immediate vicinity, and could only pray that Onulf was issuing the same orders up the line.

"More ladders!" he bellowed, and another four were passed over the throng, seized by the men in the lead ranks, and then they, too, followed their comrades of a moment before toward the walls. Over their heads, the volleys of arrows from the archery squadron hummed like a swarm of wasps, and a constant clattering and chinking of the iron arrow-heads caroming against the stone walls sounded in front of them, marking the position and distance of the walls in the darkness.

"More ladders!" Odoacer shouted hoarsely, and again ladders appeared, passed over their heads from the rapidly filling formation behind. "Fifty men to each ladder—*Go!*"

With roars of excitement, each ladder that made its way to the front ranks was seized by eager hands and borne off to the walls, followed by a small mob of fervent infantry, mixed in their legions and formations, but all desirous of one thing—to be first over the walls and into combat with the enemy they knew were awaiting them.

A sudden thought occurred to Odoacer—the archers! His troops would have positioned the first ladders at the walls by now, with more to follow within moments—the archers' withering barrage of arrows in the dark would murder his own men! Racing back to the squadron's position he hastily shouted into the ear of a man who looked to be their captain, though in the chaos he could not be sure.

"Archers—cease your arrows!"

The officer looked at him quizzically.

"But sir, the enemy sentries—"

"You can't see them—you'll hit our own men! Advance with your troops to sight range—close enough to see our ladder-scalers, directly beneath the walls if you have to. Then keep up the barrage on the sentries' positions!"

The archery captain understood, and scarcely had he shouted the order than the entire squadron, already uneasy at seeing their infantry and ladder-bearers run past them to-ward precisely the targets at which they had been shooting, ceased their volleys. The bowmen seized armloads of arrows and Odoacer led them in a sprint to a mere thirty paces from the walls, where they could discern the ladders thrown up against the stone, and the line of men beginning to climb the swaying structures.

When the arrow barrage stopped for the maneuver, the ramparts again filled with enemy defenders, who raced to the positions on the walls where the tops of each ladder had been placed. As the archery squadron reformed below the walls, Odoacer looked up impatiently. To his dismay, two garrison soldiers above the ladder nearest him inserted stout spear shafts under the topmost rung, braced them against the stone edge of the rampart as a fulcrum, and then leaned back against the shaft-ends, leveraging the top of the ladder out from the wall. With its top support gone, though lifted but a hand's-breadth from the wall, the ladder twisted from the imbalance, and the torque on the stressed poles from the weight of the ten men scaling it caused it to split with a loud crack.

It happened so quickly nothing could be done to prevent it. The lead climber, already near the top, shouted in terror as the ladder fell from beneath his feet, and throwing himself forward, he seized the edge of the wall with his hands, hoisting himself up and flopping onto the thick stone rampart with chest and belly, legs dangling below him over the outside of the wall. Before he could wriggle over, a sword sliced into his back from a defender standing above him, severing the vertebrae, and his scream of pain died abruptly in his throat. In an instant three more blows had fallen in the same spot, cutting him through at the trunk, and his lower body dropped off the edge of the wall onto the writhing men who had fallen off the ladder a moment before, all of them lying in various states of injury at the base of the wall. With a snarl of rage, the defender on the rampart leaped onto the thick edge of the wall, planted a hobnailed boot in the face of the dead man, and kicked the upper half of the body over the edge as well, reuniting it with its lower members.

The Roman had no time to exult, however—even as he loosed his roar of defiance, his voice was abruptly cut off by an arrow shot from almost directly below, piercing his throat under the chin and emerging through the top of the bronze helmet. Dead instantly, he, too, toppled over the outside of the wall, his own whole and sound limbs joining in death the severed ones of the man he had killed a moment earlier.

As the archers found their marks, the garrison troops on

the ramparts again ducked for cover, helpless to emerge into the open, or even to lift a finger to prevent the ladders from being thrown against the walls and Odoacer's troops from scaling them. The walls would be breached—there was no stopping the climbers now—and Odoacer, without remaining to confirm or even observe the results, trotted back to the infantry still forming up in front of the trenches.

As he arrived, Arderic ran forward to meet him.

"By God, Arderic," Odoacer exclaimed, relieved at seeing him. "Did you sleep well?"

Arderic ignored the jibe.

"Garrison troops have just smashed into the main camp from the south," he hastily reported. "They must have overrun our defenses on that end—"

An uneasy feeling rose in Odoacer's stomach. "I sent Gundobar and his Burgundians—"

"Who fought them every step of the way," Arderic interrupted. "The Burgundians were overwhelmed, but the bastards were too dumb or too tough to die. They were walking backward, each one taking down two or three of the garrison troops for every one of themselves who fell. When they hit the edge of the main camp, they just merged into our lines and kept on fighting alongside my boys."

"You assembled the troops in the camp, then?" Odoacer asked.

"Diverted every squadron I could find. Not enough at first, but they're still forming up, and the attack has been contained, for now. I've got a tribune and two centurions commanding them and I ran to find you—I need more men. You have five thousand here, maybe ten, and more are forming up—what the hell is that?"

His words were interrupted by trumpet signals at the front, as Ticinum's main gates burst open. Through the gap, they could see the city entirely lit up inside by torches and bonfires. Now, just as the eastern horizon behind Odoacer's men began to lighten with the coming dawn, the gates had been flung open, and the entire remaining garrison thrown into the battle in a final effort to divide and outflank the

Germanic troops opposing them. With a blare of trumpets and a concerted roar, the two thousand crack troops of the urban cohort still behind the city's walls poured through the gates, battle armor gleaming, bronze helmets shining with parade-ground polish in the torchlight.

It was the answer to Odoacer's prayers. Without stopping to further question Arderic, without stopping even to think, he turned to his men, their eyes still swollen from sleep, helmets askew and armor draped haphazardly over their sunburnt, mosquito-welted bodies. Raising his voice above the clamor of the charging Romans scarcely a hundred paces away, he roared out his challenge.

"Men, the city is yours!"

The soldiers before him, eager to join the battle they could hear raging on the ramparts above, frustrated they had been prevented from following the ladder-bearers up the walls, loosed a defiant shout. Leaping forward, lacking formation or even orders from their own captains, they lifted their swords and raced directly at the charging Romans who, upon realizing the size of the force storming toward them, more than triple their own, stopped short and assumed defensive crouches, shields up, swords and spears at the ready. With a deafening crash, the Germans slammed into the waiting Roman troops, rolling over them like a tide, the lead ranks bowling over the defenders by the size of their bodies and the momentum of their charge, and the ranks behind storming over the mounds of dead and wounded by sheer weight of numbers. In a moment, the main Roman force had been annihilated, leaving only a few of the most rearward units, who saw the fate of their comrades in the front lines, to flee in terror back through the city gates. The Germanic troops, filthy with the dirt of the march and the blood of battle, ill-armored and poorly prepared, but enraged by bloodlust, stormed after them. They forced wide the gates that had already begun closing, and joined with the ladder-scalers who had made their way down from the ramparts and leaped into the city's streets, now thronging with terrified women and bystanders.

Odoacer found himself swept along as if in a rioting mob. It was only after he had passed through the gates and penetrated far into the city's streets that he was able to step from the crush and into a side alley, where he was joined by Arderic and a handful of other officers. The sacking of the town was now beyond their control. After a moment, a gaunt figure, lacking armor, with an ill-fitting helmet propped on his head that looked as if it had been picked from the battlefield, and holding a blood-covered sword in his hand, also stepped into the alleyway, joining the small knot of officers. When Odoacer saw him he dropped his hand to his sword.

"Gilimer," he said, and Arderic turned and drew his weapon. "What the . . . ?"

"Where are his guards?" Arderic demanded.

"Your guards followed your orders," Gilimer replied to Odoacer in the Germanic tongue, "and sent me to you. Orestes' urban cohort was here in force, as I told you. I kept my promise—now let's finish this."

Odoacer eyed him suspiciously, without removing his hand from his weapon.

"What do you seek?"

"Same as you: Roman blood—from one in particular."

"If you speak of Orestes, he is mine—and is to be taken alive. I will not have Rome's highest officer murdered in an alleyway like a dog."

Gilimer smiled, nodded, and then stepped back into the street, where he was swallowed up in the crowd of rampaging men.

VIII

Orestes was led into the half-destroyed prefect's office by two burly guards, each tightly gripping his arms. One of his eyes was swollen completely shut, and a trickle of half-dried blood glittered at the corner of his mouth. The injuries he had suffered, however, did not seem to have diminished his Germanic strength, nor his fury in defeat, for he struggled vainly against his captors even as they marched him into the room. Following just behind was Gilimer, with Orestes' own jewel-encrusted sword in a scabbard swinging from his belt, his eyes boring into the back of his former patron's head.

Odoacer watched from the shadows in the corner, observing this man whom he had not seen so closely since Attila's *strava* in Hunnia many years before. He knew that his own appearance was hardly less than barbaric—his skin was burnt and bug-bitten from the long march from the Danuvius, his armor and clothing hung in tatters, and the stench of unwashed blood and sweat hovered over him like a vapid mist. This was not how he had anticipated meeting Orestes again after all these years—indeed he did not know precisely what he *did* expect in that regard—but in the end, he realized there was nothing more fitting than for the two rivals to meet thus, with their faces and their skin and their scents bearing all the strains of the struggles and battles they had endured over the years. In truth, Odoacer could not help but marvel at Orestes' ferocity as he was led, cursing, into the room, and he hoped that he, too, upon attaining such an age, might remain as strong-willed. But his regard was short-lived, for when he stepped out of the shadows to face his nemesis in the full light of the torches, he could summon nothing but scorn and hatred for this man. And Orestes himself, sensing that a person of importance had entered the limited sphere of vision of his one good eye, suddenly stopped struggling, straightened himself, and glared full into Odoacer's face.

For a long moment the two men stared at each other, scrutinizing and daring the other, searching for signs of the strength that had tormented the other for so many years. Standing motionless and expressionless, Orestes slowly, almost reluctantly turned his head to the side, to peer at Odoacer's accompanying officers in turn, but it was only a moment later that his good eye followed suit, tearing itself from Odoacer's determined gaze, and focusing one by one on the other men—on Onulf, whom he acknowledged with a slight sneer, seemingly imperceptible to all but the recipient himself; on Gundobar, with a slight look of puzzlement at the German's smoke-blackened features but with dawning recognition of an old family or tribal relationship as he stared at the piercing gray eyes and the mustaches that dangled nearly to the man's chest; at Arderic, with an expression of disdain for this man who, for years a committed officer of the Roman legions under Orestes' authority, had turned against his own commander. Last, his gaze settled on Gilimer, who had stepped forward to stand at Odoacer's side, though here Orestes did not linger even so long as to muster an expression of contempt. Hearkening deep within his chest, he summoned up a hoary, blood-streaked glob of phlegm that landed with a spatter at Gilimer's feet. The latter leaped forward in rage, but was seized and pulled back by Odoacer and Arderic, while one of Orestes' guards released his arm just long enough to fetch the captive a vicious backhanded swipe across the mouth with his mail-protected forearm, splitting Orestes' lip and shattering his two front teeth. Orestes slumped momentarily against the other guard, then looked up blearily, shook his head, and mustered a contemptuous smile from his bloodied mouth.

Odoacer had had enough.

"My only regret," he intoned gravely, in Hunnish, "is that we are not alone, or I might kill you slowly, on the spot, as you deserve. Instead, as a Roman citizen and an imperial officer, you will be subjected to a trial, found guilty, and only then executed. It prolongs the inevitable for us all. More's the pity."

"And *my* regret," Orestes snarled back through his broken teeth, "is that I did not eliminate you twenty years ago, rather than paying Ellac to take care of my business."

Odoacer and Onulf stared at him, and though the other men in the room could not understand the harsh, guttural language, they knew something enormous had been said, and all fell silent, observing the antagonists. Spitting out more blood, Orestes continued.

"Ellac failed to kill you, nearly failed to kill your dog of a father, and now the *Roman* Empire, of all things, is being punished for his stupidity, for having let you live!"

"No," Odoacer muttered almost inaudibly, eyes shooting daggers at his foe, who in return flashed him a bloody, triumphant smile. "No, it is not the entire empire being punished. Only your house, the House of Orestes. You, traitor, for having plotted against your betters. And your pathetic spawn, the *Augustulus,* for having had the misfortune to be sired by you—"

Before he could finish, Orestes leaped forward, his arms slipping from the hands of the two guards, whose grip had gone lax from their astonishment at the exchange of words between prisoner and commander. Nearly faster than the eye could follow, he slammed his left elbow into the face of one guard, simultaneously breaking his nose, blinding him, and doubling him over in an explosion of blood and pain. Before anyone could react, Orestes reached with his right hand for the maimed guard's sword, and in a single, swift movement, drew it from its scabbard, whirled, and slashed at the unprotected upper arm of the guard on his right, cutting through muscle and tissue with the broad blade and hacking deep into the shoulder socket. Dropping to his knees in shock and pain, the guard clutched at his injured shoulder, blood spurting through clenched fingers.

Orestes did not wait to be seized again. Immediately, he lunged for Odoacer, who stepped aside as he struggled to draw his own sword, which had become entangled in a shredded strip of mail hanging over his scabbard. Anticipating the feint, Orestes, too, shifted his weight, though he was unable to adjust the aim of his sword stroke, which slashed uselessly through the air, striking the stone floor with the tip in a shower of sparks. Leading with his left shoulder, his momentum carried him straight into Odoacer, who grunted as Orestes crashed into his chest, and both men fell hard to the floor. They rolled across the room, now one on top, now the other. The other officers leaped forward but, unable to gain a clear sword stroke on Orestes, they hesitated to strike, and wary of Orestes' own flailing sword, they were unable to step between the combatants to pull Odoacer away.

Finally, slamming into the stone wall at the end of the room, the antagonists were stopped in their mad grapple. Odoacer, though initially caught by surprise, was the stronger man and twenty years Orestes' junior, and finally realized his advantage. Throwing his full weight onto Orestes' chest, he heard a snap and felt the other man's sharp intake of breath at the pain of the broken ribs. As the flailing sword arm hesitated, Odoacer thrust his hips forward and planted his knee full on Orestes' elbow, grinding it into the stone floor until he felt another snap and heard the sword clatter uselessly to the floor behind him. Glancing to the side, he saw Orestes' eyes roll back in his head and his face constrict in pain, as he struggled to draw breath under the weight of Odoacer's body on his caving ribs.

For a moment, the entire room fell silent and Odoacer, stretched sideways across the torso of his panting rival, glanced down at Orestes' face, past the broken, bloodied mouth with its lolling tongue, to the jutting chin and bull neck, which retained its full strength and power despite his age and injuries. Odoacer's eyes were drawn to the chain that draped loosely around his rival's neck, a thick gold rope, from which dangled a medallion nestled into the hollow between the collarbones. A medallion like any man might wear, a simple gold disk with worn figures engraved on it, nothing to attract one's attention . . .

But something did attract his attention, even as Odoacer lay there, panting nearly as hard as his adversary; something did draw his eyes to that small golden disk, and after a moment, having ensured the sword would not be raised again and thrust into his back, he lifted his head slightly to better see the medallion at the man's neck.

It was a coin, pierced by a hole through which the chain was passed. A golden coin, unlike any ever seen in the empire. An eastern coin. Attila's coin.

For which Odoacer's father had died.

Coming to his senses, he suddenly realized that the room

was in pandemonium, with shouts erupting from the onlookers, the two injured guards roaring in pain, and Odoacer's officers still collecting their wits and racing to where the two antagonists lay. Gilimer was first to arrive, eyes flashing fury as he stepped up and placed his boot on Orestes' throat, causing the latter to gag and his eyes to bulge, and allowing Odoacer to warily release his hold on the prisoner and stand. As he staggered to his feet, face red from the exertion and anger darkening his countenance, Gilimer drew his own still-bloody sword.

"May I have the privilege?"

There was no questioning his meaning. Odoacer nodded silently, and without objection from any man in the room, Gilimer raised his sword and brought it down, once, again, three times, until the twitching body lay still and Orestes' head rolled to the side to rest against the wall in a pool of blood.

Odoacer turned away.

"We leave immediately," he said. "I do not wish to spend the night in this town, nor have the troops delayed in women and plundering and lose their discipline. Call the men to formation in the forum. We march at noon."

"And the town itself?" Onulf inquired. "It is a valuable property, with the walls still intact."

"We march on Ravenna. We do not have the men to occupy this garrison, nor any other we may conquer, and therefore it is of value only to the remaining troops of the urban cohort, who might return to reoccupy it. Burn it."

"Everything?"

Odoacer turned and looked at Onulf. "Do you remember, Brother, how we used to conquer towns and tribes that dared to rebel against Attila?"

Onulf nodded slowly.

"Every last building razed to the ground," Odoacer continued. "Houses, shops, churches. The Hunnish way. Attila's way. His final vengeance, on the man who mocked him and desecrated his grave, and on the townspeople who assisted that man."

The officers began filing out, Odoacer the last to go, but just as he began walking through the door he stopped. Turning, he strode back into the room, pausing a moment to gaze around, to recall in his mind the confrontation he had just endured, Orestes' final moments, Gilimer's revenge. Moving toward the headless body lying against the wall, he stepped through the puddle of blood, which in the heat was quickly coagulating on the porous floor, and reaching down, he seized the golden coin and chain, which slipped easily from the ragged stump of the neck. Wiping it of its bloody residue on the edge of his tunic, he stuffed it into his belt, and then turned and again strode across the room, out the door, and into the morning sun.

After the cool penumbra of the room he had just left, the stifling heat hit him like a blast furnace, but he scarcely took notice. The air was filled with the keening and wails of women whose men had been killed in the fury of the attack, and who now were being thrown from their homes and ordered to leave the city. At the nearby forum, a column of black smoke was already beginning to rise and drift into the streets with a choking, acrid odor. This was no place to linger. Slowly, he walked into the nearest side street, made his way to the city gates, which now hung forlorn and deserted, and out into the open field beyond, where already the troops were beginning to assemble.

"Orestes is dead, and the Augustulus will soon be seized; it is time to consider who will be the next emperor," Onulf said quietly.

The two brothers stood side by side on the platform of the sniper tower in their camp, observing the troops pour from the gates of Ticinum, pushing through the crowds of women and prisoners, while behind them black smoke billowed from the principal buildings and houses. Over the walls, flames were visible from the windows of the highest towers and turrets, and Odoacer knew that within moments the entire town would be an inferno. The heat from the burning buildings adjacent to the inside walls was already turning the wall mortar to powder, and here and there along the length of the structure, deep fissures were opening, accompanied by loud cracking and groaning from the suddenly stressed stones. Before evening, nothing would be left of the city—not a building standing, not a wall still erect, not a kitchen garden not filled with rubble, broken roof tiles, and the charred remains of ceiling beams. Ticinum Papiae would go the way of so many cities, of Carthage of the distant past, of Soutok of the previous decade. Odoacer felt no pity.

"What did you say?" he asked.

Onulf looked at the men gathering about them, reeking with the rancid oil they had smeared on their bodies beneath the layer of dirt, the "red men," though many looked as black as if they had been seared over a fire, and indeed it was fire, and the smoke from the burning buildings inside the city, that had lent this additional layer to their skin; some were coated so thickly that only their gray eyes and dangling mustaches identified them as men rather than demons from the underworld. Around the tower the men gathered, at first hesitantly, and then more enthusiastically, jubilant at their recent victory, exulting in the stench of the smoke, the smell of destruction and death, rejoicing in the small treasures they had collected before the licking flames had taken their share, eager to consummate the final victory, to embark on the march to the ultimate goal, to Ravenna, to the overthrow of the emperor, the last remaining symbol of their rage. The throng of men grew and expanded, and their cheering rose from a far corner and spread like a wave to the middle and then to the other end, passing through the base of the sniper tower as if it were no more than a reed or a blade of grass.

"I said it is time to acclaim a new emperor," Onulf continued. "The Augustulus will be overthrown when we arrive, if he has not been already, and there must be no gap in authority."

"I want nothing to do with naming an emperor," Odoacer spat in disgust. "I am no kingmaker, no manipulator of men, like Orestes and Ricimer."

"You needn't name one. The men would not accept that in any case. You must *be* one."

Odoacer stared at his brother.

"I? Emperor?"

"Why not?"

Odoacer scoffed.

"I am not Roman. I have no Roman bloodline, no rank, no parentage. You do not understand this civilization, Brother. The people would not accept such an emperor."

"The people? Who cares about the people? You need the troops' support and you have it. For years you have been their leader, first as crown prince of the Scyri, then as general, now as—"

"I cannot be emperor," Odoacer insisted. "It is impossible."

"The men have gathered below. They are waiting to acclaim you."

"Acclaim me as what? Not as emperor."

"As their leader, as their ruler."

"I have no time for word games. I am their commander, and that suffices. We must start the march to Ravenna now, before the Augustulus gets wind of our victory and flees the city."

"Odoacer, look around you! Look at your troops! These men will not allow you to leave unacclaimed, unrecognized for this great victory, for Orestes' defeat. You would insult them if you did so. Accepting their honors is as important as accepting their obedience."

"Not as emperor, I cannot . . ."

The chanting below them had changed, in rhythm and in words. No longer were the shouts random and disorganized, the mindless bellowing of a mob drunk with victory. Now, twenty thousand voices were raised in unison, spears thumping in clattering rhythm against shields, all eyes trained on the two men standing in the sniper tower, in unanimous acclamation.

"*Odoacer Rex!* Long live the King!"

Odoacer looked down, and for the first time that day

seemed to see his men, to truly *see* his men. Their faces shone eager, enthusiastic, even through the grime and the blood and the insect welts, men calling out to him, not forced, but as if rejoicing, rejoicing in a word that had not been heard in Italia as an acclamation for a thousand years and more, the unanimous cry of a conquering army.

"Rex, Rex, Rex!"

And as Odoacer gazed over the throng of men, smoke boiling behind them from the dying city, the air suddenly filled with a cloud of wind-borne ash, drifting over them, coating everything, men and horses and tents and ditches, covering all with a sheen of powdery white, a cleansing white, masking the horrors of the day's destruction. Gazing through the haze of powdery ash, he allowed his mind to drift, to imagine a scene, an era: one of wealth and peace, free of grasping emperors, free of rivalry with the Romans of the East, free of decrepit senators of diluted nobility serving as Augustus, free of their assassinations and replacements, of ruinous donatives, of false descent from invented bloodlines, of fabricated legacies inherited from mythical Romulus and Remus themselves.

"Rex, Rex!"

It was time for new blood, a new man, a new leader—a new title. Onulf was right. He could not refuse. Stepping forward on the rickety platform, he raised his hands in acknowledgment, and the troops' roar swelled and engulfed him like the tide. The men cheered, and in some, tears coursed down bloodied cheeks, leaving streaks in the grime, as he acknowledged their acclaim. Behind him he sensed Onulf, too, stepping forward, sensed his brother raising his own arms, and heard the crowd's noise diminish, slightly only, but enough that Onulf's voice could soar out over the crowd.

"I present to you," he shouted, and the men's voices dropped further; "I present to you: Odoacer the First, Sovereign King of Italia, *Rex Italiae!* Rome of the emperors is dead. Long live the King!"

And every man in the throng knew that at this moment, at the very instant the fateful word "*Rex*" was pronounced, an era twelve hundred years old had creaked to an inauspicious end, smothered in black smoke and blood, and a new era, like a fragile coating of white dust, had descended upon them.

AUTHOR'S POSTSCRIPT

I will here make an end of my narration. Which if I have done well and as it becometh the history, it is what I desired: but if not so perfectly, it must be pardoned me. For as it is hurtful to drink always wine or always water, but pleasant to use sometimes the one and sometimes the other: so if the speech be always nicely framed, it will not be grateful to the readers. But here it shall be ended.

—2 MACCABEES

With the death of Orestes, his son realized he could not withstand the invading Germanic army, and surrendered Ravenna without a struggle. Odoacer accepted the people's acclamation as their ruler and, as a gesture of goodwill, spared the life of the boy, whom he judged innocent of his father's wrongdoings, exiling him to a castle in Campania with a large pension. The last Western Roman emperor, Romulus Augustus, then disappeared from history.

The Roman Senate capitulated shortly afterward, and drafted a letter to the Eastern Emperor in Constantinople, renouncing any desire or need for an Emperor of the West, and declaring Italy a separate "diocese" to be governed by their conqueror. Nor did Odoacer forget the promises he had made to his troops, to distribute territory to them upon his accession. The noble families and wealthy landowners throughout

Italy were compelled to give up one third of their estates to the resettled soldiers of Odoacer's German and Ostrogoth army, who after a generation or so fully integrated themselves into the country.

Odoacer governed Italy for nearly seventeen years until his luck finally gave out. After a series of bloody clashes with none other than his distant kinsmen, the Ostrogoths, who had invaded at the behest of the still angry Eastern Roman Emperor, Odoacer was besieged in Ravenna, where he held out for four years despite the city's near starvation. He finally agreed to meet with his besieger, the Ostrogoth king, Theodoric, at a "peace banquet" held on the Ides of March, 493, at which he was treacherously murdered, setting up the final irony: that the destroyer of the Western Roman Empire was stabbed to death on the same day as had been its founder, Julius Caesar. During his lifetime, Odoacer had witnessed the collapse of three nations.

Onulf was killed by Theodoric's troops shortly afterward, breaking the royal line of succession, and the political situation in Europe then descended into chaos. Contrary to Odoacer's original hopes, the end of the Western Roman Empire did not produce relief from tyranny, but rather ushered in the bleak era of warfare, ignorance, and disease known today as the Dark Ages, from which Europe did not recover for several centuries.

ACKNOWLEDGMENTS

Over the past seven years, since I first embarked on novel writing, I have found it to be an amazing adventure, in the truest sense of the word. Like most adventures, it comprises much hard work and tedium, but it is punctuated by marvelous flights of imagination, short bursts of exhilaration, periods of discouragement alternating with triumph (it is amazing how merely hitting upon precisely the *right word* can make an author's spirit soar), and even the occasional moment of sheer terror (think public speaking here . . .). Meeting deadlines and keeping a consistent output across five novels has been, for me, largely a matter of discipline, which often means paying close attention to the "sacramentals" of writing, those external aids—a good cup of coffee or shot of Calvados, the room set at the proper level of darkness, the desk stacked with the familiar reference works—that don't necessarily contribute directly to the work, but that help make the author more receptive to the grace of inspiration. It is hard to tell whether or not these material aspects improve the writing, but it is impossible to imagine doing it without them.

Yet as necessary as certain habits and tics are, ultimately the inspiration must come from one's own life, and in this regard, few things remain the same. Evolution is constant, a fact that is both disconcerting and invigorating. My true vocation is not as an author, but rather as a *paterfamilias,* and having begun my writing career at a time when it was a struggle to find silence and solitude with two small children lolling under my desk, I now find I am faced with a new struggle: that of keeping up with the interests and intellects of two near-adults (as well as one more small child, who also enjoys lolling under my desk). My oldest, Eamon, who once helped ground me in reality by making my morning coffee and issuing me constant invitations (demands?) to play, now keeps the computers and Web site whirring, and still issues constant invitations (demands?), this time to let him practice driving. Isa, whose childish humming and bedtime hugs used to put a spring in my step, now keeps the place jumping with her renditions of Broadway show tunes, and my quads burning as I struggle to keep up with her triathlon training. (Incidentally, both Eamon and Isa contributed to proofing the galleys for this book.) Little Marie, who, four novels ago, was nothing more than a grainy photo of a bald baby on an adoption report from Mongolia, has now exceeded even Isa's career achievements in the Department of Incessant Background Noise, and has developed her own unique contributions to my work, with her dozens of samples of artwork taped to my walls, her unerring memory for movie gags, and the limitless imagination she displays in her frequent dialogs with her imaginary "little sister Al."

Yet as always, the greatest credit is owed to my wife, Cristina, the one truly stable aspect of my life. She lends order to the chaos, soothes the cranky author's soul, and tempers the discipline of running a family, a business, and a school out of the home, with her liberal doses of love, humor, and great cooking. Heaven, I believe, is the state of joy that comes about from the ultimate union of one's soul with its Creator. Until that occurs (God willing), I have a hint of it in my life with Cris, a foreshadowing of that happiness, heaven's reflection here on earth.

M.C.F.
January 2007